MW01119734

Disability and Modern Fiction

Disability and Modern Fiction

**Faulkner, Morrison, Coetzee and the
Nobel Prize for Literature**

Alice Hall

First published 2012 by
PALGRAVE MACMILLAN

Palgrave Macmillan in the UK is an imprint of Macmillan Publishers Limited, registered in England, company number 785998, of Houndmills, Basingstoke, Hampshire RG21 6XS.

Palgrave Macmillan in the US is a division of St Martin's Press LLC, 175 Fifth Avenue, New York, NY 10010.

Palgrave Macmillan is the global academic imprint of the above companies and has companies and representatives throughout the world.

Palgrave® and Macmillan® are registered trademarks in the United States, the United Kingdom, Europe and other countries.

ISBN 978–0–230–29209–3

This book is printed on paper suitable for recycling and made from fully managed and sustained forest sources. Logging, pulping and manufacturing processes are expected to conform to the environmental regulations of the country of origin.

A catalogue record for this book is available from the British Library.

A catalog record for this book is available from the Library of Congress.

10   9   8   7   6   5   4   3   2   1
21   20   19   18   17   16   15   14   13   12

Printed and bound in the United States of America

For Chris, Pete, Tom and Josh

Contents

List of Illustrations

Acknowledgements

I would like to thank the Centre for Advanced Studies at the University of Nottingham for providing me with the postdoctoral research fellowship which allowed me to write this book. At Nottingham, I received excellent advice and kind encouragement from Professor Paul Crawford and all of the staff at CAS. I am very grateful to the Arts and Humanities Research Council for their financial support, including a three-year studentship at Cambridge and a study trip to New York. Darwin College, Cambridge, has provided me with a supportive, friendly environment in which to carry out my work. I am also grateful to Benjamin Doyle and Paula Kennedy at Palgrave Macmillan for all of their work on this project.

Finally, I would like to thank my family and friends for their generous help and fantastic support, particularly Chris, Pete and Tom Hall and Joshua Freeman.

1
Disability and Modern Fiction: Charting New Territory

On 15 September 2005, the statue *Alison Lapper Pregnant* by Marc Quinn was unveiled by the Mayor of London, Ken Livingston, at a public ceremony in Trafalgar Square (Figure 1). The work is a portrait of Alison Lapper: naked and pregnant. Lapper, an artist born without arms and with shortened legs due to a congenital disorder, is sculpted in smooth, white marble. The sculpture occupied the fourth plinth in Trafalgar Square for eighteen months. It is huge: over three metres tall and thirteen tons in weight.

This representation of a disabled female body provoked uproar in the British media. For many journalists, it was the subject matter, rather than the craftsmanship of the sculpture that was problematic. On the day of the unveiling, *The Evening Standard* denounced *Alison Lapper Pregnant* as 'repellent'.[1] Roy Hattersley, a prominent Labour politician, led this media backlash against 'political correctness gone mad' objecting to 'the suggestion that we have to be taught about the disabled'.[2] Jonathan Jones in *The Guardian* summed up a widespread sense of ambivalence with his claim that 'it falls short of being art'.[3]

This book, which sets out to explore the representation of disability in the fiction and criticism of William Faulkner, Toni Morrison and J. M. Coetzee, takes Jones's question of whether the disabled body is a valid subject for aesthetic representation as a point of departure. The media reaction to the Alison Lapper statue suggests on-going anxiety about potentially sensationalist exploitations of the disabled body (and Lapper's own unborn child), but also a wider unease about the process of *representing* personal experiences of disability in a public discourse or space. Jones's rejection of the statue raises several fundamental questions: What constitutes aesthetic value? What does it mean, both ethically and politically, to bring marginalized bodies to the centre

1

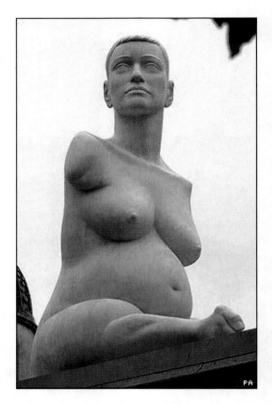

Figure 1   Marc Quinn, *Alison Lapper Pregnant*, 2005

of debate and to open up these aesthetic representations for critical analysis and public scrutiny? To what extent does this statue by an able-bodied man, Marc Quinn, raise questions about the problem of sympathizing with or imagining a pain which is not one's own?

In Coetzee's *Elizabeth Costello* (2003), the central character connects the idea of obscenity with public representation. She defines the word: 'Obscene. That is the word, a word of contested etymology...She chooses to believe that obscene means off-stage. To save our humanity, certain things that we may want to see...must remain off-stage.'[4] She employs the concept as a talisman. For Elizabeth, the salvation of humanity is assured by the exclusion of disruptive presences, by a blinkered gaze which purposefully ignores that which it wishes to scrutinize. While she hopes to 'hold onto' static concepts and fixed meanings, the certainty of Elizabeth's position is undercut by the inherent instability, malleability (and historical contingency) of language and unseen presences that wait in the wings.

Like the Lapper statue, this study seeks to bring to centre stage representations of disability which may, in the past or in the present, be perceived as obscene or unrepresentable. Despite the fact that representations of disability have been at the centre of aesthetic practice throughout the twentieth and into the twenty-first centuries, until recently they have been marginalized in critical practice. In universities, higher education for disabled students has been a high-profile priority, yet disability studies has, in the United Kingdom in particular, been largely excluded from the curriculum.[5]

The media coverage of the Alison Lapper statue highlights the wider, paradoxical place of the disabled in the history of aesthetic representation and critical reception.[6] In his newspaper article, Hattersley suggests that 'Trafalgar Square is for something else.'[7] Hattersley's objection is primarily historical: Lapper's status as an ordinary, relatively anonymous citizen means that she does not qualify for memorialization alongside national heroes such as, for example, Nelson, Shakespeare or Milton. On the other hand, Jones, an art critic, expresses his concern in aesthetic terms: far from being too ordinary, Lapper's extraordinary body is not deemed a suitable subject for art. Art is implicitly understood as a practice that excludes material which is perceived to be overtly political or aesthetically 'obscene'. The personal may be political, bold and brave, but it is certainly not viewed as beautiful. These views suggest a distinctly conservative sense that art must not be disruptive and that heroic historical figures should be privileged over the materiality of everyday lives.

The Daily Telegraph article on the Lapper statue opened with the question: 'Whatever would Nelson think?',[8] ignoring the fact that the statue of Nelson, exhibited on a column in the centre of Trafalgar Square for more than 150 years, depicts a disabled, war-wounded soldier, blind in one eye and missing an arm. This neatly highlights the extent to which disability, while prevalent in literary and artistic representations throughout the centuries, has remained, until recently, a critical blind spot. Standing alongside the Lapper Statue, Nelson's heroic white masculinity becomes reconfigured. The hierarchy of embodiment (and disability) implicit in the media response is clear: Nelson's disability, inflicted rather than congenital, is understood as a symbolic badge of military honour rather than as a marker of physical vulnerability. The visceral reaction against the representation of Lapper's pregnant, naked body suggests taboos about both the equalization of a disabled female body and Lapper's prospective role as a physically fertile, socially productive carer – a mother – rather than a passive recipient of care. In this context, the *recognition* of the presence of disability creates new connections and enriches our understanding of existing aesthetic works, including the Nelson statue. So, *Alison Lapper Pregnant* needs to be read in a wider, richer history of artistic representation, in the context for example of such works as the armless *Venus de Milo* (130 BC), as well as for its contemporary political significance in terms of disability rights activism.

It is the statue itself, rather than the negative media coverage of it, which raises the questions that are most pertinent to this book. Lapper's pregnant body suggests that we might reconceptualize the disabled body as physically, economically, aesthetically and critically productive. But how exactly can the disabled body pose imaginative challenges? Can aesthetic representation help us to better understand the experience of disability? How do able-bodied artists or writers, such as Marc Quinn, Faulkner, Morrison or Coetzee, approach the problems of mediating the experience of disability through their own aesthetic frameworks? What ethical demands are put upon viewers or readers by this process? Can literature, unlike sculpture, offer the possibility of empathizing or even entering the consciousness of another? And how does the malleability of language as a medium contrast to the stark marble of Quinn's sculpture?

The assimilation over time of a wide range of personal, public, medical and legal understandings under the modern heading 'disability', poses both problems and possibilities for literary critics, policy-makers, carers and those who identify themselves as disabled. In his unveiling speech, Ken Livingstone sought to position Lapper as both disabled and empowered, a 'modern heroine'.[9] In a literary context, this desire to identify positive role models in relation to disability has led to some instrumental and crudely political critical approaches. This book draws on a range of more recent and nuanced approaches to 'literary disability',[10] to make connections between authors from different time periods and backgrounds and explore shifting understandings of disability between 1920 and the present day. Disability is treated as a culturally and historically specific concept.

Coetzee's *Slow Man* (2005) self-consciously considers these questions through its engagement with a history of sculpture, portraiture and disability in the context of the novel. The central character, Paul, who is recovering from the amputation of his leg following a bicycle accident, rails against the contradictory aesthetic and cultural ideals that surround him:

Does he really want to feel natural?...Does the Venus of Milo feel natural? Despite having no arms the Venus of Milo is held up as an ideal of feminine beauty...Yet if it were discovered tomorrow that the Venus was in fact modelled on an amputee, she would be removed at once to a basement store. Why? Why can the fragmentary image of a woman be admired but not the image of a fragmentary woman, no matter how neatly sewn up the stumps?[11]

Paul therefore identifies both a prevailing stigmatization of disability, but also a gap in existing aesthetic theories of the beautiful in relation to impairment. The novel as a whole explores the idea that amputation and prosthesis are not just physical or medical matters of 'sew[ing] up the stumps' (59), but also need to be considered in terms of their complex and intersecting aesthetic, ethical and emotional significance.

Certain critics have made claims about the potential for literature, more than any other art form, to allow a more subtle engagement with the complexities of disabled people's experiences. Snyder and Mitchell argue that the 'characteristic intimacy with disabled characters in literature', achieved through first-person narrative perspectives, allows 'a unique space for contemplating the complexity of physical and cognitive differences'.[12] Their argument that literature *by definition* 'makes disability a social, rather than a medical phenomenon' (6) suggests a privileging of the literary over any other modes of accessing interior, personal experiences.

Derek Attridge, writing from a more general perspective on literature and ethics, makes a similar claim about the potential for literature to allow a perspective from the interior space of a character:

> [Literary works] are capable of taking us through an intense experience of these other-directed impulses and acts. The inventive literary work, therefore, should be thought of as an ethically charged act.[13]

Yet, in Faulkner, Morrison and Coetzee the experimentation with marginalized perspectives – of physically and cognitively impaired characters but also women, slaves and the dead – whilst 'other-directed' in an ethical sense also has the potential to be aesthetically exploitative and politically complex.

The representation of disability is not then a minority concern restricted to disability rights activism or the critical genre of disability studies. The fact that the ethical, aesthetic and imaginative challenges implicit in the representation of the disabled body are central to three of the most popular, celebrated authors of the twentieth century – Faulkner, Morrison and Coetzee, all Nobel laureates – is significant. Although this topic has received little attention to date other than in disability studies itself, a focus on representations of literary disability can enrich our understanding of individual texts by Faulkner, Morrison and Coetzee and suggest new connections between them. Do impaired and invalid bodies 'fall short of being art'?[14] How can a literary focus on disability work as a valid category of critical investigation? Can disability provide a perspective that draws upon and contributes to critical understandings of a wide spectrum of bodily experience and aesthetic representation and avoids universalizing the differences between people?

This book sets out to offer close readings of key texts alongside an exploration of the diverse contributions to public debates about disability that Faulkner, Morrison and Coetzee have made as academics, curators, essayists and public intellectuals. The study draws on historical and cultural contexts from the periods in which the authors were writing, ranging from the Louvre's catalogue for Morrison's *Foreign Bodies* exhibition (2006) to the will of Alfred Nobel (1895).

In an interview, Alison Lapper suggested that the representation of her body at a moment of proud maternity implies a kind of confrontation: 'Anything we're uncomfortable with, we avoid. But now I'm up there, 11ft, you can't avoid me anymore.'[15] Faulkner, Morrison and Coetzee also confront these taboos and, through their diverse critical and fictional representations, refuse to look away from the disabled body itself. Their works explore not only the sense of public discomfort in relation to disability that Lapper describes, but also shifting conceptions of health, beauty and the struggle to represent the materiality of the body in writing.

Conceptualizing disability studies

The discipline of disability studies is often traced back to the 1970s when the focus on literary texts was closely aligned with the political aims of the disability rights movement. In this period, notions of the *effect* of literary representations of disability were polarized; literature was viewed either as a source of liberation[16] or as directly colluding with structures of oppression by using disability as 'a deterministic vehicle of characterization'.[17] Moreover, the role of *affect*, an inescapable emotional and ethical dimension to any engagement with representations of disability,[18] was often ignored in the quest for intellectual authority and academic recognition.[19] The intersection between disability activism and the feminist, gay and black civil rights movements in this period provided shared, alternative models for understanding identity and more politicized modes of reading (or re-reading) texts. Henri-Jacques Stiker argues that these interconnected movements constituted a wider, cultural 'grand examination'[20] that provided a specific historical point of departure for disability studies in 1970s America.

This book argues for a far wider conception of disability studies. In fact, the study of literary representations of disability can be traced further back than the 1970s. In 1926, for example, Helen MacMurphy wrote *The Almosts*. The text begins by suggesting an exchange between literary representation and scientific discourses:

> Sometimes the poet sees more than the scientist, even when the scientific man is playing at his own game. The novelist can give a few points to the sociologist, and the dramatist to the settlement worker.[21]

This opening calls for communication across disciplines but also emphasizes the complexity of literary texts and their potential to deepen our understanding. MacMurphy focuses on the representation of disability in the work of some of the most well-known authors of her period:

> Take the case of the feeble-minded. They have been drawn from life more than once by *the great masters* already mentioned [Shakespeare and Scott], as well as by Charles Dickens, Victor Hugo, Charles Reade, and many other writers, and yet so far at least *we do not seem to have taken mentally defective persons in the world as seriously as the great writers* who immortalized Wamba, Quasimodo, Barnaby Rudge, Young Sparkler, Mr. Toots and others. (1; my italics)

She traces the concept of 'feeble-mindedness' through the literary great masters of the past including the fool in Shakespeare's plays, back to the Domesday Book. MacMurphy's concern is with social change; she urges the state to 'stop neglecting the mentally defective and reorganize charitable institutions, education' (177). Yet, her analysis is rooted in the details of the texts themselves. She emphasizes the humanity of disabled characters, and the potential for textual representation to foster a sense of similarity and empathy rather than difference: 'They are human creatures – human beings, and differ among themselves in reactions, in character, in endowment, in emotion, almost as much as the rest of us' (170). MacMurphy's first-person voice, which implicitly positions both herself and her audience as able-bodied, nevertheless suggests the ways in which literature can particularize and individual-ize experience. Difference – diverging physical states and characters – paradoxically becomes the point of similarity.

MacMurphy's work about disability took place at a time when men-tally traumatized and physically injured American soldiers were return-ing from the First World War.[22] During the war, the American military's adoption of the Binet Scale as a way of testing and categorizing soldiers had provoked wider anxieties about the 'intelligence' of the population as a whole.[23] Through this system of intelligence testing, a previously unrecognized (or at least uncategorized) class of the 'feeble-minded' became visible in post-war American society. As MacMurphy suggests:

> Great writers have recognized the feeble-minded. We must reckon with the mental defective as one of the many things in heaven and earth that are not dealt with by some philosophers, and yet that make a great difference to the community and to social progress.[24]

In some respects, MacMurphy's focus on the literary representations of disability anticipates Virginia Woolf's essay, 'On Being Ill', published in 1930. Like MacMurphy, Woolf identifies a critical gap in the treatment of disability and illness in literature. Both authors echo the language of *Hamlet* to suggest that disability and invalidity constitute both an 'undiscovered country'[25] and 'one of the many things in heaven and earth'[26] that we have so far failed to explore, even in some of the most well-known literature. For MacMurphy, this gap is between the preva-lence of representations of disability and the lack of critical engagement with the topic. For Woolf, there is an absence in contemporary fictional writing about the experience of illness and invalidity:

> Considering how common illness is, how tremendous the spiritual change that it begins, how astonishing, when the lights of health go down, the undiscovered countries that are disclosed ... It becomes strange indeed that illness has not taken its place with love and battle and jealousy among the prime themes of literature. (4)

MacMurphy's focus is on character: she identifies examples, such as Dickens's Tiny Tim, where a physically or mentally disabled character is observed from the outside, narrated by an omniscient narrator. For Woolf, the new territory that writers need to explore is the interior experience of the 'daily drama of the body [of which] there is no record' (4). She suggests that the poverty of existing language available to describe physical suffering necessitates linguistic innovation and literary creation: '[The sufferer] is forced to coin words himself, and, taking his pain in one hand, and a lump of pure sound in the other … so to crush them together that a brand new word in the end drops out … It is a new language we need, more primitive, more sensual, more obscene' (7). Language is treated here as a material that can be handled or moulded. For Woolf, the sensuality and obscenity of this alternative language roots it in the physical realm, mediated by the body.

Woolf and MacMurphy do not address the same conditions: MacMurphy's focus is on disability and cognitive impairment. Woolf's definition of illness is far more ambiguous, ranging from female hysteria to a trip to the dentist, and clearly encompassing allusions to her own suffering from depression, insomnia and various nervous diseases. Yet both authors explore how those who stand outside the 'army of the upright' (16), often deemed economically unproductive or culturally invalid, represent uncharted literary and critical territory at the beginning of the twentieth century. Through Shakespearean references, both texts explore disability and invalidity not as a personal tragedy but rather as an imaginative possibility.

At the beginning of the twentieth century then, Woolf invited authors and critics to venture into unexplored imaginative territories of illness and invalid experience. A century later, the fictional and critical landscape is quite different; the taboos that Woolf described have been challenged by, for example, the late twentieth-century explosion in the publication of illness narratives. Tales of illness and disability are far more common: in autobiographical writing and fictional accounts of disabling conditions and ill health,[27] as well as a growing critical field of 'health humanities'.[28]

Yet, Woolf's sense of the potential for writing about invalid experience to suggest new modes of perception and narration has not been fully explored. The condition of invalidity, she argues, opens up new modes of knowing and looking. Lying on one's back, for example, allows a new attention to the shifting beauty of the clouds: 'We float with the sticks on the stream … irresponsible, disinterested and able, perhaps for the first time in years, to look round, to look up – to look, for example, at the sky' (12). This peripheral position reveals 'endless activity … [a] gigantic cinema play[ing] perpetually to an empty house' (14).

This motif of staring up at the sky also appears in Faulkner's 'The Leg' (1934) and D. H. Lawrence's 'The Prussian Officer' (1914). In both stories, the protagonists are depicted as lying incapacitated and injured, flat on their backs. Faulkner relates a short, fragmented story through the consciousness of David, a British First World War soldier who is injured and has his leg amputated. Lawrence imagines a scene through the eyes of an orderly in the Franco-Prussian war (1870–1) who, following a bitter mental and physical struggle with his officer, falls from his horse and lies dying in the mountains. In both cases, the external action of combat becomes subordinated to the shifting, interior consciousness of the protagonist. Both Lawrence and Faulkner adopt a first-person perspective in which there is a blurring of the 'line between truth and delirium'.[29]

As in Woolf's essay, this recumbent position is associated with pain and suffering but also with a mystical, imaginative quality which is captured in the first-person narrative. The soldiers and Woolf's invalid find themselves in a position where 'the tools of business [have] grown remote'; both their bodies and the world have 'changed shape'.[30] Woolf's protagonist discovers new sensitivities and sensory perceptions as a result of her stillness and illness:

> The words give out their scent and distil their flavour, and then, if at last we grasp the meaning, it is all the richer for having come to us sensually first, by way of the palate and the nostrils, like some queer odour. (22)

In Lawrence's story, the landscape is endowed with a similar dream-like beauty in which different senses and memories merge to create an overwhelming impression of 'solid unreality' that resembles Woolf's swirling cinema in the sky: 'There was thick, golden light behind golden-green glitterings, and tall, grey-purple shafts, and darknesses further off, surrounding him, growing deeper.'[31] As in Woolf's essay, there is an awareness of texture, width and depth, 'thick', 'light' and 'deep' darkness (19).

In Faulkner's 'The Leg' the imaginative potential of this recumbent position, in which 'the mind concocts a thousand legends and romances...for which it has neither time nor taste in health',[32] takes on a more bitter, delusional edge. The new mental and social division[33] inaugurated by the First World War becomes incorporated into David's consciousness, as the internal voice is split between himself and the imaginary presence of his dead friend, George. As David lies in the hospital bed, his senses are sharpened and darkness becomes an almost tangible presence:

> And my nights were filled too, with nerve- and muscle-ends chafed now by an immediate cause: the wood and leather leg. But the gap was still there, and sometimes at night, isolated by invisibility, it would become filled with the immensity of darkness and silence despite me. (311)

The prosthetic leg fails to fill the gap in David's consciousness, or the blank in his memory. In David, Faulkner engages with the fear and anxieties of an individual protagonist, within a wider social and cultural context. The wood and leather leg is an example of the prostheses developed in the First World War and symbolic of the culture of rehabilitation which 'figur[ed] disability as an anomaly to be made to disappear'.[34] For David, the missing leg also comes to symbolize the death of his friend George, a loss that refuses to be easily prostheticized or replaced: 'I had lost them both' (312).

Woolf's essay and Faulkner's short story about disability provide a literary starting point for this study, rooted as they are in an early twentieth-century, post-First World War context. Woolf's metaphor of illness as an undiscovered country is frequently cited and often extended by contemporary disability studies critics. Yet, near the start of the twenty-first century, the metaphor of totally uncharted ground is inaccurate: disability studies and illness narratives are no longer entirely unexplored, but they are still relegated to the margins of critical practice. As Davis, writing in the preface to the second edition of *The Disability Studies Reader* (2006), puts it: 'Just because disability studies is on the map doesn't mean that it is easy to find' (xiii). Ato Quayson, thinking along similar lines in *Aesthetic Nervousness* (2007), suggests that what is needed is 'a provisional map of interconnections' (15).

This exchange between literary and the critical forms suggests that disability studies needs to take account of both types of writing. Close analysis of the vocabulary and imagery that are used to define, describe and articulate the experience of disabled people is central to the project of better understanding disability in both literature and culture more widely. There are undoubtedly difficulties posed by the assimilation of physically and geographically diverse experiences under the single heading of 'disability'. Yet, as Morrison argues in *Playing in the Dark* (1992), it is important to explore the role of fiction in shaping cultural perceptions and the construction of these labels within a specific historical context.

She describes a reciprocal relationship in which 'cultural identities are formed and informed by a national literature'.[35]

The challenges that MacMurphy and Woolf set up at the beginning of the twentieth century – to address the lack of critical writing about disability and to explore the imaginative potential of conditions of invalidity – remain significant for twenty-first-century critics. Whilst the growing presence of disability studies on the university curriculum in the United States[36] and the wealth of recent books on disability,[37] the history of medicine,[38] illness narratives[39] and ageing[40] indicate that the role of the invalid in literature is no longer the unmapped critical terrain that Woolf's metaphor suggests, there is still a great deal to be done. Disability is not a minority concern in demographic, historical or literary terms. This book argues for the importance of disability as a critical approach that needs to be integrated into the academy and mainstream literary criticism, and an important perspective through which we can better understand some of the most celebrated authors of the twentieth and twenty-first centuries.

The definition of disability

Disability, as a category, is fundamentally unstable. Nineteenth-century notions of 'disability' – set against a backdrop of eugenics discourses and the conflation of categories of disabled people with immigrants and the poor – encompassed congenital disorders, sensory impairments and various types of chronic disease.[41] Disability remained both under-theorized and overlooked in policy-making and public spheres.

The interplay between literal and metaphorical, physically and socially disabling factors is also central to twentieth-century institutional definitions of disability. UPIAS (the Union of the Physically Impaired Against Segregation, formed in 1976) sought to address this difficulty through the adoption of a dualistic definition, which was employed as a political tool by disability rights activists in the 1970s. This definition makes a clear division between 'impairment' as 'lacking part or all of a limb, having a defective limb, organism or mechanism of the body' and 'disability' as 'the disadvantage or restriction of activity caused by a contemporary social organization which takes little or no account of people who have physical impairments and thus excludes them from the mainstream of social activities'.[42] This focus on socially constructed barriers lends itself to political campaigns for architectural and legislative changes. The Americans with Disabilities Act (1990), a landmark act that extended the civil rights legislation of 1964 to protect disabled people from discrimination, was widely celebrated as a victory for campaigns based upon this dualistic definition. Like the medical (impairment) and social (disability) model, the law acknowledges that disability extends beyond a physical or mental medical model to include culturally constructed perceptions of limitation and certain forms of social organization.[43]

Yet, the personal, ethical and affective aspects of these processes of definition deserve closer attention. Iris Marion Young suggests that the instability of the category itself is linked to the potential for anyone to become disabled (as many of us will in old age) and a sense of abjection.[44] The resistance to naming, defining and thinking about ageing and disability that Young describes connects to what Morrison herself calls a 'fear of being outcast, of failing, of powerlessness... of boundarylessness'.[45] In this context, the drawing of boundaries and dualistic definitions takes on an arbitrary quality related to self-definition and reassurance on the part of the able-bodied definer: 'Encounter with the disabled person,' Young argues, 'produces the ambiguity of recognizing that the person whom I project as so different, so other, is nevertheless like me' (147). These encounters, whether through personal meetings or aesthetic representations, invite an intimate process of self-reflection and provide a challenge to conventional understandings of 'disability' as a homogenized category.

In some senses, then, ambiguity and a resistance to naming become defining features of disability as a category. The *Oxford English Dictionary* (2009) suggests that 'disability' as a generalized 'lack of ability, inability, incapacity, weakness' is a more common usage than disability as the 'physical or mental condition that limits a person's movements, senses, or activities'[46] which applies to millions of people around the world. In all of these cases, the underlying question of what capabilities dis-ability is defined *against* remains unclear. The relationship between 'the definers... and the defined',[47] which lies at the centre of Morrison's *Beloved*, becomes a site of political contestation in disability studies, opening up a gap between medical authority and personal experience to produce both linguistic and ethical ambiguities.

In this context, more nuanced, interactionist[48] models of disability that suggest the interconnectedness of medical and social factors become important as critical tools. In this study, the difficulty of defining disability is a further starting point. The diversity of disabled experience, which can include mobility impairments, sensory deprivation, cognitive disorders, speech problems and ageing, is emphasized to suggest both its prevalence and its importance as a critical category.

If bodily variation and vulnerability constitute a point of similarity for *all* human beings then disability shifts from an 'integrable' perspective to become 'integral' to the theorization of the human.[49]

Such a wide-ranging, shifting definition of disability is at once a problem and an opportunity. Woolf's 'On Being Ill' provides a way of thinking about how distinct separations between body and mind, between medical and social models, are problematic:

> Literature does its best to maintain that its concern is with the mind; that the body is a sheet of plain glass through which the soul looks straight and clear and is...null, and negligible and non-existent. On the contrary, the very opposite is true. (4)

For Woolf, the body is the mediator of all experience and so is inextricably bound up with the act of writing, reading, sensing and understanding. This study takes the body as a site of knowledge yet also of resistance, a standard which writers, seeking to capture experience and identity, must perpetually come up against. The political efficacy of a division between social and medical models[50] has to be balanced with the danger of physical pain, suffering and embodied experiences disappearing from disability studies.[51] In literary critical terms, the tendency towards abstraction and a focus on linguistic crisis can lead to a mode of analysis in which the body is treated merely as a figure of language.[52] It is only by challenging the boundaries of disability studies, through an exploration of intersections with critical gerontology, aesthetics, linguistics and history, that the discipline can continue to develop.

In her essay, Woolf resists the notion of a Cartesian subject, returning us to the sense that 'the creature within...cannot separate off from the body like the sheath of a knife or the pod of a pea for a single instant' (4). Given this interconnectedness, literary and cultural representations of disability can facilitate alternative understandings of the lived experience of disabled people. Interactionist perspectives emphasize bodily experience, necessarily mediated through text in a novel or critical essay. They allow a way of thinking about the relation between able-bodied author and the representation of disabled characters, but also about the relation between a text and the specific historical and cultural context in which it was written.

Each of the chapters in this book explores a different form of disability. My aim in adopting this approach is to suggest the diversity and the ambiguity of the term 'disability' within specific historical and cultural contexts. I also locate my own analyses on a wider spectrum of writing about embodiment in general. I do this by exploring cognitive impairment and war-wounded soldiers in my chapter on Faulkner; physical disability and disfigurement in my analysis of Morrison; and sensory deprivation and ageing in relation to Coetzee's later fiction. The final chapter of the book considers the relationship between materiality and metaphor, and the ethics of using disability as a metaphor in the context of the Nobel Prize lectures of all three authors.

An aesthetic dialogue between Faulkner, Morrison and Coetzee

Until now, no literary critical work has undertaken a sustained reading of the works of Faulkner, Morrison and Coetzee together. Although some comparative studies exist,[53] particularly between Morrison and Coetzee,[54] the complex interconnections between all three authors and their recurring focus on disabled bodies have not yet been explored. Little critical writing has emerged on the relationship between Coetzee and Faulkner's writing, although Coetzee himself has published an essay on 'William Faulkner and his Biographers' (2005).

Rather than an existing body of critical writing on the topic, it is the authors themselves that invite connections between their works. In 1985 Morrison attended the annual 'Faulkner and Yoknapatawpha' conference in Oxford Mississippi. Prior to reading from *Beloved*, then a work-in-progress, Morrison highlighted a complex relationship between her reading and her writing: 'There was for me not only an academic interest in Faulkner, but ... in a very personal way as a reader, William Faulkner had an enormous effect on me.'[55] As a Masters student at Cornell in 1955, Morrison had written her thesis on 'Virginia Woolf's and William Faulkner's Treatment of the Alienated'. Her fascination with the role of the outsider in a literary tradition, and in Faulkner's work in particular, is evident in *Playing in the Dark*, written over thirty years later: 'I am in awe of the authority of Faulkner's Benjy ... Melville's Pip, Mary Shelley's Frankenstein – each of us can extend the list' (4). Here she places Faulkner's representation of disability, the cognitively impaired Benjy in *The Sound and the Fury* (1929), alongside other characters who are isolated as a result of physical and mental otherness.

Coetzee's essay, 'William Faulkner and his Biographers', also focuses on disability, this time in the context of Faulkner's own life. From the compendious biographical writing on Faulkner, Coetzee chooses to highlight the story of Faulkner's feigned disability:

> He returned to Oxford [Mississippi] wearing an RAF officer's uniform and sporting a British accent and a limp, the consequence, he said, of a flying accident... He sustained the aviator legend for years; he began to play it down only when he became a national figure and the risk of exposure loomed too large.[56]

With a kind of puzzled 'astonishment' (189) that characterizes the entire essay, Coetzee explores the possibility, raised by certain biographers, that this absurd fiction of his own personal disability marked a turning point in Faulkner's development, triggering an urge to tell (and write) stories that continued for the rest of his life:

> Faulkner's biographers have made much of his war stories... The ease with which he duped the good people of Oxford, Karl says, proved to Faulkner that... one can make not only a life but a living out of fantasy. (191)

In the same essay, Coetzee describes Faulkner's literary contribution in unequivocal terms: 'The one blazing genius of American literature of the 1930s' (194).

I do not, however, intend to suggest any kind of straightforward influence or similarity between authors from different ethnic and geographical backgrounds, historical periods and with their own personal perspectives. In an interview with Nellie McKay in 1983, Morrison repudiates any simple likeness between her own work and Faulkner's writing:

> I am not like James Joyce; I am not like Thomas Hardy; I am not like Faulkner. I am not like in that sense. I do not have objections to being compared to such extraordinary gifted and facile writers, but it does leave me sort of hanging there when I know that my effort is to be like something.[57]

Here she insists that her specific identity as a female, black writer should not be erased through assimilation into a wider literary history which is largely dominated by white male authors. This objection to comparison – the endorsement of an African American woman's writing through its relation to a white male predecessor – responds to traditional linear readings of Morrison's work which see it as descending from Faulkner's 'master text'.[58] Harold Bloom, for example, employs a metaphor of family resemblance suggesting that her 'style stems from an amalgam of Faulkner and Woolf' who he views as a 'the father and mother of Morrison's art'.[59] This book takes a quite different approach, exploring a dialogic relationship between authors and shifting conceptions of disability across different times and contexts, rather than the notion of literary lineage.

Yet, in their Nobel lectures, Faulkner, Morrison and Coetzee all articulate a strong sense of their own place within a wider literary tradition. Faulkner modestly suggested that 'this award is only mine in trust'.[60] His acceptance speech not only acknowledged past masters but was also focused on a future generation of 'young men and woman already dedicated to the same anguish and travail' (119). Morrison, in her Nobel banquet speech, suggested that previous generations of authors represent an ambiguous, spectral presence, haunting her life and work: 'I entered this hall pleasantly haunted by those who have entered it before me . . . That company of Laureates is both daunting and welcoming, for among its lists are names of persons whose work has made whole worlds available to me.'[61]

Yet despite Faulkner, Morrison and Coetzee's sense of indebtedness, Bloom's linear formulation seems inadequate. My aim is to suggest fresh, mutually enriching reciprocal relationships between the authors, using the work of each to better understand and explore the representation of disability in the writing of the others. This book therefore sets out to probe points of intersection, as well as of divergence, between Faulkner, Morrison and Coetzee's works. Their recurring representation of disabled bodies that *endure*, that refuse to be removed from view even at the end of their novels and essays, will be central. Morrison's comment on Faulkner's work, that there is 'a sort of staring, a refusal-to-look-away in his writing that I found admirable',[62] is a significant feature of the uncompromising, often discomforting yet compelling nature of works by Faulkner, Coetzee and Morrison herself. These authors all examine the problems of representing disability as well as the empathetic challenge that this poses. Morrison suggests that the act of literary imagining is relational and goes beyond the visual: 'For me, imagining is not merely looking or looking at; nor is it taking oneself intact into the other. It is, for the purposes of the work, becoming.'[63] Literature can provide an enabling perspective through which to enter into this process of becoming another consciousness, but at the same time, it confronts us with the aesthetic, ethical and imaginative limits of this struggle.

Faulkner, Coetzee, and particularly Morrison, also provide critical models for thinking about literature and disability more widely. Like many disability studies critics, Morrison begins *Playing in the Dark* by positing an unspoken presence, in this case of African American characters, 'at the heart' (50) of many canonical works of American literature. She argues that: 'One likely reason for the paucity of critical material on this large and compelling subject is that, in matters of race, silence and evasion have historically ruled literary discourse' (9). 'Evasion,' she continues, 'has fostered another, substitute language, in which the issues are encoded, foreclosing open debate' (9).

There is no longer an absence of writing about race in critical studies just as there is no longer a complete critical silence about disability. Yet, there is still a lack of writing about disability in mainstream literary criticism, particularly in relation to some of the most respected authors of the last century. Morrison's critical writing on race provides a way of writing about unsettling populations that is not only an act of political resistance, but also a nuanced and productive literary critical approach. In *Playing in the Dark*, she argues that literary representation can both perpetuate and subvert prejudices, but she also suggests that alternative critical approaches might be able to shift our understanding of the place of marginalized populations in a text and in society:

> I wanted to identify those moments when American literature was complicit in the fabrication of racism, but equally important, I wanted to see when literature exploded and undermined it... Much more important was to contemplate how the Africanist presence *enriched the text*... [and] what the engagement meant for the work of the writer's imagination. (16; my italics)

In using Morrison's *Playing in the Dark* as a model for reading, I am not seeking to conflate race and disability, but rather to explore how Morrison's perspectives on these matters complicate our understanding of the categories and their place in literary history. As Morrison puts it, celebrating the pleasures and possibilities through new and enriching critical perspectives seems to 'render the nation's literature a much more complex and rewarding body of knowledge'.[64] Morrison's desire to reconfigure the critical landscape of American literature by focusing on a repressed Africanist presence returns us to Woolf's metaphor of an 'undiscovered country'[65] of invalid experience:

These chapters put forth an argument for extending the study of American literature into what I hope will be a wider landscape. I want to draw a map, so to speak, of a critical geography and use that map to open as much space for discovery, intellectual adventure and close exploration as did the original charting of the New World – without the mandate for conquest.[66]

Drawing on Morrison, MacMurphy and Woolf, I hope in this study to chart new critical territory, to explore the ways in which a focus on the representation of disability shifts our understanding of Faulkner, Morrison and Coetzee and the relationship between them, and to contribute to an emerging critical category for examining twentieth-century and twenty-first-century literature and culture.

2
Tales Told by an Idiot: Disability and Sensory Perception in William Faulkner's Fiction and Criticism

As a young man, William Faulkner created a personal myth of disability. Aged just nineteen when America joined the First World War in 1917, Faulkner found himself unable to join the United States Army because of his height (five foot five inches). Instead, he joined first the Canadian Air Force and then the British Royal Air Force. During his short time spent in air force training, Faulkner employed his skills as a writer to fabricate stories of his own injury and disability. Despite the fact that he never served in action, and probably never even flew a plane, Faulkner 'wrote home about... crashing his plane upside down in the rafters of a hangar... He arrived at Oxford railway station limping, having acquired a mythical war wound to complete his identity as hero of the air.'[1]

By the time he wrote *Soldier's Pay* in 1926, this fictionalization of his own disabled body had been expanded. Gray, a biographer of Faulkner, goes on to describe how: 'He had even adopted a second wound... His brother Jack had been injured by shrapnel while in France and severely wounded in the head... Faulkner claimed a similar injury.'[2] These stories, though revised and re-written in various versions over the course of his lifetime, were never fully refuted by Faulkner himself.

These personal fantasies need to be seen in the context of a time when there was a sudden increase in the visibility of physical disability on a national level. By 1918 four million American men had been drafted and in the aftermath of the war huge numbers of them returned home with shocking physical injuries and permanent disabilities. In a later essay, 'On Privacy' written in 1955, Faulkner looking back suggests both a physical and a linguistic crisis which followed the conflict, a fault line which disrupted gender identities and divided families. He describes a post-war world in which 'the American dream has abandoned us'[3] and the possibility of storytelling is itself in doubt: 'Now what we hear is ... the loud and empty words which have been emasculated of all meaning' (66). The narrative, historical and ethical problems, as well as possibilities generated by this attempt to narrate unspeakable experiences become central to the complex narrative structures of Faulkner's fictional writing.

This sense of a damaged and imperfect body politic – an American dream in tatters – also intersects with the rise of the eugenics movement in America. The classification and testing of American children and servicemen, most notably through the Binet Intelligence Scale (or IQ test) which was introduced in 1908, raised widespread concerns about the definition of the citizen and the responsibility of the state. These medical divisions were highly politicized: used to draw lines along racial lines and as a tool to control immigration early in the century. In 1915, for example, psychologist Robert Yerkes used intelligence testing to suggest that 37 per cent of white Americans and 89 per cent of African Americans could be classified as 'moronic', with a mental age of between eight and twelve.[4] Notions of an idealized American identity were threatened by the deviant bodies and minds of a growing class who were being designated as 'feeble-minded'. Disabled bodies and minds were increasingly visible, due to the physical and psychological trauma of modern warfare abroad but also a widespread anxiety about the perceived growth of 'idiocy' inside the borders of the United States itself.

Faulkner's performance of heroism and disability in his youth introduces a distinctively personal edge to the wider cultural concern with the representation of disability that remained with him over the course of his working life. His absurd early fictions give way to more serious concerns which are explored in his writing: concerns about what it means for the able-bodied to write about disability and to attempt to imagine experiences from the perspective of marginalized people. Yet, the ambivalence, fascination and fraudulence are also present in Faulkner's tragi-comic representations of disability, which are often poised between sensationalist exploitation and creative reimagination. His novels depict a wide range of conditions from mental impairment in the form of the 'idiots' Benjy and Ike in *The Sound and the Fury* (1929) and *The Hamlet* (1940), to the physically disabled First World War heroes in *Soldier's Pay* (1926) and *A Fable* (1954).

Soldier's Pay and *A Fable* seem to provide an imaginative outlet for unspoken desires in Faulkner's own past, as well as a chance to explore blank spots in national memory. In both novels, Faulkner depicts semi-autobiographical young pilot figures, Julian Lowe and Captain Levine, who share Faulkner's own frustration with abrupt, premature endings. Faulkner was denied the opportunity to serve by the fact that the war ended halfway through his air force training; Cadet Julian Lowe complains that: 'They had stopped the war on him.'[5] Lowe denies the pain of the individual, suffering body; instead, he jealously views the scar of his war-wounded companion, Donald, as an abstract badge of honour:

> Raising his hand he felt his own undamaged brow. No scar there... To have been him! He moaned... To have got wings on my breast... and to have got his scar, too, I would take death tomorrow. (38)

The imagined scar is understood not as the remnant of a bloody wound but as a traumatic yet heroic narrative inscribed onto the surface of the skin. This fragile narrative, which Lowe clings to, is challenged by the solid materiality of his own body.

Through this blurring of personal fantasy and literary fiction *Soldier's Pay* and *A Fable* articulate, in Faulkner's own words, 'the writer's secret life... the dark twin of a man'.[6] Just as Lowe projects his desires onto Donald as a kind of double, Levine and Lowe mirror Faulkner's own personal frustrations. The fact that *Soldier's Pay* was written near the start of his career and *A Fable* was written near the end makes any linear, strictly autobiographical reading of Faulkner's treatment of disability inadvisable. Between these two points, Faulkner shifted from external to internal narrative perspectives on impairment and disability in, for example, *The Sound and the Fury* (1929). Yet, *Soldier's Pay* and *A Fable* suggest his personal investment in the on-going problem of narrating, understanding and imagining varying experiences of disability in his fiction as well as his own life.

This chapter probes the problematic status of disability *as a fiction* played out in Faulkner's novels and critical writing. How does Faulkner, as an able-bodied white male living in the American South at the turn of the century, respond to the challenge of imagining conditions of physical otherness and social marginality? How does the representation of conditions of mental and physical impairment reconfigure modes of seeing and knowing within these texts? And how does Faulkner approach the problem of finding a form for 'a virtually unknowable ontological position'?[7]

The significance of discourses of eugenics and idiocy in Faulkner's works has been relatively unexplored. Medical records and sociological reports from the period provide an important historical context for Faulkner's shifting understandings of disability which are reflected and refracted through his fictional and critical writing. Conflations of different forms of disability were common in the period in which Faulkner was writing, when mentally and physically impaired people were often assimilated into a single category of socially 'defective delinquents'.[8] Faulkner's novels challenge these homogenizing categories both through their representation of conditions of disability and their complex structures of narration. So, the experience of disability is explored not merely as a 'problem of representation',[9] but also as an embodied condition. Time, space and sensory perception are imaginatively reconfigured to explore alternative, marginalized perspectives in his fiction including those of isolated black characters, women, the dead and the disabled. A personal, embodied fascination with disability seems to drive Faulkner's desire to perhaps sensationalize and exploit but also to experiment with form and explore the limits of empathy.

The physicality of language in Faulkner's writing

Faulkner depicts writing as an intensely bodily process that is paradoxically both pleasurable and painful: 'Good writing...worth the agony and the sweat.'[10] There is a complex intertwining of the spiritual and physical, material and metaphorical, bodily and linguistic in his writing. His focus on a wide range of conditions of physical and mental disability foregrounds those who are outside of conventional temporal, economic, narrative and linguistic structures. Disabled figures act as physical reminders of the horrors of warfare: the anonymous 'soldiers maimed and unmaimed...old men and women in black veils and armbands'[11] provide a background in *A Fable* but they also occupy the foreground of works such as *Soldier's Pay*. The centrality of traditionally marginalized perspectives in Faulkner's novels is most striking in the first section of *The Sound and the Fury* in which readers become complicit with 'idiot' Benjy's mode of perceiving the world.

Faulkner's focus on conditions of sensory deprivation and mental impairment has frequently been read by critics in terms of a representational, linguistic crisis. Benjy's inarticulate, spiralling howl, 'bellow on bellow...more than astonishment...it was horror; shock; agony eyeless, tongueless; just sound',[12] which echoes throughout the text resonates with Elaine Scarry's sense of 'the collapse of language in the face of pain':[13] 'the shapeless bellows that have no words behind them'.[14] From the beginning of his career, Faulkner's writing exhibited anxiety about the possibility of linguistic dissolution. These linguistic concerns have often overshadowed critical engagements with Faulkner's depictions of corporeal vulnerability and the insistent physicality of his imagery. Martin Halliwell, for example, reduces Faulkner's representation of Benjy to a literary device through which Faulkner deploys 'the idiot's mind as a textual vehicle'.[15] This approach risks effacing the complex interrelation between materiality and metaphor in Faulkner's writing, subsuming the suffering, individual body into an exclusively abstract, linguistic critical discourse.[16]

The visual and verbal conventions of realist fiction are challenged by the sheer prevalence of blind, visually impaired, inarticulate characters that proliferate in Faulkner's writing. Even as he describes a condition of linguistic collapse, Faulkner returns to the body as an alternative site of potential meaning and communication. In 'On Privacy', for example, Faulkner suggests the breakdown of oppositional models of identity and meaning structured around differences such as race and gender:

> The empty mouthsound of freedom ... Truth – that long clean clear undeviable unchallengeable straight and shining line, on one side of which black is black and on the other white is white, has now become an angle, a point of view ... depending solely on where you are standing when you look at it. (72)

The destabilizing hollowing out of 'old verities'[17] and values is linked here to voids within the body: the empty and gaping mouth. Voices become embodied as a series of mimed 'mouthsounds'. This representational crisis is, for Faulkner, always mediated by the body.

Faulkner frequently represents language itself in distinctly physical terms. In *The Hamlet* (1931), we are reminded that the narrative is not only mediated by an oral tradition of storytelling, but also by the body of the teller: 'You fellows don't know how good a man's voice feels running betwixt his teeth.'[18] Paradoxically, the dissolution of meaning is linked to a simultaneous 'fleshing' out of the voice in the ritualistic church scene in *The Sound and the Fury*: 'With his body he seemed to feed the voice that, succubus like, had fleshed its teeth in him' (294). The power of Shegog's Easter Service sermon lies not in its meaning, but rather in its capacity to facilitate non-linguistic, intuitive communication between bodies, 'their hearts were speaking to one another in chanting measures' allowing access to a realm 'beyond the need for words' (295).

Intervening bodies: the disruption of visual, verbal and narrative structures

Faulkner's representation of disability endows his writing with an intense narrative richness through its sensitivity to different forms of sensory perception. Language becomes significant for its shapes, abstract sounds and texture, as Faulkner seeks to represent what Maurice Merleau-Ponty describes as the 'thickness of experience'.[19] In *A Fable*, for example, the sensations of touch and the act of speech are similarly intertwined, as words are described in terms of their fluid texture and temperature, rather than their meaning:

> The pinch of his hand between the bayonet's cross guard and his own flesh told him better and so he could stop the crying now – the sweet thick warm murmur of it pouring suddenly from his mouth. (1009)

The flesh itself takes on a role as a potentially signifying surface here, the body is placed in the foreground as that which at once blurs and mediates communication: 'The thickness of the flesh between the seer and the thing . . . is not an obstacle between them, it is their means of communication.'[20]

Faulkner challenges the primacy of visual clarity or enlightened 'truth' through a focus on interior perspectives and the individual, subjective and distinctly physical aspects of disabled experience. He shifts these 'abnormal' bodies from the social margins to the centre of his fiction and criticism. As Woolf describes in 'On Being Ill', the processes of narration and perception are always mediated by the body: 'All day, all night the body intervenes' (4).

The striking presentness and experiential quality to Benjy's narrative in *The Sound and the Fury*, for example, blur the boundary between mind and body but also highlight the artificiality of conventional divisions between the senses:

> I squatted there, holding the slipper. I couldn't see it, but my hands saw it, and I could hear it getting night, and my hands saw the slipper but I couldn't see myself . . . I squatted there, hearing it get dark. (70)

Distinctions between light and dark, smell and vision are destabilized, as touch becomes a primary stimulus for memory. Like Woolf, Faulkner suggests that overlooked invalid or disabled bodies not only 'intervene' in literary conventions of seeing, but also open up alternative, rich sensory narrative modes.

In *Soldier's Pay*, *The Sound and the Fury*, *The Hamlet* and *A Fable*, Faulkner perpetually returns to the body in his struggle to imagine otherness and to depict conditions of disability conventionally placed in a realm beyond words. He explores bodies and narratives that live on beyond conventional endings. *Soldier's Pay*, his first novel, announces itself as a war story, yet, in fact, it begins after the conflict has ended. Donald Mahon, the doctor declares, 'should have been dead these three months were it not for the fact that he seems to be waiting for something. Something he has begun but has not completed' (128).

Written at the end of Faulkner's career, *A Fable* returns to the same First World War context explored in *Soldier's Pay* and to the sense of a maimed and wounded body that has lived on too long. In the final scene, dialogue is fragmented and sparse but powerfully embodied through Faulkner's focus on mouths as mediators of speech: '[The soldier] turned his head a little until he could spit out the blood and shattered teeth and speak' (1072). The disturbing presence of the disabled soldier, whose identity is stripped away until he becomes 'not a man but a mobile and upright scar...one arm and one leg, one entire side of his hatless head was one hairless eyeless and earless sear' (1072), shatters the ritual closure of the final procession scene. His last words echo a wider resistance to both narrative and bodily closure in Faulkner's writing: ' "That's right," he said: "Tremble. I'm not going to die. Never" ' (1072). So, in both *A Fable* and *Soldier's Pay*, the wounded bodies come to serve both as symbols and as literal, physical reminders of a brutal historical reality that cannot be hidden from view, a chapter in history that is not closed. The marked, maimed and inscribed bodies of the wounded soldiers act as a shocking 'hang-over of warfare in a society tired of warfare',[21] a literal 'remnant, a trace, of a distant European war'.[22]

In *The Sound and the Fury* and *The Hamlet*, mental impairment is often described in a highly physical way. The 'idiot' figures of Ike and Benjy represent 'intervening' bodies that refuse to be removed from view or assimilated into a sense of narrative closure. Their messy, uncontrolled, indeed 'uncivilized'[23] bodies constantly threaten to overflow their own corporeal boundaries, and the frame of the narrative itself: drooling, babbling, crying, howling, sexually desiring. Benjy is not hidden away and institutionalized at Jackson until the belated appendix in *The Sound and the Fury*; 'bear-like' Ike resists attempts to cage him inside the house in *The Hamlet*, and both figures refuse the constant injunction to 'hush'.

Faulkner is fascinated by liminal spaces: the gap between life and death in *Soldier's Pay*; the hiatus in the war depicted in *A Fable*; the timeless narrative of Quentin with his smashed pocket watch in *The Sound and the Fury*. In his focus on how damaged bodies live on after and disrupt fixed narrative endings, Faulkner's writing probes what Frank Kermode terms 'the interval between "tock" and "tick" [which] represents purely successive, disorganized time'.[24] His writing also goes beyond this to consider how the writer's voice will prevail over mortality, the ambivalent narrative space *after* the final 'ding dong': 'When the last dingdong of doom has clanged and faded from the last worthless rock hanging tideless in the last red and dying evening, that even then there will still be one more sound: that of [the writer's] puny inexhaustible voice, still talking.'[25]

Contextualizing Faulkner: disability and the instability of the category

In his representation of these on-going conditions of disability and his specific focus on 'idiocy' and war-wounded soldiers, Faulkner was engaging with contemporary cultural anxieties. A complex interdependence between individual and national bodies was emerging as the fragmented bodies and shattered nerves of soldiers returning from the First World War threw abstract idealized notions of heroic masculinity into doubt. Men who were incapacitated, incapable of work, of sexual relations or of controlling their own bodies disrupted conceptions of the figure at the heart of the American dream as a white male, heroic in war yet also productive: physically and economically self-supporting in an emerging domestic capitalist economy. In *Soldier's Pay*, Mrs Saunders rages to her husband:

> The idea of you driving your own daughter into marriage with a man who has nothing ... may be half dead, and who probably won't work anyway. You know yourself how these ex-soldiers are. (82)

The intrusion of the brutal realities of war, permanently inscribed on the wounded body of the soldier, into the enclosed domestic sphere, inaugurates a temporal, linguistic and bodily rupture in *Soldier's Pay*. Donald's unspeakable scar comes to symbolize a 'fault ... in American culture'.[26]

Anxieties about the perceived growth of idiocy or 'feeble-mindedness' in the American population created a sense that the American dream was not only under attack by foreign enemies in warfare, but was also from inside its own national boundaries. A study by the Juvenile Protective Association of Cincinnati published in 1915, for example, declared: 'The important thing at the present time is ... to recognize that there is a serious problem created by the feeble-minded in our midst' (18).

For Faulkner personally, this impression of 'the feeble-minded in our midst' was evident in his early life. His first-grade teacher, Annie Chandler, and her mentally impaired brother, Edwin, lived just a few streets away from his childhood home in Oxford, Mississippi. Joseph Blotner, Faulkner's biographer, depicts Edwin in a manner that is highly reminiscent of Faulkner's own fictional rendering of Benjy staring through the garden gate: '[His] mind would never grow to adulthood as his body had done years before. Faulkner had seen him behind his iron fence since childhood.'[27]

Faulkner's representation of 'idiot' figures in his fiction is therefore derived in part from his personal experience, but also from a proliferation of cultural and literary representations of mental 'defectives' and delinquents in the years preceding *The Sound and the Fury*. Faulkner's short story 'The Kingdom of God' (1925) represented a static image of the idiot; a figure incapable of speech and, as far as readers see, any kind of independent thought. This unnamed 'idiot' is a passive, silent observer of the robbery that takes place, until his fit of crying at the end of the short piece draws attention to the crime and to himself. The external positioning of the narrator, who is shut out of the consciousness of the 'idiot' figure, is characteristic of other literary representations of idiocy in the decades when Faulkner was growing up. Authors frequently depicted this topical figure of 'the idiot' for comic effect, with omniscient narrators who spoke for the silent central character; for example in the collection of short stories published by W. C. Morrow in 1897, *The Ape, the Idiot and Other People*,[28] or John Kendrick Bangs's comic illustrated novel, *The Idiot*[29] (1895) and its sequel, the domestic comedy of manners, *The Idiot at Home*[30] (1900).

The Sound and the Fury, so often celebrated for its radical innovation and originality,[31] must also be read against a background of on-going debates about the nature and definition of idiocy. The novel represents yet also challenges stereotypical understandings of idiocy that were widespread at the time of its publication. From the interior perspective represented in the first section, Benjy's narrative is rich, filled with distinct smells and sounds, as well as a diverse range of other sensory perceptions. Yet, viewed from the outside by other characters in the following sections, Benjy is dismissed. Infantilizing and animalistic discourses link Benjy to Donald in *Soldier's Pay* and Ike in *The Hamlet*. They are disparagingly described as a 'gelding', 'bear', 'rat', 'goat', 'big foolish dog', 'looney' and 'a grown child'.[32] These reductive, animalistic and infantilizing discourses echo the easy association of categories in Morrow's short stories (*The Ape, the Idiot and Other People*), but they also draw on contemporary medical understandings of idiocy which condemned sections of the population to be shut out from definitions of adult citizenship. Joseph Byers's report, 'Colony Care of the Feeble-minded' in 1915, for example, described the feeble-minded as 'grown-up children'[33] or more specifically, 'child's minds in the bodies of men and women' (13).

Reports such as Byers's, produced across the United States under the auspices of 'The National Committee for Mental Hygiene', associated mental deficiency with moral depravity, as 'idiots' were conflated with paupers, criminals, prostitutes, alcoholics and physically disabled people to form 'the defective delinquent class'.[34] J. Harold Williams, for example, titled his report 'Feeble-mindedness and Delinquency' (1915) while Henry H. Goddard explored 'Feeble-mindedness as a Social Problem' (1915).

Social and moral questions about mental and physical disability abounded. In particular, the question of how to care for dependent and marginalized groups was a matter of intense contemporary debate. Jason poses these same questions in *The Sound and the Fury*. For Jason, characters are linked and defined according to their economic dependency upon him. He groups these figures together in his imagination as parasites, speculating that if he died, Quentin would 'have to work some to feed a few invalids and idiots and niggers' (246). These concerns with social care resonate with early twentieth-century debates, as care shifted from a familial matter within the household (as at the beginning of *The Sound and the Fury*) to an increasing emphasis upon state intervention.[35] Calls for the institutionalization of 'idiots' are visually encoded in this wheel image which, like Jason's description, links idiocy, criminality and pauperism (Figure 2). The state institutions around the edge of the wheel – the jailhouse, court, hospital and workhouse – suggest the struggle by state authorities in this period to adapt medical, legal and political frameworks to control the perceived threat from a 'defective class' (15).

The animalistic insults hurled at Benjy in *The Sound and the Fury* and Ike in *The Hamlet* echo eugenics discourses in which policies of

30

Figure 2 The Juvenile Protective Association of Cincinnati, *The Feeble-Minded; or, the Hub to our Wheel of Vice, Crime and Pauperism* (Cincinnati, 1915), cover, print with text

'breeding' aimed to create an idealized norm. Davenport, writing in 1915, suggested:

> The experience of animal and plant breeders ... should lead us to see that proper matings are the greatest means of permanently improving the human race – of saving it from imbecility, poverty, disease and immorality.[36]

The landmark case of *Buck* v. *Bell* was tried in the Supreme Court in 1927, just two years before the publication of *The Sound and the Fury*, in which Dr James Hendren Bell sought the right to sterilize Carrie Bell, a 'feeble-minded' woman under his care at Virginia State Colony for Epileptics and the Feeble-minded. Against the wishes of Carrie and her guardian, who mounted a legal challenge against Bell on her behalf, Carrie was sterilized following a ruling which judged her to be 'promiscuous', 'feeble-minded' and illegitimate. The case gained immediate national attention and had shocking, lasting policy implications, as it set a legal precedent for the compulsory sterilization of the 'unfit', including the feeble-minded, in Virginia and had the effect of legitimizing the practice in many other states in the South. The case provides an important context for the castration and institutionalization of Benjy in an asylum in Jackson at the end of *The Sound and the Fury*. These were issues of national, political concern, as well as moral and social debate, which Faulkner refused to ignore in his writing.

   The homogenizing perspective of these legal, political and medical discourses, in which mental, physical and moral 'deficiencies' are perpetually linked, is implicitly challenged by Faulkner's highly individualized literary representations of 'idiot' figures. *The Sound and the Fury* dramatizes a blurring of this distinction between different forms of disability, as characters frequently presume that Benjy's mental impairment can be equated with a condition of complete sensory alienation. Luster insists on a biologically deterministic view of Benjy's condition, seeing him as isolated and unchanging: ' "He can't tell what you saying" Luster said. "He deef and dumb ... Been that way thirty-three years today ... Born looney." '[37] Similarly, in *The Hamlet*, Ike is described from the perspective of the surrounding community as having 'pale eyes which seemed to have no vision in them at all'.[38] Ike's ambiguous level of perception initiates a rush on the part of other characters to dismiss his ability to engage with the world entirely.

   Even as these discourses of homogenizing otherness are articulated in the texts, however, Faulkner exposes the 'blinding' nature of these generalizing tendencies. The sensitivity to smell, sound, light and specific detail in both Benjy's and Ike's narratives challenges widespread assumptions that equated mental impairment with complete sensory alienation. In this way, Faulkner's texts both engage with dominant medical definitions, in which the surface of the body was 'read' as a mirror of mental and moral capacity, and simultaneously disrupt this assumed mimetic correspondence between interior and exterior.

Soldier's Pay and the sciences of the surface

In *Soldier's Pay*, Faulkner confronts readers with the paradoxical possibilities and problems of 'reading' the skin as a signifying surface, by placing the scarred, silent body of war-wounded soldier Donald Mahon at the centre of the text. In *Soldier's Pay*, the so-called logic of the 'Sciences of the Surface'[39] – of craniometry, phrenology, palmistry and physiognomy – become incorporated into the narrative technique itself, as multiple characters seek to interpret and 'read' Donald's character and history through his scar.

From the opening page of the novel, Faulkner presents a fascinated compulsion to stare. The first scene, in which Donald travels back home on the train, sets up his role in the novel as a whole as both a public spectacle and an object of private scrutiny. The impulse to scrutinize coexists with a desire not to be seen looking: 'Craned heads of other passengers became again smugly unconcerned over books and papers' (14). News of Mahon's return home provokes a momentary narratorial aside, in which fascination with Donald's bodily difference recalls a wider 'freak show'[40] context where physical and racial otherness were displayed for the public gaze as a form of entertainment:

> In front of the post office the rector was at the centre of an interested circle ... The gathering was representative ... anything from a captured still to a Negro with an epileptic fit or a mouth organ attracts to itself like atoms to a magnet, in any small southern town. (92)

The imagery of magnetism suggests the simultaneous attraction and repulsion towards the disabled body; the act of looking implies a hierarchized dialectic between viewer and viewed, a morally ambiguous relationship between audience and object to which Faulkner constantly returns.

From the beginning of *Soldier's Pay*, however, Faulkner insists on the inadequacy of an exclusively visual narrative mode. The subjective nature of perception is exposed through a return to the body. The opening scene is focalized through a narrative perspective that is self-consciously mediated: Cadet Julian Lowe 'surveyed the world with a yellow and disgruntled eye. He suffered the same jaundice that many a more booted than he did' (7). Lowe's dialogue with a fellow soldier immediately turns to visual impairments caused during warfare; his companion laments: ' "I got gassed doing k.p. and my sight ain't been the same since" ' (7).

Bodies, and faces in particular, emerge as highly unstable signifiers in the novel. Despite the desire to read the skin, characters are forced to confront the illegible nature of bodily surfaces. George Farr indulges in a fantasy of the body as a transparent object, as a text which clearly yields its meaning, yet he is forced to admit his own limitations as a reader: 'George considered himself quite a man. I wonder if it shows in my face? he thought, keenly examining the faces of men who passed, trying to fancy that he did see something … But he had to admit that he could see nothing' (122). *Soldier's Pay* both sets up, and ridicules, the possibility of these superficial surface readings. The skin on Cecily's face is figured as a detachable garment: '[She] changed her expression as readily as you would a hat' (180). The correspondence between interior and exterior, implicit in the 'Sciences of the Surface', is increasingly undermined by the illegible bodily surfaces depicted in the text itself.

In parallel with the onset of Donald's blindness, therefore, readers themselves become increasingly confronted with their own condition of not seeing. As *Soldier's Pay* progresses, it becomes evident that Donald's 'unspeakable' scar is never actually going to be described by either the narrator or any of the characters. In contrast to the representation of beautiful yet shameful scars in Morrison's *Beloved*, such as the tree-like wounds inflicted on Sethe's back, Faulkner depicts scars that are perceived as heroic. In *Beloved*, the scar opens up an oral tradition of storytelling, triggering a rich combination of slave narratives, personal memories and highly vivid, visual descriptions. In *Soldier's Pay*, the story behind the scar is never told; instead, the scar is a site of fantasy. Donald's blank memory and incomplete back-narrative engage both readers and characters in an active imaginative reconstruction of fragments of the past. Readers, imagining the scar, come to resemble the wounded soldiers sitting on the sidelines at the dance, playing a dual role in relation to the narrative, as 'both participants and spectators at the same time' (159).

The condition of not seeing also initiates an act of storytelling on the part of the other characters in the novel. Donald's wounded body emerges as a void or blind spot at the centre of the text. This is the narrative of a soldier who refuses to tell war stories, a self-abnegating memoir of one who 'remembers nothing' (97). Characters around Donald rush to fill this void with their own narratives and highly subjective readings of the scar. His father, for example, sustains a delusional fantasy of rehabilitation and cure, as well as idealized romance: ' "Cecily is the best medicine he can have... he has a scar, you see. But I am confident this can be removed" ' (94).

The onset of Donald's blindness also leads to an increasing focus in *Soldier's Pay* on alternative modes of sensory perception. In the context of this darkening vision, touch becomes a mode of communication and identification in the text. One of the few moments of apparent recognition by Donald is provoked not by speech but by touch. It is the very condition of not seeing (on the part of both Donald and Cecily) that allows this moment of intimacy and non-linguistic communication between them:

> 'Donald, sweetheart,' [Cecily] said, putting her arm about Mahon. From here she could not see the scar so she drew his face to hers with her hand, laying her cheek against his. Feeling her touch... he stirred. 'It's Cecily... Put your arm around me like you used to.' (172)

The gradual destabilizing of vision over the course of *Soldier's Pay* – physically, in Donald's case and at the level of narrative perspective itself – allows touch to replace vision as the primary means of perception. Identities are traced out with the fingers rather than seen with the eyes: ' "Cecily, what is it?" Knowing a sharp premonition he raised her face, trying to see it. But it was only a formless soft blur warmly in his hands' (229). By charting the gradual decline of Donald, *Soldier's Pay* enacts, on one level, Santanu Das's sense that 'as words fail and life ebbs away, the body moves in to fill the void: touch becomes the final antidote against the desolation of death' (24).

Yet, just as visual 'reading' of the skin is rendered problematic, ultimately, touch also fails to mediate between the interior and the exterior in the novel. Faulkner sets up the possibility of touch as a mode of communicating memories that cannot be spoken, through rare intimate moments of literal and metaphorical contact between bodies. However, for most of *Soldier's Pay*, physical interiors remain impenetrable: 'There was something frozen in [Emmy's] chest like a dishcloth in winter' (112). Like Paul D in Morrison's *Beloved* (1987), who has a 'tobacco tin buried in his chest where a red heart used to be' (73), trauma solidifies the surfaces of the body, creating a mysterious space within, a 'cache or lair'[41] as a repository for memory. This sense of physical inaccessibility is manifested in the narrative perspective itself: readers are never allowed an insight into the interiors of Donald's consciousness, apart from a flash of memory in his dying moments.

In this early novel, Faulkner insists on a view of war as a phenomenon that is, ultimately, beyond the reach of *any* of the senses:

> Mankind's emotional gamut is like his auricular gamut: there are some things which he cannot feel, as there are sounds he cannot hear. And war, taken as a whole, is one of these things.[42]

Faulkner poses the problem of mediating narrative through a 'body that is already dead'.[43] Incapable of speech, Donald's fragmented body, suspended in a liminal space between life and death, can only convey momentary splintered shards of memory or narrative. Faulkner sets his novel in Georgia during peacetime, geographically and emotionally remote from the conflict. Many characters self-consciously articulate their own failure to literally, metaphorically and emotionally 'feel' another's grief. Margaret Powers laments: 'Am I cold by nature...that I don't seem to feel things like others?' (33). Cecily is utterly incapable of engaging in an act of imagining which, Gilligan suggests, is necessary if narrative is going to inspire compassion and empathetic identification: 'What does [Cecily] know about dying? She can't even imagine herself getting old, let alone imagining anybody she is interested in dying' (88). Faulkner figures these problems of communication and the mediation of experience, between combatant and non-combatant, narrator and reader, disabled and able-bodied figures, as a failure of literary imagination that, for Margaret at least, is inescapably intertwined with a sense of alienation from the body and embodied forms of perception: 'This man...this man here, sleeping beneath his scar...Where do we touch?' (38).

The Sound and the Fury: alternative forms of sensory perception

The Sound and the Fury, written three years later in 1929, marked a turning point in Faulkner's representation of disability. In contrast to the closed bodies and external narrative perspective of *Soldier's Pay*, the first section of *The Sound and the Fury* is characterized by a striking and inescapable interiority, as Faulkner seeks to represent the opening section of his narrative through the eyes and 'benighted brain of an idiot'[44] – the mentally impaired character, Benjamin Compson. In contrast to the impenetrable bodily surfaces of *Soldier's Pay*, the permeability and sensitivity of Benjy's eyes, and in fact his whole body, allow Faulkner to dramatize the relationship between exterior stimuli and interior emotional responses. This permeability also characterizes the relationship between past and present in Benjy's narrative, as realist conventions of seeing, knowing and narrating are reconfigured, and linear narrative structures are abandoned entirely.

This fresh approach to endings yields a whole new set of narrative beginnings in Faulkner's fiction. To quote Mr Compson, it seems that 'only when the clock stops does time come to life' (83). In interviews, Faulkner frequently described how he was able to write *The Sound and the Fury* because he felt liberated from economic, material and literary constraints: 'One day I seemed to shut a door between me and all publishers' addresses and book lists. I said to myself, now I can write.'[45] In contrast to the failed acts of literary imagining dramatized in *Soldier's Pay*, Faulkner suggests that *The Sound and the Fury* allowed him, through his writing, to transcend his subject position as a white, middle-class able-bodied male, to engage with and imagine the experience of a sexual or physical other:

> Previous to it I had written three novels, with progressively decreasing ease and pleasure...Now I, who had three brothers and no sisters...began to write about a little girl. (293)

This transcendence, however, was one that brought a return to the body both in the novel itself and in the process of writing, which he described as both chaotic – 'the first section, seemed to explode onto the paper in front of me' (293) – and intensely physical. *The Sound and the Fury* was 'a novel into which', as Faulkner put it, 'I had written my guts'.[46]

Writing later in his life about *The Sound and the Fury*, Faulkner remarked: 'The idea struck me to see how much more I could have got out of the idea of the blind self-centredness of innocence, typified by children, if one of those children had been truly innocent, that is an idiot.'[47] Here, Faulkner characterizes Benjy in terms of traditional associations between idiocy, child-like innocence, natural primitivism and blindness.[48] However, there is a disjunction between Faulkner's somewhat reductive critical commentary and the fiction itself which engages with a wide range of sensory impressions. The level of Benjy's comprehension is as a source of speculation amongst the other characters.

Luster associates Benjy not with symbolic blindness but rather with uncanny intuition and superior foresight: ' "He knows a lot more than folks thinks...He could tell you when his [time is] coming...Or yours. Or mine." '[49] In contrast to the liminal position that Faulkner attributes to Benjy in his later critical writing, the novel itself locates Benjy at the centre of the text as the source of an enabling new mode of reading, writing and narrating.

Much critical attention has been focused on Benjy's position outside dominant verbal and visual structures. The recurring mirror moments in *The Sound and the Fury* have led to Benjy being read, by Mellard for example, as a static 'moral mirror',[50] playing a purely mimetic role by reflecting the moral deficiency of the characters around him. Similarly, Benjy's incapacity to speak is viewed, by Wesley Morris and Barbara Alverson Morris for example, as a sign of his complete lack of agency and deficiency as a narrator, capable only of echoing other people's words: 'Surrounded by words he cannot use...Benjy's narrative is predominantly the voices of others he hears.'[51]

This critical commonplace that Benjy inhabits a 'world in which he cannot communicate',[52] relies upon a narrow understanding of communication and perception. Both Mellard's and Morris's readings implicitly privilege the verbal and the visual modes which are called into question by the novel itself. Despite these critical claims about the limitations of Benjy's perspective, it is in fact Quentin who is haunted by the recognition of his own occluded vision: 'It was like I was looking at him through a piece of colored glass I could hear my blood and then I could see the sky again' (160).

While Benjy's narrative is highly literal, both Quentin's and Jason's descriptions are perpetually mediated by obscuring metaphors. Quentin is self-conscious about this distorted visual perception and the slippage between the narrative 'I' and 'eye': 'The whole thing came to symbolize night and unrest...where all stable things had become shadowy paradoxical...I was I was not who was not was not who' (169). For Jason, the physical and material become eclipsed by a personal symbolic reading: his niece had not had 'entity or individuality for him for ten years...[she] merely symbolized the job in the bank of which he had been deprived' (306). His claim to clear-eyed rationality, as 'the first sane Compson',[53] is undermined by the subjective blind spots which are revealed in his section of the narrative. (Jason never acknowledges, for example, his own gambling losses, and is incapable of imagining the world through Quentin's consciousness.) His devotion to a narrow doctrine of rationality is exposed as a form of blinkered vision, resting upon a series of brittle logical constructs that threaten to collapse in the final scenes of the novel.

Benjy's section not only calls into question the narrative authority of those that follow it, but also challenges realist modes of seeing and conventions of narrative vision. His narrative confronts readers with their own basic assumptions about perception. His literalism highlights the fact that Jason and Quentin's 'normal' narratives are related through the screen of metaphor, but also how readers themselves are implicated in this condition of mediated vision.[54] As readers, our vision is also mediated by unreliable, subjective first-person narrators and the instability of metaphor, as the fragmented narrative perspectives in *The Sound and the Fury* constantly remind us.

Merleau-Ponty describes how the depiction of the 'pre-objective realm'[55] that Benjy seems to inhabit, stripped of mediating metaphors, can lead to a reappraisal of the basic assumptions about sensory perception. The example that Merleau-Ponty chooses is of the liminal space between sleeping and waking:

> I might in the first place understand sensation by . . . the experiencing of a state of myself. The greyness which, when I close my eyes, surrounds me, leaving no distance between me and it, the sounds that encroach on my drowsiness . . . perhaps give some indication of what pure sensation might be. (30)

Faulkner also explores this ambiguous state between sleeping and waking in which the distance between subject and object is collapsed. Benjy's intimate narrative captures the fluidity of distinctions between shapes, sounds and perceptual categories, through a focus on moments when the boundary between sleep and consciousness is blurred: 'The shapes flowed on. The ones on the other side began again, bright and fast and smooth, like when Caddy says we are going to sleep.'[56] Like Woolf's invalid in 'On Being Ill', staring up at the sky, Faulkner suggests that the condition of disability – whether physical or mental – does not foreclose, but rather opens up alternative imaginative and narrative possibilities. Narrative structures themselves become reconfigured in the shape-shifting sense that those who stand outside of the routines of daily life can 'float with the sticks on the stream . . . and look up' (12) to see clouds drifting across the sky in Woolf's essay, or experience the flowing forms passing across the retina in the semi-conscious states depicted in *The Sound and the Fury*.

As in *Soldier's Pay*, Faulkner suggests that the condition of *not seeing* enables alternative narrative possibilities. The innovative quality of Benjy's narrative, as well as its relentless immediacy (even in his representation of past events) resonates with Henri Bergson's theorization of life as a 'continuous creation of unforeseeable novelty'.[57] Bergson's description of 'pure perception'[58] is useful in the sense that experiences are perpetually 'made new' for Benjy: memories are relived, re-enacted, and almost physically re-membered. Bergson suggested that this process occurs in a 'brute consciousness' (69), highlighting a sense of natural primitivism that resonates with the use of the term 'natural' to denote someone considered mentally deficient in the period.[59] Faulkner plays upon these notions of the natural as Benjy is frequently connected with the outside space of the garden, the smell of trees and the perception of his brutish, primitive perspective by other characters. Yet, the novel also exposes how this link between mental impairment and innocence, intuition and an affinity with the natural world connects, paradoxically, to an unnatural tendency to infantilize and animalize many disabled bodies. In *The Sound and the Fury*, patronizing notions of natural simplicity are undercut by the detail and sensitivity of Benjy's narrative, as well as the complexity of his response to alternative forms of perception.

While touch gradually replaces vision as the primary communicative sense in *Soldier's Pay*, *The Sound and the Fury* also places Benjy's sensitivity to smell and sound at the forefront of the narrative. At first, it seems that smell functions solely as a means of identification: 'Caddy smelled like trees' (42). As the narrative develops, however, a more complex relationship to smell emerges. Smell takes on a symbolic capacity, acting as an index through which the superficially chaotic chronology of the narrative can be charted. The odour of the honeysuckle is, for example, introduced immediately after Caddy first has sexual intercourse with Dalton Ames. Faulkner disrupts contemporary associations between natural imagery and innocence, to depict the honeysuckle as a symbol of sexual experience. It is through his sensitivity to smell that Benjy articulates his impulse towards continuity. Benjy responds not only to the change in Caddy's odour, but also to her implicit sexual development. He articulates this resistance through cries and screams, until she is forced to wash off her new perfume:

> 'Why, Benjy. What is it' ... She took up the bottle and took the stopper out and held it to my nose. 'Sweet. Smell. Good.'

I went away and didn't hush... 'Oh.' She said. She put the bottle down... 'Of course Caddy won't'... Caddy smelled like trees. (40)

In a later scene, this employment of smell as a subtle narrative marker is highlighted once again when Benjy objects to Caddy's interactions with Charlie, bellowing until his sense of 'natural' odour and order is restored. It is only once Caddy has taken 'the kitchen soap and washed her mouth at the sink, hard' that Benjy's sense of stability returns: 'Caddy smelled like trees' (46). His power of smell slowly comes to be recognized by the other characters in the novel, not only as an expression of his desire for stasis and purity, but also as an alternative form of intuitive, almost otherworldly, knowledge and foresight which they cannot access: 'Can he smell that new name they gave him? Can he smell bad luck?' (87). It is through this form of embodied perception, a complex and multi-layered series of sensations and responses to stimuli, that Benjy asserts a narrative agency of his own in the action of the story.

The impression that 'the world does not make sense but only sensation'[60] is therefore central to the experiential (and experimental) mode of *The Sound and the Fury*. Touch, texture and temperature are related in highly specific detail; the feeling of water, for example, triggers a flood of associative impressions and memories in Benjy's interior narrative. The act of putting his foot in the creek initiates a reliving of Damuddy's funeral years earlier, in 1898. Touch becomes a trigger for storytelling here, illustrating the fluid relationship between past and present in Benjy's narrative as a whole. Literal settings in *The Sound and the Fury* echo contemporary theoretical metaphors used to describe a distinctly Modernist conception of what Bergson calls 'the bottomless bankless river'[61] of reality. There is a sense that each moment is overflowing with a rich multiplicity of sensations and impressions, necessarily leaving any literary rendering of experience incomplete. Similarly, the focus on sound, inscribed in the title of the novel itself, suggests a further sense in which Benjy's body evokes an excess of associations, through the many images and memories generated by a single smell. Rather than closing down communication, or 'signifying nothing', the depiction of Benjy inspires a diverse variety of aural, olfactory and physical impressions, as well as a complex web of intertextual echoes.

Faulkner's focus on sensation also serves to individualize Benjy's section in *The Sound and the Fury* and to locate him in a wider, meta-textual 'distinguished literary tradition of idiots',[62] ranging from

Shakespeare's fools to Dostoevsky's *The Idiot* (1868). The widespread description of mentally disabled figures as 'naturals'[63] further highlights this contemporary connection between uncivilized bodies and minds. The wider cultural tendency to focus on mental impairment from exterior perspectives – in terms of hyper-fertile, uncontrolled bodies – is challenged by Faulkner's focus on detailed interior thought processes and perceptions. Faulkner locates *The Sound and the Fury* in a literary tradition stretching back centuries, but also draws on specific medical debates about idiocy and degeneracy that were pressing in his own period. This rich interweaving of impressions, associations and echoes leads to a sense that Benjy's narrative threatens to spill over boundaries of the body and the frame of the novel itself.

The Hamlet: hyper-fertility and comic absurdity

The two most notable 'idiots' depicted in Faulkner's fiction are Benjy in *The Sound and the Fury* and Ike in *The Hamlet*. Both figures are characterized by a sense of hyper-symbolic narrative excess and also by bodies that threaten to quite literally burst out of their clothing. The physical description of Benjy as 'a big man who appeared to have been shaped of some substance whose particles would not or did not cohere... he moved with a shambling gait' (274), bears a strong resemblance to Ike's limping entrance into *The Hamlet*: 'The hulking shape – the backlooking face with its hanging mouth and pointed faun's ears, the bursting overalls drawn across the incredible female thighs' (95–6). These descriptions highlight how mental impairment was perceived in extremely physical terms, as chaotic surface appearances were read as symbolic of mental disorder.

Perceived through the eyes of external narrators, both Benjy and Ike are viewed as occupying an ambiguous place between male and female, animal and human. Rather than signifying an absence, lack or representational crisis, which his self-abnegating signature 'X' (84) might initially imply, Ike becomes associated with a narrative, imaginative and literal fertility. This excess permeates the structure of *The Hamlet* itself. The multiplicity of narrative styles, threads and modes of communal storytelling (subdivided to resemble a series of short stories) are reflected back in the settings described in the novel itself: 'A sky already breaking as if of its own rich, over-fertile weight' (204).

This sense of fertility, which characterizes Faulkner's literary style and his description of idiocy, was also played out in the contemporary political and social discourses of the period. At the time when Faulkner was writing there was a common perception that there was a correlation between low IQ and high fertility. A study by the Juvenile Protective Association of Cincinnati in 1915, for example, concluded:

> Feeble-mindedness is inherited, and the fecundity of the feeble-minded group is greater than among normal persons...the size of families among these defectives is at least twice as great as among the general population. (5)

The exploration of this supposed 'hyper-fertility'[64] amongst the feeble-minded became, itself, a highly generative area of enquiry for statisticians and politicians who sought to justify policies of institutionalization and sterilization. A report written in 1919 in Georgia for the National Committee for Mental Hygiene reworks the image of a spiralling 'wheel of vice' in the 1915 Cincinnati report to suggest cycles of 'defective progeny':

> Feeble-minded persons are especially prolific, and reproduce their kind with greater frequency than do normal persons...an endless stream of defective progeny, which are a serious drain to the resources of the nation.[65]

The notion of biological fecundity was widely equated with cultural constructions of 'the uncared-for feeble-minded...[as] a fertile source of crime, poverty, prostitution and misery, not only to themselves, but to all with whom they are brought now into contact' (3). There was a further exchange between scientific 'proof' and literary representations of stories of idiocy, as fictionalized case studies were used across the country to exemplify (and justify) social and political policies in which mental incapacity and physical deformity were consistently connected to moral and sexual irregularities including illegitimacy, adultery, prostitution, paedophilia and even incest.[66] In this context, storytelling itself became a rhetorical tool, as gossip or rumour intersected with literary representations and sociological case studies.

In *The Hamlet*, Faulkner draws on these discourses of literal and metaphorical fertility, using his own literary depiction of idiocy to more complex comic and subversive effect. In the section which focuses most closely upon Ike, 'The Long Summer', this wider narrative excess comes to a 'concentrated climax' (186). Initially, Ike is described in highly stylized, pastoral mode, as a romantic hero, awaiting the approach of his lover:

He would begin to hurry...in the growing visibility, the gradation from gray through primrose to the morning's ultimate gold...to let himself downward into the creekside mist and lie in the drenched myriad waking life of grasses and listen for her approach. (182)

The idyllic natural backdrop, however, becomes inverted, as the love-interest, which appears until this moment as an idealized female, is revealed to be a cow: 'The mist blew away and he saw her...paying no attention to where he was going, seeing nothing but the cow' (184). The narrative perspective, which has, until this point in the novel privileged visual perception, becomes shattered as the 'objective' narrator's complicity in this narrative trick is exposed. The 'malleate hands of mist',[67] which shroud the cow, become a metaphor for the depersonalized romantic literary conventions that blind the reader to the realities of the bovine body. Faulkner suggests that the bodies of both Ike and the cow are 'scaled in discourse',[68] to the extent that the physical is almost entirely effaced in the opening paragraphs of the scene. Through a disruptive narrative turn, Faulkner confronts readers with the inescapable knowledge that what was taken to be an encounter between a fertility goddess and a romantic hero is in fact a sentimental parody: 'bestial' passion between a cow and a mentally impaired man. The 'natural' is shifted to the 'unnatural' through this bathetic narrative turn, highlighting the precarious artificiality of the concept itself.

In this moment of realization, the body of the cow 'intervenes', rupturing the smooth surface of romantic discourse; the ambivalent narrative is located in the uneasy 'gap between nature and pastoral poetics'.[69] In this void of linguistic and visual uncertainty, smell and sound become the only stable identifiers of the cow's body: her 'milk-laden breath' or the 'faint, thick, hoarse moaning sound' (183) that announces her approach. Faulkner plays upon contemporary anxieties about a connection between 'feeble-mindedness' and excessive, animalistic sexual appetites. His fiction simultaneously realizes and re-writes these anxieties in a specific social context. The sexualization of the disabled body emerges as a threat to conventional sexual identities, and this leads the community to respond through acts of literal and social severance: Benjy is castrated following his 'attack' on the schoolgirls in *The Sound and the Fury*, and Ike's 'perverted' passion alienates him yet becomes an obsessive preoccupation of the community in *The Hamlet*.

So, the love scene in *The Hamlet*, which has been read as a moment of disembodied 'real love...transcendent'[70] in a community driven by material greed, in fact insists upon a bathetic return to the body. Ike falls from a pastoral mode into the comic and absurd; toppling from the heights of rhetorical splendour into a ditch, covering himself in mud and manure. The effect here is far more complex than straightforward comic disjunction or exploitation of folklore and rural myths of bestiality[71] because through Ike, Faulkner critiques the wider denial of the body which occurs in *The Hamlet*. Eula, for example, has her individuality eroded through a mediating narratorial gaze. The 'objective' narrator systematically denies her a subject-position: she is 'not a living integer' but exists instead mediated by distorting discourses of femininity 'in a teeming vacuum ... as though behind sound-proof glass' (106). In this way, Faulkner suggests that marginalized groups of women and the mentally disabled are understood in reductive, entirely physical terms. They represent a disruptive excess, inciting or experiencing sexual desire which cannot be assimilated into abstract structures of exchange, but must be broken down and framed in conventional, depersonalized romantic discourses. Like Luster's description of Benjy as an excessive body 'whose particles would not or did not cohere' (274), Eula is reduced to an assortment of fragmented, fleshy parts through a process of poetic emblazonment: 'Too much – too much of leg, too much of breast, too much of buttock; too much – of mammalian female meat' (111).

At the end of the episode, this wider denial of the body comes full circle, as the fleshy body of the cow that Ike desires is slaughtered, and Ike is given a miniaturized model as a form of substitution. It emerges, in keeping with the ironic logic of *The Hamlet*, that Ike's position outside the conventional systems of economics, ethics, signification and bodily identification exempts him from the relentless capitalist profit motive of the surrounding community and enables him to introduce an alternative notion of value into the text. Ike's ignorance of his own body, paradoxically, allows him to remain most closely in touch with it.

Through the representation of disability Faulkner therefore constantly pushes at the generic, ethical and aesthetic margins of the novel form. The second section of *The Hamlet*, called 'The Long Summer', dramatizes the impulse to frame the disabled body, as the men of the village gape through the gap in the fence, spying, with voyeuristic pleasure, on Ike inside the stall with the cow. Ratliff's simultaneous fascination with and repulsion by this spectacle, the desire to look but not be seen, returns readers to the ambivalent, self-implicating acts of staring dramatized in *Soldier's Pay*: 'He knew not only what he was going to see but ... he did not want to see it, yet ... he was going to look.'[72]

These scenes, set in 1890, locate *The Hamlet* in the middle of what Rosemarie Garland Thomson describes as '1840–1940: the century long heyday of the American Freak Show'.[73] While the body of the cow is framed in romantic discourse, Ike is dehumanized. Faulkner refuses to remove these intervening bodies from view or to assimilate them into normalizing fixed narrative endings or a single unified self. Through the sympathetic figure of Ratliff, he provides a meta-textual commentary on the growing sense of unease about the obsession with disembodied static economic ideals in the community depicted in *The Hamlet*. Ike represents an alternative vision of the body: as existing in an on-going state of flux, suffering, desiring but also relentlessly enduring and returning readers to 'that weak, nerve-raddled, yet curiously indestructible flesh' (210).

A Fable: enduring bodies and open-ended narrative structures

The open-ended structure of Faulkner's narratives suggests the 'dubious capacity of the . . . body to endure'[74] which he explored throughout his fiction. The final scene of *A Fable*, Faulkner's penultimate novel, returns to the figure of the brutally wounded and incapacitated soldier with which his writing career began in *Soldier's Pay*. The shocking image of the severely disabled soldier, who bellows and throws his badge of military honour into the crowd, acts as both a literal and symbolic, visual and aural 'disturbance'[75] in the scene. His fragmented body disrupts the aesthetic closure of the ritualistic 'rhythm and symmetry' of the arched war memorial, the procession which passes silently beneath it and the 'muffled drums' (1069) beating in the background. The policemen who surround the soldier, as he lies 'unconscious and peaceful' in the gutter at the end of the novel, articulate a wider longing for closure: ' "Maybe he will die this time" ' (1072). Yet, the soldier's eyes open and his suffering, howling laughter and 'furious progressless unrest' (1067) stretch on after the novel itself has ended. These echoings at the end of *A Fable* resonate with the final line of the appendix to *The Sound and the Fury*, 'Dilsey: they endured' (647). They also resonate with Faulkner's Nobel Prize lecture, given while he was writing *A Fable*, in which he links the legacy of an author to a body that refuses to die: 'I decline to accept the decline of man . . . I believe that man will not merely endure: he will prevail' (120).

The body that lives on emerges as a symbol of both on-going suffering and hope in Faulkner's novels and criticism. Rare moments of imagination and identification in the narratives occur amid the reductive stereotyping, marginalization and denial of the disabled body on the part of the other characters. Through momentary glimmers of recognition, Faulkner retains the possibility of pity. In *The Hamlet*, for example, Ratliff briefly considers the possibility that Ike may possess a consciousness of his own: 'For a fading instant there was something almost like recognition ... "I felt sorry for him. I thought maybe anytime he would happen to start thinking" ' (296). In *A Fable*, this empathetic moment – another fading instant – is placed in the climactic final line of the novel. Like Dilsey's silent and compassionate tears at the end of *The Sound and the Fury*, the last lines of *The Fable* blur the line between dark, comic absurdity and tragic pathos: ' "I am not laughing," the old man bending over him said. "What you see are tears" ' (1072).

Faulkner's novels invite yet also frustrate intensely literary acts of imagining otherness, as he attempts to represent the perspective of black, female or disabled characters. Like Morrison's writing, Faulkner's fiction and criticism display a fascination with the possibility and 'process of entering what one is estranged from',[76] 'the ability of writers to imagine what is not the self, to familiarize the strange and mystify the familiar'.[77] For Faulkner, the challenge is never fully realized: imagination remains an on-going personal endeavour rather than a socially transformative force. Faulkner has been accused of the 'textual abuse'[78] of Benjy by critics who consider his representations of intellectual disability reductive and inauthentic. Yet the limits, as well as the open-ended possibilities, of textual representation are always foregrounded in his work, as is the struggle to imagine alternative narrative and social perspectives in the novel itself.

Like the ritualistic Clearing scene in Morrison's *Beloved*, with its beating drums, pulsing bodies and inspiring 'unchurched preacher' (102), both *The Sound and the Fury* and *Soldier's Pay* focus on music and the rhythms and rituals of marginalized black communities. At the end of *The Sound and the Fury*, Dilsey, Frony and Benjy attend a church service which is characterized by its aural quality, 'sonorous echoes between the walls' and a visiting preacher's voice that almost seems to penetrate their bodies with its 'sad, timbrous quality like an alto horn, sinking into their hearts and speaking there again when it had ceased in fading and cumulate echoes' (295). In the closing scene in *Soldier's Pay*, Januarius Jones and Joe Gilligan pause outside a church where a black community service is going on inside. The singing of hymns transforms the 'shabby church' into a place that is 'beautiful with mellow longing, passionate and sad' (266). As in both *Beloved* and *The Sound and the Fury*, spiritual language is significant at this climactic moment of *Soldier's Pay* for its sounds and rhythmic musicality; ritualistically reiterated as part of an on-going life cycle of work and bodily suffering, as night falls on a land 'inevitable with tomorrow and sweat, with sex and death and damnation' (266).

The alternative sensory perceptions and merging perceptual categories, exemplified in *The Sound and the Fury*, allow Faulkner to explore the power of sound, smell and touch to both understand and communicate complex, lived experience. In his writing, the literally blinded soldiers (in *Soldier's Pay* and *A Fable*) and metaphorically blind innocence of 'idiocy' (in *The Sound and the Fury* and *The Hamlet*) trigger cycles of storytelling, actively shape the narrative and provide moments of clarity and insight into the chaotic, corrupt worlds that Faulkner depicts. The frequent return to memories, scenes and embodied conditions of not seeing connects Faulkner's fiction to Jacques Derrida's paradox in *Memoirs of the Blind* (1993) that: 'One sees only on the condition of not seeing when one sees.'[79] Through the representation of marginalized perspectives and impaired vision, Faulkner opens up narrative and imaginative possibilities.

Faulkner explores both the ethical and political problems but also exploits the possibilities for experimentation, sensationalism and innovation involved in the struggle to imagine otherness that runs throughout his fiction. As one contemporary review put it, *The Sound and the Fury* 'is a sordid and revolting story; and yet its sordidness has a certain tragic dignity to it'.[80] Years later, Faulkner himself reflected that the novel was 'his best failure' in its ambitious attempt to relate 'a tale told by an idiot'.[81] Remembering, communicating and understanding are depicted as on-going processes which are relived and re-written in all of his novels. Faulkner's open-ended structures resemble the aide's unfinished play in *A Fable*, which explores experience after conventional narrative endings: 'A drama...about glory, and how men got it, and how they bore it after they got it...the courage it takes to pity' (707).

In much of his writing, Faulkner is concerned with the specific historical, political complexities of this 'courage it takes to pity'. In his Nobel Prize lecture, he articulated his sense of the literary as a mode of critically and imaginatively engaging with the present, as well as the past:

> The poet's voice need not merely be the record of man, it can be one of the props, pillars to help him endure and prevail. (120)

Voice, then, is a prop, a means of summoning the courage to pity, to confront that which is deemed to be unspeakable or widely overlooked. Faulkner was both intrigued and troubled by the struggle to represent disability, returning to it in the first and very last novels that he wrote. The representation of physically and developmentally disabled characters enable him to explore alternative narrative spaces and forms of sensory perception in his fiction but also to explore what literary techniques can achieve. By imagining positions of otherness, he challenges the formal and ethical limits of the novel form, but also the narratives through which we give shape and meaning to our own lives.

3
Foreign Bodies: Disability and Beauty in the Works of Toni Morrison

Claudia, the young female narrator of Morrison's first novel, *The Bluest Eye*, is fascinated by the mysterious, seductive yet also destructive nature of beauty. As a young girl growing up in Ohio in the years following the Great Depression, she experiences a disjunction between abstract white beauty ideals and the materiality of her own female black body. Claudia asks: 'What was the secret? What did we lack? Why was it important?'[1]

This chapter explores Morrison's on-going engagement with questions of the beautiful and, in particular, the intersection between disability and beauty in her fiction and criticism. Morrison's challenge to reductive, racialized conceptions of beauty in *The Bluest Eye* is widely recognized.[2] Yet, her complex critical engagement with beauty, and its relationship to her frequent representations of physical disability, has been widely overlooked. Every single work of fiction by Morrison includes at least one character that is impaired, disabled or marked out by a distinct physical difference. In *Beloved* (1987), scarred Sethe, limping Baby Suggs and one-armed Nan all play a central role in the narrative. In *Foreign Bodies*, the exhibition curated by Morrison at the Louvre in 2006, she explored depictions of bodies that are fragmented, contorted and wounded yet also beautiful.

Taking Claudia's questions about the incommunicability and importance of beauty as a starting point, this chapter examines the effect of these enduring and recurring representations. What do disabled bodies *mean* in Morrison's novels? What effect does the beauty of Morrison's prose have on her representation of disability, trauma and race? And how does Morrison's employment of disability as a critical metaphor and an embodied physical reality work in relation to her other political concerns? Morrison's novels are rooted in the struggle to represent material bodies through writing and a specific African American literary and cultural tradition. The politics of definition and the relationship between defined and definers are at the heart of her depictions of her aesthetic vision. Like W. E. B. Du Bois in his essay 'Criteria of Negro Art' (1926), she asks: 'Who describe[s] beauty? What is it?'[3]

As a novelist, curator, academic and cultural critic, Morrison's aesthetic vision, and her conceptions of beauty and disability, are interdisciplinary. As guest curator at the Louvre in 2006, Morrison selected sketches and studies by a range of artists, including Eugène Delacroix, Charles Le Brun and Edgar Degas,[4] that depict fragments of bodies or multiple versions of the same body, writhing in pain and pleasure. These are bodies that, by virtue of the artist's close attention, suggest a level of aesthetic value. Yet, as in much of Morrison's lyrical writing, the beauty of the form and rendering is inseparable from the horror and pain etched onto the faces of the figures depicted. The choice of sketches and studies foregrounds the process of aesthetic construction through an attention to individual bodies and incomplete portraits. Delacroix's *Études de Figures Volantes Nues*, for example, depicts multiple reworkings of a single figure: armless, faceless and reduced to nothing but a few highly evocative lines and swirls of grey, disappearing into the edge of the page.

Through her conceptual, trans-historical approach, Morrison challenged modes of perceiving the body that were implicit in the categorization of artefacts in the Louvre's existing collection. She explored a multi-sensory conception of the body through dance, painting, drawing and film, including artworks ranging from Le Brun's seventeenth-century sketches to Japanese dancer Kahzuo Ohno's *Portrait of Mr O.* (1969). The 'criss-crossing'[5] that Scarry associates with her alternative notion of beauty was embedded in the structure of the exhibition itself, in the perpetual movement between different time frames, genres and disciplines. For Scarry:

> What is beautiful prompts the mind to move chronologically back in search for precedents and parallels, to move forward into new acts of creation, to move conceptually over, to bring things into relation. (30)

The subdivisions of the exhibition made this self-conscious focus on precarious, fragmented, displaced bodies even more specific. *Foreign Bodies* was organized into four sections: 'Folds', 'Falls', 'Erasures' and 'Battlefields'. Like the scarred, individualized and disabled bodies that recur throughout Morrison's novels, the exhibition focused on bodily boundaries that are fluid and constantly shifting: moving, falling, enduring and in danger. They demonstrate Morrison's fascination with the aesthetic processes of construction and the redrawing of the boundaries of beauty and the body in her works.

Morrison's exploration of the aesthetic and imaginative potential of disabled bodies needs to be read in the context of a contemporary resurgence of critical interest in beauty. Morrison engages with a wider discourse which, in the last few decades, has not only highlighted the critical problems of talking about questions of beauty, but has also called for a radical redefinition and rehabilitation of the concept. Scarry, in *On Beauty* (2000), considers beauty as an incitement to create and an active ethical principle. Umberto Eco, in his book with the same title, puts forward a 'polytheistic' model of beauty.[6] Eco suggests a relational approach, an attempt 'to see how different models of beauty could coexist in the same period and how other models refer to one another through different periods' (14). Both of these accounts shatter familiar notions of beauty as an inherently conservative, static concept, traceable through a linear, historical narrative.

This contemporary re-writing of beauty, as a potentially 'radical aesthetic'[7] suggests that like disability, beauty demands a fresh critical approach. In the past, Morrison's writing has frequently been perceived as overly concerned with aesthetic style – writing in a style almost *too* beautiful for her subject matter – or in strictly political terms. For example, James Wood, in *The Broken Estate* (1999), suggests that the sheer lushness of Morrison's novels, as beautiful objects in their own right, detracts from the specificities of character and the cultural context that they seek to represent. He extends his analysis of *Paradise* into a wider critique of Morrison's style: 'Too often, Morrison is so besotted with making poetry, with the lyrical dyeing of every moment, that she cannot grant characters their own words.'[8] This claim about Morrison's blind and 'besotted' love for language is extended to a figuration of 'the evasive abruptness' of Morrison's lyricism as 'like a rich man stuffing money into our pockets while refusing to look at us and shouting all the while, "Here, take this, and feel good"' (216). For Wood, the seductive richness of the language creates an almost delusional, deceptive 'false magic' (213), in which personal and historical details are lost amid the flood of images, impressions and memories.

By contrast, in the field of disability studies, the political efficacy and ethical directedness of Morrison's wider vision has often been emphasized. Garland Thomson's focus on independence as a defining feature of Morrison's disabled women is, for example, encapsulated in her chapter title 'Disabled Women as Powerful Women in Morrison, Petry and Lorde'.[9] This suggests a political, revisionist agenda which risks assimilating nuanced characters – often depicted as vulnerable, sexualized and implicated in complex familial networks – in the search for positive role models. In this context, notions of the disabled body as beautiful or pleasurable are, paradoxically, often excluded from the search for positive, politicized representations of disability.

I argue that these two threads in Morrison's writing – of disability and beauty, of the political and the aesthetic – are not contradictory or competing forces. The devastating lyricism of Morrison's prose draws attention to the problem of reading and interpreting bodies that are traumatized or impaired yet also beautiful. Morrison's works complicate the relationship between beauty and aesthetic pleasure; the lushness of the writing counters a loss of language in the face of pain and responds to generations of African Americans denied the luxury of literacy and the time or resources to write expansively and elaborately. In contrast to the austerities of Coetzee's style or the starkness and condensed forms of much of Faulkner's writing, Morrison's early writing is strikingly elaborate, even excessive in its style: lengthy sentences, packed with images, metaphors, layered clauses and memories re-membered in many different forms. Morrison does not allow anger to paralyse her expressiveness; instead, achingly beautiful prose becomes, in itself, a statement of resistance. By exploring moments at which Morrison's discussion of beauty and depiction of disability converge, I suggest that the representation of the disabled body can open up new aesthetic possibilities and reconfigure existing concepts of embodiment in her writing.

Morrison's focus on the disabled body creates rich, imaginatively and critically fertile moments in her fiction. In *Sula* (1973), Eva has only one leg, but her body is no less beautiful or sexual; quite the opposite:

> Whatever the fate of her lost leg, the remaining one was magnificent... Nor did she wear overlong dresses to disguise the empty place on her left side. Her dresses were mid-calf so that her one glamorous leg was always in view as well as the long fall of space below her left thigh.[10]

Here, Morrison goes beyond simply re-writing disability, often perceived as a 'lack',[11] into a positive presence. Like Eva, who places her leg in view of the community through her short dresses, Morrison implicates readers in the ambivalent act of scrutinizing the disabled, female body. Garland Thomson views Eva as a figure of empowerment: a 'goddess / queen / creatrix character' (117). Yet it is, I suggest, the sensual and material rather than the mythologized aspects of Eva's body that are placed in the foreground of the text. The distance and control of the narrative perspective highlights how physical disability is viewed exclusively from exterior perspectives in this early novel. The detached 'magnificence' and cool 'glamour' of her appearance suggest a powerful, impressive presence that transcends mere sexual admiration. Morrison does not use disability as a trigger for storytelling – the fate of the lost leg is withheld throughout the novel – but instead focuses on the material presence of both the remaining leg and the visible gap.

The interplay between absence and presence in the quotation from *Sula*, which pays equal attention to the absence of one leg and the magnificent presence of the other, conveys a sense of ambiguity that characterizes the paradoxical role of disability in literature and art more widely. Though rarely recognized as such, disability often becomes 'the very factor that establishes works as superior examples of aesthetic beauty'.[12] Disability has been a central inspiration for art and the subject matter of some of the most beautiful and celebrated art works, yet it has, until recently, been a critical blind spot. Early theories of the grotesque[13] – with their emphasis on the subversive power of the disabled body on the edges of an official language or culture – focus on the marginality of disability. Yet, this conceptual framework is not adequate to theorize the fluidity, complexity and centrality of the disabled body in Morrison's works.

Morrison's depiction of disability and beauty does not, in her own words, 'risk lobotomizing literature'[14] by excising the political, but rather generates and celebrates aesthetic pleasure through the process of writing itself. Through writing that is often shockingly beautiful and lyrical, Morrison suggests the critical and imaginative possibilities in the representation of disability. Her engagement with identity politics is a very knowing one: she challenges hierarchies of representation and embodiment, exploring the breadth of disability as a concept alongside contested definitions of beauty. Her sense that 'definitions belonged to the definers – not the defined'[15] is fundamental to the complex intertwining of aesthetics and politics, disability and beauty in her works.

Dead-end beauty: Morrison's early critical writing

Writing in *The New York Times Magazine* in 1971, Morrison denounced beauty as 'a needless cul-de-sac, an opiate that ... eventually must separate us from reality'.[16] In this early article, Morrison suggests that beauty functions as a paralysing discourse, a frivolous fiction that limits perception. Her language is historically loaded: 'Concentrating on whether we are beautiful is a way of measuring worth that is wholly trivial ... it is an irrevocable slavery of the senses.'[17] Yet, even as she denounces beauty here as a delusional fantasy, Morrison roots her discussion in the language and context of contemporary black civil rights campaigns and the women's movement. The title of her article, 'What Black Women Think about Women's Lib', itself foregrounds beauty as an important point of intersection for contemporary debates about the cultural construction of gender, race, class and disability.[18] Even in Morrison's early rejection of beauty, therefore, there is an implicit recognition of both the political and aesthetic significance of the concept.

Later in the same article, Morrison engages directly with contemporary protest discourses, in her dismissal of the 'Black is Beautiful' campaign as 'a white idea turned inside out'.[19] At this point, Morrison conceives of beauty as a hierarchized relationship between defined and definers, based upon exclusion. She suggests that the inversion of the usual white 'definers' and black 'defined' in 'Black is Beautiful' fails to address the politically problematic nature of this oppositional, negative mode of self-definition.

Morrison's dismissal of beauty in general, and the Black is Beautiful campaign in particular, located her in opposition to a central aspect of the black power movement emerging in 1960s America. The shifts in notions of beauty in this period are exemplified in *Ebony* magazine. As the bestselling African American magazine in the late 1960s and throughout the 1970s, *Ebony* featured political stories, biographies of exemplary African Americans and a diverse range of advertisements, primarily for beauty products. In September 1962, the magazine featured a black beauty queen on its front cover, celebrating black beauty in the context of a white beauty pageant.[20] Three women are pictured against the backdrop of a garden; one youthful white blonde woman standing at the back, another kneeling in the middle and then the black 'Detroit Beauty Queen', Clintera Jackson, sitting in the foreground wearing a tiara on top of her straightened hair. By 1969 the mood had shifted and advertisements in the magazine suggested the influence of a specifically black cultural and aesthetic movement.[21] Yet the paradoxical nature of the 'Black is Beautiful' movement and the inherent contradictions in marketing campaigns aimed at the newly recognized African American market are encapsulated in a single February 1969 issue. Alongside various articles celebrating black power, including an advertisement for a music compilation album bearing the caption 'Say it

Loud ... I'm Black and Proud', are advertisements for 'Bleach and Glow' skin cream and 'Hair Strate' straightening balm with the caption, 'Make Things Happen'.[22] Like the 1962 front cover, the beauty of the women in these advertisements lies, implicitly, in their resemblance to the idealized straight hair and pale skin of white women. The black pride message, promoted in the music compilation and elsewhere in the magazine, is challenged by the competing and often conflicting notions of beauty that sit side by side in the issue.

In the decades that followed, this apparent hegemony of beauty was critiqued by both feminist and disability studies critics. Naomi Wolf's *The Beauty Myth*, written in 1992, suggests that beauty functions as an outdated, immobilizing and highly damaging discourse. Wolf argues that conventional notions of beauty, as a hierarchized dialectic between a male viewer and a female as the object of the gaze, create a static, paralysing understanding of the concept, based around a further opposition between the living, material body and an abstract, disembodied ideal.[23] The first wave of disability studies writing made a similar critique of beauty as 'an oppressive cultural ideology perpetuated and enforced by a wide range of institutions and received traditions'.[24] Later theorizations from within disability studies highlighted the exclusionary nature of dominant ideals of beauty. Garland Thomson suggests that: 'Disability is more than a background ... It is the basis on which the "normal" body is constructed' (8). She goes to argue that 'the subject position of the cultural self is the figure outlined by the array of deviant others whose marked bodies shore up the normate's boundaries' (8).

This argument intersects with the oppositional paradigms articulated in Morrison's early critical writing, in which she argues that marginalized bodies construct the norm through their 'deviant' status and open up debates about beauty and disability, as well as race and identity. In *Playing in the Dark* (1992), Morrison proposes a model in which American identity itself is defined in opposition to 'unsettling populations':[25] 'Africanism is the vehicle by which the American self knows itself as not enslaved, but free; not repulsive, but desirable; not helpless, but licensed and powerful' (52). As in Garland Thomson's quotation, the notion of a 'normal' American citizen, as white, male, physically and economically self-supporting, is exposed here as being paradoxically dependent upon a process of social marginalization and fictional construction. As a critic, Morrison's early writing focuses primarily on the exclusionary nature of these structures embedded in American society and literary criticism. As a novelist, however, Morrison frequently returns to the aesthetic dimensions of the narrative, and the imaginative and ethical challenges of representing this condition of 'the not-me'.[26]

Morrison's early description of beauty as a 'cul-de-sac' and 'opiate' engages with a political and cultural trend in 1970s America in which, some argue, beauty was treated as 'the forbidden subject . . . the bad child no one wanted to talk about'.[27] Scarry's historical account of critical discussions of beauty at the end of the twentieth century echoes the sense of a critical impasse that is articulated in Morrison's writing. At a time when 'the vocabulary of beauty has been banished or driven underground in the humanities',[28] Morrison's critical, fictional and curatorial work frequently places shifting understandings of beauty in the foreground. In her novels, Morrison treats the body as both individual and material, rather than an abstract aesthetic ideal or merely as a terrain for political and ideological debate. Throughout her writing, Morrison remains committed to representing enduring, changing, imperfect and marked bodies.

Like Soaphead Church in *The Bluest Eye* (1970), readers of Morrison's fiction are implicated in a close inspection of the surfaces of the body which is described in terms of taste, texture and smell, as well as sight. The narrator of *The Bluest Eye* describes how:

> Body odor, breath odor, overwhelmed him. The sight of dried matter in the corner of the eye, decayed or missing teeth, ear wax, blackheads, moles, blisters, skin crusts – all the natural excretions and protections the body was capable of. (132)

This fascinated, almost microscopic scrutiny of the body, which demands close attention to surfaces of both the body and the text itself, provides a model for reading and writing about Morrison's works. It helps to create the 'intimacy between the reader and the page'[29] which Morrison had set out to capture from the very beginning of her career. Through this intimate focus, she explores the imaginative potential of characters who exist outside dominant discourses of normality and beauty. In *Song of Solomon* (1977), Pilate, marked out by physical difference, is able to challenge the community's superficial, capitalist definitions of beauty and value: 'She threw away every assumption she had learned and began again at zero. First off, she cut her hair . . . Then she tackled the problem of trying to decide how she wanted to live and what was valuable to her.'[30] Similarly, in *Sula* (1973), the liminal position of the two friends allows a space for self-definition and imaginative reinvention:

Because they had discovered years before that they were neither white nor male, and that freedom and triumph was forbidden to them, they set about creating something else to be. (52)

The apparent minority status of these characters is ironic: their position outside the white, male, physically and economically independent ideal, in fact applies to the majority of the American population. Morrison's representations of disability and impairment therefore have a wide scope, including the 'marks of particularity'[31] – Pauline's club foot, Pilate's navel-less stomach, Eva's amputated leg, Sethe's scarred back, Baby Suggs's twisted hip – which individualize these characters. So, the representation of disability is used to criticize normative notions of beauty but also to explore the possibility of an imaginative redefinition of the disabled body as at once painful, pleasurable and beautiful.

The Bluest Eye and *Sula*: Morrison's critique of beauty

In Morrison's first novel, *The Bluest Eye* (1970), the narrator describes:

Physical beauty. Probably one of the most destructive ideas in the history of human thought. In equating physical beauty with virtue, [Pauline] stripped her mind, bound it, and collected self-contempt by the heap... curtailing her freedom in every way. (95)

In 'Behind the Making of the Black Book', published four years later, Morrison makes an almost identical critique. Once again, she alludes to a philosophical tradition in which beauty and virtue are equated:

The concept of physical beauty as a *virtue* is one of the dumbest, most pernicious and destructive ideas of the Western world and we should have nothing to do with it.[32]

This similarity between Morrison's commentary on her editorial work for *The Black Book* and the narrative voice in *The Bluest Eye* has led some critics to read the novel as a straightforward piece of political didacticism. The vehement rejection of dominant discourses of beauty in both texts has meant that the narrator is often read as Morrison's mouthpiece; *The Bluest Eye* is viewed as a cautionary tale, a 'strain of the black antiracist tradition'[33] or an instructional novel. Lennard Davis argues, for example, that what *The Bluest Eye* 'allows students to understand is that "ugliness" is not located in any objective physical criteria but instead in the ideological systems of denigration...as a condition of racism, sexism, and classism'.[34]

In these readings, analysis of the nuances of the text itself as an aesthetic object is subordinated to the promotion of wider political ideals. In fact, *The Bluest Eye* is concerned not merely with a rejection of beauty, but also with a wider exploration of the damaging nature of ideals, and the social (and narrative) processes through which these concepts are constructed. At first glance, the treatment of Pecola, the little black girl who longs for blue eyes, appears to confirm the paradigm of identity articulated in Morrison's *Playing in the Dark*: the community defines itself in opposition to Pecola's 'unsettling' presence, and the dominant conception of beauty is confirmed by reducing Pecola to an example of ugliness:

> All of our waste we dumped on her and she absorbed. And all of our beauty which was hers first and which she gave to us. All of us...felt so wholesome after we cleaned ourselves on her. We were so beautiful when we stood astride her ugliness...her pain made us glow with health. (163)

On closer scrutiny, however, beauty is depicted as a fragile and elusive quality, based on a precarious set of shifting boundaries, rather than a static binary opposition. The plurality of the narrator's description, 'our waste we dumped', implicates readers, as well as the fictional community in the text, in this process of scapegoating and exclusion. The fluidity of beauty, a quality that 'was hers first and which she gave to us', suggests the significance of 'absorption' or internalization, as a precarious process through which the community delineates its boundaries and defines itself.

The Bluest Eye frequently returns to the mysterious, shifting and unspeakable nature of the beautiful. Claudia and her sister agree: 'All the time we knew that Maureen was not the Enemy and not worthy of such intense hatred. The *Thing* to fear was the *Thing* that made *her* beautiful, and not us' (58). Claudia's combination of repulsion and fascination is captured in her impulse to dismember the idealized white beauty of the Shirley Temple doll, 'to discover the dearness, *to find the beauty*, the desirability that had escaped me, but apparently only me' (14) (my italics).

It is, however, in relation to the physically impaired figure of Pauline that these self-conscious debates about beauty are played out to greatest effect. Pauline's slight disability, her limping club-foot, becomes central to her sense of self: 'as it was, this deformity explained many things that would have been otherwise incomprehensible...why she never felt at home anywhere, or that she belonged anyplace' (86). Pauline's foot acts as the trigger and focus for her delusional fantasies. Like Pecola, Pauline's isolation leads her to invest in commercialized notions of the beautiful, perpetuated by magazines, billboard advertisements and Hollywood films. The cinema becomes a place of fantasy and escape:

> She was never able, after her education in the movies, to look at a face and not assign it some category in the scale of absolute beauty, and the scale was one she absorbed in full from the silver screen...There the flawed became whole, the blind sighted, and the lame and halt threw away their crutches. (95)

Pauline's 'education' in the movies paradoxically inculcates a blinding set of physical ideals, based upon an exclusionary hierarchical scale. Pauline accepts a notion of beauty that perpetuates a fantasy of bodily completeness and perfection and denies the materiality of her own disabled body. The cultural vitality and black pride of the Harlem Renaissance history is relegated to the background in *The Bluest Eye*. By setting Pauline's internalized self-loathing against this historical backdrop, Morrison highlights the ways in which exclusionary, racist beauty ideals continued to dominate American culture and mass media.

Snyder and Mitchell, writing in a disability studies context, develop the notion of 'narrative prosthesis'. This term, they suggest, is 'meant to indicate that disability has been used throughout history as a crutch upon which literary narratives lean for their representational power, [and] disruptive potentiality'.[35] On a superficial level, Pauline appears to exemplify this 'prosthetic' dependence on artificial notions of beauty and disability: 'Mrs Breedlove handled hers as an actor does a prop: for the articulation of character, for support of a role she frequently imagined was hers – martyrdom' (29). Disability functions here as a kind of theatrical aid which she employs to enact the role of martyr. Pauline's 'ugliness' is figured as a symbolic costume through which she and her family cover their shame: 'It was as though some mysterious, all-knowing master had given each one a cloak of ugliness to wear, and they had each accepted it without question' (28). Their passivity is encapsulated in the conditionality of the narration here and the unquestioning omnipotence of a vague, apparently patriarchal power. Their bodies become metaphorically 'scaled in discourse',[36] as prejudices mediate their experiences of their own identities.

On closer scrutiny, however, *The Bluest Eye* provokes a more complex commentary on this 'prosthetic' reliance upon stereotype. Snyder and Mitchell suggest that literary representation often depends upon stereotypical images of disability. Morrison's novel, by contrast, explores how this process of differentiation and isolation works. Morrison develops a recurring metaphor of 'absorption', in terms of the 'waste we dumped on [Pecola which] she absorbed' (163) and 'the scale of absolute beauty... [which Pauline] absorbed from the silver screen' (95). Later, in *Beloved* (1987), Morrison provides a metaphor of growth for this process of indoctrination, likening it to a gradual colonization of individual consciousness: 'It was the jungle white folks planted in them. And it grew. It spread, until it invaded the whites who had made it' (50). Here Morrison suggests that prejudice spreads to different communities, infecting individual perspectives. *The Bluest Eye* explores precisely this interaction or 'invasion' in relation to normative definitions of beauty, to suggest the artificiality and permeability of boundaries between inside and outside, individual and community, defined and definers.

A sense of complicity in this process of definition, on the part of the character, community and readers themselves, further complicates notions of blame in the novel. Pauline is exposed not only to a highly specific definition of beauty based on Hollywood ideals (she attempts to style her hair, for example, like Greta Garbo), but also to external pressure to conform from the black, female community who are 'amused' by her unstraightened hair: 'Their goading glances and private snickers... developed in her a desire for new clothes' (92). Pauline's immersion in a consumeristic, specular culture renders her body subject to scrutiny by white men, but also vulnerable to the directed 'eye slide of black women ... on the street' (32). The external positioning of the reader, whose view of both Pecola and Pauline is almost always mediated through the narrator, forces readers into an uneasy sense of collusion. Morrison's decision 'to break the narrative into parts to be reassembled by the reader'[37] suggests that the fragmentation of the novel form itself implicates readers in a process of imaginative reconstruction.

Therefore, rather than functioning as an artificial 'crutch', 'textual obstacle'[38] or impediment, the representation of Pauline's disability mobilizes Morrison's critique. The text itself rejects a 'discursive dependency'[39] on prosthetic or stereotypical views of disability and beauty. Instead of relying on the disruptive power of the disabled body, *The Bluest Eye* dramatizes the dangers of any attempt to assimilate to a fixed, reductive ideal. It is the normalizing imperative, rather than presence of disability, which is most disruptive in Morrison's early writing.

Morrison's second novel, *Sula* (1973), has also been read as a treatise against stereotyping. Susan Wills, for example, locates the novel in the context of 'the Black Aesthetic movement' and its call 'for positive representations and role models'.[40] There are certainly moments in the novel where conventional notions of beauty, and corresponding connotations of sexual attractiveness, are challenged by the sexualization of the amputee Eva's disabled body. Eva is associated with fertility, femininity and sexual expression: 'It was manlove Eva bequeathed to her daughters' (41). In contrast to Pauline's enclosure in blinding fantasy, Eva's disabled body is exposed and admired by 'a regular flock of gentleman callers' who engage in 'a good deal of teasing and pecking and laughter' (41).

The centrality of Eva's disabled body in the narrative, as fertile, desirable and a source of pleasure as well as pain, implicitly challenges the fantasies of cure and bodily completeness that dominate *The Bluest Eye*. Yet, despite this alternative, more positive representation of disability, as a celebrated difference rather than a lack, the definition of beauty in *Sula* remains focused on the visual: 'The men wanted to see her lovely calf, that neat shoe' (41). Eva is described as sitting in:

A rocking-chair top fitted into a large child's wagon...The wagon was so low that...adults, standing or sitting, had to look down at her. But they didn't know it...They all had the impression that they were looking up at her, up into the open distances of her eyes. (31)

Some critics view this moment of inversion as an indication of empowerment for a 'poor, black, manless, disabled woman'[41] that is symbolic of a wider reversal of the power dynamic between definer and defined, viewer and viewed, carer and cared-for. But it is not until Morrison writes *Beloved*, fourteen years later, that she formulates an alternative aesthetic, which is not about inverting viewer and viewed, but redefining the terms altogether. In *Sula* and *The Bluest Eye*, positioning is highly significant. The focus is on characters who exist 'just barely within the boundaries of the elaborately socialized world of black people'.[42] Pecola finds herself on the margins of the community, where waste and beauty coexist in the same narrative frame: she lingers 'between Coke bottle and milkweed, among all the waste and beauty of the world – which is what she herself was' (205). The ambiguous nature of her position is played out in this coupling of 'waste and beauty'; the terms function not as opposites but are intertwined with one another. Morrison gestures towards an alternative conception of value here, as that which is usually overlooked or perceived as worth-less becomes endowed with aesthetic power. The description of Pecola, suspended 'somewhere between retina and object, between vision and view',[43] gestures towards a wider conception of identity and beauty.

Both *Sula* and *The Bluest Eye* express a longing for an alternative mode of articulation and perception. The childish innocence of Sula and Nel allows temporary liberation from restrictive cultural pressures of the public sphere: 'In the safe harbor of each other's company they could afford to abandon the ways of other people and concentrate on their own perceptions of things.'[44] The search for alternative forms of imaginative expression unites Pauline and Sula. Pauline 'missed – without knowing she missed – paints and crayons',[45] while Sula's 'strangeness...was the consequence of an idle imagination. Had she paints, or clay, or knew the discipline of dance, or strings; had she anything to engage her tremendous curiosity and her gift for metaphor, she might have exchanged her restlessness...for an activity that provided her with all she yearned for' (121). Metaphor is itself figured here as a creative, inventive act; part of a basic human need for self-expression. This yearning for the agency to create, to engage in imaginative 'beauty work', foreshadows Morrison's later novels.

Yet both novels return to the damage that can come from notions of beauty and a critique of the gaze. At the end of *The Bluest Eye*, Pecola is depicted as trapped inside a prismatic house of mirrors. The narrator laments:

> Thrown, in this way, into the blinding conviction that only a miracle could relieve her, she would never know her beauty. She would see only what there was to see: the eyes of other people. (35)

A gap opens up here between a metaphorically blinded, naïve character and the knowing, resigned distance of the narrator, apparently omni-scient and detached from the narrative, unable to challenge Pecola's deep-held delusions. The text itself, which ends as it begins, with Pecola's delusional search for beauty in the form of the blue eyes, sug-gests an endless chain of reflection, rather than a redefinition of the beautiful. The split between character and narrator highlights these blind spots and the narrative form itself mirrors them. Similarly, *Sula*, which closes with the return of the title character, is unable to escape the dominant visual mode in either a literal or a metaphorical sense: 'Sula's return to the Bottom...was like getting the use of an eye back, having a cataract removed...[Sula] made her see old things with new eyes' (95). The elusive ending of the novel is based around a distinction between active and passive looking: guilt becomes bound up with the question of whether observing an act implicates the viewer in it. Nel is plagued by questions: 'What did old Eva mean by you *watched*?...Eva didn't say *see*, she said *watched*. I did not watch it. I just saw it' (170). Like *The Bluest Eye*, *Sula* consistently 'pecks away at the gaze'.[46] In her later works, Morrison searches for a new language and alternative narrative forms that go beyond this critique of the visual to articulate a wider conception of identity and beauty.

'Beauty work'

Morrison's fiction in the period from 1977 to 1992 focuses on the sensations of touch, smell and sensuous pleasure. *Song of Solomon* (1977), *Tar Baby* (1981) and *Jazz* (1992) suggest an understanding of beauty as a historical and cultural process. These novels develop Morrison's earlier engagement with conventional notions of beauty, through a focus on the role played by 'codes of beautification'[47] in the lives of African American women. Morrison places beauty parlours and hairdressers at the centre of the communities she depicts in *Song of Solomon* and *Jazz*. Here, beauty is a process of working, touching, gossiping, grooming, bonding, suggesting an economic and social significance to beautifying processes that extends far beyond any final beautiful product.

Morrison's earliest critical writing sows the seeds of this later preoccupation with the beauty of moving, living and specifically working bodies. In 'What Black Women Think about Women's Lib', she suggests:

> Beauty is romanticism...I maintain that black women are already O.K. O.K. with our short necks. O.K. with our calloused hands. O.K. with our tired feet and paper bags.[48]

Beauty here rests on an opposition between bodies that bear witness to a lifetime of work, through calloused hands and tired feet, and abstract, disembodied beauty ideals. This contrast, she implies, is racialized in the sense that bodies that have been forced to labour – either through paid servitude or actual enslavement – have not been considered beautiful in a society which idealizes passive femininity, available almost exclusively to white ruling classes. *Song of Solomon*, *Jazz* and *Tar Baby* call for a political, cultural reimagination of working black female bodies as 'O.K.', but also an appreciation of them as individualized, productive and aesthetically valuable.

Katherine Stern's notion of 'beauty work'[49] is helpful in considering Morrison's reconceptualization of beauty in these novels. In economic and social terms, hairdressing salons and beauty parlours were important sites of paid employment for African American women. The emotional and imaginative work performed in these salons values bodies that work, as *Song of Solomon*, *Jazz* and *Tar Baby* consistently show. The beauty work environment maintains the focus on particular, individual experience in the novels: enduring, imperfect, yet living, functional and fertile bodies.

There is a shift from a focus on a symbolic, 'prosthetic' dependence on stereotypes in Morrison's early novels, to a concern with the significance of the cosmetic and material conditions of the beauty industry in these later novels. The sub-plot which focuses on Hagar in *Song of Solomon* echoes *The Bluest Eye* and *Sula* in its emphasis on the damaging nature of conventional beauty ideals. Hagar seeks 'beauty that would dazzle [Milkman]' (313). Like the 'cloak of ugliness'[50] that Pauline hides behind, Hagar's body becomes symbolically covered in the language of fantasy. The make-up that she applies functions as a self-abnegating mask: 'She put baby clear sky light to outwit the day light on her eyelids' (315). However, in contrast to the homogenized beauty ideals depicted in *The Bluest Eye* and *Sula*, *Song of Solomon* offers an alternative model of beauty, articulated through Pilate. Pilate's exterior position, marked out by her navel-less stomach which is viewed as a deformity by other characters, enables her to voice a more subtle, racialized critique of Hagar's destructive ideals. Confronted with Hagar's insistence that Milkman has deserted her for 'a girl whose silky copper-colored hair cascaded over the sleeves of his coat' (127), Pilate exposes the contradictions and racial disgust implicit in Milkman's tastes. It is through touch, as much as verbal reassurance, that Pilate communicates her affection and her message:

> Pilate put her hand on Hagar's head and trailed her fingers through her granddaughter's soft, damp wool. 'How can he not love your hair? . . . It's all over his head, Hagar. It's his hair too.' (315)

Malin LaVon Walther suggests that this moment in the text functions as a political call for a more authentic understanding of beauty: Pilate 'connects hair as an attribute of beauty to racial identity'.[51] In fact, while Morrison clearly gestures towards a wider 'politics of hair',[52] the text itself depicts this as a highly intimate, personal moment. Like Paul D's loving advice to Sethe in *Beloved*, ' "You your best thing" ' (322), Pilate encourages her daughter to claim ownership not only of a racial group, but an individual identity. She urges Hagar to take pleasure in her body and to widen or shift her own definition of beauty.

The first time that readers encounter Pilate in the novel is through Ruth's memory: 'Pilate was sitting on a chair; Reba was cutting Pilate's hair with barber's clippers' (131). This hair-cutting, repeated several times over the course of the narrative, takes on an almost performative significance, as Pilate strips off heavy locks of hair and layers of restrictive discourse. In contrast to Hagar who is literally and symbolically 'weighed down by her hair' (134), Pilate's existence on the margins of the community allows her a level of freedom from these oppressive definitions of beauty and femininity. Instead of a static, disembodied ideal, Pilate offers an example of a body that is individual, functional, powerful and *different*:

> Of course she was anything but pretty, yet he [Milkman] knew he could have watched her all day: her fingers pulling threads from the orange sections, the berry-black lips that made her look as though she wore make-up, the earring... And when she stood up, he all but gasped. She was as tall as his father. (38)

The cosmetic is not rejected here, but redefined: the blackness of her lips is unusual and attractive, serving as a reminder of Pilate's work in making (and selling) wine, as well as her enjoyment in drinking it. Her fingers are working, deftly moving and productive. Her jewellery is not a frivolous adornment, but a reminder of her own history: the box contains a scrap of paper bearing her own name.

These rituals of grooming, Morrison suggests, open up the possibility of imaginative self-creation, at the same time as potentially colluding with oppressive structures of definition. Through this focus on beauty as a ritualized and commercialized process, Morrison develops a historically and culturally rooted understanding of the concept of the beautiful. In her later writing, the obsessions of a popular 'culture of the beautiful body: dieting, exercise clubs, visits to the liposuctionist... methods for perfecting ourselves',[53] coexist and compete with more abstract, philosophical definitions of beauty.

So, the beauty and hair care industries are placed in the foreground of Morrison's aesthetic and political critique, as well as providing a backdrop to the action in her novels in this period. The barber's shop in *Song of Solomon* plays a key role in the narrative, acting as a surreptitious meeting place for the 'Seven Days' group. But it is the female hairdressers and shops, such as 'Lilly's Beauty Parlor', that are endowed with a greater sense of mystery and ambivalence in the novel: 'Milkman waited on the sidewalk, staring at the curtained window of the beauty shop. Beauty shops always had curtains or shades up. Barbershops didn't.'[54]

Beauty parlours in these novels provide rare moments of escape, places where the visual judgement of outsiders is replaced with grooming, touching, massaging, gossiping and gaining pleasure from each other's company and bodies. These are feminized social spaces where pleasure and self-enhancement are emphasized. As Paula Black argues in her sociological research into the beauty salon, experiences in these locations 'cannot be reduced to the catch-all phrase of "beauty" '.[55]

In *Jazz*, processes of beautification take on a similarly intimate personal and narrative function. Violet's role as a mobile hairdresser and Joe Trace's movement around the community selling beauty products become structuring devices for the novel itself. Violet's role as a beautician locates her at the centre of a social network; her work gives her agency and confidence: '[Violet] had been a snappy, determined girl and a hardworking young woman, with the snatch-gossip tongue of a beautician.'[56] These settings – Violet's 'legally licensed beauty parlor' (5) in *Jazz* and 'Irene's Palace of Cosmetology' (3) in *Sula* – suggest the significance of 'enclosed social worlds'[57] as potentially inclusive, protected spaces in which physical and emotional work is carried out: the 'hidden labour of beauty'.[58] Rather than simply condemning beauty, *Song of Solomon* and *Jazz* suggest the experiential pleasure and significant place of processes of beautification in the lives of the female characters.

Morrison's interest in these processes of 'beauty work' is indicated in *The Bluest Eye*, her first novel, through Pauline Breedlove, whose name conjures up an association with Sarah Breedlove Walker. Breedlove Walker was one of the first African American female entrepreneurs to be successful on a national scale; she was famous for marketing innovative beauty and hair care products specifically for black women. She is often represented as an innovator and champion of the black civil rights movement. For example, Kathryn Lasky's picture book, *Vision of Beauty: The Story of Sarah Breedlove Walker*, written 81 years after Breedlove's death, holds up her story as an example of resistance and triumph, 'through tenacity and faith',[59] against racism and sexism. Breedlove's entrepreneurial endeavour is linked to a political resistance to dominant models of beauty perpetuated by the media:

> Many hair-care companies, especially those owned by white people, advertised to colored women by telling them how unattractive

they were . . . Sarah believed such advertising was misleading and that what a woman did with her hair was a woman's business and not a man's. (6)

An original advertisement from Breedlove's campaign, included in Lasky's book, evokes 'beauty work' in two senses: it promotes a product that 'works' on the body to prevent hair loss, but it also includes opportunities for women to 'secure prosperity and freedom' by finding paid employment as a representative of the company or even opening their own shop. The prominence of 'Madame C.J. Walker' on the advertisement suggests the importance of this personalized branding aimed at African American women (Figure 3).

Lasky's account of Breedlove's life, a tale of rags to riches, oppression to liberation, turns a complex biography and a shifting understanding of beauty into a capitalist fable. Like the snippets from the white child's primer interwoven into the opening of each section of *The Bluest Eye*, beauty is reduced to a simple, racially divided ideal. The 'Black is Beautiful' message of Lasky's picture book is inverted in Morrison's fictional primer, as the blonde-haired, blue-eyed healthy body is idealized through a staccato opening to the novel: 'Here is the house. It is green and white. It has a red door. It is very pretty . . . See mother. Mother is very nice. See father. He is big and strong' (1).

Morrison's allusion to Breedlove in *The Bluest Eye* introduces the concept of 'beauty work' as an important concept in Morrison's fiction as a whole, highlighting an industry in which African American women were able to make a living, gain widespread national recognition and achieve economic success. (When Breedlove died in 1920, she was one of the richest and most widely recognized women in America.) 'Beauty work' functions here as a means of employment, but also a set of products through which women can 'work' on their bodies to create a sense of beauty, self-worth and indulgence.

However, on another level, *The Bluest Eye* suggests the damaging nature of *any* simple fantasy of beauty. Just as in her critical writing Morrison insists that 'Black is Beautiful is a white ideal turned inside out',[60] *The Bluest Eye* exposes the arbitrary, exclusionary nature of both white ideals (in the increasingly garbled words of the primer) and the alternative, inverted beauty myths (through the ironic allusion to Breedlove). Instead of an image of defiant black beauty, Morrison presents readers with Pauline's vulnerable disabled body that refuses to be corrected according to a fantasy American dream image, or indeed to be removed from the narrative frame. Pauline Breedlove internalizes

68

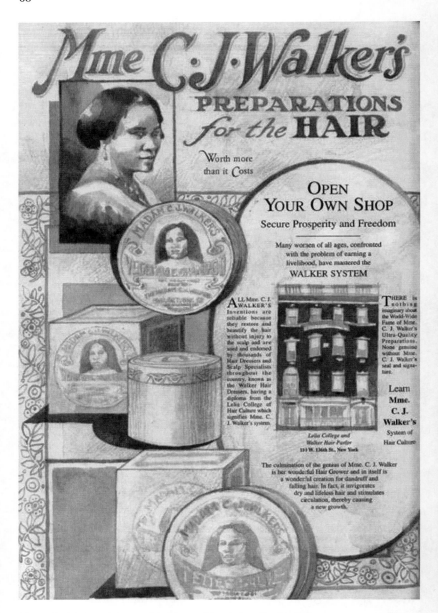

Figure 3   Vision of Beauty: The Story of Sarah Breedlove Walker

messages from precisely the same kind of damaging, racist advertisements that Sarah Breedlove stood up against. Morrison's puncturing of fantasies and fables of beauty in her fiction resists critical attempts to assimilate her individual literary aesthetic into a monologic feminist, black or disability rights discourse. The ironic naming of Pauline points to Morrison's challenge to any romanticized notion of beauty, and her commitment to representing the materiality of the living, working, feeling body itself.

Tar Baby enacts a similar shift from a focus on an idealized body, in the form of Margaret, beauty-pageant winner and 'Principal Beauty of Maine',[61] to a more sophisticated redefinition, of the beautiful by the end of the novel. As the narrative progresses, the onset of Margaret's dementia, as well as the disabling effects and signs of ageing, bring about cracks in her previously flawless self-image. Both her character and her body become fleshed out. Margaret's gradual immersion in work, taking over the household, brings about a new conception not only of her body, but of her beauty too:

> Now [Valerian] could see the lines, the ones that make-up had shielded brilliantly…She looked real. Not like a piece of Valerian candy, but like a person on a bus, already formed, fleshed, thick with a life which is not yours and not accessible to you. (164)

This change is mirrored in a corresponding shift in the descriptive vocabulary, from a specular language to an emphasis on texture: the fleshy 'thickness' of her body, and the inaccessibility of her private consciousness. *Sula* also explores the relationship between bodily surfaces and depth, though in relation to male beauty. Ajax's skin, perceived by the adoring Sula, is a complex layered surface of black skin covering 'gold leaf', followed by 'alabaster', which is gradually chipped away in her mind to reveal a richly fertile 'loam' (130). 'Ajax' shifts from a mythologized, statue-like figure to a material, flawed and very human man, 'A. Jacks', through this shifting, metaphorical relationship to bodily surfaces. Beauty is explored as a trans-gendered, highly subjective and transient quality. So, both *Tar Baby* and *Sula* chart a shift from a visual conception of flawless beauty, to a more complex appreciation of the body as a fertile, changeable, working instrument.

Morrison's novels of this period frequently return readers to bodies that are enduring, working and functional; 'tired necks' and 'calloused hands'[62] are depicted as not merely 'O.K.' but as sensuous and beautiful. While beautifying practices are presented with some ambivalence, they have an important narrative function which also suggests their social significance in the community. *Song of Solomon, Tar Baby* and *Jazz* go beyond an exclusively politicized call for a 'new way to see',[63] to open up the complex historical, social and economic dimensions of 'beauty work'. In doing so, they pave the way for a complete redefinition of the concept of beauty in Morrison's later writing.

Morrison's collaborative aesthetic: beauty and *The Black Book*

The subject of working bodies, and beauty as an industry and a social practice, is also explored in Morrison's early editorial project, *The Black Book* (1974). While an editor at Random House in the early 1970s Morrison pioneered this project which Bill Cosby, in a conversational foreword, describes as a 'scrapbook' documenting African American history. Cosby invites readers on an imaginative 'folk journey':

> Suppose a three-hundred-year-old black man had decided, oh, say when he was about ten, to keep a scrapbook – a record of what it was like for himself and his people in these United States... [64]

These introductory remarks, with their almost fairytale-like opening, immediately establish a piecemeal, collaborative model of history, in which the reader is implicated in the process of telling. Like Denver in *Beloved*, who 'giv[es] blood to the scraps her mother and grandmother had told her' (78), readers are invited to flesh out the fragments on the page through our own imaginative reconstruction. Both the topic of the book, shared experience: 'life as lived',[65] and the form of the book itself (its large size, inviting array of materials and lack of narratorial or editorial commentary), suggest a communal aesthetic of reading and storytelling. *The Black Book* breaks with conventional historical and narrative structures; it was, for Morrison, an 'organic book, which made up its own rules'.[66]

Just as the Breedlove story underpins the social and economic dimensions of beauty work explored in Morrison's novels, *The Black Book* is an important context for all of Morrison's works in their engagement with the everyday lives of the African American majority: 'The anonymous men and women ... the people who have always been viewed only as percentages would come alive in *The Black Book*.'[67] Images of beautiful and famous black stars from music and film, such as Lucille Armstrong (175), are placed alongside shocking anti-slavery images and representations of unnamed working people (97). Glamorous African American show girls sit alongside cherished photographs and family portraits; celebrations of African American achievement are interspersed with images of degradation and debasement.[68] *The Black Book* also engages with the emergence of the beauty industry and commercialized conceptions of beauty. The politics of hair are once again suggested, through the inclusion of the patent application for a hot comb hair-straightening device which is located among other examples of patents filed by African Americans. These celebrations of ingenuity, innovation and new technologies sit alongside images that remind readers of the way in which the African American body was exploited in commercial campaigns. The advertisement for Sunlight Soap (120), for example, parodies racial oppositions; it depicts a caricatured image of a very black child to make a point about the power of a detergent to achieve an idealized, pure 'whiteness'.

The Black Book draws upon the materials of everyday life to disrupt any simple, linear narrative of black history or beauty through a focus on contradiction, complexity and individual stories. Each page is packed with stories and cuttings, which include photographs, play bills, advertisements, newspaper articles, dream interpretations, letters, speeches, drawings, recipes, children's rhymes, spirituals, blues and folk songs. The coexistence and the merging of timeframes and genres – personal, political, frivolous and serious – are encapsulated in the overlapping images packed onto the front cover of the original book (Figure 4). Generically, it has been described as a 'memory book',[69] 'scrapbook'[70] and a 'genuine black history book'.[71] It was also, for Morrison, a deeply personal project. Although she is not credited in the book, she was the primary collator of materials and a portrait photograph of her own mother appears on the bottom right-hand side of the cover.

This fascination with photography and visual imagery extended throughout Morrison's career: she was the 'ghost writer'[72] of *The Black Book*, but also the official author of a foreword for the *Black Photographers Annual* (1973), James Van Der Zee's *Harlem Book of the Dead* (1978) and Robert Bergman's collection of portraits, *A Kind of Rapture*, published in 1998. In critical terms, the significance of *The Black Book*, however, goes beyond a personal connection for Morrison. *The Black Book* is usually only mentioned in passing by critics, for the fact that it introduced Morrison to the source for *Beloved*: 'A Visit to the Slave Mother Who Killed Her Child', a contemporary article documenting Margaret Garner's crime and punishment. These brief critical allusions, however, ignore the complex, productive models of history

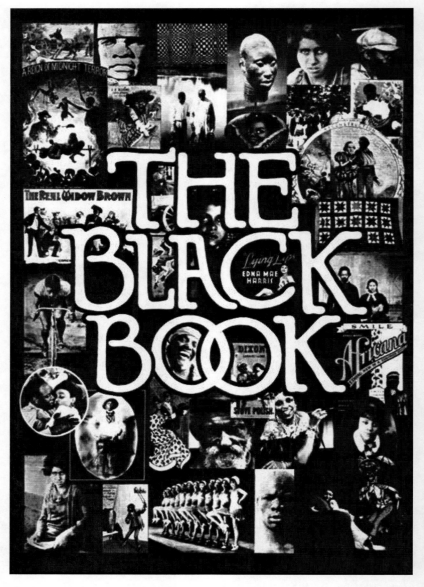

Figure 4 'Book Cover', from *The Black Book* by Middleton A. Harris, Morris Levitt, Roger Furman and Ernest Smith

and narrative that are embedded in *The Black Book* which inform all
of Morrison's fiction. An interview conducted with Morrison shortly
after its publication suggests the importance of the project to her later
work:

> I was, in completing the editing of 'The Black Book,' overwhelmed
> with the connecting tissue between black and white history. The con-
> nection, however, was not a simple one of white oppressor and black
> victim...The two histories merge in the book, as in life, in a noon
> heat of brutality and compassion, outrage and satisfaction.[73]

Here, Morrison rejects a model of history based upon false, oppositional paradigms. Instead, she insists upon an embodied perspective
which is emotionally charged and keenly aware of paradox and the
coexistence of pleasure and pain. *The Black Book* refuses the kind of
straightforward, celebratory view of African American culture articulated in a campaign such as 'Black is Beautiful'. As in *Beloved*, imagery
of the terrible suffering of slavery is placed alongside representations
of beauty and ritual celebration. For example, the shocking image of
a slave known only as 'Gordon' (9), whose back is scarred by the violence of his slave master, is followed by reproductions of pages from
the family bible of black slave-owners, but also more frivolous scenes
of dance performances. Any crude opposition between black 'defined'
and white 'definers' is complicated by the sheer range of materials and
stories in *The Black Book*, and this range symbolizes the complexity
of the ways in which Morrison's work is rooted in African American
history. The shifting dynamics explored through the content and collaborative form of *The Black Book*, between storyteller and listener,
between black and white histories and between beauty as an industry
and an abstract ideal, extend throughout her fiction. Morrison's essay,
'Rootedness: The Ancestor as Foundation', suggests that a further relationship of interdependence, between the aesthetic and the political,
is a defining feature of her literary and critical project: 'It seems to me
that the best art is political...and you ought to make it unquestion-
ably political and irrevocably beautiful at the same time.'[74] Morrison's
language is unequivocal: this interconnected, politically informed conception of beauty is at the centre of her own aesthetic as a critic and an
author.

In this sense, Morrison's aesthetic vision echoes Du Bois's essay, 'Criteria of Negro Art' (1926), in which he insists upon the right to create

art and to appreciate beauty. Like Morrison, Du Bois emphasizes the inseparability of the beautiful and the political:

> That somehow, somewhere, eternal and perfect Beauty sits above Truth and Right I can conceive, but here and now and in the world in which I work they are for me unseparated and inseparable. (293)

More recently, bel hooks has continued this political campaign for black experience, and black women's presence in particular, to be recognized as an important subject of aesthetic value, in both art and the critical discourses around it: 'The idea that there is no meaningful connection between black experience and critical thinking about aesthetics or culture must be continually interrogated.'[75] Morrison's *The Black Book* invites precisely such an 'interrogation' of this gap between critical and aesthetic thinking, in its focus on the intersection between black art and popular culture. For Morrison, the creation of beautiful objects and the exploration of beauty do not detract from political concerns but are, rather, fundamental to her commitment to 'assuming responsibility for people no one's ever assumed responsibility for'.[76] Beauty can, for Morrison, be shocking, paradoxical and difficult; a painful trigger for memories as well as a source of aesthetic pleasure.

Formulation of an alternative aesthetic: *Beloved, Foreign Bodies* and *The Dancing Mind*

In *Beloved* (1987), Morrison moves away from her critique of disabling, primarily visual definitions of the beautiful to reconceptualize beauty altogether. There is a shift from the focus on 'beauty work' in her middle novels, to a more complex, multi-sensory understanding of beauty. In *Beloved*, beauty and horror, lyrical style and traumatic memory, coexist. Here, Morrison formulates and articulates her 'alternative approach to beauty'[77] through an attention to the materiality of the black, female body: verbal and visual structures become subordinated to communication through sound, smell, movement and touch. In this way, the disabled, scarred, enslaved and displaced bodies of Sethe, Baby Suggs and Nan are reimagined, not merely as instruments of work but as sources of sensuality, beauty and pleasure.

The figure of Beloved herself encapsulates the ambivalent nature of beauty in the novel. Beloved's appearance of flawless beauty, 'new skin, lineless and smooth, including the knuckles of her hands' (61), draws attention to the surfaces of the body. Yet, this idealized exterior belies a monstrous, haunting and all-consuming interior vengeance. The crowd that gathers outside 124 observes: 'the devil child was clever...And beautiful' (309). For Denver, Beloved's body represents an excessive and threatening combination of qualities: 'Nothing was out there that this sister-girl did not provide in abundance: a racing heart, dreaminess, society, danger, beauty' (90). Sethe's motive for infanticide, the narrator suggests, lies partially in her desire to preserve an unsullied, idealized notion of the beautiful that Beloved represents:

> The best thing she was, was her children. Whites might dirty her all right, but not her best thing, her beautiful, magical best thing – the part of her that was clean. (296)

The powerful repetition of superlatives, and the appeal to an alternative, almost mystical purity here counters the brutal realities of the racism and slavery that Sethe has been forced to endure. The strength of the love contains within it the seed of destruction. Like Baby Suggs, the text itself remains ambivalent towards Sethe's 'rough choice' (296). The ghost-like figure of Beloved, suspended between the natural and supernatural worlds, is as an embodiment of the beautiful horror which haunts the text as whole.

For Barbara Johnson, this coexistence of beauty and horror constitutes a dangerous, almost seductive aesthetic: Morrison 'runs – indeed courts – the risk of transforming horror into pleasure, violence into beauty'.[78] There is certainly a sense in which the lushness and lyricism of Morrison's writing – the sheer fertility of her imagery – mediates the horror that she depicts. However, these anxieties about the transformation of horror into beauty, voiced by Johnson (and, to an extent, Wood), are anticipated in the text itself. *Beloved* introduces a principle of coexistence; Sethe's memory of 'Sweet Home', for example, introduces a paradoxical sense of 'shameless beauty'. The disturbing, unsettling nature of her description lies in the coexistence of beauty and violent exploitation in the same narrative frame:

> Suddenly there was Sweet Home...although there was not a leaf on that farm that did not make her want to scream, it rolled itself out before her in shameless beauty. It never looked as terrible as it was and it made her wonder if hell was a pretty place too. Fire and brimstone all right, but hidden in lacy groves. Boys hanging from the most beautiful sycamores in the world. It shamed her – remembering the wonderful soughing trees rather than the boys. (7)

The narrative itself highlights the deceptive nature of visual perception; the fact that the hellish farm is 'hidden' and 'never looked as terrible as it was' suggest Sethe's fear that the cumulative trauma of her abuse, as well as the particular horror of the bodies hanging in the trees, will be eclipsed in her memory by the natural beauty of the farm.

The sense of 'shameless beauty' that haunts Sethe here is revisited in the 'scandalous beauty'[79] explored in Morrison's later novel, *A Mercy* (2008). Once again, this ambivalent beauty comes in the form of a memory. Beauty and destruction are fundamentally linked as Lina, like Sethe, experiences shame at the way in which an image from the natural world (a tree, a flame) eclipses her memory of human suffering:

> Memories of her village peopled by the dead turned slowly to ash and in their place a single image arose. Fire. How quick. How purposefully it ate what had been built, what had been life. Cleansing somehow and scandalous in its beauty. Even before a simple hearth or encouraging a flame to boil water she felt a sweet twinge of agitation. (47)

The memories, like bodies soon reduced to ash, are fragile and transient. Yet, despite the paradox of Lina and Sethe's shame at their own shamelessness, it is the process of aestheticization that allows them to access these buried memories. Similarly, the figure of the tree that recurs throughout *Beloved* as a literal presence and a significant metaphor allows Sethe to speak her unspeakable memories. Garland Thomson sees this as a threat to understanding: 'Sethe's refusal to allow either spectacle to cancel out the other, her sharpening of this paradox that potentially threatens all meaning and coherence.'[80] In fact, the sycamore tree scene introduces an *alternative* mode of knowing and understanding beauty. Like Paul D's final act in the novel, of putting 'his story next to'[81] Sethe's, the text itself lays beauty and horror side by side. Rather than threatening meaning, or transforming horror into pleasure, both possibilities are left open. In the same way, historical and fictional modes coexist in the novel. The fictional representation of Sethe's scarred back recalls the historical document (and famous anti-slavery image) reproduced in *The Black Book* under the heading 'A Typical Negro': a portrait of an escaped slave from Mississippi, his 'back furrowed and scarred with the traces of a whipping administered on Christmas-day last' (9). The principle of coexistence becomes both an aesthetic strategy and a narrative mode in *Beloved*.

Most critical discussion of the role of Sethe's scar in *Beloved* tends to read the scar in abstract, historical and textual terms, as a violent inscription of a wider traumatic history of slavery onto the surface of her body: 'A metaphor for a new kind of writing, body writing.'[82] Maud Ellmann takes a wider literary overview: 'In Western literature scars traditionally... bear mute testimony to forgotten histories.'[83] She suggests, for example, that in both *Beloved* and the pivotal recognition scene in Homer's *Odyssey* scars function as triggers for rare moments of back-narration: 'At this point a kind of scar or lesion opens up within the narrative itself' (46).

Yet, through an insistence on the metaphorical significance of the tree symbol in *Beloved*, Morrison paradoxically returns readers to the fleshy materiality of the body. Sethe describes: 'I told on em. Schoolteacher made one open up my back, and when it closed it made a tree. It grows there still' (20). This unveiling of the body, and opening up of the skin, exposes many possible senses, stories and modes of knowing the scar in the text. Readers encounter the scar mediated by the metaphor of the tree, and through the consciousness of Amy Denver. Conventional notions of the beautiful are shattered, as even the most bodily of processes are reimagined. The broken skin becomes a tree trunk and the oozing pus is described as cherry blossom:

It's a tree, Lu. A chokecherry tree. See, here's the trunk – it's red and split wide open, full of sap... Leaves, too, look like, and dern if these ain't blossoms. Tiny little cherry blossoms, just as white. Your back got a whole tree on it. In bloom. (93)

As in Faulkner's *Soldier's Pay*, the scar is read from the outside, described by an observer who is shut out of the pain and memories that it signifies. The scar is perceived by others as a disabling mark of impairment; that which sets Sethe apart from bodily norms and ties to her a history of prejudice based on bodily difference. It differs from other impairments or marks of particularity in the sense that, unlike Pauline's club-foot for example, the wounds have been actively inflicted onto Sethe's body as a punishment and a mark of exploitation and ownership. The detail of the description, down to the 'tiny cherry blossoms', and the tree image risk distancing witnesses from the brutal violence of life under slavery. Yet, by linking the scar back to the natural world, through the extended metaphor of the tree, Morrison suggests that Sethe's scar can be read as something growing, changing, imaginatively fertile and even physically beautiful. The metaphorical reading allows Sethe to reclaim agency over the wound inflicted on her, to narrate her own life story and body.

So, Morrison represents Sethe's scar as simultaneously a generative metaphor and an embodied physical reality. The scar enacts the principle of coexistence, laying literal and symbolic, physical and imaginary, horrific and beautiful, next to each other. There is an opening up, through the representation of the scar, of simultaneous narrative possibilities and different modes of sensory perception. Paul D's initial insistence on a purely visual, literal reading of the scar suggests an initial failure of empathy: 'What tree on your back? Is something growing on your back? I don't see nothing growing on your back' (18). His refusal to read the metaphorical story that runs alongside the physical marking is experienced by Sethe as an act of cruelty. The descriptions of Sethe's bodily markings, mediated by Paul D's consciousness, are permeated by a sense of brutal, jarring disgust: 'a revolting clump of scars... nothing like any tree he knew' (25). At this moment, anger comes to the surface. Paul D refuses to view Sethe's body and the terrible wounds in purely aesthetic terms; he insists on a materially grounded view of the pain that she has suffered. In this way, Morrison suggests that anger (and a literal, physical focus on bodies) is an important personal and political response to the crimes of slavery.

Yet, *Beloved* remains strikingly ambiguous, as readers are suspended between literal and metaphorical readings. Paul D's perspective highlights the need to remember actual bodily pain and the very real suffering of slave life. While Sethe's metaphorical, aestheticized response to the scar not only challenges his scepticism but also subverts his reliance on visual modes of perception. Sethe's perspective enables multiple alternative imaginative readings: 'It's there all the same... I've never seen it and never will... Tiny little chokecherry leaves' (18). Morrison brings touch, imagination and empathy together through the depiction of Sethe's damaged, marked body. The soothing hands of Amy Denver, who places spider webs over the scar, mirror the maternal massaging of Sethe's wounded feet by Baby Suggs. Verbal structures are subordinated to other forms of sensory perception, as touch becomes the primary mode of communicating safety, love and intimacy: 'Wordlessly the older woman greased the flowering back and pinned a double thickness of cloth to the inside of the newly stitched dress' (110). So, through the necessarily linguistic medium of the novel, Morrison strives to depict touch, music, wordless communication and their relation to beauty.

The shift in Paul D's level of empathy towards Sethe can be charted through his increasing sensitivity to alternative forms of sensory perception over the course of the novel. Upon his return to 124, he caresses Sethe with 'educated hands' that convey what cannot be spoken, 'things neither knew about the other – the things neither had word-shapes for' (116). In a pivotal scene, Paul D engages in imaginative re-evaluation of Sethe's scar, expressing his affection and intimacy through touch:

> Bending down ... he held her breasts in the palms of his hands. He rubbed his cheek on her back and learned that way her sorrow, the roots of it; its wide trunk and intricate branches ... *He knew without seeing them or hearing* any sigh that tears were coming fast ... He saw the sculpture her back had become, like the decorative work of an ironsmith too passionate to display, *he could think but not say*, 'Aw, Lord, girl.' And he would tolerate no peace until he had touched every ridge and leaf of it with his mouth. (19; my italics)

Paul D no longer privileges visual knowledge – 'he knew without seeing or hearing' – as he is forced to confront the limits of verbal communication: 'he could think but not say'. His literal embrace of Sethe is mirrored in his symbolic embracing of her metaphorical mode of thinking about the scar as a tree, 'sculpture', or 'the decorative work of an ironsmith'. The significance and meanings attached to the scar cannot, it seems, be contained within the aesthetic frameworks that the narrator suggests in this scene: 'too passionate to display'. Sethe's sorrow is at once enclosed in the interior of her memory yet also accessible through the mediating surface of her body. Ethical and aesthetic concerns are intertwined as Morrison suggests a complex, multi-layered understanding of the body.

This multi-faceted notion of beauty is developed further in the Clearing scene. Again, trees are endowed with a symbolic significance as the community retreats to the 'emerald closet' (64) for ritualistic ceremonies. Here, bodies are depicted as simultaneously disabled and beautiful, painful and pleasurable. Baby Suggs, who 'walks like a three-legged dog' (166), represents a long line of women in the novel who are physically impaired as a result of slavery, including Nan with her 'one good arm and half of another' (74) and Sethe herself. Yet, in the Clearing, Baby Suggs's disability is reimagined as an enabling mark of distinction: 'because slave life had "busted her legs, back, head, eyes, hands, kidneys, womb and tongue," [Baby Suggs] had nothing left to make a living with but her heart – which she put to work at once ... she became an unchurched preacher' (102).

Baby Suggs offers an alternative form of authority and knowledge, rooted in the body. She counters the racial hatred perpetuated by slavery with a doctrine of self-love. In her sermons, the body is conceived of as both literally and imaginatively fertile: 'Your life-holding womb... Your life-giving private parts... Love your heart. For this is the prize' (104). Baby Suggs's association with fertility and care challenges contemporary social constructions of disabled women as lacking the capacity to fulfil procreative and maternal roles.[84] The teachings she disseminates in the Clearing challenge a racist, utilitarian view of the enslaved body as a commodity, tool or assortment of parts. At the Sweet Home plantation, Paul D 'discovers his worth... the dollar value of his weight, his strength, his heart, his brain, his penis, his future' (267). The structure of the sentence itself mirrors the sense in which his body is broken down into an inventory of parts, each with a supposedly quantifiable value. In the Clearing, by contrast, this commercialized notion of value is completely reconfigured, as traditionally marginalized bodies are placed at the centre, and are appreciated as aesthetically valuable. For Morrison, a focus on aesthetic pleasure becomes a mode of countering, even displacing, this commercial, objectifying impulse.

The beauty of the scene suggests a creative resistance to the paralysis of anger as an emotional response.[85] In this context, dancing, laughing and gaining enjoyment from the body become in themselves a form of resistance. Morrison's political and aesthetic engagements are connected here. Morrison hints at a point of intersection between impaired and enslaved bodies, in the prevailing conception of both in terms of an (in)capacity to work, or as a source of pain, rather than pleasure, beauty or sensuality. Sethe recalls:

> Slaves not supposed to have pleasurable feelings on their own; their bodies not supposed to be like that. [Baby Suggs] said for me not to listen to all that. That I should always listen to my body and love it. (247)

Aesthetic and affective experiences are privileged over economic definitions. In this way, *Beloved* encapsulates a wider shift in Morrison's outlook away from the oppositional politics and models of identity in her early fiction, towards an emphasis on celebration and imaginative redefinition. *Beloved* does not efface the sense of political anger and horror, but rather suggests that anger can fuel creative responses to suffering and prejudice.

The sensuality preached in Baby Suggs's doctrines becomes incorporated into the narrative technique itself. The Clearing scene depicts the full spectrum of sensory impressions: 'the smell of leaves simmering in the sun, thunderous feet and the shouts that ripped pods off the limbs of the chestnuts' (111). The emphasis on touch as a mode of articulation earlier in the novel is formulated into a self-conscious instruction in the Clearing. Baby Suggs urges participants to: 'Touch others...pat them...stroke them...Feet that need to rest and to dance; backs that need support; shoulders that need arms, strong arms, I'm telling you' (104). In this enclosed, alternative space, the boundaries of the body, identity and the text itself become more fluid:

> It started that way: laughing children, dancing men, crying women and then it got mixed up. Women stopped crying and danced; men sat down and cried; children danced, women laughed, children cried until, exhausted...all and each lay about the Clearing damp and gasping for breath. (103)

The Clearing scene captures the ambivalent nature of beauty in *Beloved*, by placing pleasure and pain, laughter and grief side by side, in the same actual and symbolic space. The sentences themselves, with clauses layered on top of each other, create an exhausting, exhilarating sense of bodies and emotions merging into each other. Life-giving celebration is combined with a physical form of mourning, which brings relief and helps healing. The 'criss-crossing of the senses'[86] that, Scarry suggests, characterizes the experience of beauty, becomes incorporated into the narrative technique in this scene in the interweaving of sensory perceptions, identities, emotions and bodies.

This alternative conception of beauty and the body is also explored through the medium of dance. Baby Suggs replaces verbal modes of communication with dance:

> Saying no more, she stood up and then danced with her twisted hip the rest of what her heart had to say while the others opened their mouths and gave her the music. Long notes held until the four-part harmony was perfect enough for their deeply loved flesh. (104)

The doctrine of self-love, and celebration of the disabled body, becomes physically (and aurally) articulated here. Baby Suggs's impairment individualizes her movements and enables expression. Dance in Morrison's writing is depicted not as a mode of disciplining the body, but rather as spontaneous and inclusive, a form of non-verbal, non-visual, experiential pleasure.

Inclusiveness and participation are key to the dynamic definitions of beauty that Morrison develops. Elsewhere, Morrison has commented that her aim in writing is to 'provide places and spaces so that the reader can participate'.[87] Beauty, in this sense, is also an exchange based on a reciprocal pact between active participants. Wendy Steiner has described beauty in this way: 'Beauty is not a one-way street. One discovers a valuable Other, and rises to recognize oneself in it. In doing so, one "participates" in beauty.'[88] This participatory quality works on two levels in the Clearing scene. Baby Suggs calls for all members of the community to participate in the ritual: 'Let the grown men come...' (103). Moreover, the nature of the text itself, which reaches its most lyrical and fluid at this pivotal moment of the novel, requires readers to become actively involved in the process of reading, as 'co-creator[s]'[89] of the text. Beauty here becomes an active principle, an act of re-writing, as bodies and identities have to be actively reconstructed (or indeed, re-membered) amid the dancing, writhing bodies and fluid sentence structures.

Exploration of the imaginative possibilities of this 'created space of dance'[90] continues in Morrison's later critical writing and curatorial work. There is a parallel between Morrison's redefinition of beauty in her writing, and her experimentation with an alternative aesthetic of beauty in the exhibition, *Foreign Bodies*. In both cases, Morrison explores inclusive approaches which enable the representation of bodies that are not traditionally conceived of as beautiful, though different forms of text, painting and installations. Like Morrison's novels, the exhibition explores the diversity and multi-sensory nature of beauty. As a guest curator, Morrison chose a dance installation, a collaboration between the American choreographer William Forsythe and the German sculptor and video artist Peter Welz, as the opening performance and main subject of the exhibition. The inspiration for the dance performance was Francis Bacon's last portrait, found on his easel at the time of his death in 1992 (Figure 5). The painting, which was itself exhibited in the *Foreign Bodies* exhibition, depicts a distorted, even deformed image of a face, which hides as much as it reveals. Bacon, who referred to his painting in general as a 'stenography of sensation',[91] is described by D. W. Winnicott as 'the exasperating and challenging artist of our time who goes on and on painting the human face distorted significantly'.[92] Bacon's untitled, unfinished portrait acts as a starting point for Forsythe/Welz's

Figure 5   Francis Bacon, *Untitled: Final Unfinished Portrait*, 1991–2

multimedia installation in which the boundaries of the body and of perception are constantly challenged and renegotiated. As in Morrison's fictional writing, it is the representation of bodies that disrupt the conventions of seeing and dominant discourses of beauty that prove most imaginatively fertile and aesthetically powerful.

In the installation, the painting was 'retranslated' in a dance performance by Forsythe, which was filmed from different angles, and presented on three large screens covering the entire gallery. Forsythe also wore shoes and gloves covered in graphite in order to leave traces of his movement on the floor which itself became part of the installation. Marcella Lister's essay in the exhibition catalogue describes the artistic process through textual and linguistic metaphors:

> The outcome is a complex experiment in 'translation,' from drawing to choreographic movement, back into drawing: the floor becomes part of the final installation. The process raises the question of the existing dialogue between drawing and movement.[93]

Later in the catalogue, Lister extends these textual metaphors of a 'dialogue' or 'retranslation' to describe how 'William Forsythe has teamed up with... Peter Welz to "transcribe" a painting by Francis Bacon'.[94] However, to conceive of the installation in exclusively linguistic terms, as a search for an extended 'dance vocabulary' or 'an enlarged palette of bodily language' (14) is to ignore the striking physicality and multisensory nature of the work. Morrison herself, in an interview in *The*

New York Times, suggests that the medium of dance was chosen to emphasize the centrality of the body in this project:

> It seemed to me that if we could get a choreographer as one of our disciplines, it would be a triumph...because in that field you have the body in motion and you have the obligation of seeing the body as the real and final home.[95]

Morrison's notion of 'rootedness'[96] calls for a culturally, historically and physically contextualized approach to identity and literature in which the imaginary and linguistic are intertwined with the physical. Forsythe's installation applies this principle to the body, describing *Re-translation* as: 'A reflection on the human body as the seat and last refuge of individual identity'.[97] Forsythe returns readers to Morrison's own sense of 'rootedness', in a specific culture and time, but most significantly, an individual body which is complex, unique and aesthetically challenging.

As in *Beloved*, Morrison's exhibition experiments with music, movement and touch as a mode of renegotiating the boundaries of the body, beauty and identity. The Clearing scene in the novel is mediated through text, whereas Forsythe communicates directly through the body, invoking 'movement as [a] form of knowledge about the world'.[98] This is reminiscent of Maxine Sheets-Johnstone's notion of 'kinesthetic knowledge',[99] which suggests that dance should be understood through touch, texture and movement, rather than in exclusively visual or linguistic terms: '*A spatial texture* becomes apparent: the created space of dance has a textural aspect according to the manner in which it is created' (25). The multi-media nature of Forsythe's installation, which includes video, painting, sketching, sound and dance, resonates with Morrison's sense of the diversity of beauty and the value of opening up multiple forms of sensory perception in the text of *Beloved*. In this sense, *Re-translation* responds to Morrison's on-going struggle to 'speak the unspeakable', this time through an alternative, wordless medium, 'through the body and on an experiential and kinesthetic level which precedes words'.[100] Forsythe and Welz's installation focuses on the aesthetic *process* of creating and living in the body which is always in flux, vulnerable yet beautiful as a result of its distortions.

The collaborative *Foreign Bodies* project placed different forms of knowledge and conceptions of the body side by side. Welz's photomontage (Figure 6) superimposes on Bacon's painting a video still of

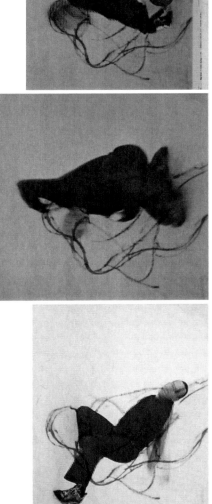

Figure 6 Peter Welz, *Studies for Re-translation/Final Unfinished Portrait (Francis Bacon)* (2006). Lambda print on paper, transparency, staples, gaffa tape. 61 cm × 86 cm

Forsythe's dancing body and drawings of his movements, suggesting different representations of the body coexisting in a single space. As in the Clearing scene in *Beloved*, the boundaries of the body are redrawn and renegotiated through dance and movement. Visitors move through the gallery, experiencing representations of the dancer's body from different angles and viewpoints but always only in fragments or glimpses. Forsythe's installation illuminates *Beloved* and the Clearing scene in particular, as both focus on coexisting perspectives, incomplete bodies and narratives. In both instances, and in Bacon's *Unfinished Portrait* which accompanies and inspired Welz's work, we are reminded of what we cannot see, but are called upon to imaginatively reconstruct.

This principle of coexistence also applies to the simultaneous suspension of many different time frames, in both *Beloved* and the installation. Forsythe argues that time and space become reconfigured through dance; his interest in form, he suggests in an interview, is with 'the sensation of formation as the body continuously moves from one state to another...I am trying to find out where these states have a place.'[101] In these art works, affect is placed above any final artistic effect, sensation above sense. Later in the same interview, Welz suggests that a multi-media, multi-dimensional approach to the body is important in breaking away from a static viewpoint:

> The reason why I filmed it from those different angles, was that it gave me the possibility to break up with sculpture as such. The three perspectives, from the front, the side and above, are a three dimensional approach to the figure. But the viewer finds the possibility to enter the figure's movement by walking through the installation. (32)

So, the visitor to the installation is invited to become an active participant in the process of constructing meaning. In this constant retracing of the lines of the (imaginary) body, the aesthetic representation brings the viewer to a self-reflexive awareness of their own physical presence in the installation. This inclusive aesthetic provides an alternative conception of beauty and the body as constructed, relational and constantly in flux.

As in the Clearing scene, Forsythe's struggle to access this 'other space of imagination' (28), returns us to Morrison's own search for alternative, inclusive 'places and spaces for the reader to participate'.[102] Alice Walker, writing at the same time as Morrison, also explores how dance, disability and alternative spaces or ways of thinking about the body intersect in 'Beauty: When the Other Dancer is the Self' (1983),[103] a semi-autobiographical essay that narrates the story of her partial blinding in an accident with an air gun as a small child. Like Morrison, Walker charts a shift from an internalized, exclusively visual notion of beauty to an alternative, inclusive and highly individualized celebration of difference. Walker narrates an initial self-loathing, reminiscent of *The Bluest Eye,* in which pain lies not in her own inability to see, but rather in the fact of being subjected to the dehumanizing stare of others:

> Where the BB pellet struck there is a glob of whitish scar tissue, a hideous cataract, on my eye. Now when I stare at people – a favorite pastime, up to now – they will stare back. Not at the 'cute' little girl, but at her scar ... I pray for beauty. (389)

Later in the essay, however, Walker suggests that this crude dichotomy between 'cute' and 'ugly', disabled and normal, becomes destabilized, when mediated through the child-like gaze of her own daughter. Just as Amy Denver describes Sethe's scar as a tree, Walker's daughter reimagines her mother's disfigurement, providing her with a metaphor that allows her to conceive of it as beautiful: 'Mommy, there's a *world* in your eye' (393). At the culmination of the essay, this approach to disability and beauty is articulated through the representation of dance:

> That night I dream I am dancing ... As I dance, whirling and joyous, happier than I've ever been in my life, another bright-faced dancer joins me. We dance and kiss ... The other dancer has obviously come through all right, as I have done. She is beautiful, whole and free. And she is also me. (393)

Walker stages a confrontation with the self, as beauty is reconceptualized through the encounter with difference and disability. The 'problem' of beauty is solved through this redefinition, as beauty is associated with a sense of completion and new-found freedom. For Walker, the mimetic process – as she encounters another version of herself through her writing and her dreaming – creates an authentic, life-like reflection. In this context, dance is employed as a metaphor for a liberated mode of thought and a site for imaginative exchange.

In Morrison's more complex, multi-layered works, beauty remains a far more ethically and aesthetically ambiguous concept, mediated by the forms of dance, language and painting. For Morrison, beauty remains both politically and aesthetically unresolved. Walker's narrative is more sentimental than Morrison's fictional and critical approach. The idea of a confrontation with the self in Walker's essay is developed into a more complex model for reciprocal ethical and narrative relationships in Morrison's *The Dancing Mind* (2003). In this speech, she suggests that aesthetic representations, this time in a literary form, can allow access to different kinds of knowledge or ways of thinking and relating to others:

> The life of the book world is quite serious. Its real life is about creating and producing and distributing knowledge; about making it possible for the entitled as well as the dispossessed to experience one's own mind dancing with another's.[104]

The implied political and social responsibility here looks forward to the *Re-translation* installation, but also links back to the impaired bodies and dispossessed characters in the Clearing. The idea of a 'dancing mind' comes from one of Sethe's childhood memories in *Beloved*. She suggests that the physical act of dancing inaugurates a mode of identifying, empathizing and even temporarily *becoming* 'something other': 'Oh but when they danced and sometimes they danced the antelope... *They shifted shapes and became something other*' (37). Dance is not merely ornamental or beautiful here but instead allows for a rethinking of relationships in which the form of the movement is inseparable from its participatory and imaginative potential. Later in the essay, Morrison places the concept of a dancing mind in a specifically literary context:

> The peace I am thinking of is the dance of an open mind when it engages another equally open one – an activity that occurs most naturally, most often in the reading / writing world we live in.[105]

The dance itself, with its collaborative, participatory quality, is linked to writing as 'a craft that appears solitary but needs another for its completion' (14). The reader or viewer of the installation becomes implicated in the 'dancing' aesthetic, as a 'fundamentally egalitarian and empowering image of dialogic interaction'[106] and an imaginative, dynamic encounter. Notions of dance, as literal movement, aesthetic representation and metaphor, are put side by side in Morrison's fiction, critical writing and curatorial work to explore its 'shape-shifting' imaginative possibilities.

Conclusion: disability aesthetics

Morrison's concern with bodies that are disabled, displaced and exiled extends throughout her career as a novelist, critic and curator. In *Playing in the Dark*, Morrison describes the on-going narrative, ethical and imaginative challenge through a critical vocabulary that foregrounds disability:

> I am interested in what prompts and makes possible this process of entering what one is estranged from – and in what disables the foray...into corners of the consciousness held off and away from the reach of the writer's imagination. (4)

For Morrison as an able-bodied writer, the challenge to imagine the condition of disability constitutes precisely this potentially 'disabling' yet compelling subject matter.

The nature of the literary project that Morrison proposes in *Playing in the Dark*, to reread canonical American literature from the perspective of the unspoken African presence, provides a theoretical framework for the *Foreign Bodies* exhibition. In the exhibition, Morrison employed a parallel strategy: re-examining celebrated works of art, with an emphasis on marginalized, unseen bodies. Through this categorization, visitors were reminded that the images were linked by their status as bodies (or parts of bodies) that are often overlooked, or deliberately avoided, in everyday life. The much-discussed motif of the unspeakable in Morrison's fiction is replicated in the unseen or unrepresented in the exhibition. The sense of the unspoken was physically embodied in Sonia Andrade's short film which was featured in the *Foreign Bodies* exhibition. Filmed in 1977 under the military dictatorship in Brazil (1964–84), the camera remains static as the female figure slowly binds her mouth with nylon thread, until her face reaches a point of extreme distortion, deformity and self-mutilation. The film is shocking for its brutal desecration of beauty. As in *Beloved* and *Sula*, aesthetic representation becomes equated with pain rather than pleasure. The unspeakable political climate of censorship and intimidation is captured even within the self-abnegating resistance to naming of the piece itself: *Untitled*.

The unseen was explored in the section of the exhibition called 'Erasures'. Morrison selected studies from Georges-Pierre Seurat, in which the figures are indistinct, preoccupied, working and turning away from the viewer. These were placed alongside Samuel Beckett's silent short *Film* which features Buster Keaton as the main character who refuses to turn his eyes to the camera, keeping his back to the viewer's (intrusive) gaze until a final, climactic moment of shocking confrontation.

As a curator, therefore, Morrison was concerned to confront visitors with their own expectations and ways of reading the body. *Foreign Bodies* adopts a multi-sensory, interdisciplinary approach to beauty and towards bodies that have been traditionally overlooked. Beauty is redefined as a complex, enriching yet also disruptive concept. Like the Clearing, the exhibition is understood as an inclusive, imaginative space in which different bodies and perspectives coexist. In these senses, Morrison's works respond to a critical trend in which the body, in its fleshy, messy materiality becomes reinserted into the discussion of aesthetics. 'Beauty,' as Eleanor Heartney comments, 'seems in need of rehabilitation today.'[107] Heartney's concern with beauty as 'an impulse that can be as liberating as it has been deemed enslaving' (xv) echoes Morrison's own early denunciation of beauty as an irrevocable 'slavery of the senses'.[108]

Morrison's writing parallels the critical shift from a denouncement of beauty as an outdated, oppressive concept in certain feminist, disability and black rights movements of the 1970s, to a redefinition and rehabilitation of the concept in much current criticism. In the first wave of disability studies, questions of beauty and pleasure in the texts themselves were frequently overlooked, understandably, in favour of a political focus on the social model of disability,[109] the collapse of language in the face of pain[110] or the establishment of the field itself.[111]

More recently, critics in the area of 'disability aesthetics' have begun to address some of the critical gaps in the field. Tobin Siebers's critical approach, for example, actively emphasizes the presence of disability in the history of aesthetics but also 'refuses to recognise the representation of the healthy body – and its definition of harmony, integrity, and beauty – as the sole determination of the aesthetic'.[112] As such, disability aesthetics operates as a critical framework for challenging 'aesthetic presuppositions in the history of art' in the past as well as a valuable perspective for exploring 'future conceptions of what art is' (71). Disability aesthetics opens up an alternative mode of viewing Morrison's work, but also a critical perspective through which a vast spectrum of texts and artworks can be re-evaluated or, in Forsythe's terms, 're-translated'. Morrison's depiction of disabled bodies as beautiful and pleasurable suggests that beauty can act as a fertile, generative area of enquiry in the expanding field of disability studies; a chance, as Davis argues, to explore the richness of experience and creativity offered by the opportunity of disability.[113]

In *Playing in the Dark*, Morrison suggests that the appreciation of beauty is central to the process of fictional construction. 'Writing and reading,' she argues, 'are not all that distinct for a writer. Both exercises require being alert and ready for unaccountable beauty...the sweaty fight for meaning and response-ability' (xiii). Even as literary processes sensitize readers and writers to beauty, they engage them in 'sweaty' physical materiality and the struggle for meaning.

Morrison's critical writing does not go so far as some critics in their arguments about the moral value of beauty. Anita Silvers, for example, posits an explicit link between moral and aesthetic concerns: 'To enlarge our aesthetic responsiveness to people...would enlarge our moral capacities.'[114] However, Scarry's sense of beauty as an enabling concept, not an impediment or obstacle but a 'lever...[or] a call'[115] chimes with Morrison's own depiction of beauty in her later works as an active principle. Scarry's sense of 'the very pliancy or elasticity of beauty – hurtling us forward and back, requiring us to break new ground' (46) also characterizes Morrison's stances as a novelist and curator. Morrison describes her multiple projects, as a novelist, critic, academic and curator, as 'constantly...evolving...aesthetically and politically unresolved'.[116] Her later works move away from the lyrical, expansive novel forms such as *Beloved*, towards more slender and condensed novellas such as *Love* and *A Mercy* in which beauty is more implicitly explored. Yet, political, ethical and aesthetic questions about beauty and the representation of disability are continually intertwined in Morrison's open-ended writerly endeavour: 'I can say that my narrative project is as difficult today as it was thirty years ago.'[117]

Twenty-three years after the publication of *The Bluest Eye*, in 1993, Morrison wrote an Afterword to the novel, to be included alongside the original text. In this Afterword she articulates the shift in her thinking about beauty and suggests an on-going struggle to redefine, rehabilitate and explore beauty as a complex imaginative process, and a potentially enabling critical tool. She recalls:

> It was the first time I knew beautiful. Had imagined it for myself. Beauty was not simply something to behold; it was something one could do. (16)

4
Dialectics of Dependency: Ageing and Disability in J. M. Coetzee's Later Writing

In Coetzee's *Slow Man*, Elizabeth Costello, the ageing author, attempts to provoke a reaction from her unresponsive, disabled companion Paul, with a parable:

> 'Do you remember, Paul, the story of Sinbad and the old man?'
>   He does not reply.
>   'By the bank of a swollen stream,' she says, 'Sinbad comes upon an old man. "I am old and weak," says the old man. "Carry me to the other side and Allah will bless you." Being a good-hearted fellow, Sinbad lifts the old man onto his shoulders and wades across the stream. But when they reach the other side the man refuses to climb down. Indeed, he tightens his legs around Sinbad's neck until Sinbad feels himself choking. "Now you are my slave," says the old man, "who must do my bidding in all things." '[1]

This dynamic, in which an ageing, frail body leads to the development of a complex, reciprocal relationship, resounds in Coetzee's later writing. For Paul in *Slow Man*, the narrative evokes a highly physical image of two bodies, master and slave, bound together, sharing a common fate: 'Vividly he remembers the illustration: the skinny old man...his wiry legs hooked around the hero's neck while the hero strides through the waist-deep torrent' (129). Paul, like the reader, is invited to consider the seductively symbolic possibilities of Costello's story. His interpretation, addressed to Elizabeth, is self-referential and confrontational:

> 'Am I to understand that I am Sinbad in the story and you are the old man? In that case you face a certain difficulty. You have no means of...getting onto my shoulders. And I am not going to help you up.'

Costello smiles a secretive smile. 'Perhaps I am already there, she says, and you don't know it.' (129)

This short parable introduces a set of complex, dualistic relationships that recur in *Slow Man* and throughout Coetzee's later fiction and criticism. The interplay between dependency and dominance, care and control, is at the heart of Coetzee's interrogation of what it means to be a citizen and a writer in twenty-first-century society. Coetzee probes moments of ethical and literary impasse, depicting bodies locked together in mutual dependency and antagonism, to explore the limits of imaginative identification and empathy.

This chapter explores how Coetzee's depiction of disability and ageing sets up a series of dynamics in the novels, structured around an initial, central relationship between carer and patient. How do these structures shift over the course of the novels? And how do dialectics of dependency work to form identity and narrative itself? The notion of a 'dialectic of dependency', introduced by Michael Davidson in the *Journal of Literary and Cultural Disability Studies* (2007), provides a productive analytical framework for exploring Coetzee's writing. Davidson argues that: 'Every relationship involves dependency – from a word's dependence on a meaning, a country's dependence on its people, a people's dependence on its political representatives' (i). This definition suggests that disability studies can be used to consider questions of universal significance: about care, bodily, linguistic and technological dependencies and the formation of narrative and identity. Davidson suggests that a specific focus on conditions of disability and disabling processes of ageing foreground the wider significance of the term: '[dependency] takes on an especially charged character for people with disabilities. For many able-bodied persons, disability is synonymous with dependency' (i).

These issues about care and dependency extend far beyond the field of disability studies. Particularized relationships of mutual dependency, the face-to-face dialogues that Coetzee depicts, also raise wider philosophical, ontological and ethical questions. Emmanuel Levinas, for example, explores the unknowable nature of the other through this same master and slave dynamic: 'The encounter with the other (autrui) consists in the fact that despite the extent of my domination and his slavery, I do not possess him.'[2] Levinas suggests that we can never have totalizing knowledge of another person. Yet, care remains at the centre of his ethical theory: 'Goodness consists in taking up a position in being such that the Other counts more than myself.'[3] The vulnerability or suffering of the other leads to a sense of obligation, Levinas suggests, that arises at an affective level: 'to nourish the hunger of another with one's own fasting'.[4] Through this image of bodily need and self-denial, the impulse to care for another person and the difficulty of imaginatively entering an other's consciousness, are placed side by side.

In Coetzee's writing, these self-sacrificing, instinctive notions of care, in which the two parties are intertwined in a complex relation, are pushed to their ethical and imaginative limits. In *Elizabeth Costello*, for example, Elizabeth relates a tale that she finds too morally ambiguous to write. Through the medium of an imaginary, unwritten letter to her sister Blanche, she describes several scenes in which she posed naked and then performed sexual favours for her mother's ageing artist friend, Mr. Phillips, as he lay dying in his hospital bed. The episodes challenge taboos about the representation of ageing and sexuality, but also continue to puzzle, even plague Elizabeth herself for years later with their sheer unrepresentability. The brutal, bodily tone of the narration is heightened by a momentary slip into a distant, third-person perspective:

> As for her, Elizabeth, crouched over the old bag of bones with her breasts dangling, working away on his nearly extinct organ of generation, what name would the Greeks give to such a spectacle? Not eros certainly – too grotesque for that. Agape? Again, perhaps not. Does that mean the Greeks would have no word for it? Would one have to wait for the Christians to come along with the right word: caritas?[5]

The competing vocabularies suggest that the definitions of care and caritas represent sites of contestation, but also form a defining feature of any civilization or ethical system. There is a sense of narrative discomfort in *Elizabeth Costello*, as both character and narrator offer more questions than answers:

> What can one make of episodes like this, unforeseen, unplanned, out of character? Are they just holes, holes in the heart, into which one steps and falls and goes on falling? (155)

Coetzee poses a linguistic, ethical and literary problem here: how can a reader be expected to understand or enter the consciousness of a character who persistently behaves 'out of character'? We are never given any indication of Mr. Phillips's response to Elizabeth's ambiguous acts of 'caritas'. Coetzee's struggle to represent unrepresentable episodes, 'holes into which one steps...and goes on falling',[6] returns us to Levinas's notion of unknowable relationships with the other: 'Our relation with the other (autrui) certainly consists in wanting to comprehend him, but this relation overflows comprehension' (6). The interplay between the impulse to care for and to control, for knowledge and an awareness of imaginative limitation, are at the fore in these moments of resistance that Coetzee depicts. Here, the relationships between carer and patient, lover and loved one, overflow into each other to create a dynamic that, even for Elizabeth herself, 'escapes comprehension'.[7]

The focus of Coetzee's novels written after his move to Australia reflects the particular preoccupation with issues of care and ageing in a developed, Westernized country in his later writing. This exploration of the ethics and social construction of care is not, however, a new concern in Coetzee's writing. His earlier novels, written under the Apartheid regime in South Africa, also explore complex experiences of ageing and disability but in the quite different context of the brutal aftermath of empire and a rapidly changing and developing country. *Waiting for the Barbarians* (1980) depicts a young woman in an unnamed frontier town whose body bears witness to 'the dark marks her torturers have left upon her, the twisted feet, the half-blind eyes'.[8] As in Morrison's *Beloved*, there is a focus on scars and the surface of the body; Magistrate eyes the marks on her body with an ambivalent fascination and revulsion: 'Too much or too little: is she what I want or the traces of a history her body bears?' (64). Mediated through his gaze, her body is inseparable from the decimated historical and political landscape that she inhabits. *Foe* (1987) is a re-written Robinson Crusoe set on an unknown desert island, yet the tongueless, traumatized figure of the silent Friday is reminiscent of this tortured, enslaved body of the barbarian girl, viewed from the outside. The namelessness of the locations invites allegorical readings and, in particular, suggests parallels with the violence and voicelessness suffered by black South Africans. In contrast to the ageing and impaired bodies of Coetzee's later novels, *Waiting for the Barbarians* and *Foe* both depict people who have had disabilities inflicted on them, rather than suffering accidents or the more gradual debilitating process of ageing. In this context, the expectation of living to an old age and the provision of high quality care, as well as the critical space to reflect upon these issues, are luxuries that only certain racial groups and sections of society are afforded.

In *Age of Iron* (1990), a novel structured around the ambiguous relationship between the elderly, dying Mrs Curren and her disabled companion, Vercueil, these debates about care are explicitly explored. Mrs Curren relates the South African landscape, in particular the abandoned farmhouses in the Karoo and the West coast, to her own dying body: barren, ageing and forgotten. She describes 'a land taken by force, used, despoiled, spoiled, abandoned in its barren later years. Loved too, perhaps, by its ravishers, but loved only in the bloomtime of its youth.'⁹ This is an earth, she suggests, to which her body will soon return. She describes South Africa as a country in which 'the spirit of charity has perished', and even the word 'charity' has been emptied of meaning, worn out: '*Charity*: From the Latin word for the heart. It is as hard to receive as to give. It takes as much effort. I wish you would learn that' (22). Mrs Curren undermines the authority of her own narration, severing the etymological link even as she attempts to establish it: 'A lie: charity, caritas, has nothing to do with the heart. But what does it matter if my sermons are based on false etymologies?' (22). Her view of caring and charity as mutually dependent has, she suggests, come under threat. The contested history and identity of the country is played out even in this loss of linguistic roots.

Like the words that she uses, Mrs Curren experiences a sense of rootlessness and a wider lack of meaning in her life. The narrative is structured around two relationships of care: her memories of caring for, and implicit desire to be cared for by, her absent daughter, Florence. This desire takes the form of the perpetual letter-writing and confessional mode of the text itself. In her daughter's absence, Mrs Curren's closest companion becomes the homeless Vercueil, a carer who, paradoxically, represents a wider national spiral of hopelessness in which caring has become impossible: 'I look for him to care, and he does not. Because he is beyond caring. Beyond caring and beyond care' (22). Again, the denial of Vercueil's capacity to care is subverted by her own frequent appeals for recognition and help from him, amid the suffering and 'indifferent squalor of old age' (35). It is only through her ultimate recognition of the interdependence that characterizes her relationship with Vercueil, like the realization of her connectedness to the horrors of Apartheid violence from which she has been sheltered for most of her life, that Mrs Curren is able to look beyond her own personal suffering.

It is in Coetzee's later novels, *Elizabeth Costello* (2004), *Slow Man* (2005) and *Diary of a Bad Year* (2007), that ageing and disability are most clearly linked and personally inflected, through the semi-autobiographical figures of JC and Elizabeth Costello. These later, post-emigration novels extend earlier concerns about disability and reciprocal relationships of care, but in a post-Apartheid, Australian context. Like the apparent 'weakness' of the elderly man in the Sinbad tale, *Elizabeth Costello*, *Slow Man* and *Diary of a Bad Year* each begin with protagonists whose physical frailty places them in positions of apparent dependency. In *Slow Man*, Paul Rayment finds himself trapped in 'a circumscribed life' (26) and a 'truncated body' (61) following the amputation of his leg. Elizabeth, appearing in both *Elizabeth Costello* and *Slow Man*, is depicted as 'frail',[10] 'grey-haired; grey-faced too, with…a bad heart'.[11] *Diary of a Bad Year* charts the process through which JC becomes increasingly physically incapacitated. He suffers from failing eyesight that renders him apparently incapable of finishing the task he has set out to do: 'There is no denying my handwriting is deteriorating. I am losing motor control…There are days when I squint at what I have just written, barely able to decipher it myself.'[12]

The reciprocity and reversibility of the dialectic in the Sinbad story suggests an ironic allusion to G. W. F. Hegel's famous essay on 'Self-consciousness' (1807) in his *Phenomenology of Spirit*.[13] Here, Hegel explores how two consciousnesses, the master and slave, depend upon each other for recognition. Hegel emphasizes the importance of this relationship in constituting identity itself:

> Self-consciousness exists in itself and for itself, in that, and by the fact that it exists for another self-consciousness; that is to say, it *is* only by being acknowledged or 'recognised'. (111)

The Sinbad story, told by Costello, signals the significance of these relationships of mutual dependency to the basic plot of these novels but also their importance as structuring principles, embedded in the form of Coetzee's writing. In *Age of Iron*, these reversible dynamics centre on a physical relationship of care: 'It is not he who fell under my care when he arrived, I now understand, nor I who fell under his: we fell under each other, and have tumbled and risen since then in the flights and swoops of mutual election' (196). In Coetzee's post-emigration fiction, this concern with reversible, unstable relationships is more specifically connected to the challenges of ageing, autobiography and the difficulties of textual representation. The liberating 'flights and swoops' of 'mutual election' in *Age of Iron* lie in stark contrast to the imprisoning, often meta-fictional relationships of care in Coetzee's later writing. This is expressed in an image of mirroring which occurs later in *Slow Man*, as Paul finds himself returning to the Sinbad story:

> And he is thinking of mirrors because of Mrs Costello's story of the old man who turned Sinbad into his slave. Mrs Costello wants to subject him to some fiction or other she has in her head. (164)

On one level, the analogy with Paul as Sinbad here is clear. Paul initially tries to help Elizabeth as she arrives panting and exhausted in his apartment one day. Yet, as *Slow Man* progresses, he realizes that he has become unwittingly enslaved, subjected to the narrative that Elizabeth seeks to impose upon him. Paul imagines an appeal to Elizabeth's children: 'Your mother has taken up residence with me, a complete stranger, and refuses to leave...Remove her, commit her, do what ever is called for as long as I am liberated' (121). Hegel's description of the master/slave dialectic as a 'freedom still enmeshed in servitude'[14] is echoed in Paul's call for 'liberation' (121) from Elizabeth, who constantly undermines his sense of narrative agency. However, the analogy works equally well in the opposite direction. Paul's own physical vulnerability and disability lead him to require physical help (like the old man) but, as the hero of the novel Elizabeth seeks to write, he is master of both of their fates. Elizabeth summarizes: 'For me Paul Rayment was born and I for him. His is the power of leading, mine of following; his of acting, mine of writing' (233).

In Coetzee's later works, the dialectic between carer and patient intersects with the dynamic between writer and character, as well as reader and writer. This ambivalent agency in the writing of *Slow Man* is replicated in *Diary of a Bad Year*. The initial relationship of writer and amanuensis, employer and employee, between JC and Anya, becomes increasingly blurred. The instability of the boundaries in their relationship, overscored with connotations of flirtation and sexual exploitation, is suggested by the linguistic slippages in Anya's description: 'At first I was just supposed to be his segretaria, his secret aria, his scary fairy, in fact not even that, just his typist, his tipitisa, his clackadackia' (28).

Coetzee's later novels are littered with complex relationships of interdependence: between writer and character (Paul and Elizabeth, Anya and JC), carer and cared-for (Elizabeth and her children, Paul and his nurse Marijana and her son, Drago), lover and the object of affection (JC and Anya, Paul and Marijana, Anya and Alan). Critical responses to the texts suggest that this reciprocity and instability become absorbed into the narrative technique itself. Zoë Wicomb describes 'a reciprocal relationship between reality and representation; writing does not only imitate, it animates and vitalises the world'.[15] Quayson focuses on a relationship between character and interlocutor to suggest that 'inarticulacy and disability...generat[e] a form of hermeneutical impasse...[a] dialectic of invitation and frustration'.[16] Attridge explores a further sense of reciprocity, in the intertwining of reader and text. He argues that 'the reader...is not a spectator of this process, but a participant, since the event of reading cannot be separated from the event of writing'.[17] Yet, it is also notable that there is an unrelenting physicality to these later novels that exists alongside the more abstract, textual concerns that dominate so much existing critical writing about Coetzee. These fragmented stories are mediated by the instabilities of language and the inconsistencies of multiple narrators but are also inseparable from the ageing, frail bodies of the writers themselves and the physical labour of care.

Coetzee confronts the fact that 'disabled' is likely to apply to '[everyone] if they live long enough',[18] but also the fact that 'our social dependencies become important in the constitution of our identities'.[19] *Slow Man*, *Elizabeth Costello* and *Diary of a Bad Year* put pressure upon fantasies of authorial, fictional or social independence. These works push at the boundaries of compassion and belief, repeatedly undermining narrative authority to call into question the ethics and process of fictional imagining itself. And like the characters that they depict, Coetzee's later novels do not stand alone but need to be considered in dialogue and complex relation to each other.

Waiting and wasting: Coetzee and contemporary dependency theory

The most striking examination of dependency and care in Coetzee's later works is played out through the semi-autobiographical author figure of Elizabeth Costello. In *Elizabeth Costello*, Elizabeth's son John is plagued by the inversion of the conventional dialectic of care between parent and child. The act of writing provides the backdrop for the exploration of these reversible dialectics. John recalls:

> For as far back as he can remember, his mother secluded herself in the mornings to do her writing...He and his sister used to slump outside the locked door...Now the scene has changed. He has grown up. He is no longer outside the door but inside, observing her as she sits, back to the window, confronting, day after day, year after year, while her hair slowly goes from black to grey, the blank page...The change came when he was thirty three. Until then he had not read a word that she has written. That was his reply to her, his revenge for locking him out. (4)

The literal and symbolic process of 'locking out' the children from her room, her writing and her consciousness, is inverted at the turning point when, at the age of thirty-three, paradoxically John becomes 'locked in' to a sense of responsibility. He echoes the language and animal imagery of his mother's own lectures as he imagines their current relationship:

> He is here, with her, out of love... He stands by her because he is her son, her loving son. But he is also on the point of becoming – distasteful word – her trainer.
> He thinks of her as a seal, an old, tired circus seal... Up to him to coax her, put heart in her, get her through the performance. (3)

Coetzee suggests both the absurdity of the academic circus, the performance required of the lecturer, and also hints at an uncomfortable 'distaste', a simultaneous duty and disgust, that characterizes many relationships of care. Like John's shift from being inside to outside of the room, the narrative perspective is destabilized by the movement between Costello and John's consciousnesses.

It is not, however, until the publication of 'As a Woman Grows Older' (2004) that these underlying anxieties in *Elizabeth Costello* are brought to the forefront of the text. This short story was read aloud by Coetzee at the New York Public Library and published in the *New York Review of Books*; the dilemma of 'what to do with an aging parent'[20] forms the central subject of the narrative. The story is itself structured around a debate, conducted over the course of a weekend in Nice, between Elizabeth and her two adult children, who urge their mother to change her lifestyle to accommodate her increasing physical vulnerability. Like John's animal and trainer analogy from the novel, the short story explores how the parental dialectic of care has become reversed and depersonalized. In this sense, the short story recalls Coetzee's earlier novel, *Age of Iron*, in which this reconfiguration of the parental relationship in later life is articulated in stark terms by Mrs Curren: 'We bear children in order to be mothered by them' (5). In 'As a Woman Grows Older', the metaphor is religious: 'Helen and John sitting her down and putting to her the scheme they had worked out for her salvation.'[21] Although published only a few months after *Elizabeth Costello* in which Elizabeth is sixty-six, Elizabeth is seventy-two in this story. Her condition has deteriorated; she is increasingly frail and unproductive: there is no mention of any publications, only the beginnings of a collection of short stories entitled 'When a Woman'. Even Coetzee's fictional characters are not immune from physical processes of degeneration. This literary trick, 'the intertextual haemorrhaging of characters from one text to another',[22] foregrounds physical degeneration. Costello, by this late stage in her career, is unable to deny that her writing and schol-arly work is mediated and, to an extent, dictated by the demands of her body: 'the body, so easy to ignore in the healthfulness of youth, compli-cates the activities of the writer ... the inseparability of mental processes from physical desire and revulsion becomes unmistakable'.[23]

The short piece ends in irresolution; Elizabeth resists change of any kind. In a sense, the story has itself become implicated in a kind of senile circularity full of repetitions and apparently inconsequential details, yet missing any central point or narrative. With characteristic bathos, the 'children' subject the episode to a puncturing self-scrutiny: 'The two children who are not children any more exchange glances. Is that all? They seem to be saying. Not much of a story.'[24] So, Coetzee removes the basic structures upon which we depend as readers for the construction of meaning. Like John, locked out of his mother's writing as a child, we as readers are confronted by our own dependency on an anonymous narrator who appears to hide as much as he reveals: 'The real story is out on the balcony, where two middle-aged children face a mother whose capacity to disturb and dismay them is not yet exhausted.'[25]

As readers, we are presented with a story with a hole in the middle, in which the inability to tell, control or finish, becomes the main topic of the narrative itself. The rare snippets of direct dialogue are merely hollowed out words, meaningless, stale clichés of ageing that substitute for actual communication: 'In this life, we do not always get what we deserve.'[26] At stake here, it seems, is the question of narrative agency over Elizabeth's life. Her son and daughter attempt, unsuccessfully, to impose a new direction on their mother's life, frustrated by her refusal to open a new chapter. Elizabeth herself suffers a similar lack of narra-tive control, apparently unable to exert power, even over the words that come out of her mouth: 'What I find eerie, as I grow older ... is that I hear issuing from my lips words I once upon a time used to hear old people say and swore I would never say myself. What-is-the-world-coming-to things.'[27] Elizabeth's words echo back to Mrs Curren's linguistic sensitiv-ity in *Age of Iron*, in which she suggests that she is herself relegated to the past tense as a result of the language that she uses: 'In my day, I thought, policemen spoke respectfully to ladies ... Old men and women, trem-bling with fury, taking up the pen, weapon of last resort. In my day, now over; in my life, now past' (53). Both Elizabeth and Mrs Curren experience loss of agency as a severance of word and meaning: 'These are just words, and we are all sick of words by now.'[28] Both women are unable to escape their own dependence on outdated clichés, ingrained patterns and cultural associations.

Yet, it is through linguistic abstraction that the story raises fundamental questions about the understanding of dependency, the modern professionalization of care and the definition of the citizen. In 'As a Woman Grows Older', *Elizabeth Costello*, *Slow Man* and *Diary of a Bad Year*, abstract textual concerns are inseparable from an embodied physical perspective: the pared down, linguistic uncertainties of Coetzee's early novels become intertwined with the depiction of physical instability. In this sense, Coetzee's later fictional writing intersects with a contemporary critical interest in aesthetic representations of old age, in the emerging fields of critical gerontology and age studies.[29] Helen Small, for example, suggests that, 'Old age is a subject with much wider dimensions. It has repercussions for what we deem to be a good life, how we measure happiness, what we think a person is . . . It touches on, and makes a difference to, how we understand epistemology, virtue, justice, self-interest, metaphysics.'[30]

Coetzee's later representations of conditions of physical impairment need to be read within these 'wider dimensions': they raise ethical, emotional, social and philosophical questions as well as offering metaphors for linguistic or existential crises. Susan Wendell suggests a link between medical and social models of impairment but also conditions of disability and ageing, in the sense that both groups suffer from stigmatization and corresponding socially disabling positions:

> A society which provides few resources to allow disabled people to participate in it will be likely to marginalize all the disabled, including the old, and to define the appropriate roles of old people as very limited, thus handicapping them. Aging is disabling. Recognizing this helps us to see that disabled people are not 'other,' that they really are 'us.'[31]

In *Slow Man*, Elizabeth Costello also draws a parallel between ageing and disability. She suggests that Paul's heightened state of dependency after the accident foreshadows a loss of physical mobility and social agency that most people suffer in old age. She reads Paul's lost leg symbolically as a 'symptom' of mortality: 'You have lost a leg . . . but after a certain age we have all lost a leg, more or less. Your missing leg is just a sign or symbol or symptom, I can never remember which is which, of growing old, old and uninteresting' (229). The instability of Elizabeth's narrow reading, which eclipses the physical, is reflected in her own confusion. Her failing memory reminds us of her individual physical frailties, even as she insists upon a detached, disembodied, reading. The unravelling of narrative agency in these texts is bound up with the ways in which the representation of disabled and ageing bodies destabilizes our concept of 'the muscular, aesthetic, and symmetrical bodies of healthy citizenry'.[32]

Yet, following the accident, his body refuses to be read as a symbol or a symptom. For Coetzee, the naked vulnerability of the body is inescapable. Paul calls the stump of his amputated leg 'le jambon' (29). Coetzee captures the struggle to represent the unrepresentability of what has happened to his leg through the use of a foreign, dehumanizing word which remains untranslated throughout the novel, suggesting Paul's alienation from his own body and his resistance to accepting the damaged limb as a part of himself. For Coetzee, the physical presence of the body exposes a corresponding lack of language through which to articulate corporeal experience. The medical and the social intersect in these contested notions of dependency.

These intersections are also explored in the focus on 'dependency work' in 'As a Woman Grows Older' and *Slow Man*. In 'As a Woman Grows Older', Elizabeth clings to a view of dependency as an asymmetrical relationship: a limited, negative, even shameful condition. She rejects offers of assistance, describing them as an 'assault' or 'burden'.[33] Elizabeth perceives any potential relationship of care, mapped onto the parent/child dynamic, as antagonistic:

'We are with you, surely you know that.'
'With you? What nonsense. Children are against their parents.'[34]

The stark layout of the lines on the page suggests the oppositional nature of the relationship but also the emotional and imaginative gap that exists between characters from two different generations. While Elizabeth experiences collusion against her, Helen and John re-write dependency as a form of open collaboration: 'our joint problem'.[35] The case that they make to Elizabeth is based on a redefined dialectic of care as reciprocal, equal exchange, in keeping with more recent critical redefinitions of dependency. These critiques explore the ways in which modern Western societies tie citizens into networks of communications and commodities which result in the majority of people living to an age where they will experience some level of social dependency. Davis, for example, argues that:

If we redefine our notions of independence to include the vast networks of assistance and provision that make modern life possible – no one can live without being dependent on these – then the seeming state of exception of disability turns out to be the unexceptional state of existence.[36]

So, 'As a Woman Grows Older' can be read as exploring the problematic nature of idealized notions of independence in societies where the experience of disability is an everyday occurrence. The anonymity of the title itself implies that Elizabeth and her children confront issues that every family must face.

Yet, despite gesturing towards a more symmetrical, reciprocal model of dependency, Helen clings to rhetoric that privileges independence above all else. She promises Elizabeth: 'We would not be living together. You would be perfectly independent. But in an emergency you would have someone to call on.'[37] This implicit assumption that Helen shares with Elizabeth, that dependency is to be avoided, marks a point of intersection between early feminist and disability rights writing. Simone de Beauvoir, for example, in *The Second Sex* (1952) poses the question: 'How can a human being in a woman's situation attain fulfilment... How can independence be recovered in a state of dependency?'[38] Wendell, writing about disability rights, suggests: 'Dependence on the help of others is humiliating in a society which prizes independence' (273).

The notion of care as a complex set of social relations, a dynamic characterized by contested control as well as mutual support, is developed in *Slow Man*. Marijana Jokic's status as a Croatian immigrant means that the poorly paid work of nursing is one of the few professions open to her. As the initial shock of the accident is followed by an increasing awareness of frailty and old age, Paul finds his sense of himself as an independent agent completely shattered. In his initial exchange with Marijana, he immediately undermines his own assertion of independence: '"Oh, I'll take care of myself." He replies. "I do not expect a lengthy old age"... But her question echoes in his mind. Who is going to take care of you?' (43). Paul not only feels alienated from his own body, but also experiences a severance between the meaning and the literal, written form of the words:

> Care: he can set the word down on paper but he would be too diffident to mouth it, make it his own speech. Too much an English word, an insider's word... The profession [Marijana] was being initiated into was in the English-speaking world known as a caring-profession. (165)

Coetzee again introduces issues of translation to suggest otherness: caring as a profession is a concept most prevalent in wealthy Anglophone countries. Care is '*too much* an English word' (my italics); like 'le jambon', foreignness captures the alienation and disjunction more accurately. Marijana's foreign perspective seems to merge into Paul's own sense of care as a business that is totally alien to him. Paul finds himself unable to reconcile a further severance between the physical intimacy of 'care' as work and the question of emotional attachment: 'caring should not be assumed to have anything to do with the heart, except of course in heart cases' (165). The commodification of care in modern Australian society is figured through a shift in the linguistic usage: caring is primarily understood as a professional contract rather than a familial duty.

In one sense then, *Slow Man* provides a social critique of the recent professionalization of care as a necessarily expanding modern industry. In contrast to the South African setting of his earlier novels, Coetzee's switch to an Australian context allows him to consider a society in which a large and increasing proportion of the population enjoys the luxury of surviving to an old age. He explores how this privilege, enjoyed in wealthy 'first world' nations, raises its own ethical, economic and aesthetic challenges, particularly in the context of a sudden increase in the proportion of elderly in society.[39] Coetzee's focus on issues of care can also be read from what Foucault would term a 'biopolitical' perspective. Foucault defines biopolitics as starting in the eighteenth century and as concerned with rationalizing the problems posed to governmental practice by phenomena characteristic of a set of living beings forming a population: health, hygiene, birth rate, life expectancy, race. Foucault traces the increasing importance of these issues of individual and collective welfare in political, social and economic terms from the eighteenth century onwards arguing that, in a biopolitical age, power is constituted not by a single sovereign force but a series of strategic relations 'of command and obedience. The relations between man and woman, master and student, doctor and patient, employer and worker.'[40] These power relations redefine the concept of humanity:

> For millennia, man remained what he was for Aristotle: a living animal with the additional capacity for a political existence; modern man is an animal whose politics places his existence as a living being into question.[41]

For Foucault then, bodies and health are inescapably politicized in a modern liberal context; the individual body and the wider social body are interdependent. Like Coetzee's representation of ageing and disabled figures, Foucault's theory interrogates 'what it means to be a living species in a living world, to have a body' (264) in contemporary society.

These relationships structure Coetzee's later works, as an interplay between writer and character is superimposed onto these overlapping power dynamics.

Elizabeth Costello, upon her abrupt entry into *Slow Man*, echoes Paul's distinction between 'caring' and loving as distinct and separate:

> We do not need love, old people like us. What we need is care: some-one to hold our hand now and then when we get trembly...Care is not love. Care is a service that any nurse worth her salt can provide, as long as we don't ask her for more. (154)

Through Elizabeth and Paul, the opening section of *Slow Man* provides a brutal critique of the modern professionalization of care in its sev-erance of mind and body, and the emotional implications of 'caring' from the material conditions of 'care'. In this context, ageing and dis-ability are met with a counter-productive rhetoric, a relentless denial of dependency: '"You're still a young man, Mr Rayment"...[Mrs Putts, his social worker] informs him in the cheery manner she must have been taught to employ upon the old' (16). Paul, systematically 'treated as an idiot' (24), finds himself desexualized, infantilized and patronized: 'Like all health professionals he has met of late, Madeleine treats the old people consigned to her care as if they were children – not very clever, somewhat morose, somewhat sluggish children in need of being bucked up' (60).

This description of Paul as 'sluggish', as implicitly physically and intel-lectually limited and lazy, feeds into a wider set of stereotypes about waste that recur in Coetzee's later fiction: the *OED* links 'waste' with a sense of 'purposelessness...the consumption or using up of material, resources, time'.[42] Coetzee explores the ways in which those on the margins of society, the elderly and disabled, are perceived as unproduc-tive, according to narrow, exclusively economic notions of value. Once again, this marks a point at which the experiences of ageing and dis-ability intersect. Both groups are relegated to a feminized private sphere, outside the world of commerce.[43] De Beauvoir, in her critique of this pre-vailing, exclusively economic definition of the citizen makes the same point, drawing a parallel between the vulnerability of individual, phys-ical bodies and their exclusion from powerful economic 'bodies': 'the aged do not form a body with any economic strength whatsoever and they have no possible way of enforcing their rights'.[44]

So, despite a huge spectrum of diverse experiences, both the ageing and the disabled are widely defined in terms of their dependency. The title, 'old age pensioner' suggests that the primary defining feature of this group is their dependency on the state and their status as 'no longer productive workers or citizens'.[45] JC, in *Diary of a Bad Year*, echoes this sense of exclusion. With biting sarcasm, he questions: 'Are old men with doddering intellect and poor eyesight and arthritic hands allowed on the trading floor, or will we just get in the way of the young?' (144). JC's perception of his 'doddering intellect' is undermined here by his own productivity as a writer. The 'poor eyesight' that he attributes to the elderly is evident only on a metaphorical level in relation to his own myopic level of self-awareness.

These stereotypes, in which ageing and disabled people are reduced to social and economic waste products, are also reflected in descriptions by the characters of their own bodies. With shocking physicality, Paul describes how part of his own body was reduced to waste after the accident: 'You anaesthetised me and hacked off my leg and dropped it in the refuse for someone to collect and toss into the fire' (10). The problem of waste recurs throughout *Slow Man*; Elizabeth Costello's marked physical deterioration is evident in her 'blue-veined, rather wasted calves' (84). Even as the accident is taking place, Paul tumbles through the air regretting that his life has not made a more valuable contribution to society: 'My life seemed frivolous. What a waste, I thought' (83). As the novel progresses, time itself becomes implicated in this condition of waste generation:

> The clock stands still yet time does not. Even as he lies here he can feel time at work on him like a wasting disease, like the quicklime they pour on corpses. Time is gnawing away at him, devouring one by one the cells that make him up. (12)

Through this recurring imagery of waste, employed as a verb, a material presence and a multi-layered metaphor, Coetzee draws (and depends) upon a web of intertextual associations with ageing and disability. De Beauvoir opens her famous analysis of old age, *The Coming of Age* (1972), with an attack upon precisely this rhetoric of waste and economic non-productivity. She cites the words of 'Dr Leach', a Cambridge anthropologist, as an example of this profit-driven perspective: 'In a changing world, where machines have a very short run of life, men must not be used too long. Everyone over fifty-five should be scrapped.' Her critique is unequivocal: 'The word "scrap" expresses his meaning admirably ... [The old man] is condemned to stagnate in boredom and loneliness, a mere throw-out.'[46]

After his accident, Paul finds himself in precisely the condition of alienation described by de Beauvoir: alone in his flat, trapped in an entropic state in which limited physical mobility is matched by a paralysing lack of narrative agency. He ferociously resists the attempts by those around him to re-write his disability into a positive presence: 'A man without sight is a lesser man, as a man without a leg is a lesser man, not a new man' (133). Paul's sense of identity and his own body are mediated by his own stereotypes of disability as a condition of inferiority, a wasted opportunity.

Samuel Beckett's writing, which formed the basis of Coetzee's doctoral thesis, explores these questions of care and dependency through the parent/child dialectic between, for example, Nagg, Nell, Clov and Hamm in *Endgame* (1957), as the ageing parents periodically interrupt the action to request food or argue between themselves. At a moment of intense self-reflexivity, Elizabeth Costello makes a direct connection to Beckett's drama, and their shared preoccupations with disability, ageing and rubbish:

> I am unhappy because nothing is happening. Four people in four corners, moping, like tramps in Beckett, and myself in the middle, wasting time, being wasted by time. (141)

In *Endgame*, the symbolic conflation of ageing and wasting becomes literalized, as the ageing, legless figures of Nagg and Nell live in rubbish bins. The dialectical relationships that characterize Beckett's drama, like the ambivalent master/slave relationship in Elizabeth Costello's Sinbad story, are frequently mapped onto a relationship of care. Clov acts as a nurse, performing an almost prosthetic function as he helps the blind, immobile figure of Hamm. They exist in an antagonistic yet dialectical relationship, in which each depends upon the other for recognition. Like Elizabeth Costello's empty threats to leave Paul, Clov's insistence that he intends to abandon Hamm ring hollow as it becomes increasingly clear that the characters are inescapably tied together. Theodor Adorno reads *Endgame* as a play about social and economic exclusion: 'The fact that both [characters] lodge in trash bins...takes the conversational phrase literally... "Today old people are thrown in the trash can" ...*Endgame* is a true gerontology.'[47] There is, he argues, a strikingly personal dimension to the play: '*Endgame* trains the viewer for a condition where everyone involved expects – upon lifting the lid from the nearest dumpster – to find his own parents. The natural cohesion of life has become organic refuse' (56).

Slow Man, *Diary of a Bad Year* and *Elizabeth Costello* confront read-ers with the frightening prospect of finding their own parents, but also themselves, on the scrap heap. These scraps of imagery, of wasted time and wasting bodies, proliferate in Coetzee's later novels. Paul, following his excursion to the shopping centre, for example, 'grips his crutches, and heaves himself up from the trash container against which he has been resting' (172). JC in *Diary of a Bad Year* imagines how Anya must perceive him as 'a crumpled old fellow in a corner who at first glance might have been a tramp off the street' (4). This waste imagery offers a paradoxically productive perspective in the struggle to understand representations of ageing and disability. In Coetzee's later writing, tra-ditional contracts, through which we understand fiction, the world and our own identity, are re-written. Coetzee self-consciously recycles scraps of Beckett's plays: the tramps, trashcans and ageing protagonists. Yet through these depictions of wasting and waiting Coetzee creates a space for the articulation of stories in which relationships between reader and writer, character and author, carer and patient, individual and society are renegotiated.

In *Diary of a Bad Year*, JC mounts a self-conscious critique of a pre-vailing social contract in which human worth is defined in exclusively economic terms. His essay attacks 'the economistic criteria which are all that count to the Liberals...The limitations of this simplistic atti-tude to society emerge in matters of race and culture' (116). He defines himself in opposition to an understanding of the citizen which is based on exclusion: 'those who chose and choose to stay outside the compact become outlaw' (3). The writer, the disabled or ageing figure are all, in a sense, treated as 'outlaws' as a result of their position outside of conven-tional codes of economic productivity. As an ageing writer, JC positions himself outside these imprisoning economic bonds, acknowledging that 'to true believers in the market, it makes no sense to say that you take no pleasure in competing with your fellow men and prefer to withdraw' (119). JC makes an impassioned call for a re-examination of the role of the ambiguous relationship between the citizen and the state:

> To regain touch, you must at every moment remind yourself of what it is like to come face to face with the state – the democratic state or any other – in the person of the state official. Then ask yourself: Who serves whom? Who is the servant, who is the master? (15)

There is an apparent contradiction between JC's wider attack on the abstract power of the depersonalized, faceless state and the example that he gives of the face-to-face encounter with an individual state official. Levinas's essay 'Is Ontology Fundamental?' (1951) captures this paradoxical status of the face through a focus on the face-to-face encounter (and speech in particular) as the 'original relation'[48] in ethics: 'A being (l'étant) is a human being and it is as a neighbor that a human being is accessible – as a face' (8). Yet, at the same time, Levinas suggests that the face also represents a site of resistance to understanding: 'In [the face] the infinite resistance of a being to our power affirms itself' (10). In Coetzee's example, the face-to-face encounter allows a physical and symbolic sense of 'regaining touch' with the individual representative of the state, yet also highlights how we can never have complete mastery or knowledge of either the state powers that we depend upon or another's consciousness. Levinas's body-centred ethics are helpful in exploring how Coetzee probes these moments of ethical, linguistic and social resistance *through* the body. In *Doubling the Point*, Coetzee described how: 'If I look back over my own fiction, I see a simple (simple-minded?) standard erected. That standard is the body.'[49] The dismissive reference to his own 'simple-mindedness' is undermined by the complexity of Coetzee's representation of bodies as points of contact and mediators of narrative but also of unrepresentable experience.

Through the representation of disability and physical frailty in *Elizabeth Costello*, *Slow Man* and *Diary of a Bad Year*, Coetzee explores how these 'economistic criteria'[50] for defining the citizen fail to accommodate disabled and ageing figures, or asymmetrical relationships of care. In their implicit challenge to literary and social contracts, Coetzee's later novels stage a debate set out in Martha C. Nussbaum's *Frontiers of Justice* (2006). Nussbaum critiques John Rawls's narrow definition of the citizen by examining the diminished rights of those who are excluded from the classical social contract. In particular, Nussbaum highlights that those described in the contract were assumed to be 'men who were roughly equal in capacity, and capable of productive economic activity'.[51] The result, she argues, was a highly exclusionary set of definitions in which 'women (understood as "non-productive"), children and elderly people ... people with severe and atypical physical and mental impairments' (15) were omitted from the bargaining situation.

Like Coetzee, Nussbaum considers the ways in which situations of physical vulnerability disrupt an idealizing fiction of 'people who are "fully cooperating ... over a complete life"' (141). In *Slow Man*, Paul voices precisely this sense of exclusion. His encounter with young

Dr Hansen, soon after the accident, is underpinned by a sense of 'not counting' in both symbolic and economic terms:

> From Dr Hansen he feels, beneath the kindly concern, the same indifference. It is as though at some unconscious level these young people who have been assigned to care for them know they have nothing left to give to the tribe and therefore do not count. (12)

Both Nussbaum's philosophical writing and Coetzee's later novels suggest that the work of care must be re-evaluated. Rather than disposing of theory, Nussbaum calls for a reworking of theoretical structures:

> Solving this problem requires a new way of thinking about who the citizen is and a new analysis of the purpose of social co-operation (one not focused on mutual advantage) and because it also requires emphasising the importance of care as a social primary good. (1)

In Coetzee's later works, this liberal imperative to re-write care as a 'primary good' is rendered more complex and ambiguous. The hope for an alternative, such as the 'capabilities' model that Nussbaum puts forward later in her argument, is absent from the enclosed fictional worlds that Coetzee depicts. The moments of resistance and the open-ended structures of Coetzee's novels challenge Nussbaum's confidence in the possibility of 'solving this problem' (1). Elizabeth and JC as ageing writers are confronted by the paradoxical condition in which their sense of self-worth is constructed through an activity perceived as marginal, even wasteful, according to dominant social and economic contracts and codes. Nussbaum's call for a 'reshaping of theoretical structures' (1) is reconfigured by Coetzee's experimentation with the novel form itself.

Reciprocal dialectics of dependency

Caring, like writing, is depicted as a fundamentally collaborative act, in which both sides are mutually implicated. *Slow Man* and *Diary of a Bad Year* disrupt conventional economic notions of care as an asymmetrical relationship. Instead, both novels explore dialectics of mutual responsibility. For Davidson:

> Dependency is never a one-way street from dependent individual to care-giving provider, but is...a dialectical one that implicates both parties in the dependency dyad...The parent who experiences

pleasure in taking care of her helpless child or the care-giver who bonds with her client are two examples that embody relations of care as both reciprocal and unequal.[52]

Davidson's use of 'dyad', a term which has strong psychoanalytic connotations, implies a level of emotional attachment that is particularly pertinent to his example of parent–child relations. In Davidson's model, the emphasis is on caring as a source of pleasure and ethical power. Coetzee explores this interdependence as more ambiguous, delusional and even destructive. In the case of Paul in *Slow Man*, the urge to reciprocate care and to extend this into affection is a central strand of the novel. Once the formal contract of employment, in which Marijana is paid to nurse Paul, seems to have 'gone up in smoke' (182), new, informal forms of mutual dependency emerge. Paul increasingly seeks to transgress the conventional carer/patient boundaries, becoming involved in Marijana's private and family life. In several episodes over the course of the novel, Paul seeks to create a situation in which the Jokic family is financially dependent upon him: first offering to pay for Drago's private education and then using bribery to save Blanka from shoplifting charges. He longs for a corresponding level of emotional dependency, fantasizing about a role for himself as a father figure to the children. The dialectic of care, in his imagination at least, becomes temporarily inverted, as Paul offers to become an active carer, rather than a passive recipient of care: 'I offered to take care of you. I offered to take care of the children too' (246). Elizabeth, with her characteristic cutting critique, highlights how visible, formal ties have been exchanged for unseen forms of attachment. She questions Paul's claim to altruism:

> 'I asked him to put Drago's interests first. I repeated that there were no strings attached to my offer.'
> 'No visible strings you mean.'
> 'No strings at all.'
> 'What about heartstrings, Paul, strings of affection?' (151)

Both of these contracts, of care and of novelistic convention, go up in smoke at precisely the same moment. At the end of chapter 12, Paul declares his love for Marijana, causing her to storm out of the house and to end their daily routine as patient and carer. Immediately after this scene, at the beginning of chapter 13, Elizabeth Costello enters the text. The entry of Elizabeth totally reconfigures both Paul's and the reader's relationship with reality in the story. Elizabeth exhibits an uncanny knowledge of Paul's past and present life. Elizabeth not only enters Paul's house without explanation, but also seems able to enter his consciousness:

> Heavily she seats herself again, squares her shoulders and begins to recite. 'The blow that catches him from the right, sharp and surprising and painful, like a bolt of electricity, lifting him up off the bicycle. Relax! He tells himself and he tumbles through the air, and so forth.' (81)

The result is a complete shattering of any 'reality effect' as Elizabeth recites back the words of the opening page. As with the recycled Beckett references, the sense of re-writing here creates a highly destabilizing, even discomforting effect for both character and reader.

Elizabeth Costello, in its ambiguous fusion of novel and lecture format, foreshadows this self-conscious crisis of realism that takes place upon Elizabeth's entry into *Slow Man*. Readers are reminded of their own dependency upon the narrator; how our experience of 'reality' is necessarily mediated on several different levels. The narrator advises:

> It is not a good idea to interrupt the narrative too often, since storytelling lulls the reader or listener into a dreamlike state in which the time and space of the real world fade away, superseded by the time and space of fiction. Breaking into the dream draws attention to the constructedness of the story, and plays havoc with the realist illusion.[53]

It is precisely this rupture, a sense of 'breaking into the dream' that occurs between chapters 12 and 13 of *Slow Man*. The scrutiny of the technical process of telling, the so-called 'constructedness of the story', paralyses the narrative itself. As in the Sinbad story, an implicit dialectic between master and slave is reversed. Paul becomes relegated to a peripheral 'character' in Elizabeth's predetermined plot; he no longer feels that he is master of his own fate:

> It is as he feared: she knows everything, every jot and tittle. Damn her! All the time he thought he was his own master he has been in a cage like a rat...with the infernal woman standing over him, observing, listening, taking notes, recording his progress. (122)

The recurring imagery of animal exploitation further binds Paul to Elizabeth, and links *Slow Man* to *Elizabeth Costello* through this shared thread of symbolism. Just as John likens his mother to a performing seal (and himself to her trainer) in *Elizabeth Costello, Slow Man* suggests that the dialectic of author and character is transfigured to become observer and observed.

Elizabeth, as author, has the power to narrate and to write Paul into existence. Yet, on another plane of reality, she is dependent upon Paul to act. This ambiguous agency shatters any notion of authorial independence as they realize that they are inescapably tied together: 'How has it come about, do you think, that I am stuck with so incurious, so unadventurous a man as you? Can you explain?' (230).

Diary of a Bad Year, structured around a similar dialectic of writing and care, also explores storytelling as a relational, collaborative act. Like Elizabeth Costello, the semi-autobiographical author figure of JC experiences a paradoxical sense of simultaneous narrative agency and dependency:

> Stories tell themselves, they don't get told... Wait for the story to speak for itself. Wait and hope that it isn't born deaf and dumb and blind. I could do that when I was younger... Nowadays I get tired. My attention wanders. (55)

The striking metaphor of disability and birth here echoes back to the literal impairments and birth imagery of *Slow Man*. The foregrounding of JC's own physical deterioration, in the opposition between his older and younger selves, suggests that disability is also a pressing literal concern in the text. Following his accident in *Slow Man*, Marijana is hired to help Paul; in *Diary of a Bad Year* Anya is employed as an amanuensis due to JC's deteriorating eyesight. As in *Slow Man*, there is a shift over the course of *Diary of a Bad Year* from a formal, rigid contract, to a more complex form of mutual dependency and unseen ties. JC's initial approach to Anya has an air of professional nonchalance: 'I happen to be a writer by profession... I need someone to type a manuscript for me and perhaps do a little editing' (17).

These lines between writer and amanuensis, and also between JC's professional, political essays and his personal commentary, are drawn out in the unusual subdivision of each page into three separate sections. Initially, the narrative told from Anya's perspective is placed at the bottom of the page and given little space, reflecting her apparently peripheral place in the text. However, this initial prosthetic understanding of Anya's function, as a neutral physical aid employed to facilitate writing, is increasingly undermined. This shift in power (the reversal of the dialectic between author and character that we see in *Slow Man*) is played out in the increasing amounts of space that Anya occupies on the page and in JC's consciousness. So, by the end of the book, two thirds of the page become devoted to a commentary on the process of writing itself and the dynamic that develops between them.

The single authorial voice of the political essays gives way to two personal diaries that challenge narrative authority through their often contradictory yet coexisting viewpoints, placed side by side. As in *Elizabeth Costello* there is a sense of generic instability, as JC desperately seeks to clarify the genre and nature of his writing: 'Alas, it is a collection of opinions I am committed to, not a memoir. A response to the present in which I find myself' (67). The linear structure through which JC seeks to trace a rational line of argument becomes tangled and the subdivisions on the page seem increasingly arbitrary as the plot lines are intertwined.

Coetzee presents a problem of writing for the disabled and ageing JC, but also a problem of reading: we are invited to read *across* rather than down the page. Moreover, as Anya herself suggests, meaning is constituted through the relation *between* these narratives. There is a sense in which the real story takes place in the gaps on the page: 'Do you think I am a dummy?...Do you think I can't read between the lines?' (91). Both Anya and Elizabeth therefore begin from a position of apparent neutrality. In *Slow Man*, Elizabeth claims a role for herself as a kind of amanuensis or 'secretary of the invisible', transcribing reality: 'I merely write down the words and then test them, test their soundness, to make sure I have heard right' (199). However, even within this claim for transparency, Elizabeth highlights the possibility for human error, particularly in the mediation of the story from oral to textual media. In fact, from the very moment that she enters the text, Elizabeth attempts to redirect Paul's controversial affection for Marijana towards her substitute, the blind Marianna.

Like Elizabeth, Anya also increasingly seeks to intervene in the text which, in principle, she is employed to write. Her complaints bear an uncanny resemblance to those voiced by Elizabeth: 'I was expecting more of a story, she says. It is difficult to get into the swing when the subject keeps changing' (30). Just as Elizabeth seeks to blot out sections of Paul's narrative, Anya realizes at the end of the novel: 'So that was what I was, a book editor...I thought I was just a humble typist' (176).

The blurring of these roles is played out in the merging of many different genres (novel, diary, essay, confession) and the way in which initially separate narrative threads become implicated in each other. Coetzee gestures towards his own paradoxical position as an author figure, everywhere and nowhere in these semi-autobiographical novels, as JC acknowledges the collaborative nature of his writing project with Anya:

> Yes, you are in the book – how could you not be when you were part of making it? You are everywhere in it, everywhere and nowhere. Like God, though not on the same scale. (181)

There are moments in both texts when this underlying parallel with Coetzee's own life, the doubling of himself with Costello and JC as ageing, white, South African author figures living in Australia, ruptures the surface of the narrative with direct references. JC, a man who describes himself as 'reserved, quiet, solitary' (170), remarks in passing: 'In the 1990s, I recall, I published a collection of essays on censorship' (22). The parallel with Coetzee himself is constantly invited, yet frustrated. Costello summarizes this sense of inescapable dependency upon autobiographical material, yet the desire to produce something that is ultimately a work of fiction:

> Of course we draw upon our own lives all the time – they are our main resource, in a sense our only resource. But no, *Fire and Ice* isn't autobiography. It is a work of fiction. I made it up.[54]

Wicomb describes how Coetzee's earlier memoirs, *Boyhood* (1997) and *Youth* (2002), which present 'Coetzee' in the third person (as in the final book of the trilogy, *Summertime*, 2009), belong to a 'hybrid genre ... where "confessing in the third person" also asserts the author's fictionality and alludes to the fluid relationship between author and character, which is also to say between author and the empirical world'.[55] This same fluidity and reciprocity extends to *Slow Man*, *Diary of a Bad Year* and *Elizabeth Costello*. In these novels, the entry of the author figures into the text has a disorienting effect, implicating readers in the kind of dizzying confusion suffered by the ageing figures that Coetzee represents. As Attridge suggests, readers of Coetzee's novels are 'denied any ethical guidance from an authoritative voice or valorizing metalanguage',[56] through narrators and novels that constantly draw attention to their own instability.

Elizabeth's first act, on entering Paul's flat, is to remove the blanket that covers Paul's mirror (163). Yet, her presence renders literal mirroring impossible; a straightforward mimetic relationship between 'reality' and an objective, omniscient narrator is completely undermined. Once again, *Elizabeth Costello* provides a commentary on the two later novels: 'The word-mirror is broken, irreparably, it seems. About what is really going on in the lecture hall your guess is as good as mine' (19). The lecture hall performance itself, documented in *Elizabeth Costello*, suggests a further distorted refraction of reality. Like the fictional contract that is torn up in *Slow Man* and *Diary of a Bad Year*, Coetzee's initial performance of the Elizabeth Costello lectures removed all basic structures (or conventions of lecturing) upon which spectators depend for the construction of meaning or identity. Attridge provides a first-hand account of the destabilizing experience of watching one of the lectures when it was delivered at Princeton in 1997. Coetzee gave the lecture in person, using the Elizabeth Costello persona:

> What made the event in which we were participating all the more disquieting was our gradual realization that it was being mirrored, in a distorted representation, in the fiction itself; the central character was revealed to be a novelist from the Southern hemisphere who had been asked to give a lecture to an American college.[57]

In *Diary of a Bad Year*, this imperfect mirroring is explored through a focus on the material conditions of production of the text itself. Anya's intervention in the process of storytelling is accidental as well as intentional. Coetzee reminds us that our experience of the text is mediated by the inaccuracies of modern technology as well as the subjectivity of her perspective. JC complains:

> As a typist pure and simple, Anya is a bit of a disappointment...the feel for the kind of thing I write, is hardly there...According to Daniel Defoe, I read, the true-born Englishmen hate 'papers and papery'. (25)

The punning on papery and popery adds to Coetzee's wider comic subversion of narrative authority here, as religion and writing become confused amid the mess of papers on JC's desk. Just as the boundaries between author and character, carer and cared-for, writer and amanuensis become blurred, language itself is shown to be prone to slippages and instability. The political opinions commissioned in *Diary of a Bad Year* are, we are told, going to be translated into German before publication. This adds yet another level of distance and mediation to the writing. Moreover, the text is an oral narrative, recited by Paul, translated into writing by Anya: 'I read through what mere hours before she translated from a record of my speaking voice into 14 point type' (137). Writing in the twenty-first century, we are reminded, is usually experienced through depersonalized and unstable digital forms.

This focus on the relation *between* oral narrative and written text is also extended to intertextual links outside of Coetzee's writing. There is a parallel between Beckett's Krapp[58] and Coetzee's JC. In Beckett's semi-autobiographical play, the ageing figure of Krapp sits alone on the stage, listening to a tape that he has made of events from his thirty-ninth year. Coetzee's JC is a similarly lonely figure, confined to his apartment and his own company. Anya provides rare moments of human interaction for a man who, she suggests, spends most of his time 'sitting by himself all day, but for the dictaphone and sometimes the birds' (209). In both cases, their enclosure in confined spaces, the limits of the stage for Krapp and the claustrophobic apartment for JC, becomes symbolic of their imprisonment in a cycle of constantly replaying and retelling the past. This entropic state parallels Paul in *Slow Man* whose 'life seems repetitive and circumscribed... because [he] hardly ever leave[s] this accursed flat' (229) and Elizabeth Costello who finds herself 'frozen in the past, as usual; frozen in the achievements of her youth'.[59]

Krapp revels in the fantasy of control over his own life that the tape-recorder allows him. Our dependency, as spectators, upon Krapp and upon the machinery he uses to tell his story, is mocked. At one point in the play, Beckett appears to bring the action to a kind of profound anagnorisis, as the recorded voice of Krapp describes:

> Spiritually a year of profound gloom and indigence until that memorable night in March... when suddenly I saw the whole thing. The vision, at last... (Krapp switches off impatiently, winds tape forward, switches on again).[60]

The parenthetical stage direction here creates a puncturing bathos, rendering Krapp's recognition scene absurd. Like the word processing technology used by Anya, which allows spell-checking, cutting, pasting, copying and deleting of text, Krapp's use of the tape-recorder highlights the dependency of the narrative (dramatic or textual) upon its medium. Both Coetzee and Beckett explore how technology renders writing yet more unstable, as it can be fast-forwarded, rewound, recorded over or lost.

Elizabeth Costello gestures towards a similar epiphany that, like Krapp's moment of recognition, is linked to the condition of ageing:

A vision, an opening up, as the heavens are opened up by a rainbow when the rain stops falling. Does it suffice, for old folk, to have these visions now and again, these rainbows, as a comfort, before the rain starts pelting down again?[61]

Yet, as in *Krapp's Last Tape*, this 'vision' is never elaborated upon; it serves only to perpetuate the cycles of uncertainty. The circular image of the spool of the tapes, looping round in *Krapp's Last Tape* or JC's dictaphone re-emerge in Elizabeth Costello's conception of herself as 'trapped'[62] in the cliché of a broken record. In 'As a Woman Grows Older' she suggests that the experience of ageing is bound up with an emptying out of language. For Elizabeth, even the technological metaphors that she employs belong to a previous age: she loathes even 'the cliché of the stuck record that has no meaning anymore because there are no gramophone needles or gramophones'.[63]

In the case of both Krapp and JC, the tape-recordings of the voice also provide a form of dialogue. In the absence of regular human contact, these recordings provide a structure for their interactions, through which they constitute their sense of identity and the narrative or play itself. This Beckettian theme, of lonely protagonists, desperate for a form through which they can affirm their identity, provides a structuring principle in much of Coetzee's writing. Vercueil in *Age of Iron* challenges Mrs Curren: 'I don't see what you need me for' (71). Her response suggests that her spoken interactions with him, as well as her writing, represent ways of combating the void of loneliness and meaninglessness in her later life: 'It is hard for me to be alone all the time. That's all' (71). The South African context for this earlier novel adds a contemporary political resonance to Mrs Curren's interrogation of the very possibility of truth, witnessing and confession: 'Is a true confession still true if it is not heard?' (166). The novel itself assumes the status of a confession, through its form as a kind of 'letter' (15) and a plea for dialogue with her absent daughter.

In 'As a Woman Grows Older', written after Coetzee's emigration to Australia, this sense of a need for dualistic structures through which to construct identity and narrative, is more explicitly formulated:

I am sorry. It is from living alone. Most of the time I have to conduct these conversations in my head; it is such a relief to have persons I can play them out with...Interlocutors. Not persons. Interlocutors.[64]

The distinction that she makes here between person and interlocutor links back to the division between loved one and professional carer explored throughout *Slow Man*. Here, Coetzee foregrounds the wider social issue of isolation in old age, but also the dramatic or narrative problem of how to construct self-hood in the absence of human interaction. Quayson, in his book on disability, argues that internalized structures of sceptical interlocution are central to Beckett's drama and to Coetzee's earlier novels set in South Africa. In a brief discussion of *Slow Man*, Quayson suggests that the entry of Elizabeth Costello disrupts these structures: 'In the case of Paul Rayment...the regular process of internal dialogism that we see in relation to Coetzee's non-disabled characters is redirected into a secondary and quite unexpected path that serves to illustrate a degree of aesthetic nervousness' (159). He suggests that Elizabeth Costello in fact 'represents something much more complicated with respect to the structures of dialogical interlocution' (159).

This problematic status of Elizabeth, I would argue, is not only a sign of 'aesthetic nervousness' but also highlights a further dimension of dependency. In Coetzee's later novels, structures of interlocution shift from an 'internal dialogism' to become externalized and superimposed onto relationships based on care and writing. Anya, Elizabeth and Marijana are carers, amanuenses and externalized 'sceptical interlocutor' figures for JC and Paul. Anya in *Diary of a Bad Year*, for example, suspects that '[JC] doesn't need a segretaria or even a tipista, he could type out his thoughts himself' (31). When Paul calls for Marijana in the middle of the night in *Slow Man*, he does not require medical attention, but human contact: 'No real emergency, just please come hold my hand' (212).

Unlike Krapp or JC, who are able to control the artificial exchanges that they create with their tape-recorders, these external dialogues often threaten to break down. The exchange between Paul and Elizabeth, for example, suggests that the longing for dialogue is coupled with an anxiety that they will not hear what they want to: 'You say you want to hear stories, I offer you stories, and I get back nothing except ridicule and scorn. What kind of exchange is that?' (202). Coetzee never allows us to forget the work of the negative here, through moments in which storytelling fails to mediate between two individuals.

Yet, at the same time, Coetzee explores how these dialectical relationships are personally and socially necessary. Anya's sense of hollowness and lack of fulfilment is, she realizes, linked to the fact that basic structures of interlocution are missing from her life: 'Señor C records his opinions (drone drone) which I dutifully type out (clickety clack)...But what about me? Who listens to my opinions?' (101). Here the reduction of language to a set of banal, nonsensical drones and clacks suggests the gap between the characters, mapped out in the subdivisions on the page. It is only in the recognition of mutual dependency, the need for exchange on both sides, that any kind of communication is achieved. The letters which follow the main text, in the 'Soft Opinions' section, suggest the impact of the relationship upon Anya's life and self-understanding. JC reciprocates with a similar admission of dependency, extending the metaphor of the birth of a text that recurs throughout *Slow Man*:

> You have become indispensable to me – to me and to the present project. I cannot imagine handing over the manuscript to someone else. It would be like taking a child away from its natural mother and putting it in a stranger's care. (121)

The careful distinction made here, in which JC acknowledges Anya as 'indispensable *to me* – and to the present project' (my italics), suggests that the initial professional and sexual dynamic between them has developed into a dialectic of appreciation and care. In *Slow Man*, Paul frequently calls for Elizabeth to leave, yet, when she does, he spends 'the best part of an hour, stumping hither and thither across the parkland, to track [her] down' (151).

These novels suggest that the definition of dependency itself is wide-ranging, implying a social as well as material, physical significance to these relationships. Eva Feder Kittay and Ellen K. Feder propose a model that 'take[s] account of the fact of dependency in our very conceptions of self'.[65] This returns us to the master and slave (or lord and bondsman) analogy of the Sinbad tale. For Hegel, this need for a structure of witnessing is fundamental to the recognition that *all* people live in a state of dependency. Kelly Oliver's essay on ethics highlights this link between Hegelian and modern dependency theory:

> Like Hegel's bondsman who realizes himself through a recognition of his dependence upon independent others ... the ethical subject as witnessing subjectivity acknowledges her dependence upon her addressee and interlocutor whom she cannot possess but upon whom she is absolutely dependent for her very subjectivity.[66]

In Coetzee's later works, the act of telling becomes bound up with a desire to both understand and construct a sense of self. Narration itself implies a series of interrelated dynamics between writer and reader, character and author, or speaker and listener that are constantly being renegotiated. In a moment of clarity, Paul sums up the sense in which this basic human impulse to tell stories is related to creativity and care: 'the need to be loved and the storytelling, that is to say the mess of papers on the table, are connected' (238).

Substitution and the sense of an ending

The urge to tell stories, narrate and engage in dialogue in Coetzee's later works is matched by a contradictory impulse to revise, erase and re-write narrative. The instability of these texts is based on their constant attempts to substitute existing stories with newer, alternative versions. As the accident is taking place, Paul imagines the process of re-writing the event in his mind. Even at this moment of extreme physical intensity, Coetzee suggests that Paul's experience is mediated by his obsession with texts and writing. As he flies through the air he imagines:

> A letter at a time, clack, clack, clack, a message is being typed on a rose-pink screen that trembles like water each time he blinks and is therefore quite likely his own inner eyelid. E-R-T-Y, say the letters. (3)

Here, the representation of the body, in a state of pain and panic, paradoxically returns us to the material, graphological qualities of the text. Wicomb suggests that: 'the letters, Q-W-E-R-T-Y, constitute a shift back to the very beginning and the first consecutive letters of the keyboard... It speaks thus of beginnings, of the raw material of writing... the difficulty of coming into being as a character through writing' (216). Wicomb highlights this focus on the mediation of text through technical devices, the keyboard and the computer, and their tendency to fragment narrative to the point when it becomes nonsensical: E-R-T-Y. For Paul, the raw material of his own body can only be imagined through these writing devices, as his eyelid itself becomes a kind of internalized 'rose-pink screen' (3).

Throughout *Slow Man*, Paul's memory of the accident is mediated by this graphological and technical focus on writing. He is plagued by the sense of language as an imperfect substitute, through which he must struggle to decipher his fate: 'he had strained, that day on Magill Road, to attend the word of the gods, tapped out on their occult typewriter!' (19). In *Diary of a Bad Year*, JC describes writing as a kind of semi-grotesque, physical straining: 'squeezing worms out of his pen' (43). JC is painfully aware that words, like worms, constantly wriggle free from their intended meaning, escaping the control of the writer.

This sense of dependency on imprecise or slippery modes of representation is also played out in relation to photography. In an episode near the end of the novel, Drago replaces a treasured photograph from Paul's Fauchery collection with a doctored copy. Like the cutting and pasting on the computer in *Slow Man* or the fast-forwarding and rewinding of the tape-recorder in *Krapp's Last Tape*, the capacity for digital enhancement shatters the straightforward narrative or historical authority of the photograph. Through the simple click of a button, Drago's immigrant relatives are inserted into Australian history and the photographic archives (218).

Paul's conception of history as a single, linear narrative is subverted through the insertion of different timeframes into the same photographic framework. The awareness of the instability of the photographic form is particularly overwhelming for a man who has devoted his working life to being a portraitist. It also calls into question the possibility of drawing or writing an authentic portrait of a character, either by an outside observer such as Elizabeth in *Slow Man* or in the form of the ambivalent self-portrait offered in *Diary of a Bad Year*. Paul fears that he holds a world-view that is in danger of unravelling: 'It is the desecration that he feels most of all: the dead made fun of by a couple of cocky, irreverent youths' (218). These shattering revelations are framed in terms of old age; Paul is forced to confront his dependency on younger generations to preserve legacies and pass on knowledge.

At the end of *Slow Man*, Elizabeth Costello seeks to impose narrative closure onto the story, of which she is co-creator, through the offer of a re-written contract of care. She offers herself, an admittedly imperfect substitute for Marijana, as a nurse and companion:

> Come and live with me in Carlton instead...I will even cook for you...serviceably enough...You can tell me more stories from your treasure-hoard, which I will afterwards tell back to you in a form so accelerated and improved that you will hardly recognise them...I will take care of you and perhaps in return you will learn to take care of me. (232)

On a superficial level, Elizabeth's contract offers a form of narrative resolution, through a 'companionate marriage' (232) contract of reciprocal exchange and care. Yet, this offer of classic, comedic narrative closure is underpinned by an on-going desire to implicate Paul in further spirals of 'accelerated and improved' storytelling. This constitutes a re-writing of his character and his life that Elizabeth attempted to do throughout the novel. Acceptance of Elizabeth's 'happily ever after' ending to the narrative would represent a complete relinquishment of the narrative agency that Paul has clung to.

This underlying desire to impose a fixed meaning on a potentially chaotic, 'inconsequential' (222) life story is undermined by the representation of on-going processes of writing and revision. *Diary of a Bad Year* ends with a similar, rather brittle possibility of narrative closure through an offer of care. Anya imagines her role in bringing about closure and narrative 'order' to JC's life and story, on the most literal of levels, in terms of overseeing funeral arrangements and clearing out the mess of his possessions: 'I will clean your flat and put everything in order...I will write to the man in Germany...to let him know that it is the end of your Opinions, there won't be any more coming in' (226). Anya's attempt to seize narrative agency here, through her letter writing, and impose an end-stop on the narrative, is subverted. JC, despite his deteriorating health, keeps on writing. Moreover, *Diary of a Bad Year* ends with a potential new beginning: 'I should thoroughly revise my opinions, that is what I should do. I should cull the older, more decrepit ones, find newer, up-to-date ones to replace them' (143). In the cases of Paul and Elizabeth, Anya and JC, the dialectic between author and character is not brought to any kind of resolution. Instead, they remain locked together at the end of these texts, like Sinbad and the old man, in an on-going battle for narrative control.

Coetzee depicts characters that are on the brink of an ending, in a physical and symbolic sense. Paul in *Slow Man* imagines his own liminal position, waiting on the borderline between heaven and earth: 'when he arrives at the gate, St Paul...will be waiting' (34). JC is similarly haunted by this image: 'last night I had a bad dream...about dying and being guided to the gateway to oblivion by a young woman' (59). In *Elizabeth Costello*, these fragmented images from the other two novels are formulated into an entire 'lesson' (193). The final section of the book takes its title from this image of characters trapped in a Beckettian condition of waiting, 'At the Gate' (193). Elizabeth finds herself imprisoned in a surreal, Kafkaesque[67] world, in which she must constantly petition the gatekeeper. Like Paul in *Slow Man* who suspects that those around him are extras, Elizabeth suffers a crisis of belief in which reality becomes substituted by an empty fictionality.

'At the Gate' does not end with any definitive crossing of boundaries but, like *Slow Man* and *Diary of a Bad Year*, is open-ended; they all finish with the image of an ageing and enduring body, that refuses to be removed from view. For Attridge, the episode does not suggest a straightforward heuristic value for literature but rather an ethical process of imagining: 'It leaves us strongly aware that what has mattered, for Elizabeth Costello and the reader, is the event – literary and ethical at the same time – of storytelling, of testing, of self-questioning, and not the outcome.'[68] Here, in Attridge's view, doubt and uncertainty become part of the ethical *process* of storytelling. In *Slow Man*, Paul offers a more sceptical opinion of this alignment of ethical and literary processes of imagining: 'with a little ingenuity ... one can torture a lesson out of the most haphazard sequence of events' (198).

This shattering of comforting fictions of fixed closure,[69] narrative authority and authorial independence, constitutes the main action of *Diary of a Bad Year* and *Slow Man*. The physical discomfort of Paul is mirrored in a corresponding narrative discomfort for the reader, as basic conventions of telling and belief are subverted. Similarly, the final scene of *Elizabeth Costello*, 'At the Gate', ends with the protagonist trapped in an on-going cycle of writing in which each day she must substitute the previous day's story for another, augmented and revised account of herself.

Narrative prosthesis

In *Slow Man*, the notion of substitution is explored as a linguistic act but also as a distinctly bodily dilemma. Paul's rejection of literal prostheses (an artificial leg and a recumbent, hand-powered bicycle) is bound up with his refusal to accept the neat, tidy narrative endings that are offered to him. The physical and the textual are mutually implicated in each other; *Slow Man* is a story that itself refuses to be prostheticized.

Recent disability studies writing discusses prostheses in terms of social and aesthetic meanings, as well as medical practicality.[70] This shift, to consider the interdependence of cultural and medical models of disability (as opposed to a crude separation of these models in some early disability theory) has led to a more complex exploration of the normalizing impulses implicit in prosthesis. David Wills suggests that prosthesis contains within it a set of ideological assumptions about deviancy and an underlying desire to erase difference, by encouraging a kind of 'passing': 'prosthesis is inevitably about belonging' (5). Elizabeth F. Emens draws an opposition between the medical and social models to identify, like Wills, this issue of prosthesis as a highly contested area: 'The medical model views disabled bodies as bodies needing a cure, whereas the social model views disability as a social category created by the context in which we live.'[71]

These are questions that have only recently received attention in disability studies circles. The first wave of disability studies often promoted counter-narratives of disability in terms of independence, wielding these alternative stories as political tools in the fight against negative stereotypes of the disabled as entirely dependent. However, nuanced discussions of these aids and prostheses, necessary in on-going conditions of disability, allow for a more complex understanding of dependency. In *Slow Man*, Paul's refusal of any form of prosthesis represents a rejection of precisely these 'narratives of overcoming'[72] and cure that, Garland Thomson suggests, are traditionally associated with literary representations of disability. Coetzee provides a mocking, momentary possibility of a fairytale ending in a rare moment of intimacy between Paul and Elizabeth at the end of *Slow Man*:

> Ever so gently, he lifts her and slips a cushion under her head.
>   In a fairy story, this would be the moment when the foul hag turns into a fair princess. But this is not a fairy story, evidently. (237)

With typical bathos, Coetzee highlights how these fairytale structures (the magical shift from witch to princess or ugly duckling to swan) provide an absurd counter-narrative of disability and ageing. Neither Paul nor Elizabeth is given a miracle cure for their conditions of old age and disability at the end of the text. Instead of a magical reversal, Elizabeth confronts Paul and the readers with an unrelenting and unchanging physicality:

> Where else in the world, at this late stage, are you going to find affection, you ugly old man? Yes, I am familiar with that word too, ugly. We are both of us ugly, Paul, old and ugly. (236)

Elizabeth's investment in conventional stereotypes means that, in her view, both age and disability exclude Paul (and herself) from conventional understandings of beauty and ability. Paul's refusal to make his body fit a normalized model suggests the disruptive potential of messy bodies in the text which Elizabeth, as 'author', and the medical professionals dealing with Paul's case seek to control. Like Kermode's assertion that 'comforting' (44) patterns of time and narrative closure are often imposed on texts, Synder and Mitchell suggest that storytelling can be perceived as an attempt to control discomforting bodies: 'The effort to narrativise disability's myriad deviations is an attempt to bring the body's unruliness under control' (5).

There is certainly a rush to narrate Paul's prosthesis in *Slow Man*, to grab narrative agency in order to define and describe it. The cheery, flippant tone of Dr Hansen suggests that prosthesis implies an under-standing of disability as a lack that needs to be cured: '"Excellent!" says Dr Hansen... "It is all coming together beautifully. You will soon be yourself again"' (10). Madeleine further perpetuates this fiction of an illusory 'normal' or idealized body: 'There are people all around in the street... who you could not even tell they are wearing prostheses, it's so natural the way they walk' (59).

This highly artificial, constructed notion of the natural allows Coetzee to explore the aesthetic dimensions of prosthesis. Interdependent models of disability, such as Tom Shakespeare's 'interactionist'[73] perspective, have also led to an examination of prosthesis specifically in terms of literary representations of disability. Mitchell and Snyder, in *Narrative Prosthesis: Disability and the Dependencies of Discourse* (2006), see prosthesis as a conservative and normalizing strategy in the novel that, they suggest, closes down narrative possibilities and open-endedness. Once again, this question of 'discomfort', both literal and metaphorical, is at the fore: 'While an actual prosthesis is always somewhat discomfort-ing, a textual prosthesis alleviates discomfort by removing the unsightly from view' (8). It is this kind of 'prosthetic' artificial narrative closure in which the unsightly is removed from view that Coetzee mocks with his allusion to the fairytale conversion of foul hag to beautiful princess. According to Mitchell and Snyder's definition, to prostheticize *Slow Man* would be to remove Paul's disruptive body from view at the end of the novel – something that Coetzee refuses to do. In his essays, as well as his fiction, Coetzee remains committed to representing, in his own words, 'people who smell wrong and look unsightly and do not have the decency to hide themselves away'.[74]

Wills's alternative model of narrative prosthesis provides a useful per-spective though which to consider Coetzee's later writing. Just as *Slow Man*, *Diary of a Bad Year* and *Elizabeth Costello* merge the novelistic form with elements of diary, essay and memoir, Wills fuses a personal account with literary theory. He defines prosthesis as a term that medi-ates between the literary and the body, as a structure on which he depends to understand his father's disability and his fascination with processes of substitution in literary criticism. Prosthesis is, for Wills, 'a doubtful enterprise', both a 'critical posture and a narrative of a father's stance' (9). In contrast to Mitchell and Snyder, who suggest that narrative prosthesis represents a closing down of the text through a return to naturalistic conventions, Wills emphasizes the artificiality of prosthesis: 'The effort is to make the prosthesis show, to flaunt its imperfect supplement as an illusion. The prosthetic relation of body to word is exposed as an artificial contrivance' (8). Thus, narrative prosthesis is associated with unsettling discomfort for Wills, in direct opposition to the comforting relief from abnormality that it allows in Mitchell and Snyder's account. Wills's sense of 'flaunting' imperfect substitutions and foregrounding 'artificial contrivance' is highly resonant of the meta-textual tricks and entry of fictionalized author figures in both *Slow Man* and *Diary of a Bad Year*.

However, the point of intersection between these two models is the way in which they use prosthesis as a metaphor through which to explore the relation of language to reality. Wills articulates this relationship: 'The word always augments a prosthetic relation to an exterior material that it cannot possess or embody' (138). In Mitchell and Snyder, this dynamic is explored by way of an analogy with Ahab's prosthetic leg in Herman Melville's *Moby-Dick* (1851): '"Reality" is merely an effect of the duplicity of language, a false leg that cannot quite replace the lost original' (12).

Diary of a Bad Year explores precisely this sense of the duplicity but also the inadequacy of language as an imperfect substitute, a collection of parts that do not quite make up a complete whole. JC has a surreal sense that even the first-person pronoun becomes unstable as 'I' is split into an artificial dualistic relationship. His description links back to the structures of internalized self-division and external interlocution in all of Coetzee's later texts:

> I have a disquieting sense that the one I hear is not the one I call myself. Rather, it is as though some other person (but who?) were being imitated, followed, even mimicked. (195)

Like the prosthetic leg that mimics the real one, the portrait that he draws of himself through his first-person descriptions, 'I', cannot quite capture his sense of 'myself'. Language acts here as a kind imitation or substitution. Wills's extended descriptions create a constant slippage between literal and metaphorical, physical and textual prostheses, amputations and substitutions. 'The writing of prosthesis,' he suggests, 'is inevitably caught in a complex play of displacements; prosthesis being about nothing if not placement, displacement, replacement, standing, dislodging, substituting, setting, amputating, supplementing' (9). Once again, there is a reminder of the cutting and pasting, fast-forwarding and rewinding, excision and substitution, that takes place in modern writing processes. The prosthetic relation to reality that JC describes is, for Wills, a universal, rather than exceptional or marginal condition. The process of writing, even for the able-bodied, is mediated by a prosthetic relationship with a keyboard and computer – human beings attached to writing machines. Wills argues that all writing is necessarily prosthetic: 'One cannot simply write about prosthesis when one is automatically, just by virtue of writing, writing prosthesis, entering into prosthetic relations, being prosthetic' (30).

Prosthesis, and the refusal of it, becomes a metaphor for the form of the texts (the refusal to provide a neat, complete narrative ending) but also the view of language expounded in them. *Diary of a Bad Year, Slow Man* and *Elizabeth Costello* explore this 'prosthetic' relationship between language and reality, but, as Wills suggests, are implicated in these same prosthetic relations merely through the act of writing itself. These novels trigger a consideration of multiple, competing understandings of the prosthetic: as a literal false limb, a mode of transport, a form of linguistic substitution or a range of complex theoretical models.

Coetzee's later writing interrogates this possibility of spiralling linguistic substitution and the 'ghostly space of the prosthetic'[75] yet, at the same time, remains grounded in a sense of the physical pain involved in Paul's decision to reject prosthesis. Readers are always brought back to the materiality of the body through the focus on disability and old age. Elizabeth, asleep on a park bench, is described as an anonymous 'old woman in [a] raincoat...Her head is sideways, her mouth open.'[76] Paul, following what he describes as 'the gross butchery of amputation' (99) at the beginning of *Slow Man*, is unable to escape the feeling of his own body as 'a lump of all too solid flesh' (198). He is plagued by a sense that his body is 'too solid' and inflexible yet, at the same time, cannot ignore its fragile vulnerability and missing parts.

It is significant, therefore, that in these most intertextual, metafictional of his novels, Coetzee chooses to represent conditions of ageing and disability – states in which the body constantly draws attention to itself. In a moment of frustration, Paul demands: 'What do you think life has consisted in ever since Magill Road but being rammed into the physical day after day?' (234–5). *Slow Man* and *Diary of a Bad Year* are not only concerned with paralysing cycles of linguistic substitution, but also with states of physical and social paralysis. David

Attwell, in his introduction to a series of interviews with Coetzee, describes how:

> Coetzee is skeptical about what he calls the 'impasse of anti-illusionism.' Once it has shaken off the tyranny of the real, radical metafiction has few options: it can simply bequeath a record of failed attempts at transcendence, or, in defiance, it can try to turn paralysis into a virtue by appealing to notions of play.[77]

Just when *Slow Man* appears to spiral off into the realms of meta-fiction, Coetzee brings it back down to earth with a bang. It is, paradoxically, the highly meta-fictional figure of Elizabeth, who insists upon the spatial and temporal limits of the text:

> 'Now let me ask you straight out, Mrs Costello: Are you real?'
> 'Am I real? I eat, I sleep, I suffer, I go to the bathroom, I catch cold. I am as real as you...This is a very ordinary story, very ordinary indeed, with just three dimensions, length, breadth and height.' (233)

Here, the playful element that Attwell describes is at the fore. Paul is being informed of his own 'reality' by the woman who seeks to create it, and who constantly treats him as merely a character or a 'puppet' (117). Paul, a man obsessed with photographs and books, clings to a notion of reality that is reminiscent of a realist novel. For him, prosthesis violates the boundaries of realism, on the grounds that 'crutches are better. Crutches are at least honest' (58). Yet, Elizabeth's words mock Paul's desperate attempts to protect narrative authority or authenticity from corrupting illusions, as she implicates him in her own fictionality. Her words echo back to *Elizabeth Costello*: 'I am as real as you' (233). Just as Paul exposes his physical dependency through the refusal of prosthesis, *Slow Man* highlights its own dependency upon unstable linguistic, technological and bodily forms of mediation through the refusal to provide narrative closure or limit itself to a single level of reality.

Style in old age

Coetzee's later works explore a fascination with the ways in which the body mediates the process of writing and how this relationship changes according to different states of health and stages of life. In *Elizabeth Costello*, the protagonist claims that the urgency and sincerity of her narrative style is a direct result of her age: 'I say what I mean. I am an old woman. I do not have the time any longer to say things I do not mean' (62). In *Diary of a Bad Year*, there is a similar sense of haste, and a desire to complete the project before JC's health deteriorates any further. Alan speculates: 'Parkinson's disease. That is what he is so worried about, your man Señor C . . . That is why he is in such a rush to get his book finished' (132).

There is a further suggestion that certain literary forms and genres are more appropriate to states in which the body is weak, vulnerable or in decay. In 'As a Woman Grows Older', Elizabeth links age to a comic sense of the absurd and an implicit duplicity: 'I am not serious, not fully serious – I am too old to be serious.'[78] In *Diary of a Bad Year*, JC depicts the process of writing as extremely physical; he dismisses the novel as a genre for younger, stronger generations:

> A novel? No. I don't have the endurance any more. To write a novel you have to be like Atlas, holding up a whole world on your shoulders and supporting it there for months and years while its affairs work themselves out. It is too much for me as I am today. (54)

Despite this unwillingness and perceived inability to shoulder the burden of a novel, political opinion is increasingly replaced by the distinctly novelistic narration of character and personal events. This interdependent relationship between the decaying body and writing is also raised in Edward Said's *On Late Style* (2006). In his discussion of 'late style', a term taken from Adorno's essay 'Spätstil Beethovens' (1934), Said posits an interdependent relationship between aesthetic style and bodily condition, but also between constructed (and interconnected) notions of nature and history:

> The body, its health, its care, its composition, functioning, and flourishing, its illnesses and demise, belong to the order of nature . . . however, how we create a sense of our life individually and collectively, subjectively as well as socially, how we divide it into periods, belongs roughly speaking to the order of history.[79]

Said suggests that the experience of the body cannot be separated from internalized myths, life-models and fictions about old age: 'there are all sorts of connections between the two realms' (3). He challenges stereotypical notions of wisdom, and a corresponding sense of narrative harmony and closure that it may suggest in literary representations

of older people: 'What of artistic lateness not as harmony and resolution but as intransigence, difficulty and unresolved contradiction?
What if age and ill health don't produce the serenity of "ripeness is
all?" ' (7).

These same myths, of old age as harmony or resolution are subverted by the unrelenting quality of *Slow Man* and *Diary of a Bad Year*.
In these novels, 'ripeness' is replaced by heightened anxiety, confusion and ambivalence. JC describes 'flickering moments when I can
see these hard opinions of mine through her eyes', imagining 'how
alien and antiquated they may seem to a thoroughly modern Millie,
like the bones of some odd extinct creature, a half bird, half reptile,
on the point of turning to stone' (137). Physical ripeness is replaced
here with a sense of himself as a decaying relic from another age. Yet,
this impression of his body as becoming increasingly solidified, 'turning to stone', paradoxically instigates a softening of his opinions and
an increasing ability to identify with others. The boundaries of the
relationship between Anya and JC, and the structure of the text itself
become more fluid in the second section of *Diary of a Bad Year*, entitled
'Soft Opinions' (155). His relationship with Anya leads to a re-writing
of these opinions, demonstrating a creative fertility that undermines
his internalized, stereotypical notions of old age as a barren period.[80]
Through the open-ended structure of his late novels, Coetzee implicitly
challenges a narrative model in which meaning is constructed according to (fixed) endings, either in terms of understanding a life or making
sense of a literary narrative.

This redefined notion of endings, a privileging of process or performance over outcome, is a recurring feature of contemporary theories of
'late' or 'old age' style. Amir Cohen-Shalev, in his book *Both Worlds at
Once: Art in Old Age* (2002), suggests that the wisdom of old age lies in a
common recognition of the impossibility of reconciliation: 'Oppositions
are dismantled and presented in their bare essentials, with no apparent
pressure to reconcile them. Where there used to be a firm, linear, and
hierarchical logic, there is now a loose, cyclical, auto telic logic' (11).
Elizabeth in 'As a Woman Grows Older' articulates this sense of the dissolution of linear narratives. History itself is not only personified, but
also implicated in the senile circularity that she fears may characterize
her own later life:

> History herself has lost her voice, Clio, the one who once upon a
> time used to strike her lyre and sing of the doings of great men, has
> become infirm and frivolous, like the silliest sort of old woman.[81]

Elizabeth's compulsion to tell or narrate, it seems, is rooted in this deep fear of voicelessness, but also a desire to cling onto these comforting, linear narrative structures for as long as possible. Her plea that she is 'losing faith in history'[82] becomes bound up with anxieties about her own loss of memory, but also the possibility that the more traditional narrative structures that she depends upon are becoming outdated. Cohen-Shalev suggests that existing literary and life models collapse with the representation of old age. The ageing and increasingly incapacitated author figures that Coetzee depicts are similarly plagued by anxieties about inauthenticity and unravelling narrative structures: 'It is a common aspect of old age that an orderly explanation of reality seems more and more implausible.'[83] Coetzee depicts the ageing author figures of Elizabeth, JC and Paul, who are all significantly older than himself, in order to endow these post-South African novels with a sense of 'lateness' but also to question the possibility of 'describing lives narratologically'.[84]

Small, in *The Long Life* (2007), argues that the literary representation of ageing reconfigures time and narrative to challenge 'the assumption of unity of lives and unity of personhood' (269). *Slow Man* and *Diary of a Bad Year* implicitly challenge the notion of a unified life or self, through their multi-layered, open-ended forms and unreliable narrators. In *Diary of a Bad Year*, the lines across the page highlight a sense of selfhood constructed not through a single biographical narrative (or personal diary entry) but as multiple coexisting and often contradictory narrative perspectives, with highly visible gaps between them. In *Slow Man*, Paul disrupts the illusion of a complete body through his refusal of prosthesis. This becomes symbolic of his wider resistance to Elizabeth Costello's attempt to assimilate his arbitrary experiences into a unified or meaningful life story.

For Small, the representation of ageing leads to a kind of tearing up of literary contracts, as we find in *Slow Man*. She suggests that the understanding of old age as a complex, embodied and enduring condition leads to a sense in which 'the quest narrative and progress narrative may cease to be appropriate models' (102). She argues for a new critical model for understanding old age; that we need 'to cease to think in terms of certain kinds of narrative progress . . . downgrading, or even rejecting altogether, a narrative view of lives as an appropriate structure for thinking about old age' (90). *In Diary of a Bad Year*, JC initially sets up a stereotypical opposition between a romantic notion of 'youth as the fountain of creation' and 'drying up in old age'.[85] However, in the second half of the quotation, pivoting around a significant 'yet', he echoes Small's sense of a need for an alternative view of lives. JC suggests that the paring down of form associated with old age style can allow liberation from constraining social and narrative models:

> Growing detachment from the world is of course the experience of many writers as they grow older, grow cooler or colder...The syndrome is usually ascribed to a waning of creative power; it is no doubt connected with the attenuation of physical powers...Yet, from inside the same development may bear quite a different interpretation: as a liberation, a clearing of the mind to take on more important tasks. (193)

JC recognizes a relationship between bodily condition and aesthetic style, but extends this to suggest that the disabling process of ageing can, paradoxically, provide an enabling freedom to focus on 'important tasks'. He self-consciously inverts a conventional narrative of decline associated with artistic production in old age. Instead, JC goes on to employ the example of Tolstoy's writing in old age: 'Far from declining, he must have felt, he was ridding himself of the shackles that had enslaved him to appearances, enabling him to face directly the one question that truly engaged his soul: how to live' (193).

This image of throwing off the shackles brings us back to the initial master and slave idea with which this chapter began, but also echoes de Beauvoir's question[86] about how to live in a state of dependency. In the context of Coetzee's later novels, the problem posed by de Beauvoir needs to be radically reformulated. Her focus on the recovery of independence is replaced by the ethical question of how life can be best lived once we have recognized dependency as a likely condition of *all* lives. When all of the layers of meta-textual playfulness and linguistic substitution are stripped away, the author is depicted not as a figure of god-like independence, but rather of embodied vulnerability. JC fears that 'he is not a novelist...but a pedant who dabbles in fiction...I have reached a stage in my life when I begin to wonder...whether, all the time I thought I was going about in disguise, I was in fact naked' (191).

As in Lucian Freud's self-portrait (Figure 7), Coetzee presents an unrelenting, close-up image of the ageing body. The position of Freud's self-image, directly facing the viewers with an interrogative stare, implies an awareness of their presence, in the same way that Coetzee's texts highlight their own dependence upon the reader to animate and reconstruct character. Both Freud, as painter, and the fictional figures of JC,

Figure 7   Lucian Freud, *Painter Working, Reflection*, 1993

the memoir-writer and Paul the photographer explore the problems of portraiture alongside their attempts to create self-portraits. The presence of the paints and palette in Freud's self-portrait suggests that the portrait is unfinished, while reminding us of the materiality of this process of construction. As in *Slow Man* and *Diary of a Bad Year*, the mimetic possibility of reflection is subverted by the physical presence of a painter or writer, and their materials, within the aesthetic frame itself.

The emerging fields of critical gerontology and age studies in literature provide alternative, re-written models of ageing, that are more in keeping with the instabilities and uncertainties of Coetzee's own later writing. For Cohen-Shalev, the representation of old age enacts a kind of reversal:

> Old age style turns sublimation inside out. Old age style is not a concealment but a 'see through' art where the tricks of the trade, the technique of 'make believe' are dropped, to make way for an art of dis-illusion. (13)

In Coetzee's writing, the exposure of bodies in pain and the bare bones of the text itself constitute precisely this art of 'dis-illusion'. This focus on the 'tricks of the trade' is played out in a series of traps in the texts themselves: the unsettling entry of Elizabeth Costello in *Slow Man* or the Marianna storyline that goes nowhere. Gullette sees ageing as an on-going process rather than any kind of fixed narrative closure: 'Age and aging as we evolve is a personal residue – of stories we have heard, received or rejected, renegotiated and retold.'[87] In *Diary of a Bad Year*, all that is left on the page is this residue: memories jotted down or half-remembered, letters that go unanswered and could easily go astray. The search for new narrative models in these texts, through the fusion of multiple narratives and literary forms, is intertwined with an on-going search for alternative understandings of old age and disability.

Conclusion: blindness and empathetic imagination

Recurring representations of blindness and visual impairment in Coetzee's later writing provide another model for exploring dependency. The relationships of mutual and reversible dependency, between carer and patient, author and character, writer and amanuensis, are explored through the dynamic between the blind person and their surroundings which are 'unimaginable but ... there to be imagined'.[88] Blindness foregrounds dependency upon processes of mediation, particularly through touch and sound, rather than through more conventional paradoxically 'invisible' modes of visual mediation, such as the computer screen or photograph. JC, for example, employs the tape-recorder as a kind of prosthesis, substituting oral for written modes of articulation as a result of his fading eyesight. His references to the blindness of Milton and Bach[89] in their later years suggest an implicit desire to locate himself within a great tradition of blind artists, for whom aesthetic production involved amanuenses and also a central role for memory. In his description of 'old age style', Cohen-Shalev invokes a metaphor of blindness:

> It is not creative ability that breaks down with age, but the perception of art as a foolproof means of providing a lasting solution to the problem of humankind. Aging artists often refrain from explicating their artistic thinking, leaving ... their scholars searching in the dark, confused. (153)

In *Slow Man*, this image of groping around in the dark becomes literalized. In the Marianna scene, Paul is forced to wear a blindfold (of flour and water stuck over his eyes) so that his encounter with his blind lover occurs entirely in darkness. This enforced blindness renders Paul more sensitive to other forms of sensory perception, not least his own hands that both symbolically grasp for clues as to her identity and literally grope Marianna as part of their sexual encounter: 'A rustling. The scent of the damp leaves over his eyes overpowers every other smell. A pressure on the frame, which he feels through his hands' (103).

This metaphor is extended as blind Marianna experiences the invasive stares of others as a kind of bodily violation: 'She is conscious of the gaze of others like fingers groping at her, groping and retreating' (96). Like the readers, both Marianna and Paul are forced to formulate an image of the other character through a few fragments of 'sense-data' (107) or snippets of speech. Through this temporary condition of blindness Paul is placed in a condition of complete dependency, forcing him to imagine another point of view. Following an attempt to imagine the scene from Marianna's perspective, Paul is left wondering 'is that enough for her to construct the image of a man from?' (107).

We are confronted here with Coetzee's paradoxical impulse to imagine otherness yet, at the same time, his sense of the limitations of this literary, empathetic act. By conducting the meeting between Marianna and Paul in darkness he plays with the conventional form of the face-to-face encounter. Meeting Marianna confronts Paul with the blind spots in his own vision. Elizabeth suggests to him that he may well have already encountered Marianna in his previous life: 'Perhaps once

upon a time you took her photograph, and it happened that your attention was concentrated on the image you were making, not on her, the
source of the image' (97). Once again, technology mediates 'reality' to
the extent that the original subject becomes eclipsed. Elizabeth's sense
of the necessarily exclusionary nature of sight is articulated in brutal
terms at the end of the text. There is a sense that, like a photograph,
Paul's vision cuts out as much as it includes in the frame:

> Let me tell you what you see, or what you tell yourself you are seeing.
> An old woman by the side of the River Torrens... But reality is more
> complicated than that, Paul. In reality you see a great deal more – see
> it and then block it out. (158)

Elizabeth seeks to control Paul's story but also his sight, controlling his
experience at every level: 'Let me tell you what you see...' Derrida,
in his *Memoirs of the Blind* (1993), explores the blindness at the heart
of vision. Through the example of drawing, Derrida suggests that aesthetic production is always based upon the condition of *not seeing*. Even
a drawing done from still life, he suggests, requires the draftsman to
look away from the object, to draw from an image that has been held
in the mind's eye. Vision is therefore substituted with, and mediated
by, memory. As in *Slow Man*, Derrida employs the image of a groping
hand to suggest that touch becomes a kind of prosthetic substitute for
sight:

> A hand of the blind ventures forth alone or disconnected... it feels
> its way, it gropes, it caresses as much as it inscribes, trusting in the
> memory of signs and supplementing sight... This eye guides the
> tracing outline; it is a miner's lamp at the point of writing, a curi-
> ous and vigilant substitute, the prosthesis of a seer who is himself
> invisible. (3)

The questionable ethics of scrutinizing the blind are present in both
Derrida's and Coetzee's writing. Elizabeth Costello articulates this
ambivalence, as well as the sense that disability has functioned as a blind
spot in the wider literary and social vision, '[Marianna] is unsightly
in the way that all blind people are unsightly' (96). Once again, we
encounter a kind of resistance in these scenes of face-to-face encounter;
Derrida explores the compulsion to look alongside the sense of repulsion at the object of scrutiny. This paradoxical impulse is described by
Elizabeth as she prepares Paul for their meeting: 'One prefers not to look

on her face. Or rather, one finds oneself staring and then withdraws one's gaze, repelled' (96).

The condition of blindness here reconfigures time, space and sensory perception, to suggest the impossibility of drawing an entirely accurate, fixed self-portrait: 'The self-portrait always appears in the reverberation of several voices.'[90] Paul, the retired portraitist, and JC, the author of a diary that is fragmented into multiple 'voices', are forced to confront these blind spots and silences in their own self-representations. In this context, a necessary imaginative dimension implicates the 'reader' of a painting, text or character in the process of construction.

This same compulsion to look, accompanied by simultaneous repulsion and the impossible desire for complete vision are also explored in Coetzee's essay 'The Dark Chamber' (1986). Here, the inability to see is discussed in relation to Gordimer's *Burger's Daughter* (1981) and scenes of torture in South African literature. These are scenes, Coetzee suggests, that we are literally and metaphorically locked out from through state secrecy and censorship yet, on an ethical level, we must seek to imaginatively reconstruct. Like Derrida, Coetzee suggests that this condition of blindness, of *not seeing*, is at the heart of aesthetic production. He describes the novelist as:

A person who, camped before a closed door, facing an insufferable ban, creates in place of the scene he is forbidden to see, a representation of that scene, and a story of the actors in it and how they come to be there.[91]

Blindness functions here as a temporary condition, something imposed by the state rather than an accidental or age-related disability. Yet, in both cases, it becomes a model for the ethical imperative to imagine states of otherness in Coetzee's works. In his introduction to *Doubling the Point* (1992), the collection that includes 'The Dark Chamber' essay, Attwell suggests that 'Coetzee speaks, in these interviews, of the struggle to "imagine the unimaginable" ' (11). For Attwell, 'The Dark Chamber' essay exemplifies the challenge of ethical imagination and identification that underpins Coetzee's works:

What is distinctive in Coetzee . . . is that he broaches the possibility of ethical reconstruction in a movement which begins with abnegation, with the recognition of unbridgeable historical constraints. It is a scrupulous position: more than conscious of the limits of its own authority. (12)

Blindness therefore becomes central to Coetzee's narrative project, as a metaphor for a condition in which it is impossible to see yet ethically necessary to *attempt* to imagine, but also as a literal, embodied condition represented in his novels. In *Age of Iron*, blindness remains symbolic: Mrs Curren's blind ignorance of the brutalities of Apartheid violence is shattered by her debilitating physical illness, and the relationship of care with Vercueil. She suggests that the process of writing and imagining, whilst shut up in her bedroom with her eyes closed in pain, is paradoxically the most insightful period of her life: 'His eyes are open and mine, though I write, are shut. My eyes are shut in order to see' (175).

For Paul in *Slow Man*, the condition of temporary blindness, in the scene with Marianna, is physically disabling yet also imaginatively liberating: '"There is no need," he begins again, "for us to adhere to any script...We are free agents"' (105). For the first time in the novel, Paul recognizes his own free will. Recognition of a reciprocal state of dependency between himself and Marianna gives him a sense of freedom and (temporary) narrative agency.

The Marianna scene, easily dismissed as a dead-end or 'a dark cul-de-sac in the narrative',[92] in fact offers a point of departure for examining the paradoxical problems of reading, representing and seeing in *Slow Man*, *Diary of a Bad Year* and *Elizabeth Costello*. These author figures are plagued with doubts about the possibility of a heuristic or ethical value to the literary. In her lecture, Elizabeth Costello suggests that any argument about the moral value of literature is fundamentally reversible: 'For surely if what we write has the power to make us better people it has the power to make us worse.'[93] Elizabeth in 'A Woman Grows Older' ends her reflections with a self-abnegating sense that 'if one truly wants to be a better person...there must be less roundabout ways of getting there than by darkening thousands of pages with prose'.[94]

This argument is most explicitly addressed in 'The Nature of Evil', an episode in *Elizabeth Costello* that is adapted from a lecture given by Coetzee at the Nexus Conference on 'Evil' in Tillburg, Holland in 2002. In *Elizabeth Costello*, there is a mirroring: Elizabeth is also taking part in a conference about the question of evil in Holland. This bookish, academic context becomes a forum for an attack on the destructive possibilities of the literary imagination. Elizabeth's target is Paul West, the author of a novel which depicts the gruesome execution of a group of men who plotted to murder Hitler in July 1944. West happens to be present at the conference. The 'dark chamber' of Coetzee's earlier critical essay re-emerges here: Elizabeth argues that West had no right to enter, through his writing, either the dark underground prison in which the plotters were killed, or to imagine the interior of their consciousnesses in these bleak final moments. She condemns his work as:

> Obscene. That is the word, a word of contested etymology, that she must hold onto as a talisman. She chooses to believe that obscene means off-stage. To save our humanity, certain things that we may want to see ... must remain off-stage. (169)

Here, the contested etymology of 'obscene' undermines the authority of Elizabeth's claim to either moral or narrative authority. Even as she attempts to anchor her argument or 'hold onto' a single word, its meaning slips away from her. Like the scenes that Elizabeth refuses to represent in writing, such as her sexual encounter with Mr Phillips or her rape by a docker (recalled later in this episode), she argues that some things challenge the ethical limits of representation: 'I take seriously the claim that the artist risks a great deal by venturing into forbidden places' (173). Yet, there is an irony at the heart of these arguments: in order to make Costello's case about the dangers of representing these scenes, Coetzee must, in part, represent them. The gap between Costello and Coetzee opens up here, to expose yet another reversible dynamic, between victim and prosecutor. Stephen Mulhall argues that: '[Coetzee] is as much the victim as the prosecutor in Costello's confrontation with West – that author whose willingness to engage to his imaginative limits with human possibilities in his writing is matched only by his refusal to say a word in his own name.'[95] In this sense, the adoption of Costello as a mouthpiece adds yet another level to the recurring self-abnegation and the reversibility of subject positions in Coetzee's later works.

Unlike Nussbaum, who suggests that fiction offers the possibility of an imaginative identification which is an ethically charged, positive process,[96] Coetzee explores how the literary imagination can have equally destructive, alienating effects. The narrative discomfort that Elizabeth suffers when reading West's book is figured as a physical shock: 'through reading him that touch of evil was passed on to me ... Like electricity' (176). The act of imagining is not in itself, Coetzee suggests, inherently moral. Instead, the representation of scenes that defy understanding enables Coetzee's narrative and his critique of liberal values to take place. Coetzee's novels explore the irrational, excessive impulses in human nature. Under state care in *Slow Man*, for example, Paul refuses to reconcile himself to his situation, preferring to cling to the impossible ideal of his previous, undamaged body rather than accept the thoughtful care of Marijana or the possibility of mobility with a prosthetic leg. His resistance to help or to progress, even against his own better judgement, is maintained throughout the novel. The forward movement of the narrative is based not on a resolution of dialectics, but rather the on-going presence and *work* of the negative.[97] In this sense, these moments of resistance become reconfigured as productive: 'Resistance is not solely a negation... To create and recreate, to transform the situation, to participate actively in the process, that is to resist.'[98]

This undermining of the ethical and imaginative power of the literary is therefore matched by an on-going compulsion to narrate. Like the bodies of these disabled and ageing figures that endure at the end of the novel, all three texts conclude with an on-going process of storytelling. *Elizabeth Costello* in particular, also articulates the potential for the literary to mediate unknowable experiences. John boasts that, through writing, his mother: '"Has been a man... She has also been a dog." "She can," he insists, "think her way into other people, into other existences... Isn't that what is most important about fiction: that it takes us out of ourselves, into other lives?"' (22). John offers a model of the literary that is concerned with the process of imagining, rather than the creation of a unified story or a form of entertaining escapism. Elizabeth's student workshop employs poetry as a way of encouraging ethical identification with the plight of animals, through a literary and imaginative process: 'The poems ask us to imagine our way into that way of moving, to inhabit that body' (96). When physical dependency is most evident, such as in cases of old age and disability, this ethical and narrative attempt to imagine states of otherness is at its most challenging yet also most important. Mitchell and Snyder suggest that:

> To represent disability is to engage oneself in an encounter with that which is believed to be off the map of 'recognizable' human experiences. Making comprehensible that which appears to be inherently unknowable situates narrative in the powerful position of mediator between two separate worlds. (5)

Here, Mitchell and Snyder make a claim for the power of the literary that is only hinted at as both a problem and a possibility in Coetzee's later writing. As an able-bodied and middle-aged writer, Coetzee engages with precisely this struggle to imagine other bodily and mental states. He is locked out of the experiences and consciousnesses of the disabled and ageing characters he creates, like the novelist locked out of the dark chamber, struggling to imagine its interior. Drago, in *Diary of a Bad Year*, articulates a similar challenge: 'If I'm sixteen, how do I know what it is like to be sixty?' (135). In this statement, Drago articulates precisely the challenge offered to readers of *Slow Man*, who are implicitly invited to identify with a character who is likely to be of a different age, temperament and physical condition to themselves.

Empathy and imaginative identification are therefore represented as a form of imaginative exchange, like the recurring relationships of dependency in the novels: at once fragile and complex, yet necessary and potentially productive. Writing and empathetic imagining are represented as collaborative acts that require recognition of mutual dependency and instability. Narrative discomfort becomes a necessary condition of reading or ethical identification. The resistance to understanding at the heart of the ethical encounter does not devalue its importance but rather accentuates the attempt to comprehend an underlying sense of shared humanity. Elizabeth exclaims: 'Easy? No. If it were easy it wouldn't be worth doing. It is the otherness that is the challenge. Making up someone other than yourself.'[99]

Coetzee's open-ended later writing does not offer solutions to the 'problems' of ageing or disability. Instead, it allows for a re-writing of the questions about issues of dependency, suggesting that existing social and literary contracts are inadequate. For Attridge, this question of imagining otherness is played out both on a level of character and in the sense of estrangement created through formal experimentation: 'Coetzee's works both stage, and are, irruptions of otherness into familiar worlds, and they pose the question: what is our responsibility towards the other?'[100]

Like the mutually dependent master and slave, the author therefore imprisoned in a paradoxical but simultaneous 'power and powerlessness'.[101] *Elizabeth Costello*, *Slow Man* and *Diary of a Bad Year* are grounded in embodied questions of the economic and social dimensions of care, nursing and prosthetics. Yet, at the same time, their broad definition of dependency allows connections to be drawn between a wide range of diverse characters and conditions, and also suggests that writing and the creation of identity are collaborative acts, part of a constellation of fluid mutually dependent relationships. These novels, produced on the cusp of the twenty-first century, demonstrate Coetzee's on-going commitment to the representation of unsightly and disruptive bodies, but also to the process of storytelling itself. As Elizabeth Costello insists:

> Have you given up reading stories? A mistake. You shouldn't.[102]

5
Disability as Metaphor: The Nobel Prize Lectures of Faulkner, Morrison and Coetzee

Harold Pinter, the Nobel Laureate for Literature in 2005, delivered his Nobel Prize lecture through a pre-recorded video in London. The image of Pinter displayed next to his speech on the Swedish Academy's website departed from the conventional single portrait shown alongside other laureates; a younger, healthier image of the dramatist was placed alongside a video still of Pinter in his wheelchair. The physical effort of the performance and unusual circumstances under which it took place were highlighted by the superimposition of an image from the lecture onto the fading portrait (Figure 8).

This spectacle of disability introduces a focus in this chapter on representations of disability in the lectures given by Faulkner, Morrison and Coetzee at the official award ceremony of the Nobel Prize for Literature. For Pinter, the condition of disability, caused by severe illness, was a pressing physical reality. For Faulkner, Morrison and Coetzee, winners of the award in 1949, 1993 and 2003 respectively, disability functioned as a central metaphor in their speeches, as a mode of conceptualizing their wider fictional and critical projects.

Pinter's Nobel Prize lecture, entitled 'Art, Truth, Politics', raises a series of important questions for an exploration of the role played by metaphors of disability in the Nobel Prize lectures of Faulkner, Morrison and Coetzee. The ethical and political issues associated with the employment of disability as a metaphor, particularly by authors who are themselves able-bodied, is central to much contemporary critical writing on illness and in disability studies. For Pinter, the 'distinction between what is real and what is unreal' is, for a writer, unclear but, he insists, 'as a citizen I must ask: What is true? What is false?'[1] By contrast, there is a layering of metaphor, myth and narrative in the speeches of Faulkner, Morrison and Coetzee that renders this distinction unstable. Morrison and Coetzee in particular resist Pinter's division between the citizen and

Figure 8   Portrait of Harold Pinter, Illuminations

the author, choosing highly literary forms for their lectures, such as a parable or extended allegory. Yet, like Pinter, Faulkner, Morrison and Coetzee, all critics and public intellectuals as well as authors, remain committed to the representation of the disabled body, in both literal and figurative forms.

When the text of Pinter's Nobel Prize lecture is set alongside the images of him on the Swedish Academy website, there appears, on one level, to be a disparity between his physical fragility and his rhetorical ferocity. Coetzee's *Diary of a Bad Year* provides an account of Pinter's performance. The narrator JC begins by describing Pinter's illness but soon shifts to focus on the courage and fearlessness of his direct attack on the British Prime Minister, Tony Blair:

> Harold Pinter, winner of the 2005 Nobel Prize for literature, is too ill to travel to Stockholm for the ceremony. But in a recorded lecture he makes what can fairly be called a savage attack on Tony Blair for his part in the war in Iraq...

> What he has done may be foolhardy but it is not cowardly. And there come times when the outrage and the shame are so great that all calculation, all prudence, is overwhelmed and one must act, that is to say, speak. (127)

Disability is not only a literal, physical presence in Pinter's lecture but also provides the metaphor through which he articulates his political attack. The power of Pinter's rhetoric lies in its position at the intersection between the literal and metaphorical, the public and the private. The act of speaking, highlighted by Coetzee's JC, was precisely what Pinter was denied by his illness; he was recovering from surgery for cancer of the throat at the time of delivering his Nobel Prize lecture. His struggle to speak was, as any observer of the lecture was reminded, an act of physical as well as political defiance. At the climax of his speech, Pinter employed a highly personal metaphor, of a malignant growth that silences and infects, to attack Western military tactics in Iraq:

> Low-intensity conflict means that ... you infect the heart of the country, that you establish a malignant growth and watch the gangrene bloom.[2]

This intertwining of the material and the metaphorical, the personal and the political, created a compelling effect. As John Sutherland comments: 'Not even carcinoma ... could silence him, or his raging Anglophobia.'[3] The foregrounding of his own suffering body in his imagery reflects Pinter's refusal to let the bloody implications of the Iraq war become assimilated into abstract military or political discourses. This unrelenting focus on taboo subjects, from political corruption to cancer, is part of a wider ethical and political commitment to the act of speaking and representation.

This intersection between literal and metaphorical disability recurs throughout Pinter's Nobel Prize lecture. He explores the condition of the writer through a cluster of metaphors of blindness: 'Truths challenge each other, recoil from each other, tease each other, are blind to each other.'[4] The relationship between author and character is, for Pinter, 'a never-ending game with them, cat and mouse, blind man's buff, hide and seek'.[5] These metaphors of play and disability are placed alongside a return to real, disabled Iraqi bodies. Pinter describes his dismay at:

> A photograph published on the front page of British newspapers of Tony Blair kissing the cheek of a little Iraqi boy ... His family had been blown up by a missile. He was the only survivor. 'When do I get my arms back?' he asked. The story was dropped.[6]

This resistance to representing disability in the media has an inescapably personal as well as political resonance for Pinter. These are both shocking true stories and disruptive, highly physical metaphors that Pinter, like Faulkner, Morrison and Coetzee before him, simply refuses to drop.

Faulkner and the centrality of bodily metaphors

When Alfred Nobel signed his last will in Paris on 27 November 1895, he left a deeply paradoxical legacy. As a philanthropist, inventor, administrator and industrialist, he was highly conscious of his own complex and often contradictory personal and professional roles: 'I am a misanthrope and yet utterly benevolent, have more than one screw loose yet am a super-idealist who digests philosophy more efficiently than food.'[7]

The nature of the ideals that this self-proclaimed super-idealist aimed to reward in his will remain ambiguous. The Nobel Medal itself, which depicts a tunnel blasted by dynamite on one side, captures this paradox of an award famous for its association with peace and benefit to mankind yet funded by technological innovations in weaponry and the art of destruction. (Nobel's father Immanuel developed sea mines used in the Crimean war and Alfred invented dynamite, used in his lifetime as a weapon in the Franco-Prussian War.)

This emphasis on the ideal was extended to the Nobel Prize for Literature in particular. In his will, Nobel specified that all of the prizes (for Literature, Physics, Chemistry, Medicine and Peace) should be awarded to those who 'have conferred the greatest benefit on mankind'[8] in the previous year. Yet, for the Literature prize he added a specific requirement: the winner must be 'the person who shall have produced...the most outstanding work in an idealistic tendency'.[9] Further layers of critical uncertainty are added by the imprecision of translation from Swedish to English. For Sutherland, the word needs to be read in the context of late nineteenth-century aesthetic concerns:

> The notion of great literature embodying the 'ideal' – or transcendent spiritual values – was very much a 19th-century aesthetic concern; and was still a live issue when the prize was set up in 1901. Conventionally 'idealistic' was opposed to 'realistic'. (xi)

The ideal here becomes associated with the abstract, imaginary and, to an extent, the perfect form that escapes us in ordinary life. The interpretation of this single word in the will is also extremely significant and highly contested; shifting understandings of Nobel's will and wider notions of the 'ideal' have been central to the selection of candidates for the award throughout the twentieth century.

This emphasis on ambiguous and abstract ideals has become a critical commonplace in the analysis of Faulkner's fiction and his Nobel lecture in particular. Wider critical readings of Faulkner have often been strangely disembodied, taking their cue from a de-contextualized extract plucked from his Nobel Prize address. At first glance, Faulkner appears to focus on spiritual concerns:

> The young man or woman writing today has forgotten the problems of the human heart in conflict with itself ... [Man is immortal] because he has a soul, a spirit capable of compassion and sacrifice and endurance. The poet's, the writer's duty is to write about these things.[10]

It has since become common in much Faulkner criticism[11] to draw a direct correspondence between this much-quoted critical paradigm and his fictional writing, emphasizing the spiritual elements of the speech to create 'an artist's credo that could have stood as a preface to any of his novels'.[12] Frequently, Faulkner's fiction and the rest of his Nobel Prize speech have been assimilated into a critical discourse of nostalgia for a lost golden age of the South, as a call for a return to the 'old verities'[13] and a series of abstract spiritual ideals.

However, read in the context of the rest of the speech and Faulkner's place in Nobel Prize history, the conception of an ideal explored in his lecture is far more complex, radical and embodied than traditional readings of these short extracts suggest. The lecture challenges an association between idealism and perfection[14] through the insistent interplay between the material and metaphorical, and an emphasis on flawed, vulnerable, living bodies. For Faulkner, linguistic concerns were always mediated by the body; communication could not be separated from shifting, living, imperfect and individual bodies.

On a historical level, the choice to honour Faulkner, a relatively unknown writer at the time in Europe, coincided with a new understanding of Nobel's conception of the ideal. Bertrand Russell, the laureate for 1950 who was awarded the Nobel Prize for Literature at the same ceremony as Faulkner due to wartime disruptions, explored the possibility of an 'ideal language'[15] in his literary and philosophical writing. Nobel Historian Kjell Espmark argues that the temporary suspension of Nobel ceremonies during the Second World War and the appointment of a new secretary to the committee, Anders Österling, ushered in a new group of pioneers.[16] In his view, this new interpretation of the ideal led to a shift away from rewarding popular taste – benefiting mankind by bringing pleasure to many – to a more nuanced sense of 'ideal' authors as those who introduced new, more experimental and challenging literary techniques.

Yet, despite this evident innovation, there remained an apparent contradiction between the bleakness of Faulkner's writing and the implicit claim that it represented an ideal form of literature. The question explored by Coetzee's Elizabeth Costello in her lecture on the gruesome writing of Paul West is applicable to Faulkner. In 'Lesson Six: the Problem of Evil'[17] Costello expresses her doubt about whether an author can write *about* evil or misdeeds, without glamorizing or becoming implicated *in* them. The announcement of Faulkner's nomination for the Nobel Prize was met with similar doubts and dismay in certain circles. Faulkner's local newspaper, *The Jackson Daily News*, for example, denounced the new Nobel Laureate as: 'The propagandist of degradation [who] properly belongs to the privy school of literature.'[18]

Even Gustaf Hellström's Presentation Speech, given at the Nobel ceremony, juxtaposed Faulkner with winners from a previous era to emphasize the bleakness of his personal, aesthetic and wider social vision:

> Faulkner's setting is so much darker and more bloody than that against which Lagerlöf's cavaliers and Bergman's bizarre figures lived...Faulkner's novels are a continuous and ever-deepening description of this painful process, which he knows intimately and feels intensely, coming as he does from a family which was forced to swallow the bitter fruits of defeat right down to their worm-eaten cores: impoverishment, decay, degeneration.[19]

The fusion of biographical and fictional contexts here is linked through a distinctly earthy cluster of images of digestion and decay. The Presentation Speech was underpinned by an implicit interrogation of how a man famous for writing about 'degenerate aberrations'[20] of the disabled, insane, dying and dishonest, could possibly be described as producing literature of an idealistic nature. Hellström depicts Faulkner as a psychologically scarred figure. He suggests that Faulkner's own fantasy of disability (the false story of his wartime injury that he had clung to since his youth) was central to the development of both his character and narrative style:

> When he was twenty he entered the Canadian Royal Air force, crashed twice, and returned home, not as a military hero but as a physically and psychically war-damaged youth with dubious prospects, who for some years faced a precarious existence.[21]

Once again, a sense of imperfection and brutal realism intrudes upon any notion of either Faulkner's life or writing as ideal in a conventional sense. Blotner, Faulkner's biographer, proposes a further incompatibility: between the hopefulness of Faulkner's speech and the portraits of misery in many of his novels. He phrases his question bluntly, highlighting what he perceives as the incongruity between the tone of Faulkner's fiction and his critical voice: 'How could he say that man would prevail, he whose works seemed to some principally a chronicle of failure, anguish and despair?'[22]

This reading, like many other critical readings of the Nobel lecture,[23] focuses on the final lines of the lecture when Faulkner offers a chink of hope amid his apocalyptic imagery:

> It is [the poet's] privilege to help man endure by lifting his heart ... The poet's voice need not merely be the record of man, it can be one of the props, the pillars to help him endure and prevail. (120)

Blotner suggests that the shift in Faulkner's language at this climactic point in the speech, from the individual to the universal, the specific 'man' to the abstract 'mankind', from misery to hope, reflects Faulkner's sense of the need to 'do the right thing'[24] at the Nobel Prize ceremony. The justification for the literary that Faulkner offers here, as possessing a transformative power and a tangible benefit to mankind, perhaps highlights his consciousness of the need to 'us[e] this moment as a pinnacle from which I might be listened to'[25] or at least a desire to justify his $30,171 prize money. Faulkner's initial refusal to attend the ceremony, his feverish symptoms, nervousness and request for speech coaching beforehand, as well as the rushed delivery of the speech itself, certainly suggest that he found the occasion an intimidating pinnacle of public exposure and media attention.

However, on a textual level, the notion of the ideal explored in Faulkner's Nobel Prize lecture as a whole is far more complex and varied than this widespread critical consensus, led by Blotner, suggests. Rather than advocating a set of nostalgic, disembodied ideals, or simply adhering to a depersonalized script of what the Swedish Academy might hope to hear, Faulkner's speech is deeply rooted in both the specific historical moment in which he was living and a powerful sense of the body. Read in context, Faulkner's Nobel address in fact displays an intense preoccupation with the physical: 'Our tragedy today is a general and universal physical fear so long sustained by now that we can even bear it' (119).

Faulkner suggests that, in the Cold War, post-nuclear setting in which he was writing, the spiritual is always mediated (and even eclipsed by) pressing material anxieties: 'There are no longer problems of the spirit. There is only the question: When will I be blown up?' (119). Instead of transcendent detachment or abstraction, Faulkner's perspective is deeply engaged in the material; he depicts his contemporary American context as an unstable world which constantly confronts readers (and authors) with the fragility of the body and the possibility of disability, or even annihilation.

This striking physicality also extends to Faulkner's depiction of the writing process itself. In his opening paragraph, Faulkner describes the act of writing as an inescapably embodied and physically arduous activity: 'A life's work in the agony and sweat of the human spirit' (119). At the end of the second paragraph, Faulkner echoes this description, suggesting that physical discomfort, even pain, is a precondition of 'good writing', 'worth the agony and the sweat' (119). Alongside the bodily metaphors, the body of Faulkner himself as author is always distinctly present in this lecture.

The damaged body emerges as an embodied 'reality' in Faulkner's fictional worlds, but also as a central metaphor through which he conceptualizes his own literary endeavour. He calls in the lecture for a return to universal, transcendent, spiritual ideals, 'love and honor and pity and pride and compassion and sacrifice' (120) through the image of a scarred, maimed body which suggests the specific post-war context in which he was speaking. Until a writer re-learns these concerns, Faulkner suggests: 'He labors under a curse. He writes not of love but of lust... worst of all, without pity or compassion. His griefs grieve on no universal bones, leaving no scars' (120). This metaphor is at the centre of Faulkner's redefinition of the ideal. For Faulkner, the recognition and representation of literal and metaphorical, scarred and imperfect bodies lies at the heart of that which writers need to re-learn. Faulkner suggests that the scar can bear witness to a historical memory or act as a record, inscribed on the surface of the body. In his lecture, Faulkner calls for compassion through a commitment to making the damaged body visible in literature and society.

The 'universal regionalism'[26] that, Hellström suggests, characterizes Faulkner's literature, is encapsulated in the interplay between the literal and metaphorical, the individual and the universal, in this metaphor of the damaged body. Faulkner's lecture shifts from individual bodies – the writer's isolated 'agony' and exertion, or the citizen's personal fear of being 'blown up' – to the universal body of the nation that is scarred by poverty, corruption and war. Like Morrison and Coetzee, Faulkner employs the disabled body as a wide-ranging metaphor but at the same time draws attention to the specificity of this body and its deviation from an ideal form, through the focus on scars. As in Pinter's lecture, the wider 'dignity of man'[27] is explored through metaphors of a suffering body.

The note of nostalgia so often identified in Faulkner's lecture is, in fact, quite complex: Faulkner does not idealize a *return* to the past, but rather a vision of the present in which enduring, damaged bodies are recognized and re-membered. The scar metaphor suggests a wider sense in which the skin becomes a 'site of metaphorical mediations'[28] but also a mode of mediating between inside and outside, past and present.

Through this emphasis on the surface of the body and the scar in particular, Faulkner prefigures an interest in the skin as a site of mediation in later critical writing.[29] In her analysis of 'epidermis'[30] modes of Modernist writing, Maud Ellmann suggests that the inseparability of the material and the metaphorical is encapsulated in the image of a scar: 'In the scar language and violence, the broken story and the broken flesh reveal themselves as inextricable from one another.'[31] Faulkner's employment of the scar as a metaphor in his Nobel Prize address recalls his depiction of Donald Mahon's shocking facial disfigurement in *Soldier's Pay*. In both the novel and the lecture, the scars, mediated by the language of the speaker or narrator, are also linked to a wider sense of visceral, physical vulnerability in the aftermath of war.

The scar, and the skin in general, also provide models for thinking about the role played by metaphor itself. Ellmann argues that metaphors of the skin are essential to our understanding of how identities and social relations are mediated: 'Our metaphors reveal the centrality of skin to our ideas of self and other: we speak of being "in touch" or "in contact" with our friends, of "rubbing" them the wrong way or "handling" them with kid gloves.'[32] These examples suggest that, like skin itself, metaphor is not merely a superficial overlay that can be stripped away from the main body of the text. Steven Connor explores the reciprocity of this relationship: he considers metaphors that involve skin but also ways in which skin resembles metaphor. He describes 'the contemporary fascination with the powers of the skin, as substance, vehicle and metaphor' (9), 'the skin is the ground against which the other senses figure: it is their milieu' (27). The skin as a kind of 'common sense' (27) provides, like metaphor, a point of contact, mediating interior experience into the public sphere.

For Faulkner, Coetzee and Morrison, the skin is represented as a literal surface but also employed as a metaphor and a site of memory. In Coetzee's Nobel Prize lecture, Robin, the author figure who spends his days scribbling down stories in his waterfront room, is described as:

> Getting on in years, [it] almost might be said he is an old man by now. The skin of his face, that had been almost blackened by the tropic sun ... [is] still leathery like parchment.[33]

Here, the skin is figured as a writing surface, upon which, as in Faulkner's lecture, a record of his own personal history is inscribed. The wrinkles and blackening of the skin act as the only physical markers of his experiences as a castaway. The body, bound up with the act of writing, becomes the central point of reference here. Faulkner's depiction of the scar in his Nobel Prize lecture can also be read in the context of Morrison's notion of 'skin memory'. In *Love* (2005), Heed's failing memory is linked to the decreasing sensitivity of her skin to touch: 'What troubled Heed ... was the loss of skin memory' (77). Without the skin to mediate between herself and the outside world, between present and past events, Heed becomes increasingly isolated. In contrast to flexible, youthful Junior, 'whose flesh was accumulating its own sexual memories like tattoos' (78), Heed has to massage her hands in an attempt to stimulate her memory:

> Lotioning her hands, trying to flex her fingers, move them apart, examining the familiar scar tissue on the back of her hand, Heed revisited the scene of the accident. (80)

Here, skin memory becomes a trigger for storytelling: 'Until recently that was all she remembered of the scene – the burn. Thirty years later, lotioning her hands, she remembered more ...' (82). As in Faulkner's Nobel Prize address, the scar functions as a point of intersection between past and present, material and metaphorical modes of knowledge.

The notion of skin as a permeable boundary or 'a double-sided entity'[34] provides a conceptual model for the constant shifting between literal and metaphorical damaged bodies in Faulkner's Nobel Prize lecture. For Elizabeth Grosz:

> The body provides a point of mediation between what is perceived as purely internal and accessible only to the subject and what is external and publicly observable, a point from which to rethink the opposition between the inside and the outside.[35]

Metaphors of the body, such as the scar in Faulkner's lecture, can offer a similar redefinition of boundaries. Instead of a strict boundary between literal and metaphorical, figures that have both literal and metaphorical significance suggest that language and the body are mutually implicated and inseparable from each other. If metaphor is defined, according to Ellmann as ' "the unknown at hand" (the tenor) conveyed by the "known far away" (the vehicle)'[36] then metaphors of the body can provide a shared point of contact, through which to comprehend or remember alien experiences, such as war. Faulkner's Nobel Prize lecture invites consideration of the relationship between disability and metaphor, as he suggests that scars on the skin can allow a mode of accessing unknown and forgotten pasts buried in the unseen interior, through the visible markings on the exterior of the body.

Blindness and insight: Morrison's Nobel Prize lecture

In Morrison's Nobel Prize lecture, which takes the form of a short story-like narrative of an encounter between a wise old woman and a group of young people, the hardening of bodily boundaries is associated with paralyzing 'dead language'.[37] Their exchange revolves around a debate about whether language can be understood as a living entity. The skin, a potentially signifying surface, is figured as a hardened empty shell that blocks communication. Morrison employs an armour metaphor in her attack against:

> Official language smitheryed to sanction ignorance and preserve privilege is a suit of armor polished to a shocking glitter, a husk from which the knight departed long ago.[38]

This is a hollow form, she suggests, an 'evacuated language',[39] emptied out of meaning with only a deceptive outer shell remaining. In her influential extended essay, *Illness as Metaphor* (1978), Susan Sontag suggests that metaphor can be conceptualized as a similarly evacuated form of language. Like Morrison's notion of a hardened outer layer of armour surrounding certain types of language, Sontag argues that 'disease is encumbered with the trappings of metaphor'.[40] She calls for metaphor to be stripped away, like removing a layer of skin or metal, from the main body of language that we use to describe the experience of illness: 'My point is that illness is not a metaphor, and that the most truthful way of regarding illness ... is one most purified of, most resistant to metaphoric thinking' (3).

Morrison's Nobel Prize lecture, structured around blindness and insight and the notion of a 'bird in the hand', demonstrates this constant interplay between the literal and the metaphorical in her writing. The initial encounter between the old woman and the children depicts a confrontation between literal and metaphorical, scientific and folkloric modes of thinking. The young people who visit the blind 'rural prophet' are 'bent on disproving her clairvoyance . . . showing her up for the fraud they believe she is'[41] by asking her to identify whether the bird that they are holding is dead or alive. Instead of answering directly, the old woman redefines the nature of the question itself. Her blindness renders all of the external markers of identity redundant, yet paradoxically sharpens her interior vision of the dilemma at the heart of the encounter:

> She still doesn't answer. She is blind and cannot see her visitors, let alone what is in their hands. She does not know their color, gender or homeland. She knows only their motive.[42]

Disability, in the form of the old woman's blindness, is at the centre of Morrison's lecture, as both a central metaphor but also a physical reality. The fairytale opening to the lecture, which begins 'once upon a time',[43] invites a series of mythological and folkloric associations, such as the parallel with the blind 'seer' Thérèse, a re-written female Tiresias from Morrison's own novel, *Tar Baby*.[44] Yet, at the same time, Morrison insists upon the specific, physical limitations of the old woman: she cannot see her visitors, let alone what is in their hands. Her wisdom, it seems, lies not in her uncanny capacity to predict the future, but rather in her ability to recognize the limits of her own knowledge and the possibilities created by her dialogic interaction with the younger generation. She insists: 'I don't know whether the bird you are holding is dead or alive, but what I do know is that it is in your hands. It is in your hands.'[45] This sense of the bird and the responsibility for its life, death or even imagined existence in *your* hands echoes throughout the Nobel Prize lecture, implicating the audience as well as the listening children.

The potential for a metaphorical reading, implied by the old woman's advice to the children, is extended by the omniscient narrator. The short-story structure and tone of the lecture is momentarily ruptured by a self-conscious, critical intervention by the omniscient narrator:

> So I choose to read the bird as language and the woman as a practiced writer . . . Being a writer she thinks of language . . . partly as a living

thing over which one has control, but mostly as agency – as an act with consequences.[46]

In contrast to the reductive literalism of the children, who are concerned only with taunting the old woman, the bird as metaphor becomes the vehicle for the narrator's extended critique of oppressive and 'policing languages of mastery'.[47] In this way Morrison links language and the bird, suggesting that both are living entities, and employs metaphor to open up many shifting narrative and critical possibilities.

The question of Morrison's own voice as lecturer and laureate is thrown into doubt by the multiplicity of voices and modes of knowledge in the lecture. From the outset, the narrative turns in on itself, expressing sceptical self-abnegation and assertion in equal quantities: 'Once upon a time there was an old woman ... Or was it an old man?'[48] Morrison refuses any fixed temporal or geographical grounding for the narrative, highlighting its place in an oral tradition: 'I have heard this story, or one exactly like it, in the lore of several cultures.'[49] We, as listeners or readers, are implicated in the process of construction, forced to choose which of the many threads to follow, and how to read the complex metaphorical significance of the bird. Our experience of the story, we are reminded, is always mediated by linguistic instabilities and the possibility of being tricked: 'Suppose nothing was in their hands? Suppose the visit was only a ruse?'[50] As Dwight McBride in his commentary on the speech suggests: 'No one is let off the hook in this scenario. All necks are on the line.'[51] Like the old woman, the audience is confronted with that which it does not know.

Even language itself, according to the narrator's description, can become implicated in a metaphorical condition of disability. Morrison employs disability as a metaphor in the attack on racist, sexist forms of language that silence certain marginalized groups. Disability is employed in a negative sense here, functioning as a figure for social paralysis and linguistic impotence:

> In her country children have bitten their tongues off and use bullets instead to iterate the voice of speechlessness, of disabled and disabling language, or language adults have abandoned altogether as a device for grappling with meaning.[52]

This symbolic silencing of oppressed groups is coupled with a distinct, shocking, self-inflicted physical impairment: 'Children have bitten their tongues off.'[53] Their condition of speechlessness is simultaneously physical and metaphorical. Yet, Morrison's lecture also explores the potential for silence, in certain circumstances, to provoke productive, dialogic communication. The old woman's silence gives the young people, often 'trivialized'[54] by wider society, a chance to speak, think and imagine for themselves:

> Nothing, no word follows her declaration of transfer. That silence is deep, deeper than the meaning available in the words she has spoken. It shivers, this silence, and the children, annoyed, fill it with language invented on the spot.[55]

Even at the end of the lecture, therefore, many possibilities are simultaneously suggested: for language to act as a paralysing force, 'blocking access to cognition', yet also to liberate: 'word-work is sublime...because it is generative'.[56] Blindness, mediated through the perception of the children, shifts from being 'a difference they regard as a profound disability' to an enabling mark of distinction: 'You, old woman, blessed with blindness.'[57] Perhaps most significant of all is the shift from an antagonistic confrontation at the beginning of the lecture, to a mutual cooperation and appreciation between the generations. Morrison's final line hints towards the ideal of an on-going process of 'grappling with meaning'[58] but also a fundamentally collaborative aesthetic:

> 'Finally,' she says, 'I trust you now. I trust you with the bird that is not in your hands because you have truly caught it. Look. How lovely it is, this thing we have done – together.'[59]

Here, Morrison foregrounds an act of collaborative creation through dialogue; she emphasizes the potential for narrative to transmit wisdom but also returns us to the earlier notion of the bird, language and responsibility 'in your hands'.[60] As in Faulkner's Nobel Prize lecture, this emphasis on skin and the surface of the body, as metaphor and point of possible mediation, means that touch supplants vision as the primary mode of knowledge at the end of the lecture. The children ask the old woman: 'Why didn't you reach out, touch us with your soft fingers, delay the sound bite, the lesson, until you knew who we were?'[61]

This emphasis on touch is also played out in the final lines of Morrison's novel, *Jazz*, published just a year before Morrison was awarded the Nobel Prize for Literature. Like Morrison's destabilizing narratorial intervention in her Nobel lecture, the narrator in *Jazz* shatters any fantasy of objective detachment on the last page of the novel, with a direct address:

> I love the way you hold me, how close you let me be to you … If I were able I'd say it. Say make me, remake me. You are free to do it and I am free to let you because look, look. Look where your hands are. Now. (229)

Here, the narrator expresses a sense of loneliness and envy at the erotic, intimate touches shared by the lovers depicted in the novel, but also draws attention to the reader's hand as it holds the book itself.

For Katherine Stern, this pivotal moment encapsulates a set of aesthetic and ethical ideals for Morrison: 'A perfect example of the beauty of imagined touch … an ethical-aesthetic innovation which draws our attention to anyone's body, rather than to any one body' (91). The interplay that Stern describes between 'one body' and 'anyone's body' is reminiscent of the shifting between the individual and the 'universal body'[62] in Faulkner's Nobel Prize lecture, and also directly echoes Morrison's own Nobel address. Both *Jazz* and Morrison's lecture end with a call to look at that which we hold in our hands. Whereas the book that the reader holds in *Jazz* is a tangible, physical presence, the existence of the bird at the end of the lecture retains its ambiguous, metaphorical status. Morrison presents us with the paradoxical struggle to capture a meaning or a concept that we can never quite grasp.

Like Faulkner's sense of himself momentarily at the pinnacle of his critical influence and literary powers in his Nobel Prize lecture, Morrison shows a distinct awareness of the significance of this moment in defining her wider academic project and aesthetic vision. In the anecdote that she chose to tell in her short Nobel banquet speech she returns, once more, to the image of holding responsibility in one's hands:

> Early in October an artist friend left a message which I kept on the answering service for weeks … 'My dear sister,' she said, 'the prize that is yours is also ours and could not have been placed in better hands.'[63]

Like the children, blind woman, narrator, readers and listeners, Morrison suggests that she herself is also implicated in this literary and ethical imperative to investigate and employ language both responsibly and imaginatively. The Nobel Prize, she reflects, is something that she holds temporarily in her hands, in trust for future generations of authors.

The instruction at the end of *Jazz*, to 'make' and 're-make' (229) that which we hold in our hands, therefore extends to Morrison's wider sense of language as a material which can be moulded, polished and handled. Morrison's Nobel banquet speech acknowledges 'the company of Laureates yet to come. Those who, even as I speak, are mining, sifting and polishing languages.'[64] Metaphor, Morrison suggests, cannot be dispensed with, but rather must be dismantled and remade. The wisdom of the blind woman, and her story, brings the children to a revelation about the necessary role of language, and metaphor in particular, as a mediator of experience:

> You, old woman, blessed with blindness, can speak the language that tells us what only language can: how to see without pictures. Language alone protects us from the scariness of things with no names. Language alone is mediation.[65]

In this sense, language, like blindness, provides an escape from exclusively visual modes of knowledge. Blindness is perceived as a blessing by the end of the lecture in that it enables this insight. Their claim that metaphor can allow access to experiences and concepts 'with no names'[66] resonates with a contemporary resurgence of critical interest in metaphor[67] as a potential means of articulating unspeakable experiences. Like literary representations of disability, metaphor has often been perceived as liminal. In fact, as George Lakoff and Mark Johnson argue, metaphors are central to our entire conceptual system[68] but also provide an enabling perspective through which to envisage abstract and unknown experiences: 'conceptual metaphor is one of the greatest of our intellectual gifts'.[69]

At first glance, Morrison's *Playing in the Dark* (1992) appears to exemplify the arguments made by both Sontag and many early disability studies texts about the destructive, seductive power of metaphor and its tendency to 'flatten'[70] the complex and diverse lived experience of disability.[71] In her exploration of the treatment of race as a metaphor in American literature, Morrison identifies the potentially oppressive 'literary techniques of othering' (58) that are highly applicable to the treatment of *any* minority group:

> Estranging language, metaphoric condensation, fetishizing strategies, the economy of stereotype, allegorical foreclosure; strategies employed to secure ... characters' (and readers') identities. (58)

Her attacks on the reductive, stereotypical and exclusively metaphorical uses of race, in which 'symbolic figurations of blackness are markers for the benevolent and the wicked; the spiritual ... and the voluptuous' (xi), provide a model for similar critiques of disability as a metaphor in disability studies writing. Jenny Morris, for example, argues that female disability has frequently been employed as a reductive 'metaphor for vulnerability'[72] in the modern visual media. Garland Thomson, focusing on twentieth-century American literature, suggests that 'the modernist gargoyle is the physically disabled figure, a metaphor for depravity, despair, and perversion ... Depoliticized and aestheticized'.[73]

However, Morrison's attacks are directed at 'metaphorical shortcuts' (xii) in which the metaphor becomes static, relying upon 'shorthand, the taken-for-granted assumptions that lie in their usage' (xii). In fact, the main point of intersection between Morrison's *Playing in the Dark* and Sontag's *Illness as Metaphor* lies in Sontag's call for 'an elucidation of ... metaphors' (3). In contrast to Sontag, Morrison's project is centred not on a dismissal (or stripping away) of metaphor, but rather an exploration of how metaphorical processes work in social and literary spheres. Metaphor, she suggests, is not only a necessary part of literary representation, but also crucial to the formation of identity: 'race has assumed a metaphorical life ... completely embedded in daily discourse' (63). Here, Morrison differs from other African American critics in this period, such as Hortense Spillers, who calls for a rejection of race-inflected discourses: 'In order to speak a truer word concerning myself, I must strip down through the layers of attenuated meanings.'[74] In contrast, Morrison argues that racial metaphors are constitutive of American identity. *Playing in the Dark* outlines a critical ideal in which metaphor is not dispensed with but, instead, scrutinized and redefined:

> I remain convinced that metaphorical and metaphysical uses of race occupy definitive places in American literature, in the 'national' character, and ought to be a major concern of the literary scholarship that tries to know it. (63)

Morrison suggests that Sontag's ideal of 'a liberation from metaphor' (3) is not only impossible but is also fundamentally undesirable. *Playing in the Dark*, written just one year before she became the ninetieth Nobel Laureate in 1993, establishes Morrison's commitment to an engagement with controversial, constitutive metaphors, as a politicized and *necessary* part of literary and social life.

Writing ten years after the publication of *Illness as Metaphor*, in *Aids and its Metaphors* (1988), Sontag revised her position to take account of this more nuanced understanding of metaphor. She qualifies her earlier rejection of metaphor, yet retains the core of her argument:

> Rereading *Illness as Metaphor* now, I thought: of course, one cannot think without metaphors. But that does not mean there aren't some metaphors we might well abstain from or try to retire. As, of course, all thinking is interpretation. But this doesn't mean that it is not sometimes correct to be 'against' interpretation. (91)

By contrast, Morrison's Nobel Prize lecture constitutes precisely such an invitation to interpret, for the children and the audience. Throughout her writing, Sontag defines metaphor in an Aristotelian sense, as a kind of deviant misnaming: 'metaphor...consists in giving the thing a name that belongs to something else' (91). Morrison's employment of metaphor in her Nobel Prize lecture appears more in keeping with Lakoff and Johnson's more wide-ranging understanding of the term as a potentially enabling relational perspective: 'The essence of metaphor is understanding and experiencing one kind of thing in terms of another.'[75] Morrison's project of remoulding language is linked to a reappropriation of metaphors.

Like Faulkner, Morrison uses her Nobel Prize lecture to challenge conventional understandings of the ideal on both a linguistic and bodily level. Morrison does not aim to find one fixed language or one fixed metaphor to explain experience, but rather a shifting constellation of metaphors and a network of meanings. At the climax of her lecture, Morrison offers a typically re-written version of paradise, through an alternative version of the Tower of Babel story:

> Perhaps the achievement of Paradise was premature, a little hasty if no one could take the time to understand other languages...Complicated, demanding, yes, but a view of heaven as life; not heaven as post-life.[76]

Unlike Sontag's aim to 'calm the imagination',[77] Morrison expresses a commitment to multilingualism, multiple metaphors and the 'complicated, demanding'[78] yet enriching process of interpretation throughout the Nobel Prize lecture. Through her fusion of narrative and lecture forms, she calls for a reinvigoration of critical vocabularies and suggests that 'metaphor [can] create new meaning, create similarities, and thereby define a new reality'.[79]

Speaking the unspeakable: Coetzee and the necessity of metaphor

In his critical writing, Coetzee explores a fascination with the workings of metaphor. His training in linguistics provides the basis for his critical analysis, which takes the constitutive nature of metaphor in language and thought as a point of departure. In an early essay, 'Isaac Newton and the Ideal of a Transparent Scientific Language' (1986) Coetzee acknowledges a critical trend in scientific writing that parallels Sontag's project of stripping away metaphor: 'The overall movement in modern science has been toward a language purged of metaphoric content.'[80] Yet, Coetzee immediately counters this view by suggesting the importance of metaphor in conveying certain concepts and modes of understanding:

> Some metaphors are, as Richard Boyd points out, 'constitutive of the bodies of theories that they express, rather than merely exegetical'...We may thus properly ask whether a metaphor-free language in which anything significant or new can be said is attainable. (193)

Coetzee, like Faulkner and Morrison, interrogates the notion of the 'ideal' through his critical writing. He not only challenges the 'classically inherited conception of language as a transparent medium for thought' (181) but also suggests that even 'the ideal creature, the fully bilingual person' must, nevertheless, 'live at any given moment within one or the other of his languages' (182). For Coetzee, in this early essay at least, there is no way out of language as a 'circle, a closed system' (182).

This fascination with the metaphorical potential of language, and its relation to the disabling condition of speechlessness, is explored in Coetzee's Nobel Prize lecture (2003). The problematic nature of any ideal of a transparent language, either scientific or literary, connects Coetzee's critical viewpoint to the anxieties expressed in Pinter's Nobel Prize lecture. At the climactic moment of the lecture, Pinter shatters any such mimetic fantasy, in a call for ethical and political action:

> When we look into a mirror we think the image that confronts us is accurate. But move a millimetre and the image changes. We are actually looking at a never-ending range of reflections. But sometimes a writer has to smash the mirror – for it is on the other side of the mirror that the truth stares at us.[81]

The press release from the Swedish Academy that accompanied Coetzee's nomination for the Nobel Prize employs a similar vocabulary of mirrors and reflections, to describe a diametrically opposite effect:

> Coetzee's interest is directed mainly at situations where the distinction between right and wrong, while crystal clear, can be seen to serve no end. Like the man in the famous Magritte painting who is studying his neck in a mirror, at the decisive moment Coetzee's characters stand behind themselves, motionless, incapable of taking part in their own actions.[82]

Whereas Pinter urges action, the Swedish Academy suggests here that Coetzee's work is characterized by an endless, paralysing chain of reflections. The simile of 'the man in the famous Magritte painting' suggests a layering of representation and aesthetic frameworks, even within a single text. Pinter's call for citizens to 'smash' the mirror directly contracts with Coetzee's distinctly literary figures: 'motionless', mesmerized by their reflections, politically and ethically impotent. While the Swedish Academy's gloss on Coetzee's work does not provide a definitive description of his complex oeuvre, and perhaps expresses the Academy's own desire to maintain the apolitical reputation of the prize, the statement does provide a useful point of contrast. Coetzee's focus on the process of representation itself, and his assertion that 'all definition is, of course, a displacement',[83] suggests that this act of standing behind a reflection of oneself becomes incorporated into Coetzee's critical and narrative technique.

In contrast to the first-person position adopted by Pinter throughout his Nobel Prize speech, Coetzee's performances as a lecturer are frequently mediated through a fictional persona. *Elizabeth Costello: Eight Lessons*, published in 2003 immediately prior to the announcement of Coetzee's Nobel Prize, consisted of a 'series of meta-generic lectures...the volume incorporates respondents to, or "critics" of, Costello/Coetzee'.[84] The parallels between Costello and Coetzee himself, as white South African writers now living in Australia, are obvious, as is the echoing (or warped reflection) of their similar names. Less widely recognized is Costello's role in *Eight Lessons* as both a lecturer *and* an audience member. In Lesson Five, 'The Humanities in Africa', Elizabeth attends a lecture given by her sister, Blanche, in which she accepts an honorary degree.[85] As in Morrison's Nobel Prize lecture, the mutually implicating roles of listener and speaker are emphasized here, as the actual audience members attending the lecture are incorporated into the fictional frame.

As both a listener and a speaker, Costello expresses her frustration with the lecture form itself. For Coetzee, the choice to mediate his lectures through this fictional framework creates a destabilizing effect, notably in the prestigious Tanner Lectures at Princeton in 1998, where he introduced his fictional persona of Costello for the first time. Yet, this ambiguous form also suggests Coetzee's sense that displacement is necessarily at the heart of *any* literary narrative. This intellectual and critical 'non position[ality]'[86] resonates with Coetzee's consistent (and much-criticized) refusal to be politically positioned as a public intellectual throughout the Apartheid regime in South Africa. Yet, the fictional characters that Coetzee creates to mediate these performances are perhaps no less artificial (or indeed dishonest) than the public persona adopted by any Nobel Prize winner for the performance of the Nobel lecture.

In the Nobel Prize lecture, the 'fiction-as-lecture'[87] format of *Elizabeth Costello* is replaced with what initially appears to be a short story style narrative (as in Morrison's Nobel Prize lecture) but gradually emerges as a series of ambiguous reports *of* reports. Once again the process of displacement and the layering of different aesthetic frameworks are central to Coetzee's technique. Coetzee, like Morrison, begins his Nobel Prize lecture with the image of a bird. Coetzee's image is not of a conventional duck, but rather a hybrid representation of a wild bird, a semi-comic 'duckoy'. The narrator 'Robin', named after a bird himself and a shortened form of 'Robinson', explains:

> The fens are home to many other kinds of birds too, writes his man, duck and mallard...to capture which the men of the fens, the fen-men, raise tame ducks, which they call decoy ducks or duckoys.[88]

The linguistic play here, with the internal rhyme 'fen-men' and punning on 'decoy' creates a sense of absurdity which punctures the formality of the Nobel ceremony. Coetzee employs this opening report as, in itself, a kind of decoy. It is the first of many narrative tricks in a Nobel lecture that disrupts interpretation and shifts attention away from its own author as an object of scrutiny.

The notion of a decoy, or indeed a 'duckoy', is incorporated into the narrative structure and characterizes Coetzee's use of metaphor throughout the lecture. The reportage structure acts as a kind of decoy, distracting attention away from the question of the actual identities of either the narrator or the report-writer. The beginning of the lecture suggests that the anonymous writer of the reports, 'his man',[89] is Friday. The opening quotation from Defoe's *Robinson Crusoe* sets up this expectation, as Coetzee selects a passage in which Crusoe expresses his 'delight' at his 'new companion'.[90] As in Morrison's lecture, listeners are distinctly aware that this is a story that has been told in various places by many different authors, including Coetzee himself in his fictional reworking of the novel, *Foe* (1986). Attridge describes this initial trick that the title of the lecture, 'He and His Man', sets up:

> 'He and His Man' begins with a quotation from *Robinson Crusoe* – which misleads the hearer or reader into thinking that the title refers to Crusoe and Friday – but then plunges into a report of a report.[91]

In this sense, Coetzee uses the listeners' own knowledge of intertextual references in the lecture (such as Defoe's *Tour through the Whole Island of Great Britain*, 1726–6, and *Robinson Crusoe*, 1719, but also Coetzee's *Foe*) against the audience, raising expectations only in order to subvert them. The opening of the lecture, which depicts an anonymous writer hunched over his work in a rented room, conjures up a scene from Coetzee's *Foe*, in which Friday is seated at a desk, writing reports:

> The man seated at the table was not Foe. It was Friday, with Foe's robes on his back and Foe's wig...on his head. In his hand, poised over Foe's papers, he held a quill with a drop of black ink glistening at its tip.[92]

Friday, tongueless and apparently silenced for ever, initially seems to be able to communicate through report-writing. In the novel, this is always left ambiguous: the section that follows the scene of Friday writing is never attributed to a specific narrator. In the Nobel lecture, Friday is denied a voice of any kind. Instead, Friday's mutilated disabled body becomes the unspoken presence that haunts the entire speech.

As the lecture develops, it emerges that the dynamic is more complex: Defoe is apparently sending reports to Crusoe. Yet, 'his man'[93] doing the reporting is in fact a projection of Crusoe's imagination, as he sits drinking and scribbling in the *Jolly Tar* on the Bristol waterfront. This fantasy figure who 'gallops about the kingdom making his inspections'[94] acts as a kind of decoy, allowing Crusoe to displace his own identity (and imagined narratives) onto a fictional persona. The dialectical structure of reporting established between 'Him and his Man' enables Crusoe to write. Once again, the notion of authenticity, of what is faux/Foe, is constantly called into question by the lecture, as in the case of the 'duckoys'.

Through this layering of ambiguous authorship, Coetzee mocks the act of complex, confusing critical interpretation that it triggers; he parodies the tendency to read a metaphorical, personal significance into the most physical and material of situations. This tendency is particularly evident in critical receptions of Friday in *Foe*. Lewis McLeod summarizes: 'Attridge uses "Friday's tonguelessness [as] the sign of his oppression"... Spivak uses "Friday's loss" to distinguish between different understandings of marginality.'[95] McLeod goes on to explore how critical templates of colonialism and power relations have been mapped onto *Foe*, reducing Friday's mutilated body to a symbol. Friday, he suggests, has been read not as a disabled character depicted with a distinct physical impairment, but merely as a metaphor for a wider post-colonial condition of speechlessness: 'The postcolonial critic wants a tongueless Friday because of the critical opportunities such a character would provide' (6). In this case, these critics are guilty of the kind of 'metaphoric opportunism'[96] that is widely condemned in disability studies texts of this period.

In the Nobel Prize lecture, Friday occupies a similar position of paradoxical absent presence. He is arbitrarily edited out of the story, on the whim of yet another bird, a speaking parrot:

> The years in the island and then the years travelling with his serving-man Friday (poor Friday, he laments to himself, squawk-squawk, for the parrot would never speak Friday's name, only his), had made the life of a landed gentleman dull for him.[97]

Friday's speechlessness leads the other to tell, or refuse to tell, his story. Moreover, this critical tendency to read a metaphorical status into any event is exaggerated to the point of absurdity in Coetzee's Nobel Prize lecture. The most physical of situations, a palsy or a plague, are read by Crusoe as a metaphor for his own predicament: previously shipwrecked on the island and now isolated as a writer. For example, the narrator reads a report of the sudden change in fortunes for a merchant:

> The Thames rises one winter, the kilns in which the tiles are baked are washed away... [A]ll of this – the wave of water, the ruin, the flight,

the pennilessness, the tatters, the solitude – *let all of this be a figure* of the shipwreck and the island where he, poor Robin, was secluded from the world for twenty-six years.[98]

This tendency towards metaphorical reading of events, to 'let all of this be a figure', is repeated frequently throughout the lecture. Later, in response to a gruesome report of a man buried alive amid plague-ridden dead bodies, the narrator clings to these reductive, highly personal metaphorical readings: '*But am I dead then?* says the man. And this too is a figure of him on his island.'[99]

Even in this most bodily of reports, the material becomes eclipsed by the metaphorical when mediated through Crusoe's perspective. The failure to comprehend the bodily *alongside* the metaphorical, Coetzee suggests, creates a set of bizarre (mis)readings and a kind of 'madness' of writerly solitude. Coetzee frequently returns to the potential for language to be rendered nonsensical through endless, meaningless repetition, such as in the case of Crusoe's parrot who constantly chants: 'Poor Poll!'[100]

Yet, the narrator then shifts to consider a more nuanced understanding of the role of metaphor, not as a distracting decoy but instead as a potential means of accessing unspeakable experiences and bodies. Significantly, it is through a bodily image that this realization is articulated. Initially, the narrator likens plagiarism to cannibalism, in an image that once again recalls Friday (and the accusations of cannibalism made against him in *Foe*):

> When the first bands of plagiarists and imitators descended upon his island history and foisted on the public their own feigned stories of the castaway life, they seemed to him ... a horde of cannibals falling upon his own flesh ... *figures* ... *that would gnaw at the very substance of truth*.[101]

This act of metaphorically feasting on the story of another implies a further, grotesque cycle of regurgitation in the constant retelling of the castaway narrative, in both the Nobel lecture and *Foe*. Coetzee draws on a common analogy between the corporeal body and the body of a text, yet he also shifts this figure onto a fleshy, bloody, literal level. However, the narrator's perspective shifts to view this cycle as a potentially productive one, necessary for communication and the preservation of certain narratives between generations:

But now, reflecting further, there begins to creep into his breast a touch of fellow-feeling for his imitators. For it seems to him now that there are but a handful of stories in the world; and if the young are to be forbidden to prey upon the old then they must sit forever in silence.[102]

As in Morrison's Nobel Prize lecture, we are returned to the question of the role of narrative and acts of storytelling in mediating relations between the young and the old. The question of what is literal or metaphorical, authentic or fraudulent is subordinate to a creative act of imagining alternative experiences. Coetzee demonstrates a commitment to redefinition and retelling, above authenticity, in ways that draw attention to the details of language but also challenge conventional power relations.[103]

Even in this most excessively figurative of speeches, Coetzee does not allow the body to become lost. As in Faulkner's critical writing, there is an emphasis on the physicality of writing itself. Coetzee frequently returns to scenes of writing: an old man sitting hunched over his desk, writing in 'a neat, quick hand with quills that he sharpens with his little pen-knife'.[104] The end of the lecture is characterized by the sense of a reciprocal relationship between the material and the metaphorical. Once again, this experience is mediated by the body, through a condition of temporary disability in which imaginative and physical perceptions become blurred:

> Only days later did he understand ... he had suffered a palsy of a passing kind, and being unable to move his leg concluded there was some creature stretched out upon it ... Of which the lesson would seem to be that ... a visitation by illness may be figured as a visitation by the devil, or by a dog figuring the devil, and vice versa, the visitation figured as an illness ... and therefore that no one who writes stories of either, the devil or the plague, should forthwith be dismissed as a forger or a thief.[105]

Those who use figures, he suggests, should not be 'dismissed' for forgery or stealing narratives. Instead, he explores how metaphors help us to understand different forms of experience. The narrative turn at the end of the lecture shifts from a cycle of storytelling and absurdity to an appreciation of how metaphor may allow access to unspoken presences in a text. We are returned to the duckoys: 'What did he, Robinson, know of decoy ducks? Nothing at all, until this man of his began sending in reports.'[106] These are not merely coincidental events; the knowledge of the decoy ducks and the sending of reports are actually co-dependent. Crusoe, like Coetzee, confronts the fact that he needs these distracting displacements, the ducks or the fictional veil of 'his man', to enable him to write. Crusoe comes to realize that these figures and fictional techniques are not dispensable or superficial, but they are in fact necessary for the process of creation itself: 'Only when he yields himself up to this man of his do such words come.'[107] Metaphor, Coetzee suggests, is not any more dishonest or fraudulent than realist representation; it is a necessary and enabling tool for the articulation of character and critical interpretation.

Coetzee's Nobel Prize lecture therefore ends with an on-going search for a metaphor through which to articulate the complex relationship between 'Him and His Man'. For McLeod, Friday's speechless condition provides a metaphor for Coetzee's own position as a public figure, on the peripheries of his own lectures:

> Operating under his own procedures, Friday, like Coetzee, both protects and asserts his own story, resisting the persistent demands of an overriding discourse through a much more localized and idiosyncratic form of writing and storytelling. (8)

Yet, the Nobel lecture itself offers no such certainty or closure, ending with a question, an open-ended search for a figure to capture this shifting dynamic between the writer and narrator:

> How are they to be figured, this man and he? As master and slave? As brothers, twin brothers? As comrades in arms? Or as enemies, foes? What name shall he give this nameless fellow with whom he shares his evenings...?[108]

In this sense, the Nobel lecture captures an on-going dilemma on the part of Coetzee, of how to create 'figures' for his own critical persona, such as Robin or Elizabeth Costello. The simultaneously productive and problematic relationship between these figures, of the author and the narrator, of the reports and the unspoken (and unspeakable) experience of Crusoe and Friday on the island, are at the centre of Coetzee's Nobel Prize lecture. His insistence that the bodies he depicts should be read as neither entirely literal nor in exclusively metaphorical terms creates an effect that is destabilizing yet imaginatively generative.

Literature in an ideal direction: compassion and empathetic identification

In their critical writing, Faulkner, Morrison and Coetzee all focus on compassion and the complex process of empathetic identification through their use of disability as a metaphor. The final lines of Faulkner's Nobel lecture emphasize empathy and endurance: '[Man] is immortal because he has a soul, a spirit capable of compassion and sacrifice and endurance' (120).

The presentation speech given by Sture Allén when Morrison was awarded the Nobel Prize suggested that: 'The most enduring impression [Morrison's novels] leave is of empathy, compassion with one's fellow human beings.'[109] Metaphors of disability are central to this attempt to move towards an ideal of empathetic identification in these lectures. The critical emphasis on defining (and redefining) the ideal often ignores the fact that the translation of Nobel's will suggests a process, a movement in a direction towards an ideal. Morrison articulates her aim in a critical language that foregrounds disability:

> I am interested in what prompts and makes possible this process of entering what one is estranged from – and in what disables the foray, for the purposes of fiction, into corners of the consciousness held off and away from the reach of the writer's imagination.[110]

Once again, the sense of a process, of entering, imagining, empathizing, is foregrounded here. Disability, it seems, is precisely one of these points at which imaginative and empathetic identification is pushed to its limits. The complex, diverse lived experience of disability may be that which 'disables' attempts by the able-bodied majority to understand alternative bodies and lives. The press release from the Swedish Academy following the nomination of Coetzee for the Nobel Prize highlights a similar sense of an attempt to understand alternative experiences: 'The capacity for empathy that has enabled Coetzee time and again to creep beneath the skin of the alien and the abhorrent.'[111]

This metaphor of the skin, as a surface that we must aim to get beneath, works slightly differently from Faulkner's focus on the scar or Morrison's emphasis on hands, in which it is the skin itself that becomes the mediator of memory. Yet, all of these representations of the skin suggest that literary narrative may allow a point of mediation between inside and outside, symbolically 'entering what one is estranged from'[112] or creeping beneath the skin to explore other perspectives and experiences.

The final scene of Coetzee's Nobel lecture explores this problem of mediating between two different consciousnesses or concepts. Like Morrison's Nobel Prize lecture, which can be read as a literalization of the 'bird in the hand is worth two in the bush' aphorism, the final section of Coetzee's Nobel lecture takes the saying 'passing like two ships in the night' on a literal level. Coetzee presents a fantasy scene that is at once a metaphor – a figure for the relationship of paradoxical proximity between 'Him and his Man' – but is also imagined as an actual physical confrontation:

> If he must settle on a likeness for the pair of them, his man and he, he would write that they are like two ships sailing in contrary directions... Or better, that they are deckhands... Their ships pass close, close enough to hail. But the seas are rough, the weather is stormy: their eyes lashed by the spray, their hands burned by the cordage, they pass each other by, too busy even to wave.[113]

Here, Coetzee explores the problem of communicating over a divide; the expanse of sea could be read as a gap between consciousnesses, bodies or backgrounds, or the space between the narrator and 'his man', the speaker and the audience. The multi-layered nature of this metaphor suggests a wider slippage between the literal and the many metaphorical levels throughout the Nobel lecture. The problem of mediation that it poses is bound up with the frequent return to metaphor as a mode of accessing or narrating the experience of another. The significance of the face-to-face encounter, a point at which, for Levinas, we are required to confront the incomprehensible nature of the presence of the other, is explored as a potentially ethically and imaginatively productive position:

> The relation with the face, with the other absolutely other which I cannot contain, the other in this sense is infinite... The 'resistance' of the other does not do violence to me, does not act negatively, it has a positive structure: ethical.[114]

Like the uncanny confrontation in *Slow Man*, where Elizabeth Costello is brought face-to-face with Paul Rayment, the man she has written into existence, the final scene of the Nobel Prize lecture explores the problem posed by a fictional persona that 'seems to become increasingly independent of the one who is supposed to be inventing him'.[115] As doubles or fictional personae, Elizabeth Costello and 'his man' constitute, for Coetzee, 'other[s] which I cannot contain'.[116] Yet this uncontainability, the difficulty of linking two similar personae or concepts, is fundamental to the critical challenges that these dramatic lecture performances pose.

The prevalence of disabled, scarred, mutilated bodies in these Nobel Prize lectures reflects a wider commitment to the representation of disability in the fictional writing of these authors, but also suggests that the disabled body is a central metaphor for the articulation of their critical projects. Faulkner, Morrison and Coetzee all delivered their Nobel lectures in later life, when the demands of the body could not be ignored: Morrison, at 62, walked with a stick; Faulkner, though only 52, suffered from poor health, connected to his lifelong alcohol problem. Coetzee, a Nobel laureate at 63, has been famously obsessed with maintaining his physical fitness in his later life, through cycling and healthy vegetarian eating regimes. These 'able-bodied' authors all employ metaphors of disability with a distinct contextual and political awareness, to explore the possibility of storytelling as a mode of mediating between old and young, disabled and non-disabled, or across the divide between *any* two consciousnesses.

In all of these Nobel lectures figurative language is depicted as potentially both paralysing and enabling: Coetzee in particular articulates an awareness of the dangers of reading literary works exclusively in terms of metaphor. This ambiguity is encapsulated in Denver's shifting relationship to language in *Beloved*: 'The last time … words blocked up her ears. Now they opened her mind' (252). Reformulated in a Nobel Prize context, Sutherland also suggests that literary language can be at once liberating and imprisoning: 'Literature's power, like dynamite, depends on those who use it. On "idealism," or the lack of it. One returns to Stockholm's original formulation' (xviii).

Once again, we are brought back to Morrison's recurring, self-implicating image of carrying responsibility both literally and metaphorically 'in your hands'.[117] In all of these lectures, language is depicted as an act with consequences; a raw material that we all hold in our hands which must be remoulded and redefined. Faulkner's Nobel lecture suggests that this *process* of on-going innovation, as well as empathetic imagination, is at the heart of his work 'to create out of the materials of the human spirit something which did not exist before' (119).

For Faulkner, Morrison and Coetzee, metaphor and materiality are inextricably linked: to read disability as a metaphor is not to eclipse its physical implications entirely. Instead, a varied and shifting constellation of literal and metaphorical depictions of the disabled body become central to the way in which all of these authors approach the ethical, narrative and critical problem of how to conceptualize their dual roles as authors and critics, as well as the process of imagining central to writing itself. Through the body, with the skin as a mediating surface and a shared point of reference for all human beings, these writers seek out the possibility of 'a common language...shareable imaginative worlds'.[118] For Faulkner, Morrison and Coetzee, the disabled body emerges as a metaphor that, as both authors and critics, they simply 'cannot do without'.[119]

6
Conclusion: 'You Can't Just Fly on off and Leave a Body'

In Faulkner's last novel, *A Fable* (1954), a military aide describes the play that he has written, a piece of work which he cannot finish: 'A drama...about glory, and how men got it, and how they bore it after they got it...the courage it takes to pity' (707). The aide's play, like the novel itself, is open-ended in structure and addresses the question of how to live on after conventional narrative endings. The enduring bodies and injured soldiers that refuse to be removed from view at the end of the novel highlight Faulkner's compelling exploration of the 'courage it takes to pity'.

Faulkner explores this ambivalent, 'dubious capacity of the...body to endure'[1] throughout his fiction. In *A Fable*, the wounded soldier lives on, disrupting the final memorial scene with his screams of rage and pain. In an earlier short story, 'The Leg' (1934), the protagonist David is haunted by a sense that his amputated limb cannot be laid to rest:

> 'It's my leg,' I said. 'I want you to be sure it's dead...They might bury it and it couldn't lie quiet. And then it would be lost and we couldn't find it to do anything.' (309)

The capacity of the body to endure endows this short fragment with a dubious horror; there is a hallucinatory quality to David's descriptions. This intersection between enduring bodies and the process of empathizing is also identified by Coetzee in his essay on Faulkner:

> Courage and honor and pride: to this litany Ike might have added endurance, as he does elsewhere in the same story...The exemplary figure in *A Fable* is Jesus reincarnated in and re-sacrificed as the unknown soldier; elsewhere in the work he is the simple, suffering

black man or, more often, black woman, who by enduring the unendurable present keeps alive the germ of the future.[2]

For Coetzee, this paradoxical condition of 'enduring the unendurable' suggests a capacity for perseverance that Faulkner demonstrated in his own life. Coetzee cites Joseph Blotner:

> What most impresses about Faulkner as writer is the sheer persistence, the will-to-power that brought him back to the desk each day, year after year ... [His] grit was ... as much physical as mental. (203)

For Coetzee, this fictional focus on enduring bodies offers a 'germ' of hope for the future, as well as representations of on-going pain and suffering.

The motif of two bodies locked together in mutual support and dependency, living on at the end of the novel, recurs in the closing scenes of a number of works by Faulkner, Morrison and Coetzee. In the penultimate scene of *The Sound and the Fury*, Dilsey embraces Benjy, shielding him from Luster's mockery but also offering the maternal care denied to him by his own family: 'Dilsey led Ben to the bed and drew him down beside her and she held him, rocking back and forth, wiping his drooling mouth upon the hem of her skirt' (316). The embrace suggests both physical affection and Dilsey's sense of human equality and spiritual reciprocity: 'You's de Lawd's chile, anyway. En I be His'n too' (317). Dilsey, protector of Benjy and a certain set of moral values in the novel, is given the final word. Seventeen years after the original publication of *The Sound and the Fury* in 1929, Faulkner wrote this short history of the Compsons as an appendix to Malcolm Cowley's *The Portable Faulkner* (1946). In contrast to the lengthy descriptions of the lives and histories of Quentin, Jason, Caddy and many other fictional characters that did not appear in the original novel, Dilsey's life and family are described in just two words, the final words of the entire collection: 'They endured' (647). This striking brevity suggests, on one level, Dilsey's marginalization as a character on the grounds of race. The preceding description of Frony is prefaced with a dismissive narratorial commentary: 'Those others were not Compsons. They were black' (647). Like the other figures in the appendix, Dilsey is not allowed to speak for herself as a character, but is instead described by an anonymous narrator. Yet it is Dilsey's capacity for endurance that distinguishes her and is highlighted above all else. '*They* endured' suggests both her endurance of an almost unendurable racial and economic exploitation alongside other black characters in the text, but also a potentially hopeful capacity for them to live on as part of a community.

Morrison's *Love* also ends with a scene that affirms a sense of enduring bodies and lives. As in *The Sound and the Fury*, the novel ends with the two protagonists locked together. The novel depicts a conflict between two ageing women, living in a decaying seaside resort: 'A fairytale that lived on' (43). Their story is one of failed pity and empathy; Heed and Christine inhabit the same property yet they spend decades bitterly fighting over its ownership. In a climactic scene, the rotten floor gives way and Heed's fall leaves her bones shattered and her body prostrate on the ground below:

> The falling is like a silent movie and the soft twisted hands with no hope of hanging on to rotted wood dissolve, fade to black as the movies always do, and the feeling of abandonment loosens a loneliness so intolerable that Christine drops to her knees peering down at the body arching below. She races down the ladder, along the hall, and into the room. On her knees again, she turns, then gathers Heed in her arms ... Each searches the face of the other ... Old, decrepit, yet sharp. (177)

The shattering of the wood brings about a 'loosening' (177) of the mutual antagonism between them, a shift in perspective that, Morrison suggests, resembles the cinematic technique of fading out a scene. The embrace silently recognizes their mutual dependency. Their position in this climactic scene: imprisoned and paralysed by bones that have 'splintered like glass' (183), provides a metaphor for their wider condition, locked for years in stultifying mutual love and loathing. Their physical incapacity following the fall brings about a new potential for recognition and understanding between Heed and Christine, mediated by touch: 'Wordlessness continues ... "Hold my hand"' (194). At this point, even time becomes subject to a sense of dissolution: 'the future is disintegrating along with the past' (194). All that is left at the end of the novel is an image of two bodies physically and symbolically bound together in on-going uncertainty.

In Coetzee's *Diary of a Bad Year* (2007), the parting embrace between the ageing author, JC, and Anya his amanuensis, initially appears to offer a kind of closure for their relationship and the novel itself. The scene is mediated through JC's consciousness:

> Then I took the required step forward and embraced her, and for a whole minute we stood clasped together, this shrunken old man and this earthly incarnation of heavenly beauty ... But I thought, 'Enough is Enough,' and let her go. (190)

The embrace suggests their interdependence, tied together contractually as employer and employee, but also socially and emotionally as carers and confidants for each other. In fact, JC's desire to 'let her go' is undermined by the structure of the novel: their dialogue continues at a distance, through letters. Anya fantasizes about JC's worsening health and death yet at the same time suggests that she is bound to him through a sense of emotional responsibility: 'I will fly to Sydney. I will do that. I will hold his hand' (226). Yet JC's body endures: he is not removed from the narrative frame, he continues living and writing. The novel itself refuses to let go of the themes of ageing or let the readers off the hook. Instead, we are confronted with JC's enduring loneliness and disintegrating body.

Snyder and Mitchell suggest that the desire to impose closure on a narrative is a feature of many narratives of disability. They describe how 'recent narrative work in disability studies examines formulas for their drive toward the solution of curing or killing off disabled characters'.[3] In his Foreword to *A History of Disability*, Mitchell identifies a similar impulse in the social treatment of the disabled: 'Disability and disabled populations continue to surface as that which must be assimilated or made to disappear ... the social ideal of erasure' (xi). He associates modern discourses of rehabilitation and prosthesis with an 'integrationist ideal' (xii) in which difference is assimilated to the point of invisibility. By contrast, in their representation of disabled, enduring bodies, Faulkner, Morrison and Coetzee refuse to conform to this impulse towards social or literary erasure. Through their formal experimentation and the focus on otherness in their writing Faulkner, Morrison and Coetzee all sustain an 'unflinching gaze [which] creates profound discomfort in readers'.[4]

In a twenty-first-century cultural context, any engagement with literary depictions of disability raises uncomfortable debates about the boundaries of medical ethics, as well as the limits of aesthetic representation.[5] For Stiker, the representation of disability suggests the vulnerability of *all* bodies: '[Disabled people] are the tear in our being that reveals its open-endedness, its incompleteness, its precariousness.'[6] In studies of disability in literature, this sense of precariousness has been registered as a kind of linguistic impasse or, more recently, 'aesthetic nervousness'.[7] Woolf's claim that 'to hinder the description of illness in literature, there is a poverty of the language',[8] is echoed in Scarry's claim that 'there is ordinarily no language for the body in pain'.[9] Quayson begins his book on literary disability from a similar sense of 'an aesthetic problematic ... an interpretive difficulty or impasse' (14). He suggests that, in the writing of certain twentieth-century novelists and drama-tists, these anxieties have been absorbed on an unconscious level, to generate 'a series of crises in the protocols of representation' (14).

Faulkner, Morrison and Coetzee confront these problems of articu-lating physical suffering, 'speaking the unspeakable'[10] or 'enduring the unendurable',[11] yet also suggest the possibility of empathetic identifi-cation through the representation of enduring disabled bodies. Early in the twentieth century, Woolf's 'On Being Ill' posed the challenge of imagining conditions of illness or invalidity in literature: 'to look these [issues] squarely in the face would need the courage of a lion tamer' (5). Faulkner, Morrison and Coetzee take up this challenge. The attempt to imagine disability from *within*, from Faulkner's rendering of Benjy's nar-rative in *The Sound and the Fury* to Coetzee's ageing JC, engages with the aesthetic and ethical difficulties but also the imaginative possibilities of 'the courage it takes to pity'[12] for both a reader and a writer.

The notion of pity can be seen as patronizing. The *Oxford English Dictionary* etymology suggests that the earlier definition 'to be merci-ful or compassionate'[13] is now outdated, replaced by a more specific, relational understanding of 'pity' as: 'tenderness or concern aroused by suffering, distress, or misfortune of another, and *prompting a desire for its relief*, compassion, sympathy'[14] (my italics). The emergence of the sense of a desire for relief as a defining feature of pity supports Stiker's argument about the emergence of contemporary discourses of rehabilitation and an underlying desire for an erasure or assimilation of difference.[15] In a disability studies context, these terms are ethically charged and politically contested. Sue Halpern suggests that a distinc-tion between sympathy and empathy is connected to the relationship between able-bodied and disabled people:

> Physical health is contingent and often short-lived. But this truth eludes us as long as we are able to walk by simply putting one foot in front of another. As a consequence, empathy for the disabled is unavailable for most able-bodied persons. Sympathy, yes, empathy, no, for every attempt to project oneself into that condition, to feel what it is like not to be ambulatory, for instance, is mediated by an ability to walk.[16]

The line that Halpern draws between sympathy and empathy relies upon a clear division between able-bodied and disabled. Given the instability of the category of disability, encompassing invisible and vis-ible impairments, temporary injuries and cognitive disorders, Halpern's dismissal of the possibility of empathy does not give due weight to the wide spectrum of embodiment and the diverse, shifting nature of *all* human bodies.

For Wendell, the widespread lack of empathy towards disabled people is not the result of a quantifiable physical difference, but rather a mental resistance to identifying oneself with those who are labelled 'disabled':

> It is not simply because they are in able bodies that the able-bodied fail to identify with the disabled. Able-bodied people can often make the imaginative leap into the skins of people physically unlike themselves; women can identify with a male protagonist in a story, for example...Something more powerful than being in a different body is at work. Suffering caused by the body, and the inability to control the body, are despised, pitied, and above all, feared. This fear, experienced individually, is also deeply embedded in our culture. (248)

For Wendell, 'pity' is a derogatory term, associated with despising and fearing. For both Wendell and Halpern, empathy between disabled and able-bodied people is blocked by either physical or social, imaginative obstacles. Yet, this difficult process of empathy, 'the power of projecting one's personality into...the object of contemplation',[17] is precisely what is being asked of readers and writers engaging with individualized literary representations of disability. The fact that Faulkner, Morrison and Coetzee are able-bodied novelists writing about disabled characters highlights the ethical and imaginative challenge that they undertake. Pity, in Faulkner's earlier sense, does not suggest a sentimental or infantilizing understanding of disability, but rather foregrounds the relational aspect of impairment as constructed through a relationship between an individual and their social and cultural environment.

The difficult, discomforting nature of this challenge – of representing disabled bodies and attempting empathetic identification – inspires literary innovation and experimentation, as well as a degree of aesthetic freedom. For Woolf, in illness, 'words give out their scent and distil their flavour'.[18] Woolf offers a multi-sensory description of her own experience of being an invalid to make a wider argument about why more writers should engage with illness. This sensuality and creativity is also reflected in Faulkner's comments about representing disability in *The Sound and the Fury*: he felt that 'the novel was generating a new narrative kind that would ideally be printed in 28 coloured inks'.[19] If we dismiss even the possibility of empathetic identification with the lived experience of disability as Halpern suggests, the body as a source of 'sensuous potentiality... and knowledge about the world'[20] is lost from disability studies. The materiality of the body is central to the process of empathy, as the body represents the shared point of mediation and contact between individuals and their surroundings.

The role of the literary in enabling this process of imagining and empathizing is explored in Faulkner, Morrison and Coetzee's critical writing about each other. Morrison, admiring Faulkner's 'refusal-to-look-away',[21] explains that:

> My reasons, I think, for being interested and deeply moved by all [Faulkner's] subjects had something to do with my desire to find out something about this country and that artistic articulation of its past that was not available in history, which is what art and fiction can do.[22]

For Morrison then, art and fiction provide uniquely enabling per-spectives through which to think about difficult cultural and ethical questions; the complexity and messiness of human life cannot be cap-tured in the factual discourses of history. Coetzee, in his essay on Faulkner, makes a similar point about the unique value of the novel, in this case as a mode of addressing political questions. He contrasts the crude political statements made by Faulkner in the press with the rich, nuanced observations in his fiction:

> [The] appropriate vehicle for his political insights was not the essay, much less the letter to the editor, but the novel, and in par-ticular the kind of novel that he invented, with its unequalled rhetorical resources for interweaving past and present, memory and desire. (199)

Coetzee suggests that Faulkner's novels should be read, not as politi-cal tracts, but rather as perspectives through which political debates are focused and particularized. Quayson takes a similarly complex view of the potential efficacy of novels; he suggests that literary representations of disability do not necessarily correspond with the actual experience of disabled people but can help us to engage with some attitudes and issues about disability, as well as the problem of representation: 'Disability scholarship allows us to glean certain repeated features from the general social treatment of the disabled... the literary domain invokes some of these attitudes but dissolves them into the tapestry of representation'

(5). He highlights the problem of mediating the experience of physical bodies through text. Yet, the prevalence and cultural influence of representations of disability in literature in itself suggests that a focus on literary disability should form a central aspect of disability studies. Snyder and Mitchell list American classics, including *Of Mice and Men* (1937), *Catcher in the Rye* (1951), *To Kill a Mockingbird* (1960) and *One Flew Over the Cuckoo's Nest* (1960) to argue that: 'This list of influential scenes from "contemporary classics" reminds us that Americans learn disability perspectives from books more than policies.'[23] Close reading of the novels themselves deepens our understanding and frequently helps to complicate the theoretical paradigms that critics seek to impose upon them.

Today, disability studies has moved beyond a directly politicized 'search for a more "positive" story of disability'[24] to explore a more complex, nuanced understanding of the relationship between literary representations of disability and their specific cultural contexts. Disability studies is a field that is expanding beyond the boundaries of identity politics, as a discourse which 'can potentially speak to everything from dyslexia to dystopia, from prosthetics to aesthetics'.[25] This expansion has allowed critics to explore new definitions of disability and ethics. It has also encouraged analysis of new technologies and alternative forms of digital writing which provide a wide scope for future research on disability.[26] The notion of translation between media provides another mode of thinking about the relational nature of the processes of empathizing and reading. Davis suggests that the understanding of *all* types of human identity is reconfigured by a focus on disability.[27] Quayson argues that disability is central to our understanding of *all* literary writing: 'the plot of social deformation as it is tied to some form of physical or mental deformation ... [is] relevant for the discussion of all literary texts' (22). Both of these arguments suggest that a focus on disabled bodies in texts is an enabling and productive critical perspective through which a wide range of political, ethical and aesthetic questions can be addressed. The representation of the disabled body does not suggest an obstacle or linguistic impasse, but rather 'a lever to elevate debate'.[28]

There is still much work to be done in disability activism in terms of fighting social oppression and economic injustices, as well as addressing the critical, philosophical gap in relation to the theorization of disability. In the United States in 2009, for example, the employment–population ratio for people with disabilities was 19.2 per cent, as opposed to 64.5 per cent of people without disabilities employed in the same year.[29] In the UK, the 2008 Labour Force Survey found that disabled people are approximately twice as likely not to hold any qualifications compared to non-disabled people, and around half as likely to hold a degree-level qualification.[30] In academic circles, the array of publication, curriculum and epistemological absences[31] means that much remains to be explored.

Yet the writing of Faulkner, Morrison and Coetzee suggests a commitment to the representation of the disabled body in literature which spans the twentieth century and raises important issues and debates about disability for the twenty-first century. Morrison's *Song of Solomon*, with its exploration of family history and geographical rootedness as a means of transcendence, provides a way of thinking about how Faulkner, Morrison and Coetzee should be read in their specific cultural contexts, but also as global, trans-historical authors. As Morrison remarks:

> Faulkner wrote what I suppose could be called regional literature and had it published all over the world. It is good – and universal – because it is specifically about a particular world. That's what I wish to do.[32]

Analysis of literary representations and shifting understandings suggest the importance of disability as a 'travelling concept',[33] which can be traced across different regions, time frames and disciplines. Faulkner, Morrison and Coetzee, in their different times and places, explore how disability can lead to imprisoning social and economic conditions for the sufferer or carer, or to an individual being trapped inside a painful or marginalized body. Yet they also represent disability as a kind of imaginative liberation, which enables new modes of sensory perception and embodied knowledge, creative experience and critical energy. The fictional and critical writing of all three authors exists at the intersection between the literal and the metaphorical, yet their writing remains rooted in an ethical and aesthetic commitment to an engagement with and representation of enduring, disabled bodies. In keeping with the wisdom of the children's song in *Song of Solomon*, Faulkner, Morrison and Coetzee all remind us that:

> You can't just fly on off and leave a body. (149)

Notes

1 Disability and Modern Fiction: Charting New Territory

1. Robin Simon, 'Alison Lapper, the New Icon of Trafalgar Square', *The Evening Standard*, 15 September 2005.
2. Bill Mouland, 'Nelson Looks Down as Statue of Disabled Mother is Unveiled in the Rain', *The Daily Mail*, 16 September 2005.
3. Jonathan Jones, 'Bold, Graphic but Bad Art', *The Guardian*, 16 March 2006.
4. J. M. Coetzee, *Elizabeth Costello: Eight Lessons* (London: Vintage, 2004), 169.
5. David Bolt, 'The Aims and Scope', *Journal of Literary Disability* 1, 1 (2007): i.
6. David T. Mitchell and Sharon L. Snyder, *Narrative Prosthesis: Disability and the Dependencies of Discourse* (Ann Arbor: University of Michigan Press, 2000), 6.
7. Mouland, 'Nelson Looks Down', 27.
8. Nigel Reynolds, 'Whatever Would Nelson Think?', *The Daily Telegraph*, 16 September 2005, 3.
9. Ibid.
10. Tom Shakespeare, *Disability Rights and Wrongs* (London: Routledge, 2006); Tobin Siebers, *Disability Theory* (Ann Arbor: University of Michigan Press, 2008); Ato Quayson, *Aesthetic Nervousness: Disability and the Crisis of Representation* (New York: Columbia University Press, 2007).
11. J. M. Coetzee, *Slow Man* (London: Secker & Warburg, 2005), 59.
12. Sharon L. Snyder and David T. Mitchell, 'Disability Haunting in American Poetics', *Journal of Literary Disability*, 1, 1 (2007), 6.
13. Derek Attridge, *J. M. Coetzee and the Ethics of Reading: Literature in the Event* (Chicago: University of Chicago Press, 2004), xi–xii.
14. Jones, 'Bold, Graphic but Bad Art'.
15. Alison Lapper, 'Bold, Brave, Beautiful', AlisonLapper.com, http://www.alisonlapper.com/statue/, accessed 16 April 2008.
16. Rosemarie Garland Thomson, *Extraordinary Bodies: Figuring Disability in American Culture and Literature* (New York: Columbia University Press, 1997), 6.
17. Mitchell and Snyder, *Narrative Prosthesis*, 51.
18. Henri-Jacques Stiker, *A History of Disability*, trans. William Sayers (Ann Arbor: University of Michigan Press, 1997), 2.
19. Lennard J. Davis (ed.), *The Disability Studies Reader*, 2nd edn. (London: Routledge, 2006), xvi.
20. Ibid., 233.
21. Helen MacMurphy, *The Almosts: A Study of the Feeble-Minded* (Boston: Houghton Mifflin, 1926), 1.
22. Estimates suggest that 204,000 American soldiers were physically wounded in the conflict. ('The Stars and Stripes: American Soldiers' Newspaper of World War One 1918–1919', Library of Congress, http://memory.loc.gov/ammem/sgphtml/sashtml/, accessed 22 August 2008).

23. Stiker, *A History of Disability*, 121.
24. MacMurphy, *The Almosts*, 169.
25. Virginia Woolf, 'On Being Ill', ed. Hermione Lee (Ashfield: Consortium, 2002), 3.
26. MacMurphy, *The Almosts*, 169.
27. Michael Bérubé, *Life as we Know it: A Father, a Family and an Exceptional Child* (New York: Vintage, 1998); Robert F. Murphy, *The Body Silent* (New York: W. W. Norton and Co., 1987); Kenzaburō Ōe, *A Personal Matter* (New York: Grove Press, 1969).
28. P. Crawford, B. Brown, V. Tischler and C. Baker, 'Health Humanities: The Future of Medical Humanities?' *Mental Health Review* 15, 3 (2010): 4–10.
29. William Faulkner, 'The Leg', in *Dr Martino and Other Stories* (London: Chatto & Windus, 1965), 311.
30. Woolf, 'On Being Ill', 8.
31. D. H. Lawrence, *The Prussian Officer and Other Stories*, ed. John Worthen (London: Penguin, 1983), 19.
32. Woolf, 'On Being Ill', 6.
33. Stiker, *A History of Disability*, 125.
34. Ibid., 137.
35. Toni Morrison, *Playing in the Dark: Whiteness and the Literary Imagination* (New York: Vintage, 1993), 15.
36. For example: Master of Arts in 'Disability Studies' at The City University of New York; Undergraduate minor in 'Disability Studies' at UCLA and the University of California at Berkeley; University of Illinois at Chicago offers Masters of Science in 'Disability and Human Development' and PhD in Disability Studies.
37. Colin Barnes and Geoff Mercer, *Disability* (London: Polity Press, 2002); Maddie Blackburn, *Sexuality and Disability* (Oxford: Butterworth-Heinemann, 2002); Michael Davidson, *Concerto for the Left Hand: Disability and the Defamiliar Body* (Ann Arbor: University of Michigan Press, 2008).
38. Laurinda S. Dixon and Gabril P. Weisberg, *In Sickness and in Health: Disease as Metaphor in Art and Popular Wisdom* (Newark: University of Delaware Press, 2004); Mary Klages, *Woeful Afflictions: Disability and Sentimentality in Victorian America* (Philadelphia: University of Pennsylvania Press, 1999); Stiker, *A History of Disability*.
39. G. Thomas Couser, *Recovering Bodies: Illness, Disability and Life Writing* (London: University of Wisconsin Press, 1997); Arthur W. Frank, *The Wounded Storyteller: Body, Illness, and Ethics* (Chicago: University of Chicago Press, 1995).
40. Thomas R. Cole, Robert Kastenbaum and Ruth E. Kay (eds.), *Handbook of the Humanities and Aging* (New York: Springer Publishing, 2000); Helen Small, *The Long Life* (Oxford: Oxford University Press, 2007).
41. Teresa Meade and David Serlin, 'Introduction', *Radical History Review: Disability and History* 94, 4 (2006), 3.
42. Bill Hughes and Kevin Paterson, 'The Social Model of Disability and the Disappearing Body: Towards a Sociology of Impairment', *Disability and Society* 12, 3 (1997), 328.
43. Garland Thomson, *Extraordinary Bodies*, 6.

44. Iris Marion Young, *Justice and the Politics of Difference* (Princeton: Princeton University Press, 1990), 147.
45. Morrison, *Playing in the Dark*, 37.
46. 'Disability', OED.com, http://www.oed.com/, accessed 21 May 2009.
47. Toni Morrison, *Beloved* (New York: Alfred A. Knopf, 1987), 190.
48. Shakespeare, *Disability Rights and Wrongs*, 2.
49. David T. Mitchell, 'Foreword', in Stiker, *A History of Disability*, xi.
50. Hughes and Paterson, 'The Social Model of Disability and the Disappearing Body', 326.
51. Ibid.
52. Siebers, *Disability Theory*, 2.
53. Carol A. Kolmerton, Stephen M. Ross and Judith Bryant Wittenberg (eds.), *Unflinching Gaze: Morrison and Faulkner Re-Envisioned* (Jackson: University Press of Mississippi, 1997), xi.
54. Quayson, *Aesthetic Nervousness*; Sam Durrant, *Postcolonial Narrative and the Work of Mourning: J. M. Coetzee, Wilson Harris and Toni Morrison* (Albany: State University of New York Press, 2004).
55. John N. Duvall, 'Toni Morrison and the Anxiety of Faulknerian Influence', in Kolmerton, Ross and Wittenberg (eds.), *Unflinching Gaze*, 7.
56. J. M. Coetzee, 'William Faulkner and his Biographers', in *Inner Workings: Literary Essays, 2000–2005* (London: Vintage, 2008), 190.
57. Cited in Duvall, 'Toni Morrison and the Anxiety of Faulknerian Influence', 6.
58. Ibid., 3.
59. Harold Bloom (ed.), *Toni Morrison* (New York: Chelsea House Publishers, 1990), 4.
60. William Faulkner, 'Address upon Receiving the Nobel Prize for Literature', in *Essays, Speeches and Public Letters*, ed. James B. Meriwether (New York: W. W. Norton, 2001), 119.
61. Toni Morrison, 'Banquet Speech', UMich.edu, http://www.umich.edu/~eng 217/student_projects/nobel%20prize%20winners/morrisonres.htm, accessed 20 March 2011.
62. Duvall, 'Toni Morrison and the Anxiety of Faulknerian Influence', 7.
63. Morrison, *Playing in the Dark*, 4.
64. Ibid., 53.
65. Woolf, 'On Being Ill', 3.
66. Morrison, *Playing in the Dark*, 3.

2   Tales Told by an Idiot: Disability and Sensory Perception in William Faulkner's Fiction and Criticism

1. Richard Gray, *The Life of William Faulkner* (Oxford: Blackwell, 1994), 4.
2. Ibid., 5.
3. William Faulkner, 'On Privacy', in *Essays, Speeches and Public Letters*, ed. James B. Meriwether (New York: Random House, 2004), 66.
4. Stephen Jay Gould, *The Mismeasure of Man* (London: Penguin, 1997), 227.
5. William Faulkner, *Soldier's Pay* (London: Vintage, 2000), 7.
6. Gray, *Life of Faulkner*, 5.

7. Martin Halliwell, *Images of Idiocy: The Idiot Figure in Modern Fiction and Film* (Aldershot: Ashgate, 2004), 18.
8. The Juvenile Protective Association of Cincinnati, *The Feeble-Minded; or, the Hub to our Wheel of Vice, Crime and Pauperism, Cincinnati's Problem: A Study by the Juvenile Protective Association of Cincinnati* (Cincinnati, 1915), 22.
9. Halliwell, *Images of Idiocy*, 18.
10. Faulkner, 'Address upon Receiving the Nobel Prize', 119.
11. William Faulkner, *A Fable*, in *Novels, 1942–1954: Go Down, Moses, Intruder in the Dust, Requiem for a Nun, A Fable* (New York: Library of America, 1994), 803.
12. William Faulkner, *The Sound and the Fury* (London: Vintage, 2005), 320.
13. Elaine Scarry, *The Body in Pain: The Making and Unmaking of the World* (Oxford: Oxford University Press, 1985), 6.
14. Ibid., 96.
15. Halliwell, *Images of Idiocy*, 21.
16. Santanu Das, *Touch and Intimacy in First World War Literature* (Cambridge: Cambridge University Press, 2005), 6.
17. Faulkner, 'Address upon Receiving the Nobel Prize', 120.
18. William Faulkner, *The Hamlet* (New York: Vintage International, 1991), 88.
19. Maurice Merleau-Ponty, *Phenomenology of Perception*, trans. Colin Smith (London: Routledge, 2002), 503.
20. Maurice Merleau-Ponty, *The Visible and the Invisible: Followed by Working Notes*, ed. Claude Lefort; trans. Alphonso Lingis (Evanston, IL: Northwestern University Press, 1968), 135.
21. Faulkner, *Soldier's Pay*, 165.
22. Trudi Tate, *Modernism, History and the First World War* (Manchester: Manchester University Press, 1998), 113.
23. Norbert Elias, 'Homo Clausus and the Civilizing Process', in *Identity: A Reader*, ed. Jessica Evans, Paul du Gay and Peter Redman (London: Sage, 2000), 293.
24. Frank Kermode, *The Sense of an Ending: Studies in the Theory of Fiction* (Oxford: Oxford University Press, 1967), 45.
25. Faulkner, 'Address upon Receiving the Nobel Prize', 120.
26. Faulkner, 'On Privacy', 68.
27. Joseph Blotner, *Faulkner: A Biography* (London: Chatto & Windus, 1974), 210.
28. W. C. Morrow, *The Ape, the Idiot and Other People* (Philadelphia: J. P. Lippincott Company, 1897).
29. John Kendrick Bangs, *The Idiot* (New York: Harper, 1895).
30. John Kendrick Bangs, *The Idiot at Home* (New York: Harper, 1900).
31. Donald M. Kartiganer and Ann J. Abadie (eds.), *Faulkner and the Natural World: Faulkner and Yoknapatawpha* (Jackson: University Press of Mississippi, 1999).
32. Faulkner, *The Hamlet*, 83; *The Sound and the Fury*, 253; *The Hamlet*, 352; *The Sound and the Fury*, 298; *The Sound and the Fury*, 52.
33. Joseph P. Byers, 'Colony Care of the Feeble-minded', in *Report of the 1915 Legislature Committee on Mental Deficiency and the Proposed Institution for the Care of Feeble-minded and Epileptic Persons* (California, 1917), xi.
34. J. Harold Williams, 'Feeble-Mindedness and Delinquency', in *Report of the 1915 Legislature Committee on Mental Deficiency*, 63.

35. Sharon L. Snyder and David T. Mitchell, *Cultural Locations of Disability* (Chicago: University of Chicago Press, 2006), 53.
36. Charles B. Davenport, 'Eugenics and Euthenics', in *Report of the 1915 Legislature Committee on Mental Deficiency*, 18.
37. Faulkner, *The Sound and the Fury*, 47.
38. Faulkner, *The Hamlet*, 90.
39. Snyder and Mitchell, *Cultural Locations of Disability*, 39.
40. Garland Thomson, *Extraordinary Bodies*, 58.
41. Jean Starobinski, 'The Inside and the Outside', *The Hudson Review* 28, 3 (1975), 337.
42. Faulkner, 'Literature and War', in *Essays, Speeches and Public Letters*, 255.
43. Faulkner, *Soldier's Pay*, 128–9.
44. Andre Bleikasten, 'A European Perspective', in *The Cambridge Companion to William Faulkner*, ed. Philip M. Weinstein (Cambridge: Cambridge University Press, 1995), 83.
45. Faulkner, 'Introduction to *The Sound and the Fury*, 1946', in *Essays, Speeches and Public Letters*, 299.
46. Frederick L. Gwynn and Joseph Blotner (eds.), *Faulkner in the University* (Charlottesville: University of Virginia Press, 1995), 61.
47. Robert A. Jeliffe (ed.), *Faulkner at Nagano* (Tokyo: Norwood Editions, 1977), 103–4.
48. Cleanth Brooks, 'Primitivism in *The Sound and the Fury*', in *English Institute Essays 1952*, ed. Alan S. Downer (New York: AMS Press, 1954), 5–28.
49. Faulkner, *The Sound and the Fury*, 30.
50. James Mellard, 'Caliban as Prospero: Benjy and *The Sound and the Fury*', *Novel: A Forum on Fiction* 3, 3 (1970), 239.
51. Wesley Morris and Barbara Alverson Morris, *Reading Faulkner* (London: University of Wisconsin Press, 1989), 136.
52. Ibid.
53. Faulkner, 'Appendix: The Compsons', in *The Portable Faulkner*, ed. Malcolm Cowley (London: Penguin, 2003), 643.
54. Donald M. Kartiganer, '*The Sound and the Fury* and Faulkner's Quest for Form', *ELH* 37, 4 (1970), 622.
55. Merleau-Ponty, *Phenomenology of Perception*, 14.
56. Faulkner, *The Sound and the Fury*, 10.
57. Henri Bergson, *The Creative Mind: An Introduction to Metaphysics*, trans. Mabelle L. Andison (London: Greenwood Press, 1968), 104.
58. Henri Bergson, *Matter and Memory*, trans. Nancy Paul and W. Scott Palmer (London: Allen & Unwin, 1911), 69.
59. Myra Jehlen, 'Faulkner and the Unnatural', in *Faulkner and the Natural World*, ed. Kartiganer and Abadie, 143.
60. Lawrence Bowling, 'Faulkner and the Theme of Innocence', *Kenyon Review* 20, 2 (1958), 466–7.
61. Henri Bergson, *Introduction to Metaphysics*, trans. T. E. Hulme (London: Macmillan, 1913), 62.
62. Mellard, 'Caliban as Prospero', 237.
63. Jehlen, 'Faulkner and the Unnatural', 143.
64. Snyder and Mitchell, *Cultural Locations*, 86.

65. National Committee for Mental Hygiene, *Report of the Georgia Commission on Feeble-Mindedness and of the Survey Conducted by the National Committee for Mental Hygiene* (Atlanta, 1919), 16.
66. Committee on Protection of the Feeble-Minded of the Massachusetts Society of the Prevention of Cruelty to Children, *The Menace of the Feeble-minded in Massachusetts: The Need of a Program* (Cambridge, MA, 1913), 1.
67. Faulkner, *The Hamlet*, 183.
68. Young, *Justice and the Politics of Difference*, 128.
69. Jehlen, 'Faulkner and the Unnatural', 145.
70. Ibid.
71. Gray, *Life of Faulkner*, 262.
72. Faulkner, *The Hamlet*, 217.
73. Garland Thomson, *Extraordinary Bodies*, 58.
74. Faulkner, *A Fable*, 904.
75. Ibid., 1071.
76. Morrison, *Playing in the Dark*, 4.
77. Ibid., 15.
78. Maria Truchan-Tataryn, 'Textual Abuse: Faulkner's Benjy', *Journal of Medical Humanities* 26, 2/3 (2005), doi: 10.1007/s10912-005-2916-0.
79. Jacques Derrida, *Memoirs of the Blind: The Self Portrait and Other Ruins*, trans. Pascale-Anne Brault and Michael Naas (London: University of Chicago Press, 1993), 16.
80. Thomas M. Inge, *William Faulkner: Contemporary Reviews* (Cambridge: Cambridge University Press, 1995), 37.
81. Gwynn and Blotner, *Faulkner and the University*, 61.

3 Foreign Bodies: Disability and Beauty in the Works of Toni Morrison

1. Toni Morrison, *The Bluest Eye* (London: Vintage, 1999), 57.
2. Paul C. Taylor, 'Malcolm's Conk and Danto's Colors; or, Four Logical Petitions Concerning Race, Beauty and Aesthetics', in *Beauty Matters*, ed. Peg Zeglin Brand (Bloomington: Indiana University Press, 2000), 62; Katherine Stern, 'Toni Morrison's Beauty Formula', in *The Aesthetics of Toni Morrison: Speaking the Unspeakable*, ed. Marc C. Connor (Jackson: University Press of Mississippi, 2000), 78.
3. W. E. B. Du Bois, 'Criteria of Negro Art', *The Crisis* 32 (1926), 293.
4. Eugène Delacroix, *Études de Figures Volantes Nues* (1836–40); Charles Le Brun, *Groupes D'hommes Précipités* (1672); Edgar Degas, *Femme Nue, Échevelée, Penchée en Avant à Droite* (1860–2).
5. Elaine Scarry, *On Beauty and Being Just* (London: Duckworth, 2000), 30.
6. Umberto Eco (ed.), *On Beauty: A History of a Western Idea*, trans. Alastair McEwen (London: Secker & Warburg, 2004), 14.
7. Isobel Armstrong, *The Radical Aesthetic* (Oxford: Blackwell, 2000), 3.
8. James Wood, *The Broken Estate: Essays on Literature and Belief* (New York: Random House, 1999), 218–19.
9. Garland Thomson, *Extraordinary Bodies*, 103.
10. Toni Morrison, *Sula* (London: Vintage, 1998), 31.

11. Davis (ed.), 'Constructing Normalcy: The Bell Curve, the Novel and the Invention of the Disabled Body in the Nineteenth Century', in *The Disability Studies Reader*, 9.
12. Tobin Siebers, 'Disability Aesthetics', *JCRT* 7, 2 (2006), 65.
13. Wolfgang Kayser, *The Grotesque in Art and Literature* (New York: Columbia University Press, 1981).
14. Morrison, *Playing in the Dark*, 12.
15. Morrison, *Beloved*, 190.
16. Toni Morrison, 'What Black Women Think about Women's Lib', *The New York Times Magazine*, 22 August 1971.
17. Ibid.
18. Susan Willis, *Specifying: Black Women Writing the American Experience* (Madison: University of Wisconsin Press, 1987); Toni Morrison, 'Rediscovering Black History', in *Toni Morrison: What Moves at the Margin*, ed. Toni Morrison and Carolyn C. Denard (Jackson: University Press of Mississippi, 2008), 39–55; Davis (ed.), *The Disability Studies Reader*, xvi.
19. Morrison, 'What Black Women Think about Women's Lib'.
20. 'September 1962 Edition', *Ebony* magazine archive, accessed 22 June 2009, http://books.google.com/books?id=9eEDAAAAMBAJ&source=gbs_navlinks_s.
21. 'February 1969 Edition', *Ebony* magazine archive, accessed 22 June 2009, http://books.google.com/books?id=9eEDAAAAMBAJ&source=gbs_navlinks_s.
22. Ibid.
23. Naomi Wolf, *The Beauty Myth* (London: Anchor Books, 1992), 17.
24. Davis (ed.), *The Disability Studies Reader*, 297.
25. Morrison, *Playing in the Dark*, 6.
26. Ibid., 38.
27. Peg Zeglin Brand (ed.), *Beauty Matters* (Bloomington: Indiana University Press, 2000), 7.
28. Scarry, *On Beauty and Being Just*, 52.
29. Morrison, 'Afterword', in *The Bluest Eye*, 169.
30. Toni Morrison, *Song of Solomon* (London: Vintage, 1998), 149.
31. Garland Thomson, *Extraordinary Bodies*, 121.
32. Toni Morrison, 'Behind the Making of the Black Book', *Black World* 23, 1 (1974), 89.
33. Taylor, 'Malcolm's Conk and Danto's Colors', 59.
34. Davis (ed.), *The Disability Studies Reader*, 304.
35. Mitchell and Snyder, *Narrative Prosthesis*, 49.
36. Young, *Justice and the Politics of Difference*, 153.
37. Morrison, 'Afterword', 168.
38. Mitchell and Snyder, *Narrative Prosthesis*, 49.
39. Ibid.
40. Willis, *Specifying*, 103.
41. Garland Thomson, *Extraordinary Bodies*, 124.
42. Morrison, *Song of Solomon*, 149.
43. Malin LaVon Walther, 'Out of Sight: Toni Morrison's Revision of Beauty', *Black Literature Forum* 24, 4 (1990), 777.
44. Morrison, *Sula*, 55.

45. Morrison, *The Bluest Eye*, 86.
46. Morrison, 'Afterword', 167.
47. Brand (ed.), *Beauty Matters*, 1.
48. Morrison, 'What Black Women Think about Women's Lib'.
49. Stern, 'Toni Morrison's Beauty Formula', 79.
50. Morrison, *The Bluest Eye*, 28.
51. Walther, 'Out of Sight', 782.
52. Bertram D. Ashe, ' "Why Don't He Like My Hair?" Constructing African-American Standards of Beauty in Toni Morrison's *Song of Solomon* and Zora Neale Hurston's *Their Eyes Were Watching God*', *African American Review* 29, 4 (1995), 2.
53. Armstrong, *The Radical Aesthetic*, 6.
54. Morrison, *Song of Solomon*, 62.
55. Paula Black, *The Beauty Industry: Gender, Culture, Pleasure* (London: Routledge, 2004), 2–3.
56. Toni Morrison, *Jazz* (London: Vintage, 2005), 23.
57. Black, *The Beauty Industry*, 7.
58. Ibid., 18–19.
59. Kathryn Lasky, *Vision of Beauty: The Story of Sarah Breedlove Walker*, illus. Nneka Bennett (New York: Walker Books, 2000).
60. Morrison, 'What Black Women Think about Women's Lib', 14.
61. Morrison, *Tar Baby* (London: Vintage, 2004), 9.
62. Morrison, 'What Black Women Think about Women's Lib', 14.
63. Wolf, *The Beauty Myth*, 19.
64. Bill Cosby, 'Introduction', in *The Black Book*, ed. Middleton A. Harris (New York: Random House, 1974), i.
65. Morrison, 'Rediscovering Black History', 41.
66. Ibid.
67. Ibid.
68. Cheryl A. Wall, 'Toni Morrison, Editor and Teacher', in *The Cambridge Companion to Toni Morrison*, ed. Justine Tally (Cambridge: Cambridge University Press, 2007), 144.
69. Cosby, 'Introduction', i.
70. Ibid.
71. Sara Blair, *Harlem Crossroads: Black Writers and the Photograph in the Twentieth Century* (New Haven: Princeton University Press, 2007), 259.
72. Ibid.
73. Cheryl A. Wall, *Worrying the Line: Black Women Writers, Lineage and Literary Tradition* (Chapel Hill: University of North Carolina Press, 2005), 102.
74. Toni Morrison, 'Rootedness in the Ancestor', in *Black Women Writers (1950–1980): A Critical Evaluation*, ed. Mari Evans (Garden City, NY: Anchor Books, 1984), 345.
75. bel hooks, 'Postmodern Blackness', *Postmodern Culture* 1, 1 (1990), 23.
76. Toni Morrison, *Conversations with Toni Morrison*, ed. Danille Taylor-Guthrie (Jackson: University Press of Mississippi, 1994), 247.
77. Stern, 'Toni Morrison's Beauty Formula', 78.
78. Barbara Johnson, *The Feminist Difference: Literature, Psychoanalysis, Race and Gender* (London: Harvard University Press, 1988), 86.
79. Toni Morrison, *A Mercy* (London: Chatto & Windus, 2008), 47.

80. Garland Thomson, *Extraordinary Bodies*, 116.
81. Morrison, *Beloved*, 273.
82. Claudine Raynaud, 'Beloved or the Shifting Shapes of Memory', in *The Cambridge Companion to Toni Morrison*, ed. Tally, 51.
83. Maud Ellmann, 'The Power to Tell: Rape, Race and Afro-American Women's Fiction', in *An Introduction to Contemporary Fiction: International Writing in English since 1970*, ed. Rod Mengham (Oxford: Polity Press, 1999), 46.
84. Anita Silvers, 'From the Crooked Timber of Humanity, Beautiful Things Can be Made', in *Beauty Matters*, ed. Brand, 211.
85. 'Interview with Toni Morrison by Don Swaim', CBS Radio, 15 September 1987, http://www.wiredforbooks.org/tonimorrison/.
86. Scarry, *On Beauty and Being Just*, 4.
87. Morrison, 'Rootedness', 341.
88. Wendy Steiner, *The Trouble with Beauty* (London: Heinemann, 2001), xxii.
89. Judylyn S. Ryan, 'Language and Narrative Technique in Toni Morrison's Novels', in *The Cambridge Companion to Toni Morrison*, ed. Tally, 154.
90. Maxine Sheets-Johnstone, *The Phenomenology of Dance* (London: Dance Books Ltd., 1966), 119.
91. 'A Figure in Space: Interview with William Forsythe and Peter Welz', in *Corps Étrangers: Danse, Dessin, Film*, ed. Marcella Lister (Paris: Musée du Louvre Éditions, 2006), 28.
92. D. W. Winnicott, *Playing and the Reality* (London: Routledge, 1971), 133–4.
93. 'A Figure in Space', 20.
94. 'Foreign Bodies', in *Corps Étrangers*, ed. Lister, 14.
95. Alan Riding, 'Entr'acte: At Louvre, Toni Morrison Hosts a Conversation on Exile', *The New York Times*, 15 November 2006.
96. Morrison, 'Rootedness', 339–45.
97. Henri Loyrette, 'The Foreigner's Home: A Proposal by Toni Morrison for the Louvre', in *Corps Étrangers*, ed. Lister, 12.
98. 'Foreign Bodies', 14.
99. Sheets-Johnstone, *The Phenomenology of Dance*, 118.
100. Sondra Horton Fraleigh, *Dance and the Lived Body: A Descriptive Aesthetics* (Pittsburgh: University of Pittsburgh Press, 1987), 51.
101. 'A Figure in Space', 36.
102. Morrison, 'Rootedness', 341.
103. Alice Walker, 'Beauty: When the Other Dancer is the Self', in *In Search of Our Mother's Gardens: Womanist Prose* (London: Harcourt, 1983), 385–94.
104. Toni Morrison, *The Dancing Mind: Speech upon Acceptance of the National Book Foundation Medal for Distinguished Contribution to American Letters* (New York: Alfred A. Knopf, 1996), 16.
105. Ibid., 7.
106. Sami Ludwig, 'Toni Morrison's Social Criticism', in *The Cambridge Companion to Toni Morrison*, ed. Tally, 133.
107. Eleanor Heartney, 'Foreword: Cutting Two Ways with Beauty', in *Beauty Matters*, ed. Brand, xv.
108. Morrison, 'What Black Women Think about Women's Lib'.
109. Susan Wendell, 'Towards a Feminist Theory of Disability', in *The Disability Studies Reader*, ed. Davis.

110. Scarry, *The Body in Pain*, 6.
111. Mitchell and Snyder, *Narrative Prosthesis*.
112. Siebers, 'Disability Aesthetics', 64.
113. Davis (ed.), *The Disability Studies Reader*, 5.
114. Silvers, 'From the Crooked Timber of Humanity, Beautiful Things Can be Made', 200.
115. Scarry, *On Beauty and Being Just*, 109.
116. Toni Morrison, 'Home', in *The House that Race Built: Original Essays by Toni Morrison, Angela Y. Davis, Cornel West and Others on Black Americans and Politics in America Today*, ed. Lubiano Waheema (New York: Pantheon Books, 1997), 5.
117. Morrison, 'Afterword', 172.

4   Dialectics of Dependency: Ageing and Disability in J. M. Coetzee's Later Writing

1. Coetzee, *Slow Man*, 129.
2. Emmanuel Levinas, *Basic Philosophical Writings*, ed. Adrian T. Peperzak, Simon Critchley and Robert Bernasconi (Bloomington: Indiana University Press, 1996), 9.
3. Emmanuel Levinas, *Totality and Infinity: An Essay on Exteriority*, trans. Alphonso Lingis (Pittsburgh: Duquesne University Press, 1969), 247.
4. Emmanuel Levinas, *Otherwise than Being or Beyond Essence*, trans. Alphonso Lingis (Pittsburgh: Duquesne University Press, 1999), 128.
5. J. M. Coetzee, *Elizabeth Costello: Eight Lessons* (London: Vintage, 2004), 154.
6. Levinas, *Basic Philosophical Writings*, 6.
7. Ibid., 9.
8. J. M. Coetzee, *Waiting for the Barbarians* (London: Secker & Warburg, 1980), 64.
9. J. M. Coetzee, *Age of Iron* (London: Secker & Warburg, 1990), 26–7.
10. Coetzee, *Elizabeth Costello*, 2.
11. Coetzee, *Slow Man*, 82.
12. J. M. Coetzee, *Diary of a Bad Year* (London: Harvill Secker, 2007), 31.
13. G. W. F. Hegel, *Phenomenology of Spirit*, trans. A. V. Miller (Oxford: Oxford University Press, 1977), 111.
14. Ibid., 119.
15. Zoë Wicomb, '*Slow Man* and the Real: A Lesson in Reading and Writing', in *Austerities: Essays on J. M. Coetzee*, ed. G. Bradshaw and Michael Neil (London: Ashgate Publishing, 2010), 226.
16. Quayson, *Aesthetic Nervousness*, 149.
17. Attridge, *J. M. Coetzee and the Ethics of Reading*, 200.
18. Martha C. Nussbaum, *Frontiers of Justice: Disability, Nationality, Species Membership* (Cambridge, MA: The Belknap Press of Harvard University Press, 2006), 101.
19. Eva Feder Kittay and Ellen K. Feder (eds.), *The Subject of Care: Feminist Perspectives on Dependency* (Oxford: Rowman & Littlefield Publishers, 2002), 4.

20. J. M. Coetzee, 'As a Woman Grows Older', *The New York Review of Books*, 15 January 2004, accessed 6 March 2010, http://www.nybooks.com/articles/archives/2004/jan/15/as-a-woman-grows-older/.
21. Ibid.
22. Quayson, *Aesthetic Nervousness*, 159.
23. Derek Attridge, 'A Writer's Life', *The Virginia Quarterly Review* 80, 4 (2004), 258.
24. Coetzee, 'As a Woman Grows Older'.
25. Ibid.
26. Ibid.
27. Ibid.
28. Ibid.
29. Kathleen Woodward, *Aging and its Discontents: Freud and Other Fictions* (Bloomington: Indiana University Press, 1991); Margaret Morganroth Gullette, *Declining to Decline: Cultural Combat and the Politics of the Midlife* (Charlottesville: University Press of Virginia, 1997).
30. Small, *The Long Life*, 272.
31. Wendell, 'Towards a Feminist Theory of Disability', in *The Disability Studies Reader*, ed. Davis, 263.
32. Mitchell and Snyder, *Narrative Prosthesis*, 63.
33. Coetzee, 'As a Woman Grows Older'.
34. Ibid.
35. Ibid.
36. Lennard J. Davis, 'Dependency and Justice', *Journal of Literary and Cultural Disability Studies* 1, 2 (2007), 4.
37. Coetzee, 'As a Woman Grows Older'.
38. Simone de Beauvoir, *The Second Sex*, trans. H. M. Parshley (London: Vintage, 1997), 35.
39. In Australia, for example, 'much alarm was aroused by the predictions that the proportions of older people, aged 60 and over, would rise from, in 1990, 15.5 per cent in Australia...to, in 2020, 18.2 per cent'. Cited in Pat Thane, *The Long History of Old Age* (London: Thames & Hudson, 2005), 279.
40. Maurizio Lazzaranto, 'From Biopower to Biopolitics', *Pli: The Warwick Journal of Philosophy* 13 (2002), 104.
41. Michel Foucault, *The Foucault Reader*, ed. Paul Rabinow (London: Penguin, 1991), 265.
42. 'Waste', *Oxford English Dictionary*, accessed 12 January 2009, http://dictionary.oed.com.
43. Wendell, 'Towards a Feminist Theory of Disability', 266.
44. Simone de Beauvoir, *The Coming of Age*, trans. Patrick O'Brian (New York: Putnam, 1972), 3.
45. Thane, *The Long History of Old Age*, 268.
46. De Beauvoir, *The Coming of Age*, 6.
47. Theodor W. Adorno, 'Trying to Understand Endgame', in *Modern Critical Views: Samuel Beckett*, ed. Harold Bloom (New York: Chelsea House Publishers, 1985), 56.
48. Levinas, *Basic Philosophical Writings*, 6.

49. J. M. Coetzee, *Doubling the Point: Essays and Interviews*, ed. David Attwell (London: Harvard University Press, 1992), 248.
50. Coetzee, *Diary of a Bad Year*, 116.
51. Nussbaum, *Frontiers of Justice*, 15.
52. Michael Davidson, 'Introduction: Dialectics of Dependency', *Journal of Literary and Cultural Disability Studies* 1, 2 (2007), ii.
53. Coetzee, *Elizabeth Costello*, 16.
54. Ibid., 12.
55. Wicomb, '*Slow Man* and the Real', 217.
56. Attridge, *J. M. Coetzee and the Ethics of Reading*, 7.
57. Attridge, 'A Writer's Life', 255.
58. Samuel Beckett, 'Krapp's Last Tape', in *Samuel Beckett: The Complete Dramatic Works* (London: Faber, 1990), 213–23.
59. Coetzee, *Elizabeth Costello*, 161.
60. Beckett, 'Krapp's Last Tape', 220.
61. Coetzee, *Elizabeth Costello*, 192.
62. Coetzee, 'As a Woman Grows Older'.
63. Ibid.
64. Ibid.
65. Kittay and Feder (eds.), *The Subject of Care*, 10.
66. Kelly Oliver, 'Subjectivity as Responsivity: The Ethical Implications of Dependency', in *The Subject of Care*, ed. Kittay and Feder, 325.
67. Coetzee's 'At the Gate' echoes Franz Kafka's *The Trial* (1925), trans. Idris Parry (London: Penguin, 2000).
68. Attridge, 'A Writer's Life', 260.
69. Kermode, *The Sense of an Ending*, 43.
70. David Wills, *Prosthesis* (Stanford: Stanford University Press, 1995); Mitchell and Snyder, *Narrative Prosthesis*.
71. Elizabeth F. Emens, 'Shape Stops Story', *Narrative* 15, 1 (2007), 125.
72. Garland Thomson cited in Emens, 'Shape Stops Story', 125.
73. Shakespeare, *Disability Rights and Wrongs*, 2.
74. J. M. Coetzee, 'Into the Dark Chamber: The Writer and the South African State', in *Doubling the Point*, 361.
75. Wills, *Prosthesis*, 12.
76. Coetzee, *Elizabeth Costello*, 33.
77. David Attwell (ed.), 'Editor's Introduction', in *Doubling the Point*, 6.
78. Coetzee, 'As a Woman Grows Older'.
79. Edward W. Said, *On Late Style: Music and Literature against the Grain* (London: Bloomsbury, 2006), 3.
80. Amir Cohen-Shalev, *Both Worlds at Once: Art in Old Age* (Lanham: University Press of America, 2002), 3.
81. Coetzee, 'As a Woman Grows Older'.
82. Ibid.
83. Cohen-Shalev, *Both Worlds at Once*, 152.
84. Small, *The Long Life*, 268.
85. Cohen-Shalev, *Both Worlds at Once*, 5.
86. De Beauvoir, *The Second Sex*, 35.
87. Margaret Morganroth Gullette, 'Age Studies as Cultural Studies', in *Handbook of the Humanities and Aging*, ed. Cole, Kastenbaum and Kay, 218.

88. Coetzee, *Slow Man*, 44.
89. Coetzee, *Diary of a Bad Year*, 221.
90. Derrida, *Memoirs of the Blind*, 64.
91. Coetzee, 'Into the Dark Chamber', 364.
92. Wicomb, '*Slow Man* and the Real', 13.
93. Coetzee, *Elizabeth Costello*, 171.
94. Coetzee, 'As a Woman Grows Older'.
95. Stepehn Mullhall, *The Wounded Animal: J. M. Coetzee and the Difficulty of Reality in Literature and Philosophy* (Woodstock: Princeton University Press, 2009), 211.
96. Nussbaum, *Frontiers of Justice*, 141.
97. See André Green, *The Work of the Negative*, trans. Andrew Weller (London: Free Association Books, 1999).
98. Lazzaranto, 'From Biopower to Biopolitics', 111.
99. Coetzee, *Elizabeth Costello*, 12.
100. Attridge, *Coetzee and the Ethics of Reading*, xii.
101. Ibid., 18.
102. Coetzee, *Slow Man*, 96.

5   Disability as Metaphor: The Nobel Prize Lectures of Faulkner, Morrison and Coetzee

1. Harold Pinter, 'Nobel Prize Lecture', *The Guardian* (London), accessed 2 March 2011, http://www.guardian.co.uk/stage/2005/dec/08/theatre.nobel prize.
2. Ibid.
3. John Sutherland (ed.), *Nobel Lectures: Twenty Years of the Nobel Prize for Literature* (Cambridge: Icon Books Limited, 2007), xii.
4. Pinter, 'Nobel Lecture'.
5. Ibid.
6. Ibid.
7. Kenne Fant, *Alfred Nobel: A Biography*, trans. Marianne Ruuth (New York: Arcade Publishing, 2006), 2.
8. 'Nobel's Will', *Encyclopedia Britannica's Guide to the Nobel Prizes*, accessed 2 March 2011, http://www.britannica.com/nobelprize/article-9098434.
9. Ibid.
10. Faulkner, 'Address upon Receiving the Nobel Prize', 119–20.
11. Warren Beck, *Faulkner: Essays* (Madison: University of Wisconsin Press, 1976); Irving Howe, *William Faulkner: A Critical Study* (Chicago: University of Chicago Press, 1975) and Edmond L. Volpe, *A Reader's Guide to William Faulkner: The Novels* (New York: Syracuse University Press, 2003).
12. Warren Beck cited in 'Foreword', in Faulkner, *Essays, Speeches and Public Letters*, ed. Meriwether, xii.
13. Faulkner, 'Address upon Receiving the Nobel Prize', 120.
14. See Definition 2.a. 'Ideal' (adj.): 'Conceived or regarded as perfect or supremely excellent in its kind; answering to one's highest conception'. *Oxford English Dictionary*, oed.com, accessed 12 April 2009, http://www.oed.com/view/Entry/90958?redirectedFrom=ideal#.

15. See example given for definition 2.a. 'Ideal' (adj.): 'e.g. 'Ideal language' (Philosophy – B. Russell) 'a supposed language that would mirror the world perfectly.' Ibid.
16. Kjell Espmark, *The Nobel Prize in Literature: A Study of the Criteria Behind the Choices* (Boston: G. K. Hall and Co., 1991).
17. Coetzee, *Elizabeth Costello*, 156–82.
18. *Jackson Daily News* (November, 1950) cited in Blotner, *Faulkner: A Biography*, 526.
19. Gustaf Hellström, 'Presentation Speech', Nobelliterature.com, accessed 2 March 2011, http://nobelliterature.com/nobelliteraturelist/1941-1950/118-1949william-faulkner-.html.
20. Ibid.
21. Ibid.
22. Blotner, *Faulkner: A Biography*, 533.
23. Beck, *Faulkner: Essays*; Howe, *William Faulkner*; Volpe, *William Faulkner: The Novels*.
24. Blotner, *Faulkner: A Biography*, 532.
25. Faulkner, 'Nobel Prize Lecture', 119.
26. Hellström, 'Presentation Speech'.
27. Pinter, 'Nobel Prize Lecture'.
28. Sheri Hoem, 'Disabling Postmodernism: Wideman, Morrison and Prosthetic Critique', *Novel: A Forum on Fiction* 35, 2 (2002), 196.
29. Merleau-Ponty, *The Visible and the Invisible*; Maureen Curtin, *Out of Touch: Skin Tropes in Woolf, Ellison, Pynchon and Acker* (London: Routledge, 2003); Steven Connor, *The Book of Skin* (London, Reaktion Books, 2004).
30. Maud Ellmann, 'Skinscapes in "Lotus-Eaters"', in *Ulysses: En-gendered Perspectives*, ed. Kimberley J. Devlin and Marilyn Rizbaum (New York: University of South Carolina Press, 1999), 60.
31. Ellmann, 'Rape, Race and Afro-American Women's Fiction', 46.
32. Ellmann, 'Skinscapes in "Lotus-Eaters"', 55.
33. J. M. Coetzee, 'Nobel Prize Lecture', *The Guardian* (London), accessed 2 March 2011, http://www.guardian.co.uk/books/2003/dec/09/fiction.nobelprize.
34. Ellmann, 'Skinscapes in "Lotus-Eaters"', 55.
35. Elizabeth Grosz, *Volatile Bodies: Towards a Corporeal Feminism* (Bloomington: Indiana University Press, 1994), 20.
36. Ellmann, 'Rape, Race and Afro-American Women's Fiction', 49.
37. Toni Morrison, 'Nobel Prize Lecture', GiftsofSpeech.com, accessed 2 March 2011, http://gos.sbc.edu/m/morrisont.html.
38. Ibid.
39. Ibid.
40. Susan Sontag, *Illness as Metaphor and Aids and its Metaphors* (London: Penguin, 2002), 5.
41. Morrison, 'Nobel Prize Lecture'.
42. Ibid.
43. Ibid.
44. Morrison, *Tar Baby*, 105.
45. Morrison, 'Nobel Prize Lecture'.
46. Ibid.

47. Ibid.
48. Ibid.
49. Ibid.
50. Ibid.
51. Dwight McBride, 'Morrison, Intellectual', in *The Cambridge Companion to Toni Morrison*, ed. Tally, 166.
52. Morrison, 'Nobel Prize Lecture'.
53. Ibid.
54. Ibid.
55. Ibid.
56. Ibid.
57. Ibid.
58. Ibid.
59. Ibid.
60. Ibid.
61. Ibid.
62. Ibid.
63. Morrison, 'Banquet Speech'.
64. Ibid.
65. Morrison, 'Nobel Prize Lecture'.
66. Ibid.
67. Ellmann, 'Rape, Race and Afro-American Women's Fiction', 49.
68. George Lakoff and Mark Johnson, *Metaphors We Live By* (Chicago: University of Chicago Press, 2003), 3.
69. George Lakoff and Mark Johnson, *Philosophy in the Flesh: The Embodied Mind and its Challenge to Western Thought* (New York: Basic Books, 1999), 129.
70. Garland Thomson, *Extraordinary Bodies*, 10.
71. Leonard Kriegal cited in David Mitchell and Sharon L. Snyder, 'Representation and its Discontents', in *The Handbook of Disability Studies*, ed. Gary Albrecht, Katherine Dolores Seelman and Michael Bury (London: Sage Publications, 2001), 197; Linda Rogers and Beth Blue Swadener (eds.), *Semiotics and Dis/ability: Interrogating Categories of Difference* (Albany: State University of New York Press, 2001).
72. Jenny Morris, 'A Feminist Perspective', in *Framed: Interrogating Disability in the Media*, ed. Ann Pointon and Chris Davis (London: BFI Publishing, 1997), 23.
73. Garland Thomson, *Extraordinary Bodies*, 112.
74. Hortense Spillers, 'Mama's Baby, Papa's Maybe: An American Grammar Book', in *African American Literary Theory: A Reader*, ed. Winston Napier (New York: New York University Press, 2000), 257.
75. Lakoff and Johnson, *Metaphors We Live By*, 5.
76. Morrison, 'Nobel Prize Lecture'.
77. Sontag, *Illness as Metaphor*, 99.
78. Morrison, 'Nobel Prize Lecture'.
79. Lakoff and Johnson, *Metaphors We Live By*, 211.
80. J. M. Coetzee, 'Isaac Newton and the Ideal of a Transparent Scientific Language', in *Doubling the Point*, 192.
81. Pinter, 'Nobel Prize Lecture'.

82. Swedish Academy cited in 'J. M. Coetzee Wins the Nobel Prize', SouthAfrica.Info.com, accessed 2 March 2011, http://www.southafrica. info/about/arts/nobel-jmcoetzee.htm.

83. Coetzee, 'Censorship in South Africa', in *Doubling the Point*, 321.

84. Jane Poyner, 'J. M. Coetzee, Elizabeth and that Prize', *African Review of Books*, accessed 10 April 2009, http://www.africanreviewofbooks.com/Review.asp? book_id=62.

85. Coetzee, *Elizabeth Costello*, 116.

86. Poyner, 'J. M. Coetzee, Elizabeth and that Prize'.

87. Attridge, 'A Writer's Life', 254.

88. Coetzee, 'Nobel Prize Lecture'.

89. Ibid.

90. Ibid.

91. Attridge, 'A Writer's Life', 256.

92. J. M. Coetzee, *Foe* (London: Penguin, 1987), 151.

93. Coetzee, 'Nobel Prize Lecture'.

94. Ibid.

95. Lewis MacLeod, ' "Do We of Necessity Become Puppets in a Story?" or Narrating the World: On Speech, Silence and Discourse in J. M. Coetzee's *Foe*', *Modern Fiction Studies* 52, 1 (2006), 6.

96. Mitchell and Synder, 'Representation and its Discontents', 197.

97. Coetzee, 'Nobel Prize Lecture'.

98. Ibid. (my italics).

99. Ibid.

100. Ibid.

101. Ibid.

102. Ibid.

103. Philomena Mariani (ed.), *Critical Fictions: The Politics of Imaginative Writing* (Seattle: Bay Press, 1991).

104. Coetzee, 'Nobel Prize Lecture'.

105. Ibid.

106. Ibid.

107. Ibid.

108. Ibid.

109. 'Toni Morrison: Author Among Authors', *FacetoFace: A Blog for the National Portrait Gallery Smithsonian Institution*, accessed 2 March 2 2011, http:// face2face.si.edu/my_weblog/2009/02/toni-morrison-author-among-authors.html.

110. Morrison, *Playing in the Dark*, 4.

111. Swedish Academy cited in 'J. M. Coetzee Wins the Nobel Prize'.

112. Morrison, *Playing in the Dark*, 4.

113. Coetzee, 'Nobel Prize Lecture'.

114. Emmanuel Levinas, 'Ethics and the Face', in *The Phenomenology Reader*, ed. Dermot Moran and Timothy Mooney (London: Routledge, 2002), 517.

115. Attridge, 'A Writer's Life', 256.

116. Levinas, 'Ethics and the Face', 517.

117. Morrison, 'Nobel Prize Lecture'.

118. Morrison, Preface to *Playing in the Dark*, xii.

119. Morrison, *Playing in the Dark*, 47.

6   Conclusion: 'You Can't Just Fly on off and Leave a Body'

1. Faulkner, *A Fable*, 904.
2. Coetzee, 'William Faulkner and his Biographers', 200.
3. Snyder and Mitchell, 'Disability Haunting in American Poetics', 6–7.
4. Kolmerton, Ross and Wittenberg (eds.), *Unflinching Gaze*, xi–xii.
5. Davis (ed.), *Disability Studies Reader*, xiii.
6. Stiker, *History of Disability*, 10.
7. Quayson, *Aesthetic Nervousness*, 14.
8. Woolf, 'On Being Ill', 6.
9. Scarry, *The Body in Pain*, 3.
10. Morrison, *Beloved*, 58.
11. Coetzee, 'Faulkner and his Biographers', 200.
12. Faulkner, *A Fable*, 707.
13. 'Pity', OED.com, accessed 10 June 2009, http://www.oed.com/.
14. Ibid.
15. Mitchell, 'Foreword', xii.
16. Sue Halpern, 'Portrait of the Artist: Review of *Under the Clock* by Christopher Nolan', *The New York Review of Books*, 30 June 1988, 3.
17. 'Empathy', OED.com, accessed 10 June 2009, http://www.oed.com/.
18. Woolf, 'On Being Ill', 22.
19. Faulkner cited in Snyder and Mitchell, 'Disability Haunting in American Poetics', 2.
20. Hughes and Paterson, 'Disability and the Disappearing Body', 334.
21. Duvall, 'Toni Morrison and the Anxiety of Faulknerian Influence', 7.
22. Morrison cited in ibid., 7.
23. Snyder and Mitchell, 'Disability Haunting in American Poetics', 6.
24. Mitchell and Snyder, *Narrative Prosthesis*, 59.
25. Michael Bérubé, *Rhetorical Occasions: Humans and the Humanities* (Chapel Hill: University of North Carolina Press, 1996), 155.
26. Lennard J. Davis, 'The End of Identity Politics and the Beginning of Dismodernism', in *Disability Studies Reader*, ed. Davis, 237–9.
27. Ibid., 241.
28. Siebers, *Disability Theory*, 2.
29. United States Department of Labor: Bureau of Labor Statistics, 'Employment among the Disabled by Age in 2009', The Editor's Desk, last modified 31 August 2010, http://www.bls.gov/opub/ted/2010/ted_20100831.htm.
30. Office for Disability Issues: HM Government, 'Disability Facts and Figures', Department for Work and Pensions, accessed 2 March 2011, http://odi.dwp.gov.uk/disability-statistics-and-research/disability-facts-and-figures.php.
31. David Bolt, 'Introduction', *Journal of Literary Disability* 1, 1 (2007), 3.
32. Morrison cited in Duvall, 'Toni Morrison and the Anxiety of Faulknerian Influence', 6.
33. Mieke Bal, *Travelling Concepts in the Humanities: A Rough Guide* (Toronto: University of Toronto Press, 2002).

Select Bibliography

Primary texts

Coetzee, J. M. *Age of Iron*. London: Secker & Warburg, 1990.

——'As a Woman Grows Older'. *The New York Review of Books*, 15 January 2004. Accessed 6 March 2010. http://www.nybooks.com/articles/archives/2004/jan/15/as-a-woman-grows-older/.

——*Boyhood: Scenes from Provincial Life*. London: Secker & Warburg, 1997.

——*Diary of a Bad Year*. London: Harvill Secker, 2007.

——*Disgrace*. London: Secker & Warburg, 1999.

——*Doubling the Point: Essays and Interviews*. Edited by David Attwell. London: Harvard University Press, 1992.

——*Dusklands*. London: Secker & Warburg, 1974.

——*Elizabeth Costello: Eight Lessons*. London: Vintage, 2004.

——*Foe*. London: Penguin, 1987.

——*Giving Offense: Essays on Censorship*. London: University of Chicago Press, 1996.

——*In the Heart of the Country*. London: Secker & Warburg, 1977.

——*Inner Workings: Literary Essays, 2000–2005*. Introduced by Derek Attridge. London: Vintage, 2008.

——*The Life and Times of Michael K*. London: Secker & Warburg, 1983.

——*The Lives of Animals*. London: Princeton University Press, 1999.

——'The Making of Samuel Beckett'. *The New York Review of Books*, 30 April 2009, 13–16.

——*The Master of Petersburg*. London: Secker & Warburg, 1994.

——'Nobel Prize Lecture'. *The Guardian* (London). Accessed 2 March 2011, http://www.guardian.co.uk/books/2003/dec/09/fiction.nobelprize.

——*Slow Man*. London: Secker & Warburg, 2005.

——*Stranger Shores: Essays, 1986–1999*. London: Vintage, 2002.

——*Summertime*. London: Harvill Secker, 2009.

——*Waiting for the Barbarians*. London: Secker & Warburg, 1980.

——*White Writing: On the Culture of Letters in South Africa*. London: Yale University Press, 1988.

——*Youth: Scenes from Provincial Life II*. London: Vintage, 2003.

Faulkner, William. *Absalom, Absalom!* London: Vintage, 2005.

——'Address upon Receiving the Nobel Prize for Literature'. In *Essays, Speeches and Public Letters*. Edited by James B. Meriwether, 119–20. New York: W. W. Norton, 2001.

——*As I Lay Dying*. London: Vintage, 2004.

——*Dr Martino and Other Stories*. London: Chatto & Windus, 1965.

——*Essays, Speeches and Public Letters*. Edited by James B. Meriwether. New York: W. W. Norton, 2001.

——*A Fable*. In *Novels, 1942–1954: Go Down, Moses, Intruder in the Dust, Requiem for a Nun, A Fable*. New York: Library of America, 1994.

——*Faulkner at Nagano*. Edited by Robert A. Jelliffe. Tokyo: Kenkyusha, 1956.

——*Faulkner in the University*. Edited by Frederick L. Gwynn and Joseph Blotner. Charlottesville: University of Virginia Press, 1995.

——*Go Down, Moses*. New York: Literary Classics of the United States, 1994.

——*The Hamlet*. New York: Vintage International, 1991.

——*Intruder in the Dust*. New York: Literary Classics of the United States, 1994.

——*Light in August*. London: Vintage, 2005.

——*The Mansion*. New York: Literary Classics of the United States, 1998.

——*Mosquitoes*. London: Picador Books, 1989.

——*New Orleans Sketches*. Edited by Carvel Collins. Jackson: University Press of Mississippi, 2002.

——*The Portable Faulkner*. Edited by Malcolm Cowley. London: Penguin, 2003.

——*Pylon*. London: Vintage, 1987.

——*The Reivers: A Reminiscence*. New York: Literary Classics of the United States, 1998.

——*Requiem for a Nun*. New York: Literary Classics of the United States, 1994.

——*Sanctuary*. London: Vintage, 1993.

——*Sartoris*. London: Vintage, 1973.

——*Selected Short Stories*. New York: Random House, 1993.

——*Soldier's Pay*. London: Vintage, 2000.

——*The Sound and the Fury*. London: Vintage, 2005.

——*Thinking of Home: William Faulkner's Letters to his Mother and Father, 1918–1925*. Edited by James G. Watson. New York: W. W. Norton, 1992.

——*The Town*. New York: Literary Classics of the United States, 1998.

——*The Unvanquished*. London: Vintage, 1995.

——*The Wild Palms*. London: Vintage, 2000.

Morrison, Toni. 'Banquet Speech'. UMich.edu. Accessed 2 March 2011. http://www.umich.edu/~eng217/student_projects/nobel%20prize%20winners/morrisonres.htm.

——'Behind the Making of the Black Book'. *Black World* 23, 1 (1974): 86–90.

——*Beloved*. New York: Alfred A. Knopf, 1987.

——*The Bluest Eye*. London: Vintage, 1999.

——'City Limits, Village Values: Concepts of the Neighborhood in Black Fiction'. In *Literature and the American Urban Experience: Essays on the City and Literature*. Edited by Michael C. Jaye and Ann Chalmers Watts, 35–43. New Brunswick: Rutgers University Press, 1981.

——*Conversations with Toni Morrison*. Edited by Danille Taylor-Guthrie. Jackson: University Press of Mississippi, 1994.

——(curator). *Corps Étrangers*. The Louvre, Paris. November 2006–January 2007.

——*The Dancing Mind: Speech upon Acceptance of the National Book Foundation Medal for Distinguished Contribution to American Letters*. New York: Alfred A. Knopf, 1996.

——'Foreword'. In *Black Photographer's Annual*. Edited by Joe Crawford, i–ix. New York: Another View, 1972.

——'Foreword'. In *The Harlem Book of the Dead*. Edited by James Van Der Zee, Owen Dodson and Camille Bishops, i–vi. New York: Morgan and Morgan, 1978.

——'Interview'. By Don Swaim. CBS Radio, 15 September 1987. http://www.wiredforbooks.org/tonimorrison/.

——*Jazz*. London: Vintage, 2005.

——*Love*. Toronto: Vintage Canada, 2005.

——*A Mercy*. London: Chatto & Windus, 2008.

——'Nobel Prize Lecture'. GiftsofSpeech.com. Accessed 2 March 2011. http://gos.sbc.edu/m/morrisont.html.

——*Paradise*. London: Random House, 1998.

——*Playing in the Dark: Whiteness and the Literary Imagination*. New York: Vintage, 1993.

——(ed.) *Race-ing Justice, En-gendering Power: Essays on Anita Hill, Clarence Thomas, and the Construction of Social Reality*. New York: Pantheon Books, 1992.

——'Rediscovering Black History'. In *What Moves at the Margin: Selected Nonfiction*. Edited and introduced by Carolyn C. Denard, 39–55. Jackson: University Press of Mississippi, 2008.

——'Rootedness in the Ancestor'. In *Black Women Writers (1950–1980): A Critical Evaluation*. Edited by Mari Evans, 339–45. Garden City, NY: Anchor Press, 1984.

——*Song of Solomon*. London: Vintage, 1998.

——*Sula*. London: Vintage, 1998.

——*Tar Baby*. London: Vintage, 2004.

——'What Black Women Think about Women's Lib'. *The New York Times Magazine*, 22 August 1971.

Morrison, Toni and Claudia Brodsky Lacour (eds) *Birth of a Nation'hood: Gaze, Script, and Spectacle in the O.J. Simpson Case*. London: Vintage, 1997.

Morrison, Toni and Gloria Naylor. 'A Conversation'. *Southern Review* 21, 1 (1985): 567–93.

Secondary texts

Abbott, James. *The Handbook of Idiotcy*. London: W. S. Orr and Co., 1856.

Adams, Rachel. *Sideshow USA: Freaks and the American Cultural Imagination*. Chicago: University of Chicago Press, 2001.

Adorno, Theodor W. 'Trying to Understand Endgame'. In *Modern Critical Views: Samuel Beckett*. Edited by Harold Bloom, 51–81. New York: Chelsea House Publishers, 1985.

Albrecht, Gary, Katherine Dolores Seelman and Michael Bury (eds.) *Handbook of Disability Studies*. London: Sage Publications, 2001.

Anzieu, Didier. *The Skin Ego: A Psychoanalytic Approach to the Self*. Translated by Chris Turner. New Haven: Yale University Press, 1989.

Armstrong, Isobel. *The Radical Aesthetic*. Oxford: Blackwell, 2000.

Ashe, Bertram D. ' "Why Don't He Like My Hair?" Constructing African-American Standards of Beauty in Toni Morrison's *Song of Solomon* and Zora Neale Hurston's *Their Eyes Were Watching God*'. *African American Review* 29, 4 (1995): 579–92.

Attridge, Derek. 'J. M. Coetzee's *Disgrace*: Introduction'. *Interventions: International Journal of Postcolonial Studies* 4, 3 (2002): 315–20.

——*J. M. Coetzee and the Ethics of Reading: Literature in the Event*. London: University of Chicago Press, 2004.

——*The Singularity of Literature*. London: Routledge, 2004.

——'A Writer's Life'. *The Virginia Quarterly Review* 80, 4 (2004): 254–65.

Attwell, David. 'Race in Disgrace'. *Interventions: International Journal of Postcolonial Studies* 4, 3 (2002): 331–41.

Bakerman, Jane. 'The Seams Can't Show: An Interview with Toni Morrison'. *Black Literature Forum* 12, 2 (1978): 56–60.

Bakhtin, Mikhail. *Rabelais and His World*. Bloomington: Indiana University Press, 1984.

Bal, Mieke. *Looking In: The Art of Viewing*. London: Routledge, 2001.

——*Travelling Concepts in the Humanities: A Rough Guide*. Toronto: University of Toronto Press, 2002.

Banet-Weiser, Sarah. *The Most Beautiful Girl in the World: Beauty Pageants and National Identity*. Berkeley: University of California Press, 1999.

Bangs, John Kendrick. *The Idiot*. New York: Harper, 1895.

——*The Idiot at Home*. New York: Harper, 1900.

Barker, Francis. *The Tremulous Private Body: Essays on Subjection*. Ann Arbor: University of Michigan Press, 1984.

Barnard, Rita. 'Coetzee's Country Ways'. *Interventions: International Journal of Postcolonial Studies* 4, 3 (2002): 384–94.

Barnes, Colin and Geoff Mercer. *Disability*. London: Polity Press, 2002.

Bateman, Frederick. *The Idiot: His Place in Creation and his Claims on Society*. London: Jarrold and Sons, 1897.

Bauer, Margaret Donovan. *William Faulkner's Legacy: 'What Shadow, What Stain, What Mark'*. Gainesville: University Press of Florida, 2008.

Baynton, Douglas. 'Slaves, Immigrants and Suffragists: The Uses of Disability in Citizenship Debates'. *PMLA* 120, 2 (2005): 562–7.

Beaulieu, Elizabeth Ann. *The Toni Morrison Encyclopedia*. Westport: Greenwood Press, 2003.

Beauvoir, Simone de. *The Coming of Age*. Translated by Patrick O'Brian. New York: Putnam, 1972.

——*The Second Sex*. Translated by H. M. Parshley. London: Vintage, 1997.

Beck, Warren. *Faulkner: Essays*. Madison: University of Wisconsin Press, 1976.

Beckett, Samuel. *Samuel Beckett: The Complete Dramatic Works*. London: Faber 1990.

Bergson, Henri. *The Creative Mind*. Translated by Mabelle L. Andison. London: Greenwood Press, 1968.

——*Introduction to Metaphysics*. Translated by T. E. Hulme. London: Macmillan, 1913.

——*Matter and Memory*. Translated by Nancy Margaret Paul and W. Scott Palmer. London: Allen & Unwin, 1911.

Bérubé, Michael. *Life as we Know it: A Father, a Family and an Exceptional Child*. New York: Vintage, 1998.

——*Rhetorical Occasions: Humans and the Humanities*. Chapel Hill: University of North Carolina Press, 1996.

Beuf, Ann H. *Beauty is the Beast: Appearance Impaired Children in America*. Philadelphia: University of Pennsylvania Press, 1990.

Bhabha, Homi K. *The Location of Culture*. London: Routledge, 1994.

Black, Paula, *The Beauty Industry: Gender, Culture, Pleasure*. London: Routledge, 2004.

Blackburn, Maddie. *Sexuality and Disability*. Oxford: Butterworth-Heinemann, 2002.

Blair, Sara. *Harlem Crossroads: Black Writers and the Photograph in the Twentieth Century*. New Haven: Princeton University Press, 2007.

Bleikasten, Andre. 'A European Perspective'. In *The Cambridge Companion to William Faulkner*. Edited by Philip M. Weinstein, 75–95. Cambridge: Cambridge University Press, 1995.

Bloom, Harold (ed.) *Toni Morrison*. New York: Chelsea House Publishers, 1990.

Blotner, Joseph. *Faulkner: A Biography*. London: Chatto & Windus, 1974.

——and Frederick Gwynn (eds.) *Faulkner in the University*. Charlottesville: University of Virginia Press, 1995.

Boesenberg, Eva (ed.) *Gender-Voice-Vernacular: The Formation of Female Subjectivity in Zora Neale Hurston, Toni Morrison and Alice Walker*. Heidelberg: Universitätsverlag C. Winter, 1999.

Bogdan, Robert. *Freak Show: Presenting Human Oddities for Amusement and Profit*. Chicago: University of Chicago Press, 1988.

Bolt, David. 'The Aims and Scope'. *Journal of Literary Disability* 1, 1 (2007): i–ii.

——'Introduction'. *Journal of Literary Disability* 1, 1 (2007): 1–5.

Bouson, J. Brooks. *Quiet as it's Kept: Shame, Trauma, and Race in the Novels of Toni Morrison*. New York: State University of New York Press, 2000.

Bowling, Lawrence. 'Faulkner and the Theme of Innocence'. *Kenyon Review* 20, 2 (1958): 466–87.

Bradshaw, G. and Michael Neil (eds.) *J. M. Coetzee's Austerities*. London: Ashgate Publishing, 2010.

Brand, Peg Zeglin (ed.) *Beauty Matters*. Bloomington: Indiana University Press, 2000.

Bronfen, Elisabeth. *Over Her Dead Body: Death, Femininity and the Aesthetic*. Manchester: Manchester University Press, 1992.

Brooks, Cleanth. 'Primitivism in *The Sound and the Fury*'. In *English Institute Essays 1952*. Edited by Alan S. Downer, 5–28. New York: AMS Press, 1954.

Brown, Calvin S. 'Faulkner's Idiot Boy: The Source of Simile in Sartoris'. *American Literature* 44, 3 (1972): 474–6.

Burke, Kenneth. 'On Literary Form'. In *The New Criticism and After*. Edited by Thomas Young, 80–90. Charlottesville: University of Virginia Press, 1988.

Burke, Lucy. 'Introduction: Thinking About Cognitive Impairment'. *Journal of Literary Disability* 2, 1 (2008): i–iv.

Butler, Judith. *Bodies that Matter: On the Discursive Limits of Sex*. London: Routledge, 1993.

——*Gender Trouble: Feminism and the Subversion of Identity*. London: Routledge, 1990.

Byers, Joseph P. 'Colony Care of the Feeble-Minded'. In *Report of the 1915 Legislature Committee on Mental Deficiency and the Proposed Institution for the Care of Feeble-minded and Epileptic Persons*, xi–xvii. California, 1917.

Cavell, Stanley. *Disowning Knowledge in Seven Plays of Shakespeare*. Cambridge: Cambridge University Press, 2003.

Charlton, James I. *Nothing About us Without us: Disability Oppression and Empowerment*. London: University of California Press, 1998.

Chenge, Anne. 'Wounded Beauty: An Exploratory Essay on Race, Feminism and the Aesthetic Question'. *Tulsa Studies in Women's Literature* 19, 2 (2000): 191–217.

Childs, Peter. *Modernism*. London: Routledge, 2000.

Cohen-Shalev, Amir, *Both Worlds at Once: Art in Old Age*. Lanham, MD: University Press of America, 2002.

Cole, Thomas R. *The Journey of Life: A Cultural History of Aging in America.* Cambridge: Cambridge University Press, 1992.
——Robert Kastenbaum and Ruth E. Kay (eds.) *Handbook of the Humanities and Aging.* New York: Springer Publishing Co., 2000.
Committee on Protection of the Feeble-Minded of the Massachusetts Society of the Prevention of Cruelty to Children. *The Menace of the Feeble-minded in Massachusetts: The Need of a Program.* Cambridge, MA, 1913.
Connor, Marc C. (ed.) *The Aesthetics of Toni Morrison: Speaking the Unspeakable.* Jackson: University Press of Mississippi, 2000.
Connor, Steven. *The Book of Skin.* London: Reaktion Books, 2004.
Couser, G. Thomas. *Recovering Bodies: Illness, Disability and Life Writing.* London: University of Wisconsin Press, 1997.
Cowart, David. 'Faulkner and Joyce in Morrison's *Song of Solomon*'. *American Literature* 62 (1990): 87–100.
Critchley, Simon (ed.) *The Cambridge Companion to Levinas.* Cambridge: Cambridge University Press, 2006.
Crutchfield, Susan and Marcy Epstein (eds.) *Points of Contact: Disability, Art and Culture.* Ann Arbor: University of Michigan Press, 2000.
Curtin, Maureen. *Out of Touch: Skin Tropes in Woolf, Ellison, Pynchon and Acker.* London: Routledge, 2003.
Das, Santanu. *Touch and Intimacy in First World War Literature.* Cambridge: Cambridge University Press, 2005.
Davenport, Charles B. 'Eugenics and Euthenics'. In *Report of the 1915 Legislature Committee on Mental Deficiency and the Proposed Institution for the Care of Feeble-Minded and Epileptic Persons,* 18–29. California, 1917.
Davidson, Michael. *Concerto for the Left Hand: Disability and the Defamiliar Body.* Ann Arbor: University of Michigan Press, 2008.
——' "Every man his Speciality": Beckett, Disability and Dependence'. *Journal of Literary and Cultural Disability Studies* 1, 2 (2007): 55–68.
——'Introduction: Dialectics of Dependency'. *Journal of Literary and Cultural Disability Studies* 1, 2 (2007): i–vi.
Davie, Maurice R. *Social Aspects of Mental Hygiene.* New Haven: Yale University Press, 1925.
Davis, Lennard J. *Bending Over Backwards: Disability, Dismodernism and Other Difficult Positions.* New York: New York University Press, 2002.
——'Dependency and Justice'. *Journal of Literary and Cultural Disability Studies* 1, 2 (2007): 1–4.
——(ed.) *The Disability Studies Reader.* 2nd edn. London: Routledge, 2006.
——*Enforcing Normalcy: Disability, Deafness, and the Body.* London: Verso Books, 1995.
Derrida, Jacques. *Memoirs of the Blind: The Self Portrait and Other Ruins.* Translated by Pascale-Anne Brault and Michael Naas. London: University of Chicago Press, 1993.
——'Unforseeable Freedom'. In *For What Tomorrow: A Dialogue.* Edited by Jacques Derrida and Elisabeth Roudinesco and translated by Jeff Fort, 47–61. Stanford: Stanford University Press, 2004.
Dickson, Harris. *The House of Luck.* Oxford: Small, Maynard and Co., 1916.
Diderot, Denis. *Diderot's Early Philosophical Works.* Edited by Margaret Jourdain. London: Lenox Hill Publishing, 1972.

Dixon, Laurinda S. and Gabril P. Weisberg. *In Sickness and in Health: Disease as Metaphor in Art and Popular Wisdom*. Newark: University of Delaware Press, 2004.

Douglass, Frederick. *My Bondage and My Freedom*. London: Penguin, 2003.

Du Bois, W. E. B. 'Criteria of Negro Art'. *The Crisis* 32 (1926): 290–7.

Durrant, Sam. *Postcolonial Narrative and the Work of Mourning: J. M. Coetzee, Wilson Harris and Toni Morrison*. New York: State University of New York Press, 2004.

Duster, Troy. *Backdoor to Eugenics*. London: Routledge, 2003.

Duvall, John N. 'Toni Morrison and the Anxiety of Faulknerian Influence'. In *Unflinching Gaze: Morrison and Faulkner Re-Envisioned*. Edited by Carol A. Kolmerton, Stephen M. Ross and Judith Bryant Wittenberg, 3–16. Jackson: University Press of Mississippi, 1997.

Ebony Magazine. 'Archives 1962–1969'. Accessed 22 June 2009. http://books.google.com/books?id=9eEDAAAAMBAJ&source=gbs_navlinks_s.

Eckard, Paula Galland. *Maternal Body and Voice in Toni Morrison, Bobbie Ann Mason and Lee Smith*. London: University of Missouri Press, 2002.

Eco, Umberto (ed.) *On Beauty: A History of a Western Idea*. Translated by Alastair McEwen. London: Secker & Warburg, 2004.

Elias, Norbert. 'Homo Clausus and the Civilizing Process'. In *Identity: A Reader*. Edited by Jessica Evans, Paul du Gay and Peter Redman, 293–301. London: Sage, 2000.

Ellmann, Maud. 'The Power to Tell: Rape, Race and Writing in Afro-American Women's Fiction'. In *An Introduction to Contemporary Fiction: International Writing in English since 1970*. Edited by Rod Mengham, 32–52. Oxford: Polity Press, 1999.

——'Skinscapes in "Lotus-Eaters"'. In *Ulysses: En-gendered Perspectives*. Edited by Kimberley J. Devlin and Marilyn Rizbaum, 51–66. New York: University of South Carolina Press, 1999.

Emens, Elizabeth F. 'Shape Stops Story'. *Narrative* 15, 1 (2007): 124–32.

Espmark, Kjell. *The Nobel Prize in Literature: A Study of the Criteria Behind the Choices*. Boston: G. K. Hall and Co., 1991.

Evans, James. *Spiritual Empowerment in Afro-American Literature: Frederick Douglass, Rebecca Jackson, Booker T. Washington, Richard Wright, Toni Morrison*. New York: Edwin Mellen Press, 1987.

Fant, Kenne. *Alfred Nobel: A Biography*. Translated by Marianne Ruuth. New York: Arcade Publishing, 2006.

Fargnoli, A. Nicholas and Michael Golay. *William Faulkner: The Essential Reference to his Life and Work*. New York: Econo-Clad Books, 2002.

Fielder, Leslie. *Freaks: Myths and Images of the Secret Self*. London: Penguin, 1981.

Folks, Jeffrey J. *From Richard Wright to Toni Morrison: Ethics in Modern and Postmodern American Narrative*. Oxford: Peter Lang, 2001.

Foster, Hal. *Compulsive Beauty*. Cambridge, MA: MIT Press, 1993.

Foucault, Michel. *The Birth of Biopolitics: Lectures at the Collège de France, 1978–79*. Edited by Michel Senellart, translated by Graham Burchell. New York: Palgrave Macmillan, 2008.

——*Discipline and Punish*. Translated by Alan Sheridan. New York: Penguin, 1979.

——*The Foucault Reader*. Edited by Paul Rabinow. London: Penguin, 1991.

Fraleigh, Sondra Horton. *Dance and the Lived Body: A Descriptive Aesthetics*. Pittsburgh, University of Pittsburgh Press, 1987.

Frank, Arthur W. *The Wounded Storyteller: Body, Illness, and Ethics*. Chicago: University of Chicago Press, 1995.

Fraser, Nancy and Axel Honneth. *Redistribution or Recognition: A Political-Philosophical Exchange*. London: Verso Books, 2003.

Freud, Sigmund. 'The Uncanny'. In *The Standard Edition of the Complete Works of Sigmund Freud*, vol. 12. Edited by James Strachey, 219–56. London: Hogarth Press, 1973.

Fuery, Patrick and Kelli Fuery. *Visual Cultures and Critical Theory*. London: Bloomsbury Academic, 2003.

Garland Thomson, Rosemarie. *Extraordinary Bodies: Figuring Disability in American Culture and Literature*. New York: Columbia University Press, 1997.

——(ed.) *Freakery: Cultural Spectacles of the Extraordinary Body*. New York: New York University Press, 1996.

Gardner, Sarah, E. *Blood and Irony: Southern White Women's Narratives of the Civil War, 1861–1937*. Chapel Hill: University of North Carolina Press, 2004.

Gilman, Sander L. *Creating Beauty to Cure the Soul: Race and Psychology in the Shaping of Aesthetic Surgery*. London: Duke University Press, 1998.

——*Disease and Representation: Images of Illness from Madness to Aids*. Ithaca: Cornell University Press, 1998.

Goddard, Henry H. 'Feeble-Mindedness as a Social Problem'. In *Report of the 1915 Legislature Committee on Mental Deficiency and the Proposed Institution for the Care of Feeble-Minded and Epileptic Persons*, 19–23. California, 1917.

Goffman, Erving. *Stigma: Notes on the Management of Spoiled Identity*. Englewood Cliffs: Prentice-Hall, 1963.

Gottfried, Amy S. *Historical Nightmares and Imaginative Violence in American Women's Writings*. London: Greenwood Press, 1998.

Gould, Stephen Jay. *The Mismeasure of Man*. London: Penguin, 1997.

Gray, Richard. *The Life of William Faulkner*. Oxford: Blackwell, 1994.

Green, André. *The Work of the Negative*. Translated by Andrew Weller. London: Free Association Books, 1999.

Gresset, Michel and Patrick Samway (eds.) *Faulkner and Idealism*. Jackson: University of Mississippi Press, 1983.

Grossberg, Lawrence, Cary Nelson and Paula Treichle (eds.) *Cultural Studies*. London: Routledge, 1992.

Grosz, Elizabeth. *Volatile Bodies: Towards a Corporeal Feminism*. Bloomington: Indiana University Press, 1994.

Guerrero, Edward. 'Tracking "The Look" in the Novels of Toni Morrison'. *Black American Literature Forum* 24, 4 (1990): 761–73.

Gullette, Margaret Morganroth. *Declining to Decline: Cultural Combat and the Politics of the Midlife*. Charlottesville: University Press of Virginia, 1997.

Halliwell, Martin. *Images of Idiocy: The Idiot Figure in Modern Fiction and Film*. Aldershot: Ashgate, 2004.

——*Modernism and Morality: Ethical Devices in European and American Fiction*. New York: Palgrave Macmillan, 2001.

Halpern, Sue. 'Portrait of the Artist: Review of *Under the Clock* by Christopher Nolan'. *The New York Review of Books*, 30 June 1988: 3–5.

Harding, James M. 'Trying to Understand Godot: Adorno, Beckett and the Senility of Historical Dialectics'. *CLIO* 23 (1993): 1–4.

Harris, Middleton A. (ed.) *The Black Book*. New York: Random House, 1974.

Heartney, Eleanor. 'Foreword: Cutting Two Ways with Beauty'. In *Beauty Matters*. Edited by Peg Zeglin Brand, xiii–xv. Bloomington: Indiana University Press, 2000.

Hegel, G. W. F. *Phenomenology of Spirit*. Translated by A. V. Miller. Oxford: Oxford University Press, 1977.

Hellström, Gustaf. 'Presentation Speech'. Nobelliterature.com. Accessed 2 March 2011. http://nobelliterature.com/nobelliteraturelist/1941-1950/118-1949william-faulkner-html.

Hendley, Steven. *From Communicative Action to the Face of the Other: Levinas and Habermas on Language, Obligation and Community*. Oxford: Lexington Books, 2000.

Hillman, David and Carla Mazzio (eds.) *The Body in Parts: Fantasies of Corporeality in Early Modern Europe*. New York: Routledge, 1997.

Hoem, Sheri. 'Disabling Postmodernism: Wideman, Morrison and Prosthetic Critique'. *Novel: A Forum on Fiction* 35, 2 (2002): 193–210.

hooks, bell. 'Postmodern Blackness'. *Postmodern Culture* 1, 1 (1990): 23–4.

Hope, Christopher. *The Garden of Bad Dreams and Other Stories*. London: Atlantic Books, 2008.

Howe, Irving. *William Faulkner: A Critical Study*. Chicago: University of Chicago Press, 1975.

Hughes, Bill and Kevin Paterson. 'The Social Model of Disability and the Disappearing Body: Towards a Sociology of Impairment'. *Disability and Society* 12, 3 (1997): 325–40.

Inge, Thomas M. *William Faulkner: Contemporary Reviews*. Cambridge: Cambridge University Press, 1995.

Inness, Sherrie (ed.) *Disco Divas: Women and Popular Culture in the 1970s*. Philadelphia: University of Pennsylvania Press, 2003.

Iser, Wolfgang. *The Implied Reader: Patterns of Communication in Prose Fiction from Bunyan to Beckett*. Baltimore: Johns Hopkins University Press, 1976.

'J. M. Coetzee Wins the Nobel Prize'. SouthAfrica.Info.com. Accessed 2 March 2011. http://www.southafrica.info/about/arts/nobel-jmcoetzee.htm.

Jacobus, Mary, Evelyn Fox Keller and Sally Shuttleworth (eds.) *Body/Politics: Women and the Discourses of Science*. London: Routledge, 1990.

Jeliffe, Robert A. (ed.) *Faulkner at Nagano*. Tokyo: Norwood Editions, 1977.

Jennings, La Vinia Delois. *Toni Morrison and the Idea of Africa*. Cambridge: Cambridge University Press, 2008.

Jesser, Nancy. 'Violence, Home and Community in Toni Morrison's *Beloved*'. *African American Review* 33, 2 (1999): 325–45.

Johnson, Barbara. *The Feminist Difference: Literature, Psychoanalysis, Race and Gender*. London: Harvard University Press, 1988.

Johnson, Mark. *The Body in the Mind: The Bodily Basis of Meaning, Imagination and Reason*. Chicago: University of Chicago Press, 1992.

Jones, Jonathan. 'Bold, Graphic but Bad Art'. *The Guardian* (London), 16 March 2006.

Kafka, Franz. *The Trial*. Translated by Idris Parry. London: Penguin, 2000.

Kartiganer, Donald M. '*The Sound and the Fury* and Faulkner's Quest for Form'. *ELH* 37, 4 (1970): 613–39.

——and Ann J. Abadie (eds.) *Faulkner and the Natural World: Faulkner and Yoknapatawpha*. Jackson: University Press of Mississippi, 1999.

Kayser, Wolfgang. *The Grotesque in Art and Literature*. New York: Columbia University Press, 1981.

Kella, Elisabeth and Joy Kogawa. *Beloved Communities: Solidarities and Difference in Fiction by Michael Ondaatje, Toni Morrison and Joy Kogawa*. Uppsala: Uppsala Universität, 2000.

Kermode, Frank. *The Sense of an Ending: Studies in the Theory of Fiction*. Oxford: Oxford University Press, 1967.

Kevles, Daniel J. *In the Name of Eugenics: Genetics and the Uses of Human Heredity*. Harmondsworth: Penguin, 1986.

Kittay, Eva Feder and Ellen K. Feder (eds.) *The Subject of Care: Feminist Perspectives on Dependency*. Oxford: Rowman & Littlefield Publishers, 2002.

Klages, Mary. *Woeful Afflictions: Disability and Sentimentality in Victorian America*. Philadelphia: University of Pennsylvania Press, 1999.

Kolmerten, Carol A., Stephen M. Ross and Judith Bryant Wittenberg (eds.) *Unflinching Gaze: Morrison and Faulkner Re-envisioned*. Jackson: University Press of Mississippi, 1997.

Kossew, Sue. *Writing Women, Writing Place: Contemporary Australian and South African Fiction*. London: Routledge, 2004.

Krumland, Heidi. ' "A Big Deaf-Mute Moron": Eugenics Traces in Carson McCullers's *The Heart is a Lonely Hunter*'. *Journal of Literary Disability* 2, 1 (2008): 32–43.

Lakoff, George and Mark Johnson. *Metaphors We Live By*. Chicago: University of Chicago Press, 2003.

——*Philosophy in the Flesh: The Embodied Mind and its Challenge to Western Thought*. New York: Basic Books, 1999.

Lapper, Alison. 'Bold, Brave, Beautiful'. AlisonLapper.com. Accessed 16 April 2008. http://www.alisonlapper.com/statue/.

Lasky, Kathryn. *Vision of Beauty: The Story of Sarah Breedlove Walker*. Illustrated by Nneka Bennett. New York: Walker Books, 2000.

Lawrence, D. H. *The Prussian Officer and Other Stories*. Edited by John Worthen. London: Penguin, 1983.

Lazzaranto, Maurizio. 'From Biopower to Biopolitics'. *Pli: The Warwick Journal of Philosophy* 13 (2002): 100–11.

Ledbetter, Mark. *Victims and the Postmodern Narrative, or, Doing Violence to the Body: An Ethic of Reading and Writing*. Basingstoke: Macmillan, 1996.

Lee, Hermione. *Body Parts: Essays on Life-Writing*. London: Chatto & Windus, 2005.

Leusmann, Harold. 'J. M. Coetzee's Cultural Critique'. *World Literature Today* 78, 3 (2004): 60–3.

Levenson, Michael (ed.) *The Cambridge Companion to Modernism*. Cambridge: Cambridge University Press, 1999.

Levinas, Emmanuel. *Basic Philosophical Writings*. Edited by Adrian T. Peperzak, Simon Critchley and Robert Bernasconi. Bloomington: Indiana University Press, 1996.

——'Ethics and the Face'. In *The Phenomenology Reader*. Edited by Dermot Moran and Timothy Mooney, 515–28. London: Routledge, 2002.

——*Otherwise than Being or Beyond Essence*. Translated by Alphonso Lingis. Pittsburgh: Duquesne University Press, 1999.

——*Totality and Infinity: An Essay on Exteriority*. Translated by Alphonso Lingis. Pittsburgh: Duquesne University Press, 1969.

Lister, Marcella (ed.) *Corps Étrangers: Danse, Dessin, Film*. Paris: Musée du Louvre Éditions, 2006.

Louvel, Liliane. 'Photography as Critical Idiom and Intermedial Criticism'. *Poetics Today* 29, 1 (2008): 31–46.

Lubiano, Waheema (ed.) *The House that Race Built: Original Essays by Toni Morrison, Angela Y. Davis, Cornel West, and Others on Black Americans and Politics in America Today*. New York: Pantheon Books, 1997.

Ludwig, Sami. 'Toni Morrison's Social Criticism'. In *The Cambridge Companion to Toni Morrison*. Edited by Justine Tally, 125–38. Cambridge: Cambridge University Press, 2007.

Macaulay, Rose. *Told by an Idiot*. London: Virago, 1983.

MacDonald, Arthur. *Hearing on the Bill to Establish a Laboratory for the Study of the Criminal, Pauper, and Defective Classes*. Washington, 1902.

MacLeod, Lewis. ' "Do We of Necessity Become Puppets in a Story?" or Narrating the World: On Speech, Silence and Discourse in J. M. Coetzee's *Foe*'. *Modern Fiction Studies* 52, 1 (2006): 1–18.

MacMurphy, Helen. *The Almosts: A Study of the Feeble-Minded*. Boston: Houghton Mifflin, 1926.

Mariani, Philomela (ed.) *Critical Fictions: The Politics of Imaginative Writing*. Seattle: Bay Press, 1991.

Massumi, Brian (ed.) *Shock to Thought: Expression after Deleuze and Guattari*. London: Routledge, 2002.

Matthews, Eric. *Merleau-Ponty: A Guide for the Perplexed*. New York: Continuum International Publishing, 2006.

Mattingly, Cheryl and Linda C. Garro. *Narrative and Cultural Construction of Illness and Healing*. London: University of California Press, 2000.

Matus, Jill. *Toni Morrison: Contemporary World Writers*. Manchester: Manchester University Press, 1998.

McBride, Dwight. 'Morrison, Intellectual'. In *The Cambridge Companion to Toni Morrison*. Edited by Justine Tally, 162–74. Cambridge: Cambridge University Press, 2007.

McCullers, Carson. *The Heart is a Lonely Hunter*. London: Penguin, 2008.

McKee, Patricia. *Producing American Races: Henry James, William Faulkner, Toni Morrison*. London: Duke University Press, 1999.

Meade, Teresa and David Serlin (eds.) 'Introduction'. *Radical History Review: Disability and History* 94, 4 (2006): 1–8.

Meer, Sarah. *Uncle Tom Mania: Slavery, Minstrelsy, and Transatlantic Culture in the 1850s*. Athens, GA: University of Georgia Press, 2005.

Mellard, James. 'Caliban as Prospero: Benjy and *The Sound and the Fury*'. *Novel: A Forum on Fiction* 3, 3 (1970): 233–48.

Mengham, Rod (ed.) *An Introduction to Contemporary Fiction: International Writing in English since 1970*. Oxford: Polity Press, 1999.

Merleau-Ponty, Maurice. *Phenomenology of Perception*. Translated by Colin Smith. London: Routledge, 2002.

——*The Visible and the Invisible: Followed by Working Notes*. Edited by Claude Lefort. Translated by Alphonso Lingis. Evanston, IL: Northwestern University Press, 1968.

Miller, Edgar. 'Idiocy in the Nineteenth Century'. *History of Psychiatry* 7, 27 (1996): 361–73.

Millgate, Michael. *The Achievement of William Faulkner*. London: University of Georgia Press, 1989.

Mills, Nicolaus (ed.) *Arguing Immigration: The Debate over the Changing Face of America*. New York: Prentice Hall, 1994.

Mitchell, David T. 'Disability Studies in the Humanities'. *Disability Studies Quarterly* 17, 3 (1997): 94–8.

——'Foreword'. In *A History of Disability* by Henri-Jacques Stiker, translated by William Sayers, vii–xiv. Ann Arbor: University of Michigan Press, 1997.

——and Sharon L. Snyder. *The Body and Physical Difference: Discourses of Disability*. Ann Arbor: University of Michigan Press, 1997.

——and Sharon L. Snyder. *Narrative Prosthesis: Disability and the Dependencies of Discourse*. Ann Arbor: University of Michigan Press, 2000.

——and Sharon L. Snyder. 'Representation and its Discontents: The Uneasy Home of Disability in Literature and Film'. In *The Handbook of Disability Studies*. Edited by Gary Albrecht, Katherine Dolores Seelman and Michael Bury, 195–218. London: Sage Publications, 2001.

Mol, Annemarie. *The Body Multiple: Ontology in Medical Practice*. Durham, NC: Duke University Press, 2002.

Moran, Dermot and Timothy Mooney (eds.) *The Phenomenology Reader*. London: Routledge, 2002.

Morris, Wesley and Barbara Alverson Morris. *Reading Faulkner*. London: University of Wisconsin Press, 1989.

Morrison, Jago and Susan Watkins. *Scandalous Fictions: The Twentieth-Century Novel in the Public Sphere*. Basingstoke: Palgrave Macmillan, 2006.

Morrow, W. C. *The Ape, the Idiot and Other People*. Philadelphia: J. P. Lippincott Company, 1897.

Mouland, Bill. 'Nelson Looks Down as Statue of Disabled Mother is Unveiled in the Rain'. *The Daily Mail* (London), 16 September 2005.

Mulhall, Stephen. *The Wounded Animal: J. M. Coetzee and the Difficulty of Reality in Literature and Philosophy*. Woodstock: Princeton University Press, 2009.

Murakami, Yoshiko. *Les Mains pour voir: Collection de la Fondation CCF pour la Photographie*. Paris: Actes Sud, 1999.

Murphy, Robert. *The Body Silent*. New York: W. W. Norton and Co., 1987.

National Committee for Mental Hygiene. *Report of the Georgia Commission on Feeble-Mindedness and of the Survey Conducted by the National Committee for Mental Hygiene*. Atlanta, 1919.

Nekola, Charlotte and Paul Rabinowitz (eds.) *Writing Red: An Anthology of American Women Writers, 1930–1940*. New York: Feminist Press at the City University of New York, 1987.

Noll, Stephen. *The Feeble-Minded in Our Midst: Institutions for the Mentally Retarded in the South, 1900–1940*. Chapel Hill: University of North Carolina Press, 1996.

Nussbaum, Martha C. *Frontiers of Justice: Disability, Nationality, Species Membership*. Cambridge, MA: The Belknap Press of Harvard University Press, 2006.

O'Donovan-Anderson, Michael. *The Incorporated Self: Interdisciplinary Perspectives on Embodiment*. New York: Rowman & Littlefield Publishers, 1996.

Ōe, Kenzaburō. *A Personal Matter*. New York: Grove Press, 1969.

Office for Disability Issues: HM Government. 'Disability Facts and Figures'. Department for Work and Pensions. Accessed 2 March 2011. http://odi.dwp. gov.uk/disability-statistics-and-research/disability-facts-and-figures.php.

Peach, Linden (ed.) *Toni Morrison: Contemporary Critical Essays*. New York: Macmillan, 1988.

Peterson, Nancy J. *Against Amnesia: Contemporary Women Writers and the Crisis of Historical Memory*. Philadelphia: University of Pennsylvania Press, 2001.

——(ed.) *Toni Morrison: Critical and Theoretical Approaches*. Baltimore: Johns Hopkins University Press, 1997.

Pinter, Harold. 'Nobel Prize Lecture'. *The Guardian* (London). Accessed 2 March 2011. http://www.guardian.co.uk/stage/2005/dec/08/theatre.nobelprize.

Pointon, Ann and Chris Davis (eds.) *Framed: Interrogating Disability in the Media*. London: BFI Publishing, 1997.

Polk, Noel (ed.) *New Essays on 'The Sound and the Fury'*. Cambridge: Cambridge University Press, 1993.

Poyner, Jane. 'J. M. Coetzee, Elizabeth and that Prize'. *African Review of Books*. Accessed 10 April 2009. http://www.africanreviewofbooks.com/Review.asp?book_id=62.

——(ed.) *J. M. Coetzee and the Idea of the Public Intellectual*. Athens: Ohio University Press, 2006.

Prettejohn, Elizabeth. *Beauty and Art, 1750–2000*. Oxford: Oxford University Press, 2005.

Price Herndl, Diane. *Invalid Women: Figuring Feminine Illness in American Fiction and Culture, 1840–1940*. Chapel Hill: University of North Carolina Press, 1993.

Quayson, Ato. *Aesthetic Nervousness: Disability and the Crisis of Representation*. New York: Columbia University Press, 2007.

Ramadanovic, Petar. *Forgetting Futures: On Memory, Trauma, and Identity*. Oxford: Lexington Books, 2001.

Rancière, Jacques. *The Politics of Aesthetics: The Distribution of the Sensible*. Translated by Gabriel Rockhill. New York: Continuum, 2006.

Raynaud, Claudine. 'Beloved or the Shifting Shapes of Memory'. In *The Cambridge Companion to Toni Morrison*. Edited by Justine Tally, 43–58. Cambridge: Cambridge University Press, 2007.

Reynolds, Nigel. 'Whatever Would Nelson Think?' *The Daily Telegraph* (London), 16 September 2005.

Richet, Charles. *Idiot Man: or The Follies of Mankind*. London: T. W. Laurie Ltd., 1925.

Riding, Alan. 'Entr'acte: At the Louvre, Toni Morrison Hosts a Conversation on Exile'. *The New York Times*, 15 November 2006.

Roe, Sue and Susan Sellars (eds.) *The Cambridge Companion to Virginia Woolf*. Cambridge: Cambridge University Press, 2000.

Rogers, Linda and Beth Blue Swadener (eds.) *Semiotics and Dis/ability: Interrogating Categories of Difference*. Albany: State University of New York Press, 2001.

Romm, Sharon. *The Changing Face of Beauty*. St. Louis: Mosby, 1991.

Rushdy, Ashraf H. A. 'Daughters Signify(ing) History: The Example of Toni Morrison's *Beloved*'. *American Literature* 64, 3 (1992): 567–97.

Ryan, Judylyn S. 'Language and Narrative Technique in Toni Morrison's Novels'. In *The Cambridge Companion to Toni Morrison*. Edited by Justine Tally, 151–61. Cambridge: Cambridge University Press, 2007.

Said, Edward. *Joseph Conrad and the Fiction of Autobiography*. New York: Columbia University Press, 2007.

——*On Late Style: Music and Literature against the Grain*. London: Bloomsbury, 2006.

Samuels, Robert. *Writing Prejudices: The Psychoanalysis and Pedagogy of Discrimination from Shakespeare to Toni Morrison*. New York: State University of New York Press, 2001.

Scarry, Elaine. *The Body in Pain: The Making and Unmaking of the World*. Oxford: Oxford University Press, 1985.

——(ed.) *Literature and the Body: Essays in Population and Persons*. Baltimore: Johns Hopkins University Press, 1988.

——*On Beauty and Being Just*. London: Duckworth, 2000.

Seguin, Edward. *Nervous Diseases*. New York, 1869.

Shakespeare, Tom. *Disability Rights and Wrongs*. London: Routledge, 2006.

——Kath Gillespie-Sells and Dominic Davies. *Untold Desires: The Sexual Politics of Disability*. New York: Continuum, 1996.

Shakespeare, William. *The Tempest*. Edited by Brian Gibbons. Cambridge: Cambridge University Press, 2002.

Sheets-Johnstone, Maxine. *The Phenomenology of Dance*. London: Dance Books Ltd., 1966.

Shillingsberg, Peter. 'Textual Criticism, the Humanities and J. M. Coetzee'. *English Studies in Africa: A Journal of the Humanities* 49, 2 (2006): 13–28.

Siebers, Tobin. *The Body Aesthetic: From Fine Art to Body Modification*. Ann Arbor: University of Michigan Press, 2000.

——'Disability Aesthetics'. *JCRT* 7, 2 (2006): 63–73.

——*Disability Theory*. Ann Arbor: University of Michigan Press, 2008.

Silvers, Anita. 'From the Crooked Timber of Humanity, Beautiful Things Can be Made'. In *Beauty Matters*. Edited by Peg Zeglin Brand, 197–223. Bloomington: Indiana University Press, 2000.

Simon, Robin. 'Alison Lapper, the New Icon of Trafalgar Square'. *The Evening Standard* (London), 15 September 2005.

Singal, Daniel J. *William Faulkner: The Making of a Modernist*. Chapel Hill: University of North Carolina Press, 1997.

Small, Helen. *The Long Life*. Oxford: Oxford University Press, 2007.

Smith, Bonnie and Beth Hutchison (eds.) *Gendering Disability*. New York: Rutgers University Press, 2004.

Snyder, Sharon L. and David T. Mitchell. *Cultural Locations of Disability*. Chicago: University of Chicago Press, 2006.

——'Disability Haunting in American Poetics'. *Journal of Literary Disability* 1, 1 (2007): 1–12.

——Brenda Jo Brueggemann and Rosemarie Garland Thomson. *Disability Studies: Enabling the Humanities*. New York: Modern Language Association of America, 2002.

Sontag, Susan. *Illness as Metaphor and Aids and its Metaphors*. London: Penguin, 2002.

——*Regarding the Pain of Others*. London: Penguin, 2004.

Spillers, Hortense. 'Mama's Baby, Papa's Maybe: An American Grammar Book'. In *African American Literary Theory: A Reader*. Edited by Winston Napier, 257–79. New York: New York University Press, 2000.

Spivak, Gayatri. 'Ethics and Politics in Tagore, Coetzee and Certain Scenes of Teaching'. *Diacritics* 32, 3 (2002): 17–31.

Starobinski, Jean. 'The Inside and the Outside'. *The Hudson Review* 28, 3 (1975): 333–51.

Steiner, Wendy. *The Trouble with Beauty*. London: Heinemann, 2001.

Stern, Katherine. 'Toni Morrison's Beauty Formula'. In *The Aesthetics of Toni Morrison: Speaking the Unspeakable*. Edited by Marc C. Connor, 77–91. Jackson: University Press of Mississippi, 2000.

Steuart, W. M. *Feeble-Minded and Epileptics in Institutions*. Washington, 1923.

Stiker, Henri-Jacques. *A History of Disability*. Translated by William Sayers. Ann Arbor: University of Michigan Press, 1997.

Suleri, Sara. 'Woman Skin Deep: Feminism and the Postcolonial Condition'. In *Colonial Discourse and Post-Colonial Theory: A Reader*. Edited by Patrick Williams and Laura Chrisman, 244–56. Hemel Hempstead: Harvester Wheatsheaf, 1993.

Sutherland, John (ed.) *Nobel Lectures: Twenty Years of the Nobel Prize for Literature*. Cambridge: Icon Books Limited, 2007.

Tally, Justine (ed.) *The Cambridge Companion to Toni Morrison*. Cambridge: Cambridge University Press, 2007.

Tate, Trudi. *Modernism, History and the First World War*. Manchester: Manchester University Press, 1998.

Taylor, Paul C. 'Malcolm's Conk and Danto's Colors; or, Four Logical Petitions Concerning Race, Beauty and Aesthetics'. In *Beauty Matters*. Edited by Peg Zeglin Brand, 57–65. Bloomington: Indiana University Press, 2000.

Taylor-Guthrie, Danille (ed.) *Conversations with Toni Morrison*. Jackson: University Press of Mississippi, 1979.

Thane, Pat. *The Long History of Old Age*. London: Thames & Hudson, 2005.

The Juvenile Protective Association of Cincinnati. *The Feeble-Minded; or, the Hub to our Wheel of Vice, Crime and Pauperism, Cincinnati's Problem: A Study by the Juvenile Protective Association of Cincinnati*. Cincinnati, 1915.

The Oxford English Dictionary. OED.com. Accessed 6 January 2009. http://www.oed.com/.

'The Stars and Stripes: American Soldiers' Newspaper of World War One 1918–1919'. *Library of Congress*. Accessed 22 August 2008. http://memory.loc.gov/ammem/sgphtml/sashtml/.

Thurber, S. 'Disability and Monstrosity: A Look at Literary Discourses of Handicapping Conditions'. *Rehabilitation Literature* 41, 1 (1980): 12–15.

'Toni Morrison: Author Among Authors'. *FacetoFace: A Blog for the National Portrait Gallery Smithsonian Institution*. Accessed 2 March 2011. http://face2face.si.edu/my_weblog/2009/02/toni-morrison-author-among-authors.html.

Treffert, Donald A. *Extraordinary People: Understanding 'Idiot Savants'*. New York: Ballantine Books, 1985.

Tremaine, Louis. 'The Embodied Soul: Animal Being in the Work of J. M. Coetzee'. *Contemporary Literature* 44, 4 (2003): 587–612.

Trent, James W. *Inventing the Feeble Mind: A History of Mental Retardation in the United States*. Los Angeles: University of California Press, 1994.

Truchan-Tataryn, Maria. 'Textual Abuse: Faulkner's Benjy'. *Journal of Medical Humanities* 26, 2/3 (2005). doi: 10.1007/s10912-005-2916-0.

Trumbo, Dalton. *Johnny Got His Gun*. New York: Citadel Press, 2007.

Turner, Victor. *The Forest of Symbols: Aspects of Ndembu Ritual.* Ithaca: Cornell University Press, 1970.

United States Department of Labor: Bureau of Labor Statistics. 'Employment among the Disabled by Age in 2009'. The Editor's Desk. Last modified 31 August 2010. http://www.bls.gov/opub/ted/2010/ted_20100831.htm.

Volpe, Edmond L. *A Reader's Guide to William Faulkner: The Novels.* New York: Syracuse University Press, 2003.

Wainwright, Michael. *Darwin and Faulkner's Novels: Evolution and Southern Fiction.* Basingstoke: Palgrave Macmillan, 2008.

Walker, Alice. *The Colour Purple.* Cambridge: Cambridge University Press, 1990.

——*In Search of Our Mother's Gardens: Womanist Prose.* London: Harcourt, 1983.

Wall, Cheryl A. 'Toni Morrison, Editor and Teacher'. In *The Cambridge Companion to Toni Morrison.* Edited by Justine Tally, 139–48. Cambridge: Cambridge University Press, 2007.

——*Worrying the Line: Black Women Writers, Lineage and Literary Tradition.* Chapel Hill: University of North Carolina Press, 2005.

Walther, Malin LaVon. 'Out of Sight: Toni Morrison's Revision of Beauty'. *Black Literature Forum* 24, 4 (1990): 775–89.

Waskul, Dennis and Phillip Vannini (eds.) *Body/Embodiment: Symbolic Interaction and the Sociology of the Body.* London: Ashgate, 2006.

Webster, Richard. 'New Ends for Old: Frank Kermode's *The Sense of an Ending*'. *The Critical Quarterly* 38, 1 (1974): 311–12.

Weil, Kari. 'Killing Them Softly: Animal Death, Linguistic Disability and the Struggle for Ethics'. *Configurations: A Journal of Literature, Science and Technology* 14, 1/2 (2006): 87–96.

Weinstein, Philip M. (ed.) *The Cambridge Companion to William Faulkner.* Cambridge: Cambridge University Press, 1995.

Welles, James F. *The Story of Stupidity: A History of Western Idiocy from the Days of Greece to the Present.* New York: Mount Pleasant Press, 1988.

Wendell, Susan. *The Rejected Body: Feminist Philosophical Reflections on Disability.* London: Routledge, 1996.

Wicomb, Zoë. *David's Story.* New York: The Feminist Press, 2000.

——'*Slow Man* and the Real: A Lesson in Reading and Writing'. In *Austerities: Essays on J. M. Coetzee.* Edited by G. Bradshaw and Michael Neil, 215–30. London: Ashgate Publishing, 2010.

Williams, J. Harold. 'Feeble-Mindedness and Delinquency'. In *Report of the 1915 Legislature Committee on Mental Deficiency and the Proposed Institution for the Care of Feeble-Minded and Epileptic Persons*, 63–71.California, 1917.

Williams, Lisa. *The Artist as Outsider in the Novels of Toni Morrison and Virginia Woolf.* London: Greenwood Press, 2000.

Williams, Raymond. *Keywords: A Vocabulary of Culture and Society.* London: Fontana Press, 1988.

Wills, David. *Prosthesis.* Stanford: Stanford University Press, 1995.

Willis, Paul. *Common Culture: Symbolic Work at Play in the Every Day Cultures of the Young.* London: Open University Press, 1990.

Willis, Susan. 'Eruptions of Funk: Historicizing Toni Morrison'. *Black American Literature Forum* 16, 1 (1982): 34–42.

——*Specifying: Black Women Writing the American Experience.* Madison: University of Wisconsin Press, 1987.

Wilson, James C. and Cynthia Lewiecki-Wilson (eds.) *Embodied Rhetorics: Disability in Language and Culture.* Chicago: University of Chicago Press, 2001.

Winnicott, D. W. *Playing and the Reality.* London: Routledge, 1971.

Wolf, Naomi. *The Beauty Myth.* London: Anchor Books, 1992.

Wood, James. *The Broken Estate: Essays on Literature and Belief.* New York: Random House, 1999.

Woodward, Kathleen. *Aging and its Discontents: Freud and Other Fictions.* Bloomington: Indiana University Press, 1991.

Woolf, Virginia. *Mrs Dalloway.* Oxford: Oxford University Press, 2008.

——'On Being Ill'. Introduced by Hermione Lee. Ashfield: Consortium, 2002.

Young, Iris Marion. *Justice and the Politics of Difference.* Princeton: Princeton University Press, 1990.

Žižek, Slavoj. *The Sublime Object of Ideology.* London: Verso Books, 2009.

Index